Midnight Requisition

Holly Copella

To my wonderful sister,
Denise Koch

ACKNOWLEDGMENTS

Copella Books: First Paperback Edition 2018
Printed by CreateSpace, An Amazon.com Company
Cover Artist: Daniela Owergoor
Dani-owergoor.deviantart.com

PUBLISHER'S NOTE

Chapter 1

Not far from the small coastal town in Maine, a twenty-bed hotel sat atop the hill nestled against the bluff. Although the large, old building was in desperate need of repairs, the view of the ocean was spectacular, particularly during sunrise. The towering ocean view seemed to extend for miles. The three-story, stately mansion had been converted into a small hotel decades ago and had been abandoned almost nearly as long. The old hotel was rustic both inside and out. Natural wood seemed to be the theme. All the doors, trim, and floors throughout the hotel were original despite their charming creaks from age. Although the kitchen and bathrooms had been updated, the updates were sorely in need of updates.

A breathtaking, sculpted wood, grand staircase led to the second floor landing then branched off both right and left to the third floor. For those seeking adventure, there was an old, gate style elevator that seemed to malfunction more than it functioned. Its rustic appeal kept it from being dismantled or covered over. Although there were many master suites, the current owners took the second floor, back corner, ocean view suite with a balcony overlooking the cliffs. Once the hotel was again operational, the owners would have to consider giving up their coveted room in favor of the money renting it would bring.

The corner suite was massive and remained one of the few rooms to be completely renovated. It contained a shared bath with the connecting room, which hadn't been touched in years. The master bedroom itself contained a marble fireplace, high ceiling with several ceiling fans, its own private balcony, and a garden tub in the semi-private bathroom. The heavy, detailed furniture was possibly antique and gave the room a medieval sort of appeal. A young couple was entwined beneath the sheets of the excessively large bed. By the position of their bodies and the moans of pleasure, they were having an intimate moment together.

Calvin panted while on top of the young, naked woman. He met her gaze while grinning almost boyishly. Cal was a moderately muscular man with bronzed skin, neatly trimmed light brown hair, and a rugged, manly beard. Despite only being in his mid-twenties, the tattoo on his forearm indicated he'd served in the Navy. He smiled at the beautiful, dark-haired woman beneath him and gently caressed her face before giving her a small, loving kiss.

"Why don't we blow off that thing with your grandparents tomorrow, and we'll spend the entire day naked in bed together," Cal teased.

The young woman touched his face then kissed him quickly on the lips and met his gaze. "We did that the last time they asked us to their house," she remarked.

He groaned while happily reflecting on the moment in question. "Hmm, yeah," Cal announced. "That was one hell of a weekend."

She patted his bearded face with added vigor and raised her brows. "No," she announced firmly. "We aren't blowing them off again."

Cal groaned and rolled off his young girlfriend. "Has anyone ever told you, you're no fun, Scorpio?"

Scorpio clutched the sheets to her naked body and turned on her side to face him where he lay on his back staring at the ceiling.

"You didn't say that a minute ago," she teased.

Scorpio was mature looking for a woman only twenty-two years of age. She had long dark hair, which was now pleasantly mussed from their aggressive lovemaking. She was moderately petite alongside her somewhat muscular boyfriend. Despite barely making five foot four, Scorpio was excessively toned, indicating the young woman was fairly athletic.

"I don't know what you have against my grandparents," she remarked while staring at him.

"They don't seem to like me very much," he replied with a sigh and tensed at the thought. "I think they resent me for supporting the whole bed and breakfast remodel plan of yours."

"I wouldn't read too much into it," Scorpio replied. "My grandfather doesn't like anyone."

"The only thing I have in common with your grandfather is our hatred for Carson Davenport," Cal announced.

Scorpio's look turned demanding. "Were his goons harassing you again?" she asked with disgust then shook her head. "I don't know what he has against you or my grandfather."

"He's just a corrupt, vile man," Cal replied. "I wish I'd never worked for him. Once you're under his thumb, it's hard to get out." He managed a smile and rolled onto his side facing her. "I don't want to talk about him anymore. One day, he'll be out of our lives."

"I don't see how," she remarked and rolled onto her back. "He's only in his fifties and seems pretty damned healthy at that. I sincerely doubt he intends to move either."

Cal leaned over Scorpio where she lay on their bed and kissed her briefly but warmly. He pulled away and smiled sweetly.

"Don't worry about Carson Davenport," he announced. "He's my problem, not yours. I'll deal with him." Cal rolled out of bed and slipped into his discarded clothing on the floor. "I'm going downstairs to catch the end of the game."

"You can watch the game up here," she replied while gently caressing the empty spot alongside her in the bed. "I promise not to roll my eyes too loudly when you yell at the players."

He chuckled, leaned across the bed, and again kissed her. "It's late already," he informed her. "I don't want to disturb your sleep. You have to get up early. I'll be up in an hour or so."

She nodded and watched him leave the room, partially closing the door behind him. Scorpio slipped into her tank top and shorts pajama set, turned out the light, and climbed back under the covers. Although she no longer felt tired, she seemed to fall asleep almost instantly. A little while later, Scorpio heard the bedroom door creak open. She had a difficult time waking herself and even considered not commenting on how the game had ended. She rolled onto her back as her eyes opened and saw a strange man standing over her. Scorpio suddenly gasped and attempted to leap up in bed.

The man grabbed her by the throat and slammed her back onto the mattress. With his free, gloved hand, he raised a hunting knife above his head. Scorpio struggled against the hand on her throat while gasping for air then saw the knife. She caught his wrist as he plunged the knife downward and kept him from stabbing her, although his strength and leverage was working against her. As she gasped for air beneath the crushing hand on her throat, she knew she only had seconds to react before losing the fight.

There was a blur alongside her. Cal punched the man in the nose. Her attacker jerked from the pain, releasing her throat, and pulled the knife away from her as he stumbled backward. Scorpio scrambled out from under the covers, rolled across the bed to the far side, and leaped to her feet, putting as much distance between her and her attacker as possible. The man removed his hand from his bloodied nose and glared at Cal, who stood alongside the bed not far from him. In the split second the man was thrown off Scorpio, Cal had snatched the baseball bat from alongside the bed. He swung the bat for the lunging man and struck him in the hip, dropping him to the bed with a bounce. The intruder recovered from his position on the bed, reclaimed his knife, and straightened.

Cal again swung the bat, struck him on the side of his head, and projected him face first into the headboard, snapping his neck. Scorpio grabbed the phone from the bedside table but discovered there was no dial tone. She stared at the phone with a horrified look on her face.

"They cut the phone lines," Cal told her what she had just learned for herself.

"There's no cell phone reception in the hotel either," she gasped with alarm.

"There are other intruders in the house," he gently informed her while keeping his voice down so as not to alert the others. "I'll get you out of here. Stay close by my side and don't make a sound."

She nervously nodded. Cal hurried Scorpio from the bedroom, through the never-ending hallway, and down the main stairs. He kept the baseball bat clutched in both hands close to his shoulder, prepped for action. They hurried for the main door in the foyer when they heard someone running across the front porch for the already open door. Cal pulled Scorpio down the hall just past the elevator and into the office. Both stopped when they surprised the man already in the room. The man spun for Cal with a knife in his hand. Cal was about to swing the baseball bat when he was suddenly tackled across the desk by a second man entering the room. The baseball bat flew from his hand. Scorpio screamed as the men fought, punching one another. Cal seemed to hold his own against the two men for a brief moment but was losing the battle. Scorpio ran for the discarded bat as Cal defeated the first man.

The second man slashed Cal across the arm. Scorpio saw the attack and cried out with alarm. Despite his injury, Cal continued to fight both men, as neither would stay down. The first and second man recovered at the same time and came at him. Cal seized the opportunity to escape, clutched his bleeding arm, and ran for Scorpio. He grabbed her arm rushing her from the room and away from the men. She ran with him down the hallway toward the foyer, but a third man was standing before the open door. He bolted for them. Cal forced Scorpio into the front sitting room, slammed the door behind them, and locked the door. He then hurried her toward the large side window on the far side of the room past the portable, antique bar.

"Go, Scorpio," he gasped softly. "Run for town and don't stop."

"Not without you," she whispered.

There was a thump against the sitting room door. It was immediately followed by another thump. Cal cast a look across the room at the pair of samurai swords hanging on the wall. The matching pair of swords had faux ivory, Chinese dragonhead handles, although one had a black scabbard and the other had a red scabbard. Several gunshots were fired, splintering the lock on the door. Both jumped with alarm, knowing they only had seconds to make a decision.

Chapter 2

As the bullet-riddled door flew open, two home invaders stood in the open doorway and looked into the front sitting room, scanning the massive room for the escaped couple. Not far from the portable bar, the large window stood open, and a gentle breeze blew the white, sheer curtains inward. A bloodstain was visible on the lightly flapping curtains.

"They've escaped," the leader, Argyle, announced with irritation. "Go outside and help those idiots find them. They've seen our faces. We can't let them get away."

The second man nodded and hurried from the room. Argyle again scanned the room then approached the open window and peered outside into the darkness. The excessively large grandfather clock on the other side of the fireplace struck one in the morning. Argyle glanced at the grandfather clock and saw Cal standing before him with a sword in each hand. He aimed his gun at Cal. Cal swung the sword, striking the gun, and knocking it from his hand. He slashed with both swords, slicing into his abdomen. Argyle wheezed with pain and surprise before collapsing to the floor.

Cal helped Scorpio out from under the old sofa and herded her from the room. As they hurried into the hallway, they heard someone running across the front porch just beyond the open door. Cal forced Scorpio into the small, gated elevator, jumped in with her, and closed the gate. He hit the button, and, with a loud grinding sound, the elevator disappeared for the second floor as the first man entered the foyer. He saw the elevator heading up a level and ran up the stairs; his feet loudly thumping on each step, so he could catch the elevator before whoever was within it could get away. If they got away, it would be a lot of ground to cover to find someone hiding within the hotel.

Cal opened the elevator gate on the second floor and stared into Scorpio's eyes. His look was almost as commanding as it was pleading.

"Hide in one of the rooms," he announced firmly. "I'll come and get you when it's safe."

She nodded and was about to hurry down the hallway when they heard the man running up the stairs. Cal ran to the grand stairs to greet him. As the intruder stepped onto the landing, Cal swung the sword, connecting with his neck. The man took the hit and tumbled down the stairs, striking the man standing at the bottom. The stunned man stared at his dead comrade and then ran for the sitting room.

"Argyle," he cried out as he entered through the open doorway.

Cal bolted down the stairs after the intruder and met him as he appeared from the sitting room. The intruder was possibly stunned to find his leader dead as he bolted from the room. He saw Cal with the bloodstained swords and aimed his gun at him. Cal slashed the man across the neck, allowing blood to spill from his throat. His eyes rolled back as he collapsed to the floor.

Scorpio ran down the stairs and reached the bottom then saw a man standing in the doorway. He caught a glimpse of her and aimed his gun. As the gun fired, she screamed and ran into the front sitting room with Cal on her heels. The man chasing them paused before the open doorway and aimed his weapon into the room. His eyes fell upon the gruesome fate of his leader, but Cal and Scorpio seemed to have vanished. He frowned and slowly stepped into the room while looking around. Scorpio could be seen hiding behind the sofa. He immediately aimed his weapon at the sofa and fired four shots into it.

Cal leaped out from behind the open sitting room door and attempted to defeat the man with his swords. The man leaped away from the first sharp blade and fell to the floor, dropping his gun as the blade slashed his calf. He sprang to his feet and scrambled for his discarded gun as Scorpio darted across the room and hid behind the portable bar. The man kicked Cal in the abdomen, sending him across the floor, which gave him enough time to reclaim his gun. He turned and fired several shots into the portable bar. Scorpio screamed even though the bullets didn't penetrate the thick wood. The man leaped into the opening behind the bar and aimed his gun at Scorpio where she cowered. He sneered and squeezed the trigger. The gun clicked empty. His expression dropped. Cal was suddenly standing behind him and slashed his arm as he reached for another magazine from his pocket. He clutched his bleeding arm with surprise and dropped the weapon.

Cal plunged the sword through his eye and out the back of his skull. Cal looked at Scorpio where she remained crouched behind the portable bar. He offered a tiny smile and extended his hand to her. She reached up to accept his hand then looked behind him and suddenly gasped. Cal spun around and saw the supposedly dead leader, Argyle, standing behind him with his hunting knife clutched in his hand. Argyle stabbed Cal in the abdomen. Scorpio screamed and stared with horror as Cal collapsed to his knees. She met the man's evil gaze. As he lunged for her, she ran out from behind the bar. Argyle cut off her path and was about to stab her when Cal shoved her out of the way and slashed the man across the abdomen with his sword. Argyle gasped and collapsed to the floor.

"Cal," Scorpio gasped and rushed to his side before he could fall to his knees. "You can make it to the car. I'll get you to the hospital."

She attempted to help him across the room but didn't make it far before he fell to his knees while clutching his bleeding abdomen. Scorpio kneeled alongside him and attempted to help him to his feet.

"You can make it," she cried out.

He shook his head then looked into her eyes and smiled warmly. "I love you," he whispered.

"I love you too," she gasped as tears streaked her face knowing his fate.

His eyes closed and he was gone. Scorpio gathered him into her arms, pulled his head to her chest, and sobbed softly while holding him.

§

Scorpio sat on the porch steps with a blanket wrapped around her, concealing her once white tank top now stained with blood. The local sheriff leaned against the support beam across from her and wrote on his tablet, eyeing her periodically. Sheriff Nevin Horton was a robust man in his mid-forties. Although he'd put on some weight over the years while working in the small town with a low crime rate, he still had some body mass behind him. His ginger beard helped conceal his slightly round face, and his official sheriff's cowboy hat helped cover his thinning hair.

"I'm sorry you had to relive that, Scorpio," the sheriff announced while frowning. "Would you like a ride to your grandmother's house?"

She shook her head, feeling oddly numb, while staring at nothing in particular. "No, they're on their way," Scorpio replied and shivered slightly despite the blanket and the moderately warm, early morning air.

The coroner and his men came out of the house with the stretcher containing the black body bag. Scorpio stared at the bag as if knowing that was the one containing the man she loved. She didn't take her eyes off the stretcher until they shut the back door on the coroner's wagon. She finally met the sheriff's sympathetic gaze.

"You know who's responsible for this, right?" she announced in a slightly sedate tone.

Sheriff Horton straightened while holding his breath. "We don't have any proof it was Carson Davenport. I didn't recognize any of those men," the sheriff informed her. "I know some of Davenport's employees are a little rough around the edges, but there weren't any witnesses to them ever having harassed Cal."

"He told me," she insisted while glaring at Sheriff Horton not caring if there had been any witnesses. Of course, there wouldn't be any. "They came around here and caused trouble on several occasions. I witnessed it. Doesn't that count for something?"

"I'm sorry, Scorpio," he replied gently. "You're asking me to question our most prominent citizen about a hit on one of his former employees. Cal didn't even leave his employment under bad circumstances. There's nothing to indicate there was any bad blood between them."

She shook her head then rubbed her burning eyes from crying and lack of sleep. "I should have suspected nothing would happen," Scorpio muttered.

"Your grandfather and Davenport were pretty close at one time," the sheriff remarked. "Do you honestly think he'd order a hit against his good friend's future grandson-in-law?"

"They don't get along anymore," she reminded him. "So, yes, I believe he's capable of ordering a hit on Cal in spite of my grandfather or even to hurt him."

"You've been through a traumatic experience, Scorpio," Sheriff Horton announced gently. "Go home with your grandparents and surround yourself with family and friends. You need a solid support system after an ordeal like this." He fidgeted slightly. "At least you'll have some peace knowing the men responsible are dead." He hesitated a moment then drew a tense breath. "Cal really cleaned house. He was one heroic man. Remember that."

Scorpio nodded and avoided looking at the sheriff. "Yes, he'll always be my hero."

Chapter 3

Three days later. The funeral home's front parlor was filled with large vases of flowers and two dozen folding chairs. Along the back wall was the open casket with a large flower blanket resting on the top edge of the open lid. Cal was dressed in a new, black suit. Even in death, he was handsome. Scorpio sat sedately in the front row wearing a simple black dress and black pumps. She stared at the casket containing her boyfriend, unable to take her eyes off him. To her left were her grandparents on her mother's side.

Newman and Patricia Wayland were in their mid-sixties, although they seemed younger than their years suggested. Patricia colored her shoulder-length hair, so she looked more silver than gray. She was still an attractive woman who obviously took care of herself. She wasn't as thin as she used to be, but she wasn't overweight either. Newman was completely gray. Although his hair was receding and thinning, he still had plenty of hair on his head. He was clean-cut, maintaining his youthful appearance.

Scorpio watched more than half the town show up for Cal's funeral. Cal had moved to their town when he was a teenager. Shortly after he'd graduated high school, his father died. He joined the Navy and spent the next four years on various military bases. Once his tour ended, he'd spent a couple of years in his childhood hometown to be close to his uncle. Two years ago, he returned to their small town. He was only twenty-five when he went to work for Carson Davenport. Although he never really discussed his work with Davenport, Scorpio knew he was used by the influential man to do his dirty work. Something from his past employment was, undoubtedly, what brought Davenport's hired goons to their place three nights ago. Proving his former employer had anything to do with Cal's death would be difficult. Everyone in town loved Davenport, with the exception of the few who actually knew the sort of person he was.

While keeping careful watch of those visiting Cal's casket to pay their final respects, Scorpio noticed several men she'd never met before. They weren't from town. Two men, in particular, caught her attention. There was something solemn about the moderately intimidating men in their mid to late twenties. Although neither man was built muscular, the first man was about six foot four and built sturdy. He was a clean-cut, moderately attractive African-American man with his black hair kept short.

Although the man looked at home in his dress pants and freshly pressed shirt, Scorpio thought he'd make a more convincing cowboy than a businessman. That was enough to scream hired henchman to her. The other man was devilishly handsome with flowing dark brown hair in a short, businessman cut. Although not as tall as the first man, he had a solid, athletic build as well. In his stylish suit, he looked more like a hitman for the mob than a friend of Cal's.

"I'm surprised he had the nerve to show up," Patricia scoffed taking Scorpio's attention away from the two suspicious strangers.

Her grandfather reached across her grandmother and tapped Scorpio's knee. She jumped with surprise and looked at her grandfather. He gave a slight nod across the room, indicating Carson Davenport and his trophy wife, Celine. Davenport was a distinguished looking man in his fifties. Although his brown hair was showing signs of graying, it wasn't much of a secret that he colored his hair to keep it from appearing too gray. His much younger wife would make him look older if he didn't attempt to keep the gray away. Despite being a businessman, Davenport looked more like the hired muscle than a criminal mastermind.

Women in town were smitten with the handsome, wealthy man. His muscular build only added to the attention he received.

Celine was the perfect trophy wife for a man like Davenport but stood out in their small town. The woman only a few years older than Scorpio was definitely city material from her clothes to her carefully manicured fingernails. Not a blonde hair was out of place, and her makeup was perfectly applied. Her ample breasts were as fake as her hair color. Despite attending a funeral, her black dress readily revealed her cleavage. Although Scorpio's grandfather made a face while eyeing Celine's choice of funeral wear, it was obvious he was secretly taking in a healthy gaze of her revealing dress. Any living, breathing man would notice her. Patricia rolled her eyes, although it was uncertain if she were rolling them at Celine or her husband old enough to be the blonde bombshell's grandfather.

"I can't believe he's here," Scorpio scoffed as her eyes narrowed.

Her grandmother gave her lower arm a firm squeeze. "Be civil," she announced under her breath. "Remember where we are."

"It's because of where we are that I'm not in the mood to be civil," Scorpio huffed to her grandmother.

While Scorpio was busy killing Davenport with slanted glares across the room, she hadn't realized she'd been approached by the two strangers she'd seen at Cal's casket.

"You must be Scorpio," the devilishly handsome man announced catching her attention.

Scorpio looked up and stared at the dark-haired man standing before her where she sat. He offered his best, sympathetic movie villain smile and extended his hand to her in a polite gesture.

"I'm Blake Maverick," he announced politely as she accepted his hand and shook it. "And this is Ben Stone." Maverick stared into her eyes a silent moment as if expecting her to know who they were. "We were Cal's friends growing up."

Scorpio smiled and shook Stone's hand as well. "It's a pleasure to meet some of Cal's childhood friends," she replied while studying both men. Oddly enough, Cal hadn't mentioned either of them--ever.

"Cal had left some of his belongings with us after he'd moved back here. We thought you might want them," Stone announced. "Would it be okay if we stopped by your place tomorrow and dropped them off?"

"Oh," she announced with surprise then cast a look at her grandparents, who seemed almost as skeptical as she was. She looked back at the two men and managed a polite smile. "Uh, yeah, that'd be fine. You could stop by after the funeral for the gathering if you'd like."

The two men exchanged looks then smiled back in response. "We'd love to," Maverick replied.

"Do you need the address?" Scorpio asked.

"That won't be necessary," Stone informed her. "Cal told us all about the old hotel on the bluff. We'll get together later."

Both men politely nodded and excused themselves.

Scorpio raised a suspicious brow and eyed her grandparents. "Don't leave me alone with either of those men," she announced.

"Did Cal ever mention them?" her grandmother asked with surprise.

"No, not once," she informed her and cast a glance after the men. "There must be a reason why he never mentioned them."

Davenport and Celine approached them. Scorpio was immediately set on edge the moment the man approached. She knew he had something to do with her boyfriend's murder, but there wasn't any proof or even a proper motive.

"I'm very sorry for your loss, Scorpio," Davenport announced while extending his hand to her.

Scorpio accepted his hand, although his touch was almost enough to chill her entire body. Despite her feelings, she managed a tiny smile.

"Thank you, Mr. Davenport," she announced.

"Please, call me Carson," he insisted. His look then turned serious. "If there's anything you need, anything at all, don't hesitate to call me."

Scorpio could almost hear her grandfather rolling his eyes. She was worried she'd cause a scene, but it was possible her grandfather would be the first to react.

"Thank you, Mr. Davenport," she replied.

Thankfully, there was a line of people waiting to give their condolences, so he was forced to move on. There was no telling what would have happened if she were forced to continue a conversation with the vile man.

Chapter 4

The after funeral gathering took place in the hotel's banquet hall, which had access to the outside patio. Although the room desperately needed repairs, no one seemed to notice with all the flowers from the viewing positioned along the walls. Scorpio's grandmother took care of all the gathering responsibilities. Since she was used to large formal parties, an informal gathering was easy for her. Scorpio's grandparents were one of the wealthiest families in town, second only to Carson Davenport. Her grandfather was a respected member of the community, which was why so many people showed up for Cal's funeral. Once her grandfather had a few drinks in him, he started a series of rants regarding the attack on Scorpio that resulted in Cal's death.

"If Cal hadn't killed those men, I would have found them and given them a slow, painful death," Newman announced a little louder than necessary.

Her grandmother attempted to rein him in, but his temper was already spiking.

"No one and I mean no one touches my granddaughter and gets away with it," Newman continued.

Two of his country club friends managed to guide him outside onto the lesser traveled patio, leaving Patricia relieved. Once they got some food into him, he'd be back to his usual grouchy self rather than the man who'd pick a fight with anyone right about now. At least Scorpio knew where she got her temper.

Scorpio and her twin brother never knew their parents. Their father died before they were born and their mother died only a few months after, so their grandparents were the only family they'd ever known. Scorpio's friends from college attended the gathering as well as her childhood friends. Even her best friend had driven in from Portland, where she now worked and lived. Davenport invited himself to the after funeral gathering and entertained the crowd since just about everyone thought he was an awesome guy. Scorpio had finally had enough and walked down the hall. She paused within the hallway and stared at the recently repaired sitting room door, which had been shut and locked.

Since the investigation had concluded, the room was no longer a crime scene, and a cleanup crew had been out to erase any physical signs of what had happened. Scorpio approached the door, placed her hand on the newly replaced doorknob, and attempted to open it. When it didn't open, she remembered she'd locked the door. She approached the grand staircase and sat on one of the lower steps with her drink in her hand. She couldn't deny she was well on her way to getting drunk. Her best friend, Trudy, leaned on the banister and stared at her a moment before Scorpio realized she was there.

Trudy was an attractive woman with long, wavy sandy brown hair. She stood an inch or two taller than Scorpio, although most women in town seemed to be taller than Scorpio. Trudy had been the popular girl in school and was now a successful stockbroker in Portland.

Trudy managed a sympathetic smile. "How are you holding up?" she asked gently.

Scorpio eyed her friend, held up her half-empty glass of brandy, and smirked. "A little better with each drink," she remarked.

Trudy rounded the banister and joined her on the step. She placed her arm around Scorpio and pulled her against her side. "I wish I had some magic cure," Trudy announced with a sigh. "But there's nothing I can say or do that'll change what happened or make it hurt any less."

"I know," Scorpio whispered then eyed her friend. "I'm just glad you're here."

"Of course I'm here," Trudy chirped. "I wouldn't be anywhere else at a time like this, and I'll be here as long as you need me."

"I appreciate that," Scorpio replied then managed a smile. "I miss him."

"I know," Trudy replied gently.

"Maybe we could talk about something else," Scorpio announced.

Trudy nodded and removed her arm from Scorpio's shoulder then looked around. "Where's that brother of yours?" she asked as her eyes lit up at the mention of him. "I didn't see him at the funeral."

Scorpio groaned and took another large swallow of her drink. "Who the hell knows? He's never around when I need him most," she announced and shook her head. "He took off and no one's heard from him in weeks. What else is new? He's always doing something stupid."

"Pity he's so damned cute," Trudy announced with a sigh. "He was never going to stick around a town like this anyway. He's more of the adventurer type."

"Yeah, like a plundering pirate," Scorpio teased then giggled. Her frown immediately returned. "We used to be so close before we went away to college. I don't know what prompted his need to know more about our father, but he changed after that."

"I suppose he's trying to find himself," Trudy remarked. "It's a guy thing. He never knew his father, and he feels he has to find out all he can."

"I didn't know our father either," Scorpio announced with some irritation and eyed her friend. "You don't see me attempting to hunt down his relatives." She shook her head. "I wish he'd let it be."

"It's different for him than it is for you," Trudy insisted. "Guys want to know who they are and they think that comes from knowing their father." She pressed her shoulder against Scorpio's shoulder and laughed. "He'll be back after he's blown through his inheritance."

Scorpio rolled her eyes and laughed. "You're probably right."

"He's a twenty-two-year-old man with a million dollar trust fund from your uncle's estate," Trudy boldly announced and raised her brows. "You'd better believe he's out there seizing the world."

"Trying to get himself killed is probably more accurate," Scorpio muttered.

"He was living with you and Cal before he took off for parts unknown, wasn't he?"

"Yeah," Scorpio replied and nodded up the stairs behind her. "He took one of the corner suites on the third floor. I was going to pack up his things and move them into another room, but it doesn't look like this bed and breakfast will ever be a reality."

"Don't say that," Trudy announced. "You'll make it work."

"I don't know if I want to do it on my own," she remarked sadly. "My brother was supposed to help me manage the place, and Cal was going to be in charge of repairs. Now I don't have either of them."

"Is there anything in your brother's room that might tell you where he went on his latest quest?"

"His desktop computer is in his room, but it's password protected," she announced. "He took his laptop with him when he left. Other than a variety of dirty dishes growing mold, there's not much in his room."

"Gotta love men," Trudy moaned.

"Well, there was one thing," Scorpio remarked then eyed her friend. "There was an old folder on his desk. Nothing in it."

"Old?"

"Yeah, really old," Scorpio remarked. "It had a red 'confidential' stamp across the front, so naturally I had to look inside. Just an empty folder."

"An unnamed empty folder marked confidential?" Trudy questioned then laughed. "Probably some spy stuff he didn't want to tell you about."

"That's how it looked," Scorpio announced with a chuckle. "Well, it did have a name typed on the tab."

"What did it say?"

"Midnight Requisition," Scorpio informed her and raised her brow. "Weird, huh?"

"I'm telling you," Trudy again announced. "Spy stuff. Knowing your brother, it's possible."

They exchanged looks then laughed. Scorpio glanced at her watch. The grandfather clock from the landing chimed in time with the one within the closed sitting room.

"Thankfully this day is almost over," Scorpio remarked. "I just want to go to bed and sleep for a week." She then considered the comment and eyed her friend. "Two of Cal's friends from school were supposed to show up tonight. I guess they changed their minds." She laughed and hid her grin. "You should see these guys. As handsome as they are intimidating."

"You don't say," Trudy announced with some interest and grinned slyly.

"Trust me; you don't want anything to do with these guys," Scorpio informed her. "I swear they were up to something. I'll need to sleep with my baseball bat tonight."

"Did you want me to stay tonight?"

"Would you?" Scorpio asked with enthusiasm. "I didn't want you to feel obligated."

"No, I'd love to stay," Trudy replied. "We can watch movies and eat popcorn like we used to do."

"I'd like that."

Chapter 5

The following morning, Scorpio and Trudy sat at the kitchen island counter huddled over their cups of tea. Both were still wearing their sleepwear despite it being nearly ten in the morning. Scorpio wore her tank top and sleep shorts while Trudy wore an oversized t-shirt as a nightgown. Scorpio was a little hungover, having had too much to drink at the after funeral gathering, but it helped her through a difficult day. There was a knock on the kitchen door, startling both women since few people came to the out-of-the-way hotel.

"Who'd be here at this hour of the morning?" Trudy practically demanded.

"It's almost ten," Scorpio responded while standing. "Everyone's up at this hour. It's probably my grandmother looking for leftovers to serve Grandpa for lunch."

She headed for the door and opened it without even looking to see who was on the other side. She stared at the unfamiliar man standing on her patio. Although undeniably handsome, the man in his early thirties had a nerdish genius sort of look about him. His light brown hair was cut short, and his face was clean-shaven to the point of meticulous. His expensive suit suggested wealth with a hint of snob potential. The man stared at Scorpio a moment as if he'd been expecting someone else to answer the door.

"I'm looking for Scorpio Wayland," the neatly dressed man announced.

Scorpio leaned against the doorframe while folding her arms across her chest. "You found her," she remarked while eyeing him suspiciously. "Can I help you?"

He stared at her a moment longer then immediately fidgeted and managed a smile as he handed her his business card. "I'm Rayner Roderick."

Scorpio raised her brows at the name and almost laughed. She then eyed the card but didn't uncross her arms. "I'm not interested in buying anything today, next week, or next month," she announced boldly. "I'm hungover and extremely bitchy. Now that we've been formally introduced, what do you want, Rayner Roderick?"

Rayner stared at her with some surprise then snapped out of his mild trance. "I'm here to install your new security system," he informed her.

She allowed her arms to fall to her sides as she straightened. It was her turn to be surprised. "Security system?" Scorpio asked with a curious look. "I didn't make arrangements for a security system." She then considered the comment. "Although it's not a bad idea."

He removed his clipboard and turned it toward her. "I have an order here to install exterior security cameras, a four-screen monitor system, and an alarm system for the doors and windows."

Scorpio only briefly glanced at the requisition order and shook her head. "I didn't order this."

"Uh, no," he responded and turned the clipboard back to face him so he could read it. "It was paid for by Carson Davenport." He looked at her and managed a smile. "He paid cash up front for the installation."

"Carson Davenport?" she gasped while staring at the man as if he were a monster then shook her head. "I don't want anything from that man." She again eyed him with distrust. "Who are you? You're not from around here. Why did he send you?"

Rayner seemed surprised by the line of question. "I recently moved here from Portland," he replied. "I have a small shop I just opened in town." He again extended his card to her. "Mr. Davenport commissioned me to install security systems all around town, although my specialty is computer programming."

Trudy approached Scorpio from behind and gently touched her bare shoulder. "Come on, Scorp," she announced timidly and attempted a smile. "Cut the guy a break. He's new in town; not a hitman for the mob."

"Hitman for the mob?" Rayner asked with surprise. "I can't even pick out a lobster from the tank at seafood restaurants without feeling bad."

Trudy giggled and rubbed Scorpio's shoulder. "Come on," she announced. "Lighten up. He's cute."

"If you want to refuse the installation, I understand," Rayner informed her. "You'll just need to sign that you're declining the service. I'll send the installation crew home and refund Mr. Davenport's money minus an inconvenience fee for the crew." He again extended the clipboard to her.

Scorpio stared at the innocent look on the man's face. Maybe it was because he was cute or just that he smelled good, but she suddenly felt bad for her behavior. She groaned and ran her fingers through her moderately mussed hair. "You'll end up losing money if I cancel the order, huh?"

"It's one of my larger projects," he delicately informed her. "It'll sting a little, but I don't want to make you uncomfortable."

"Carson Davenport has ruined enough lives for one week," she scoffed and waved him in. "No point making you suffer because of him."

Rayner gave her a strange look but didn't question the comment. Rayner motioned the crew of six men standing on the patio to start working on setting up exterior cameras then turned to Scorpio as she collapsed on her chair at the island counter.

"If you wouldn't mind telling me where you would like the four-monitor station set up, I'll get out of your way," he announced.

"Sure," she casually replied. "There's an office just down the hall."

"I'll get my gear," he announced and hurried from the kitchen.

Scorpio shook her head and eyed her friend as she returned to the island counter as well.

"Unbelievable," Scorpio scoffed. "Carson Davenport is trying to buy me off with an expensive security system. Like that'll make up for him killing Cal?"

Trudy held her breath while staring at her friend. "You can't go around saying things like that, Scorpio," she informed her. "He could sue you. That would certainly be the easy route to obtaining the hotel for himself."

"He'd love to get his hands on this place," Scorpio scoffed. "I heard he tried to buy it off my uncle. After he died, he tried to buy it off my grandfather, and then he tried to buy it off me." She groaned and shook her head. Scorpio then hesitated and eyed her friend. "What's with the geeky computer guy anyway? He seemed a little off to you, didn't he? It wasn't just me, right? He seemed nervous."

Trudy snorted a laugh and allowed her eyes to stray to Scorpio's white tank top. "Probably had something to do with that nearly see-through shirt you're wearing," her friend announced while grinning. "I'm thinking he was blinded by your high beams."

Scorpio looked down at her shirt and immediately gasped. She insecurely covered her chest with her arms. "My God! Why didn't you say something?"

"In front of the poor guy?" Trudy cried out then shook her head. "That would have been embarrassing for everyone." She then shrugged. "The poor guy looked like he could use the thrill anyway."

"You're awful," Scorpio announced and hurried for the back stairs.

§

Rayner and his team were at the hotel most of the day installing cameras and door and window alarms. As the men were finally packing up, Trudy returned to her parents' house to spend some time with her mother and father. Scorpio entered the study and paused in the doorway. Rayner worked on securing the panel onto four television monitors within a decorative cabinet that resembled an armoire. Although she seemed to be watching Rayner, she drifted back to her last time within the study. She could still see the intruders near the desk punching Cal. She could almost feel the knife as it cut him. When she looked down, she swore she saw his blood on her hands as he pulled her from the room and away from their attackers.

Scorpio shivered and ran trembling fingers through her hair. Despite having showered and changed, her hair was already a mess after she'd subconsciously ran her fingers through it for possibly the one thousandth time today. Pulling out her hair was turning into a nervous twitch. Rayner saw her, straightened proudly, and offered a pleasant smile.

"I'll need to come back tomorrow and tie everything together," he informed her. "Once I'm finished, you'll be able to digitally record everything the security cameras see. If you'd like, I can even tie it into your cell phone, alerting you to activity even when you're not here in the study or when you're away from home."

"Unfortunately," she announced, "cell phone service is spotty around here."

"You don't need cell phone service," he replied while grinning. "This works off your wireless router. You have internet, right? It'll all tie into that."

"I don't have wireless internet," she corrected. "The man who installed the internet gave me an outrageous quote to cover the entire hotel. People come here to get away from technology, so it wasn't worth it."

He waved her off as he leaned against the corner of the desk. "I'll throw it in for free," Rayner informed her. "Since I'm already hooking up the entire system, it's really just one more piece of equipment. It won't take much to add it for you."

"Really?"

Rayner nodded.

She laughed and shrugged. "Hell, yeah," Scorpio announced with enthusiasm. "Do it then."

He straightened and packed up his toolset. "Alright then. I'll be back in the morning to finish setting up the terminals."

As Rayner was about to leave, Scorpio took a quick step toward him. She had a serious look in her eyes. "What about inside cameras?" she asked. "Can you install inside cameras without disrupting the rustic appeal of the hotel?"

"Everything is wireless these days," he informed her. "Most hotels install cameras to catch the corridors, stairwells, and elevators for security reasons."

"How much would that cost?" she eagerly asked.

"I could take a quick walk through the hotel before I leave and have a figure for you in the morning when I return," he informed her.

She stared at him a moment and felt relief sweeping through her. "Thank you."

He smiled and nodded. Rayner walked past her and entered the hallway. Scorpio turned and followed him to the foyer. He hesitated by the front door then turned to face her with an oddly sympathetic look.

"Have you ever heard of a panic room?" he asked and raised his brows.

"Yeah, of course."

"I have a friend in security who installs panic rooms, bunkers, and other types of personal safety," he informed her. "With all the rooms you have in this place, it wouldn't take much to convert one of the rooms adjoined to your bedroom into a safe haven. If someone breaks into your house, you can remain safely locked away until help arrives."

"You heard about what happened here?" she asked with a curious raise of her brow.

He fidgeted slightly and nodded. "Yes, I had," Rayner replied. "It's a small town."

"I appreciate the suggestion and your concern," Scorpio announced. Her eyes then turned almost hateful. "But if there is a *next time*, I assure you I won't be hiding in some panic room. If there's a next time, I'll be ready for it."

Rayner stared at her a moment as if attempting to read her harsh expression. He then casually looked around the foyer and grand hallway before meeting her gaze.

"I noticed you've been renovating this old place," he remarked then raised his own brow. "I'll bet you could come up with a dozen secret passageways. They might come in handy." He handed her a card and smiled slyly. "I have a friend who's a carpenter--and a survivalist."

She accepted the card and returned the knowing smile. "Thank you."

§

Later that evening, the phone's relentless ringing sent Scorpio hustling down the hall to answer it before the machine picked up. She picked up the old-fashioned phone from the hall table.

"Hello?"

"Hey, it's me," Trudy announced from the other end. "My parents want me to stay for dinner, and they asked if you wanted to join us."

Scorpio fidgeted. She didn't feel like being entertained by more people feeling sorry for her, and she especially didn't feel like putting on a bra and going out.

"Tell them thanks, Trudy, but it's been a long day," she replied. "I think I'd like to take a hot bath and go to bed early tonight. That security guy is coming back in the morning to finish the installation, so I should get some sleep."

"You still want me to come back tonight, right?" Trudy asked. "I could use the spare key if you still keep it hidden in the same spot."

"No, I removed that key," Scorpio informed her. "I'll be fine. Stay with your parents tonight. I'm sure you have a lot of catching up to do. Since the security guy posted nearly a dozen security signs around the house, I'm actually feeling safer."

"Okay," Trudy announced with a sigh. "I'll drop by late morning and keep you company while they finish the work on your place."

They exchanged goodbyes before Scorpio hung up the phone. She looked around the hallway then stared at the closed sitting room door. She gently rubbed her chilled arms. She was suddenly cold. That hot bath sounded better and better, especially if it were accompanied by a glass of wine or two.

Chapter 6

Scorpio lounged in the large garden tub beneath a layer of bubbles. The tub comfortably seated two with plenty of additional room. She knew it for a fact since she and Cal had spent several romantic evenings within the tub. Despite being by herself, she had the lights dimmed and several candles burning on the broad ledge before the stained glass window. She sipped her wine while fighting her tears as romantic memories of her and Cal in the tub flooded her mind. She finished her second glass of wine and was about to pour a third when she thought better of it. She didn't need to drown in the tub. She stared across the large tub at the vacant end and imagined Cal soaking across from her. His rugged, manly beard covered in a beard of bubbles and his Navy tattoo glistening on his muscular arms. She shut her eyes and recalled their last romantic soak.

Three months ago, Scorpio and Cal soaked in the large tub together. She saw the sly, lustful grin on Cal's bubble-covered face as he caressed her legs beneath the water while moving across the tub for her. He loved stalking her in the tub. She could feel his hands firmly caressing her lower legs and traveling beyond her knees. She loved the way he touched her; firm but loving.

"Scorp," a familiar male voice called out from the bedroom. "Hey, Scorp. You in here?"

Cal groaned and moved back to his side of the tub. "Please tell me you locked the bathroom door."

"I have a twin brother who knows no boundaries," Scorpio announced. "The day he moved into the hotel, I started locking doors."

"Scorpio?" came the voice from the next room. Without fail, there was a knock on the door. "Hey, Scorp, you in there?"

"Taking a bath, Kane," she announced loudly with some irritation.

"Oh, good," he announced. "I was afraid you were on the toilet."

The bathroom door opened, surprising them both. Cal covered his eyes with his sudsy hand and groaned as Scorpio immediately sank down in the tub while screaming at her brother.

"What the hell?" she cried out.

Kane eyed the couple in the tub but showed little reaction. "Oh, hey, Cal," he announced then focused his attention on his sister now sunken in the tub up to her neck. "You won't believe what I found tonight."

"Whatever it is, I'm not interested, Kane," she snarled as her eyes pierced through his. "Cal and I are taking a bath. Take the hint!"

Kane was a handsome young man in his own rights with an almost steampunk sort of appeal. His brown hair was kept short although moderately spiky on top, and his neatly trimmed beard looked more like a five o'clock shadow. He was slightly shorter than average, being a tick over five foot eight. Kane wasn't built very muscular and his moderately worn clothes kept in theme with his whole steampunk look. He stared at her through innocent blue eyes as if he didn't understand her hostility toward him at that moment.

"It wasn't like I was asking Cal to leave," Kane announced and rolled his eyes with a groan. "Trust me; no one wants to see that." He eagerly sat on the edge of the tub facing Scorpio and grinned almost boyishly. "I was able to find some information on the men and the team our father served with in the military."

She shirked back to keep distance between her and her brother now sitting on the edge of the tub near her. "Kane," she snarled. "Out!"

"But I discovered there was this mission," he attempted to explain.

"I don't care," she practically screamed and splashed tub water at him.

Kane jumped from the edge of the tub and shook the water from his hands. "You're certainly touchy tonight." He then eyed Cal, who had his temple propped on his fist while attempting to ignore the entire conversation. "You're slacking in your duties, Cal," he announced. "She's obviously not getting enough."

"I would be," she launched hotly, "if you'd stop interrupting!"

"Okay, fine," he scoffed and threw his hands in the air. "It can wait. You used to be more approachable." Kane left the bathroom then poked his head back inside. "And if you want privacy, you should try locking the door." He flicked the lock into place and shut the door behind him.

Scorpio groaned, straightened within the tub, and leaned her head against the back. "I love him dearly, but sometimes I'd like to kill him."

She eyed Cal across the tub while fidgeting. Cal still had his head propped against his fist with a strange smirk on his face. She stared at him with surprise.

"You think that's funny?" she suddenly demanded.

"A little," Cal replied while holding back his laugh. "He reminds me of a chipmunk on speed." Cal leaned forward and again caressed Scorpio's legs while moving his way across the tub for her.

She glared at him and raised her brow.

He hesitated and gave her a strange look. "What's wrong?" Cal asked. "The door's locked." He grinned seductively. "I'll put you back in the mood."

Scorpio held her sudsy hand up revealing four fingers. She counted down from four. "Three, two, one--"

There was a light tapping on the bathroom door. "Hey, I'm going to order some pizza," Kane announced through the door. "You guys want some? You probably will. I know I get hungry after sex."

Scorpio covered her eyes and groaned.

"Yeah," Cal called out with enthusiasm. "Get one with pepperoni!"

She glared at him through squinting eyes. He caught her look and managed an innocent smile.

"What?" he asked. "Well, he's not wrong about getting hungry after sex."

Present day. A faint crash brought Scorpio out of her mostly enjoyable recollection of a time not so long ago and back to reality. She looked around the candlelit bathroom, realizing she'd momentarily dozed off in the tub, which was dangerous. She then heard another sound and realized it was the floorboard creaking outside her bedroom door. Scorpio sprang up within the tub and snatched her towel. She immediately regretted the action as the wine hit her hard. She practically stumbled out of the tub, barely running the towel over her body before slipping into her satin robe. She tied the robe that only came halfway down her thighs and hurried for the bathroom door. She reached for the knob when she heard what definitely sounded like someone inside her bedroom.

Scorpio flipped the lock on the door and quickly backed away from it. She stared at the door a moment and listened for any sounds. Was she just hearing things? She then heard another floorboard creak now closer to the bathroom door. Scorpio looked around the bathroom for anything she could use as a weapon, but there was nothing readily available. She then looked to the connecting door to the shared bathroom. She hurried for the door, silently unlocked it, and peered into the adjoining bedroom. The adjoining room hadn't been touched in years. It was dark, dirty, and filled with cobwebs.

She entered the room, silently shutting the door behind her, and turned the lock. Scorpio hurried across the dingy room with sheet-covered furniture still intact. She paused before the bedroom's main door and silently opened it, peering into the dimly lit corridor. When she didn't see anyone, she hurried down the hall for the back kitchen stairs. She heard another floorboard creak, causing her to look back. An unfamiliar man stepped into the hallway from her bedroom, spotted her, and shouted to someone. He obviously wasn't alone. Scorpio held back her gasp and ran along the hallway with her satin robe clinging to her wet body. She reached the less impressive back stairs and hurried down them.

Scorpio wanted to make as little noise as possible, but she couldn't slow in fear of the man catching up to her. She reached the bottom of the kitchen stairs, swung the corner, and suddenly skidded to a stop. There were two more men in the kitchen already heading for the stairs, having heard her coming down them. She spun toward the kitchen door but the two men from the second floor came down the steps and cut off her path to the door. Scorpio turned several times while assessing her rather grim situation. Her head was foggy from the two glasses of wine. She knew she needed to elude the men. She'd never make it past the two men to the kitchen door or up the back stairs.

Her only hope was making it past the two men blocking her path across the massive kitchen, where she'd have room to outmaneuver them. Scorpio faked a dodge to the right then bolted left directly for the heavy kitchen table. She threw herself onto the table, rolled across it past the men, and leaped off the other side. Despite the alcohol, she was able to catch her balance and bolted for the swinging door, knowing she wouldn't have to slow to stop and open it. She plowed through the door and into the hallway, colliding with a fifth man, taking them both to the floor. He was as startled as she was when they hit the floor.

Scorpio was already on her knees while hovering over him and attempted to ram her knee into his groin. He suddenly grabbed a handful of her long hair and pulled back, momentarily stopping her plan. He reversed their position and tackled her to the floor, landing on top of her. Scorpio thrashed beneath him, attempting to free herself while he made an effort to catch her wrists before she could hit him. He pinned her wrists to the floor on either side of her head and hovered over her, restraining her to the floor with his body as well. She attempted to break free, but she was held immobile. She could hear the four men from the kitchen enter the hallway.

"You got her?" one of the intruders asked.

"Yeah, I got her," the man on top of her announced while breathing heavily as he kept her pinned to the floor. His eyes then strayed to her satin robe clinging to her wet, naked body.

A twisted smile crossed his face. He then eyed the other men not far from them. "The security cameras aren't even connected yet. We're clear."

"What about her?" one of the other men asked.

The man again eyed her wet body through the robe. "I'll take care of her," he announced a little too eagerly. "Get the zip-ties." He smiled deviously. "I want her a little less squirmy."

Without releasing her wrists, he stood and pulled her to her feet. Before she could even react, he slammed her against the wall near the stairs. He forced her hands up to the rung just above her head and stared into her eyes as his man approached with a pair of zip-ties. He again looked over her body while pressing his hips against hers as he grinned.

"This evening is going to be more fun than I thought," the man announced and chuckled.

"I call seconds," the man with the zip-ties announced while grinning.

He swiftly zip-tied her wrists to the rung above her head while she fought to keep him from restraining her. Both men watched her struggle, enjoying catching glimpses of flesh as she fought her restraints. The man before her nodded to the three men who seemed to keep their distance. They didn't appear pleased with what was about to happen.

"Search the occupied bedrooms and the study," the first man announced.

The three remaining men dispersed. Two headed upstairs while the other entered the nearby study.

Chapter 7

The remaining two men, who were only a few years older than Scorpio, watched her attempt to free herself. Although they kept an eye on her, she wasn't even paying attention to them. She'd already seen enough of them to know they weren't very big nor were they overly intelligent. She just needed to concentrate on freeing herself. She eyed the rung above her head while clinging to it with both hands. The rung was loose. All the rungs were loose on the staircase. With the right amount of pressure, she could break the rung, freeing her hands. Both men exchanged sly grins and chuckled.

"It's cute," the first man announced. "She's trying to figure a way out of her predicament."

"I like when they struggle," the second man remarked while scanning her body. "My girlfriend just lays there like a sack of potatoes."

The first man laughed and unbuckled his belt as he took a step closer to her. Scorpio gripped the rung above her head and kicked out with both feet, striking the man in the chest. He was thrown across the hallway and struck the table with a crash. The rung cracked slightly beneath her weight. The second man sneered with annoyance and charged for her. Scorpio attempted to kick him in the crotch. He caught her foot and laughed while holding her leg in the air. He ran his hand along the leg he held and caressed her thigh.

"What are you going to do now, baby?" he announced while grinning.

Scorpio sneered while supporting her weight by holding onto the rung and kicked him in the face with her free foot. He fell to the floor and appeared somewhat dazed as well as surprised. As her feet touched the floor, she felt the rung crack a little more. She eyed the rung then looked back at both men as they recovered.

"Enough screwing around," the first man snarled. "Grab her legs!"

"I may not be an expert," a male voice announced from across the grand hallway.

All eyes were suddenly on the foyer and the man standing within the doorway. Maverick kept his hands in his pockets as he casually walked down the foyer steps.

"But I don't think that's the best way to win a woman's heart," Maverick informed them.

"Who the hell are you?" the first intruder suddenly demanded.

"Me?" Maverick announced then shrugged. "I'm no one of any importance. In fact, I just met the young lady yesterday at the funeral."

The first intruder pulled his gun and aimed it at Maverick who was now halfway to them and close to the bottom of the grand stairs.

"If you were smart, you would have just walked away," the man announced. "Now I'm afraid you're going to die with her."

Maverick casually removed his hands from his pockets causing the second man to pull his weapon as well. Maverick simply raised his brows almost humored and chewed the side of his fingernail.

"Yeah, about that," Maverick announced and spit out a fragment of fingernail. "I've never been extremely bright, and you got the second part half right."

Both stared at him with bewilderment. "What do you mean 'half right'?" the first man demanded. "I don't have time for this. Kill the bastard."

"I predict someone will die," Maverick announced while grinning. "But I don't think it's going to work out quite the way you think it should." He then eyed Scorpio while placing his hands on his hips. "Do you just intend to hang around all night? When Cal bragged about you, I sort of had someone more badass in mind."

"Yeah, well," Scorpio muttered with irritation while pulling on the partially broken rung. "We all have our off days."

"Should I kill him?" the second man demanded while casting a look at the first man.

Maverick's eyes shifted to the ceiling almost reflectively as he pointed a finger. "Did you hear that?"

Both men cast a look at the ceiling but didn't hear anything. Maverick suddenly grinned and leaned on the end of the staircase banister.

"I didn't hear anything," the first man snarled then glared at his partner. "Shoot him already."

"Really?" Maverick remarked with surprise. "You didn't hear that?"

"Stop playing games," the first man snarled.

One of the intruders from upstairs sailed over the second floor railing and swan dived to the hallway floor between them. He landed face first. Both men jumped with surprise. Scorpio gasped and stared at the broken, bloodied man who had landed on the floor near her feet. Maverick straightened while grinning.

"You're right," Maverick announced almost mockingly at the distracted men. "Playtime is over."

Maverick pulled a gun from his hidden shoulder holster and shot both men. Scorpio screamed with surprise and stared at the two men as they hit the floor with bullet holes between their eyes. Maverick eyed Scorpio and indicated both men with his gun while grinning.

"Great shot, right?"

The remaining downstairs intruder bolted from the study and aimed his weapon at Maverick. He stared with horror at his three dead teammates on the floor then aimed his gun at Maverick with more conviction.

"You're so dead," the man announced and tightened his finger on the trigger.

Maverick rolled his eyes and appeared almost bored. The last intruder from upstairs fell from the second floor landing and struck the man with the gun, crushing him. Stone peered over the railing to the hallway below.

"Did I get him?" Stone asked then suddenly grinned and held his hands in the air. "Strike. I love bowling with bodies!"

Stone walked down the steps and casually kicked the rung Scorpio struggled against, snapping it in two. She leaped away from the stairs and immediately tiptoed through the hallway littered with dead bodies and rapidly spilling blood. Stone joined Maverick at the bottom of the stairs and eyed Scorpio who fought to free her wrists still tied together with the unforgiving plastic ties.

"I thought Cal said his girlfriend was as vicious as a pit-bull," Stone remarked while indicating Scorpio with a mocking smile. "Looks more like a froo froo little poodle to me. About the size of one too."

"What the hell do you want?" she snarled while momentarily giving up her struggle. "Tell me now, or I'll kill you both!"

They stared at her with surprise then watched her again fight her bindings.

"Well, she's optimistic," Stone announced then chuckled at her expense.

Maverick replaced his gun to his shoulder holster and removed a knife from his boot. Scorpio threw herself across the floor, snatched one of the discarded guns, and rolled into a crouched position with the gun aimed at Maverick.

"That's close enough," she growled while staring him down. The look in her eyes was wild and unpredictable.

Maverick and Stone exchanged looks then grinned actually humored by her actions.

"She's feisty," Stone announced. "I like her. Can we keep her?"

"You could shoot us, if you'd like," Maverick informed her, "but we did just save your ass, so you may want to reconsider. Remember, I didn't shoot you."

Scorpio lowered the gun and groaned. "Forgive me," she huffed with hostility. "I'm having a bad day."

"You're forgiven," Maverick announced while smiling charmingly. He held up the knife while raising his brows. "If you'll permit me--?"

Scorpio tossed the gun aside and held her bound hands out to him while groaning. Maverick approached and cut the zip-ties from her wrists. He replaced the knife to his boot as she nervously ran her fingers through her damp hair.

"How do I know you're not with these guys?" she asked. "You showed up the same time they did. It's an amazing coincidence."

"I suppose because you're still alive would be the appropriate response," Maverick informed her almost mockingly. "We didn't want to intrude last night during the gathering, so we thought we'd stop by tonight and drop off some of Cal's things."

She stared at both men and shook her head. "And you just happened to show up the same time as the men who tried to kill me?"

"Yeah, our timing is quite amazing," Stone informed her then chuckled. "Actually, we saw them sneaking into the hotel and assumed they weren't invited."

"Are you going to stop me from calling the police?" she asked.

Maverick indicated the faux antique phone on the hall table and smiled charmingly. "Be my guest. In fact, I insist," he announced. "We've nothing to hide."

The two men considered the comment then exchanged looks as if reading each other's minds.

"Bodyguards?" Stone asked.

"Yeah, that'll do," Maverick replied then looked at Scorpio and smiled. "We've nothing to hide, but if you'd be so kind as to tell the sheriff you hired us as additional security after what happened to Cal, we'd be grateful."

Scorpio picked up the phone on the hall table and eyed them while dialing the old-fashioned phone. "Are you really Cal's childhood friends?"

"Absolutely," Stone announced.

"So why didn't he ever mention you?" she demanded while waiting for the sheriff to pick up.

"We're part of the life he was trying to leave behind," Maverick explained. "If someone from our past is responsible for Cal's death, we want a piece of him."

She stared at them a long moment with some surprise. "You know, I think we need to sit down and compare notes," Scorpio remarked.

"Do you have a few hours?" Stone asked.

"No, but I'll make the time," she announced. "It seems to me they were after something that belonged to Cal. The man in charge instructed them to search the bedrooms and the study."

"But you don't know what it could be?" Maverick asked her.

"Not a clue," she replied. "But whatever they were looking for, it doesn't exist. I went through this place paper by paper after Cal was killed trying to find proof that Davenport was responsible, but there's nothing here."

"Give us two days," Maverick announced. "We'll find out what they were looking for and why Cal was killed."

"You have until tomorrow evening," she countered.

Chapter 8

One month later. Kane Wayland sat in a booth against the wall near the back of the all-night trucker diner just off the highway. It was late, and the diner only had a few weary patrons, which were probably all truck drivers looking to fuel up before continuing their journey. The diner was a popular truck stop since it had free wireless internet. Kane typed into his laptop computer and watched several screens appear than disappear. His fingers suddenly stopped as he stared at the screen with alarm on his face. His expression shattered at Cal's month-old obituary. Kane firmly ran his fingers through his spiky hair while nearly pulling some out as he read the obituary.

"Murdered during a home invasion," Kane gasped softly aloud. He shook his head and continued to read the article. "Survived by--" Kane shut his eyes and exhaled with relief at word that his sister was still alive. "Thank God you're okay." He shook his head and slammed the laptop shut. "I'm coming, Scorpio. Hold on."

Kane leaped out of the booth, slipped his laptop into his backpack, and hurried from the diner. He headed across the remote parking lot where his black 1967 Chevy Camaro muscle car was parked practically hidden among the massive eighteen-wheeler trucks. He removed his car keys from his pocket and manually unlocked the car door. Being it was a classic car, he didn't have the luxury of remote locks or an alarm system. He was about to toss his backpack into the passenger seat when he heard someone approach. Kane instinctively turned to see two men standing before him.

"Nice car," the man in his early twenties announced while grinning. "How about letting us take her for a ride?"

§

Kane's black sports car was parked in the abandoned parking lot of a vacant warehouse. The warehouse was in the middle of nowhere just off some back road in Virginia. Flames from inside the car with its dead driver swiftly engulfed its exterior. Had there been anyone living nearby or driving past they would have seen the flames reaching to the sky. As it was, there was no one within miles.

§

Scorpio tossed beneath the covers on her excessively large bed within the master bedroom. She whimpered in her sleep then cried out and flew up in bed.

"Kane!"

Scorpio clutched her chest while staring into the darkness and breathing heavily. She started sobbing uncontrollably while running trembling fingers through her hair. The bedroom door flew open, but she didn't even notice or care. Maverick, who was dressed in a t-shirt and shorts, hurried to her bedside while a shirtless Stone darted across the room with his semiautomatic in his hand. Maverick sat on the bed facing her and attempted to calm her in a soothing tone.

"Scorpio, it's okay," he announced gently. "It was just another bad dream. You're fine."

She sobbed and threw her arms around his neck, clinging to him. Maverick was slightly startled by her emotional reaction and uncertainly placed his arms around her. Despite having moved into her hotel a month ago, Scorpio hadn't bonded with the guys on that sort of level, so her emotional reaction was a bit surprising. Stone lowered his gun, eyed them on the bed together in a warm embrace, and shook his head.

"Next time you get to play the muscle while I console the hysterical woman," Stone scoffed and turned on the bedroom light, brightening the room considerably.

Scorpio was jolted back into reality along with the light. She pulled away from Maverick and gave him a warning shove as if he'd been the one to reach out emotionally.

"I'm fine," she snapped while angrily wiping the tears from her cheeks.

"Must've been one hell of a nightmare," Maverick remarked while studying her. Despite her reaction, he still remained on the bed while facing her.

Stone, who only wore pajama bottoms, collapsed into the nearby chair and allowed his gun to rest on his lap. "The fourth one this week," he reminded her. "The car wreck again?"

"Maybe we should discuss these nightmares," Maverick insisted. "They seem to be getting worse. If you talk about it, maybe they'll stop."

"The underlying issue is her mother's death," Stone announced to his friend. "She needs to discuss her mother. Once she brings the underlying issue out into the open, *then* the nightmares will stop."

"When did you become the nightmare authority?" Maverick demanded while glaring at his friend.

Scorpio groaned and fell back onto the bed and shut her eyes. "Will you two take it someplace else?" she scoffed. "I'm trying to have an emotional breakdown here, and neither of you are helping."

Both men stared at her in silence. When she didn't hear any further bickering, she opened her eyes and looked at her friends.

"Did that actually work?" she remarked and again sat up in bed. She sighed and held her head. "I know you're trying to help, and I do appreciate it." Scorpio drew a deep, shaken breath. "The dream wasn't about my mother." She lifted her head and eyed both men. "It was about my brother. I keep having this dream about my brother's car running off the road and exploding into a fiery inferno." She clutched her head in her hands. "I can hear him screaming as the flames slowly burn him alive."

"We have all our best connections attempting to find him," Stone informed her. "Trust me when I tell you, if a man has enough resources and he doesn't want to be found, you're not going to find him."

"What reason would he have to hide?" Scorpio demanded. "If he's alive, why wouldn't he call and say he's okay?"

"Personally, I like the tropical island paradise scenario," Stone informed her while grinning. "Too many girls and not enough hands."

"You can stop trying to cheer me up," Scorpio scoffed while casting a stray look at both men. "It's bad enough when Kane would share the X-rated version of his romantic interludes with me. I don't need to relive them."

"I can't believe your brother gave you graphic details about his sex life," Maverick remarked with a look of distaste. "You're his sister. Makes my skin crawl a little."

She rolled her eyes while waving him off. "It's a twin thing," Scorpio huffed then shook her head. "That was his excuse for all the weird things he would do. Some bullshit about two halves of the same person." She sighed and considered the comment. "I'm pretty sure I smothered him in the womb. His brain must not have gotten enough oxygen." She straightened and looked at both weary men. "I don't need you here. I'm fine, really. Go back to bed."

Stone and Maverick reluctantly left her room, leaving the door open behind them.

"Shut the door," she called after them with an irritated groan.

Maverick returned, flashed a charming smile, and closed the door. Scorpio shook her head. There were times over the last month that the two men had gotten on her nerves, but she honestly didn't know if she would have survived without them. Although, she sometimes wished they'd let her find that out. She didn't understand her relationship with Maverick and Stone. She'd never become so close so fast to complete strangers before. She wished she could say it was because they were close to Cal, and she felt that bond. That wasn't the case.

Their quest to avenge Cal was what brought them together, but their bond was difficult to explain. Even though it was only two in the morning, Scorpio knew she wasn't getting any more sleep that night. She'd had too many of those nights since Cal's death.

Chapter 9

Eight months later. It was early morning or technically in the middle of the night. Scorpio wearily walked down the dimly lit, second floor hallway in her sleep shorts, tank top, and bare feet. Ever since Cal's murder, Scorpio was certain to keep emergency lights on within the hallways, keeping the hotel's main areas partially lit. The additional lighting also helped with the security cameras Rayner had installed a few days after the second attack. With the security cameras operational and additional alarms on the doors and windows, the hotel had been incident free in nine months. Of course, some of that may have had something to do with her new roommates. Although she referred to Stone and Maverick as her general manager and head of maintenance, most people in town chose to believe they were her bodyguards. She didn't mind that rumor circulating. It worked in her favor, and the men *were* overly protective of her.

She approached the grand stairs and headed down them, grateful for the dim light, so she didn't need to turn on actual lights in order to see. She'd spent many nights awake and wandering the halls. After more than eight months, the common areas on the first floor were transforming nicely from extensive renovations. Maverick and Stone pulled their weight when it came to renovating the old place, which put the hotel back on schedule. After Cal's death, Scorpio was about ready to give up on the dream that began with her uncle. Maverick and Stone were lifesavers in many ways, restoring her purpose and even giving her a little hope.

Scorpio paused before the front sitting room and stared at the closed and locked door. The room still hadn't been touched since Cal's death. She touched the doorknob and turned it. She wasn't surprised that it was locked, because it had been locked ever since the crime scene, cleanup crew left nine months ago. If the door hadn't been locked, she would have been surprised, but she routinely checked it anyway. Scorpio continued down the grand hallway and entered the nearby study, immediately approaching the decorative armoire. She opened the double doors and stared at the four security monitors. Each monitor revealed security camera viewpoints from different areas of the hotel's exterior. One monitor was devoted solely to the few interior cameras in the common areas. She sat on the edge of the desk and watched the night vision cameras switching views.

Everything appeared peaceful both inside and out, which had a calming effect on her most restless nights. As she watched the monitors for no particular reason, she saw a blur of someone walking past the kitchen camera. Scorpio stood and squinted at the monitor, uncertain she had actually seen something. She fiddled with the controls and kept the view locked on the kitchen camera. She caught a glimpse of someone heading up the back stairs. Scorpio leaped for the control panel and picked up the phone connected to it. She pressed a button and waited while scanning the monitors for more activity.

"Yeah," a weary Maverick announced into the phone. "Something wrong?"

"Someone's heading up the back stairs," Scorpio informed him. "I don't think it's Stone. Alert him. I'm on my way up."

"No, Scorpio," Maverick announced firmly while coming to life. "Just stay where you are. We'll handle it."

Scorpio hung up the phone and approached the nearby bookcase. She pulled a book from the shelf, opened the fake book cover, and removed a semiautomatic handgun. Scorpio tossed the fake book aside and hurried from the study. Rather than head for the kitchen, she hurried for the grand stairs to cut off the intruder with a frontal assault. Her adrenaline was rushing at the thought of an intruder in the hotel. Whoever it was had managed to slip past the security alarm connected to the doors or windows. It didn't seem possible.

Scorpio silently scaled the stairs, attempting to make as little noise as possible. She knew which steps creaked, successfully bypassing each one. She reached the second floor landing and heard a loud thump followed by a sharp scream. Scorpio bolted up the last few steps and ran along the hallway with the gun in her hand while keeping her finger in line with the trigger. The main hall lights suddenly came on, startling her. She reached the commotion and saw Stone straddling the intruder on the floor.

"Help," Trudy screamed from beneath the large man.

Scorpio suddenly gasped and ran for them. She saw Trudy face down on the floor with her arm pinned behind her back as Stone crushed her against the floor.

"Trudy," Scorpio cried out with horror then glared at the big man on top of her. "Stone, get off her!"

Stone immediately released Trudy and stood. Trudy flipped onto her back, sat up, and kicked Stone in the shin. He jumped with surprise and let out a yelp.

"What the hell?" Stone cried out.

"You nearly broke my arm, you big ox," Trudy screamed back at him.

Maverick approached and extended his hand to her. "Forgive Stone," he announced and offered a charming smile. "He doesn't know his own strength."

Trudy glared at Maverick then looked at Scorpio from where she remained sitting on the floor. "Who the hell are these guys?" she demanded. "I thought the hotel was still closed."

"It is," Scorpio explained. "I forgot you hadn't met Stone and Maverick the last time you were home."

Trudy glared at both men, who offered sympathetic looks. When Stone offered his hand, she reluctantly accepted it, allowing him to help her to her feet.

"I'm sorry," Stone explained and attempted a smile. "I don't typically wrestle women to the floor and sit on them. Well, not without permission."

"Really?" she snapped with irritation. "You seem pretty good at it."

Scorpio approached her friend and gave her a serious look. "Trudy, how did you get past the alarm system?"

"What alarm system?" Trudy demanded. "You gave me a key after Cal's funeral, remember? It was for the back door, so I let myself in."

Scorpio suddenly eyed both guys, who appeared equally curious. "The alarm was set," she announced. "I set it myself."

"Why didn't the alarm sound?" Maverick questioned.

§

All four entered the dimly lit kitchen and approached the monitor on the wall alongside the outer door. The system indicated it was armed and functioning properly. With that being the case, it should have gone off when Trudy didn't enter the code.

"I don't get it," Scorpio announced. "Why didn't it go off?"

Maverick approached the alarm monitor and started pushing buttons. Scorpio watched him and the messages that flashed past. She had no idea what he was doing even though Rayner had explained all the buttons and functions to her. She would need the instruction manual in order to figure out the damned thing. Maverick paused and pointed to the message on the monitor.

"This door has been disarmed," he announced while looking back at her. "It was set for bypass."

"Who would have done that?" Scorpio demanded then looked at Stone.

He shrugged and held his hands in the air defensively. "Don't look at me," he announced. "Electronics aren't my specialty."

Maverick again pressed several buttons and reactivated the kitchen alarm. "Well," he announced with a sigh, "it's armed now."

Scorpio stared at the monitor and shook her head. "Maybe the kitchen alarm was never set," she remarked now questioning her usual nightly habits. "The three of us are the only ones with access to the codes."

There was a beep from the monitor. All four looked at it. It flashed that the kitchen zone was bypassed and disarmed. Maverick again set the alarm. Within a few seconds, it switched off.

"Okay, you have a defective monitor," Maverick informed her. "Either that or there's something wrong with the door sensor."

Scorpio shook her head and groaned. "I'll call that Rayner guy out in the morning."

Stone flipped the deadbolt on the door. "There. Problem solved," he proudly announced then eyed the others. "Now we can go back to bed."

Chapter 10

Scorpio's jeep pulled up to the old country mansion just on the outskirts of town early that morning. It didn't look like the home of the second wealthiest couple in town, but it was considered ritzy to those within the small town. Looking more like a plantation home; the country mansion was nearly one hundred years old and still in amazing condition. Scorpio got out of her jeep and hurried toward the front door where her grandmother waited in the doorway for her. The look on her grandmother's face was concerning to Scorpio.

"Grandma, what's wrong?" Scorpio asked while studying the older woman, attempting to read her emotions. "Did something happen? Is Grandpa okay?"

Patricia threw her arms around Scorpio's neck and sobbed softly. Scorpio held her a moment then pulled away just enough to meet her gaze.

"Grandma, what is it?" she practically gasped. "What happened?"

Her grandmother sniffed and dabbed her eyes then met Scorpio's frightened gaze. "Early this morning, they found your brother's car," she announced gently. "The car and the driver were burned beyond recognition, but they're sure it was Kane. He'd been dead maybe six months or longer before someone found the car last night at the abandoned factory."

"Are they sure it was him?" Scorpio choked on her words. "If the car was burned, couldn't--?"

Patricia held back her sobs. "They found what was left of his wallet in the center console and were able to identify the car by the VIN number."

Scorpio stared at her grandmother as the nightmares she'd had eight months ago played out in her mind. Some claimed twins were able to sense when their sibling died. Perhaps that was the significance of her nightmares. She knew her brother had died. The first thing Kane bought with his inheritance was that damned muscle car. He was addicted to high speeds and thrilling chases. Plenty had suspected he'd one day die in a fiery crash.

Scorpio held back her sobs and sniffed. "I always hated that damned car," she scoffed while wiping the tears from her eyes. She almost felt more angry than sad. "Where did it happen? Was he driving too fast?"

"It happened in Virginia."

Scorpio stared at her grandmother with some surprise. "Virginia? What was he doing in Virginia?"

She shook her head unable to guess an answer. "Your grandfather caught the first flight out this morning to identify him and bring his remains home for a proper burial." Her grandmother then seemed to tense and fidgeted slightly. "I really don't want to tell you this, but you're bound to find out eventually once it hits the papers."

"Find out what?"

Patricia held her breath a moment while staring into Scorpio's eyes. "He'd been shot several times," she gently remarked. "The car was purposely set on fire after he was dead."

Scorpio stared at her grandmother a moment unable to speak then nearly choked on her words. "Are you sure?" Her horror at that moment was beyond description.

Her grandmother nodded while staring into her eyes. "The homicide detective said it looked like a professional hit."

Those words would be forever burned in Scorpio's mind. For a moment, she was numb and actually felt nothing. Was it shock or just that she somehow knew it?

§

While waiting for word from her grandfather, Scorpio and her grandmother sat on the wicker furniture in the sunroom and flipped through old photo albums from her childhood. She found herself staring at her brother and missing him even more now that she'd never see him again. She held back her tears, so she could be strong for her grandmother since she could see the older woman was barely holding it together. Patricia held a framed photo of Kane to her chest and reflected fondly.

"I remember the day your mother gave birth to you and your brother," she announced while smiling as she drifted off into a happier time. "Your grandfather's heart just melted when he held each of you." She cast a look at Scorpio where she sat on the sunroom sofa huddled over the coffee table littered with photo albums. "Your grandfather was so upset when he first found out your mother was pregnant, but that all went away the moment the two of you were born."

"He didn't approve of our father?" Scorpio asked.

It was odd she asked since she rarely asked questions about her father. Perhaps that was because Kane was the one obsessed with him. Having never met either of her parents, Scorpio was mostly indifferent toward them.

"Approve?" her grandmother asked and chuckled. "We'd never even met the young man. She'd only been with him about six months. He'd died before we even knew she was pregnant." She looked around the coffee table at the photo albums. "I couldn't even tell you what he looked like. I'd never even seen a picture of him. We collected some of your mother's belongings from her apartment in Boston, but she didn't really have that much. If she had any photos, we didn't find them. Your mother wasn't much of a pack rat like me. She didn't collect trinkets and bobbles."

"Seems odd, don't you think?" Scorpio asked.

"Some people don't like knick-knacks," her grandmother replied then shrugged. "They do collect a lot of dust. I spend hours cleaning mine."

"No, I meant that you didn't find any pictures of him," Scorpio remarked. "She dated this man for over six months and didn't have any pictures of him. Didn't he talk her into moving to Virginia with him? You used to say that was why Grandpa didn't care for him. I don't understand how she didn't have any pictures of him."

"Your mother wasn't much for taking pictures, and she used to say he was camera shy," she replied. "Besides, cameras on cell phones weren't all the rage before you were born. Things were less, uh, technical back then. We talked to people face-to-face not on the Skype."

Scorpio held back her laugh but didn't bother correcting her grandmother who still referred to Yahoo as Yoo-Hoo. Scorpio suddenly tensed and eyed her grandmother.

"Why Virginia?" she suddenly asked.

Her grandmother shrugged. "I don't know," she replied. "I suppose he had family there. Why else?"

"Virginia," she again announced. "Where Kane was murdered?"

Patricia suddenly tensed and avoided looking at Scorpio. She didn't comment.

"Did he go to Virginia looking for our father's family?" Scorpio practically demanded.

"I really don't know, honey," her grandmother replied. "Your brother did things first and asked for permission after the fact."

"Is it a coincidence? Kane goes off looking for our father's family and dies?" She sharply eyed her grandmother. "What do you know about my father, Grandma?"

"I told you, I'd never even met him," she replied. "Your mother said he'd retired from the military. That's as much as I know."

Scorpio set the photo album down and sank into thought. She cast a look at her grandmother, who seemed preoccupied now while staring at the framed photo she held.

"How did my mother die?" Scorpio asked while staring at her grandmother and watching her expression. She saw the older woman tense.

"I told you many times about that night," Patricia announced while staring at Kane's photo. "I don't like to be reminded of it. It's too painful."

"She was my mother," Scorpio insisted. "Please, tell me again."

"It was twenty-two years ago," her grandmother began. "Your uncle had traveled to Boston to help your mother get her affairs in order. While bringing her home here to us, your uncle lost control of the car, possibly from a blown tire, and they crashed down an embankment. The car rolled several times, killing them both." The older woman looked back at her with tears in her eyes. "I lost both my children that horrible night."

§

Twenty-two years ago. Scorpio's Uncle Drew hurried his sister through the dimly lit, nearly silent parking garage. Drew Wayland was a mature looking twenty-seven-year-old man with dark hair and a lean frame. He was almost certainly a younger version of his father, Newman. Maggie Wayland clung to her carry-on bag while casting looks over her shoulder. Maggie was only a couple of years younger than her brother, although she took after their mother with her smaller stature. She was a beautiful woman with long, dark hair that had been hastily pulled up into a ponytail and concealed beneath a baseball cap. As they hurried through the parking garage in the late hour, they could hear movement followed by the squealing of tires. Drew rushed his sister toward his car.

"What about my car?" Maggie practically gasped.

"Leave it," Drew shouted, the fear now showing. "We have to go!"

A black sedan suddenly raced through the parking garage for them. They bolted between rows of vehicles and away from the speeding car. The sedan skidded to a stop and raced backward in reverse. Drew opened his car door and shoved his sister across the front seat to the passenger side then dove into the driver's seat after her. He threw the car into reverse and slammed into the sedan doubling back for them. As his car jetted down the aisle of the parking garage, Maggie fastened her seatbelt then looked out the side mirror at the sedan now attempting to turn, not caring how many cars it sideswiped. The wailing of car alarms filled the garage and seemed to echo from every corner.

Drew raced from the garage and narrowly missed an oncoming car. Maggie screamed. The other car slammed on its horn, angered by the narrow miss, and was immediately t-boned by the pursuing sedan. It was enough to get the pursuing car off their tail. While driving at high speeds, Drew struggled with the seatbelt. Maggie grabbed the end and fastened it for him, allowing him to concentrate on his driving. It was late at night, so traffic was light.

"I'm sorry I got you involved," Maggie gasped while staring at her brother.

"Don't be," Drew announced without looking at her then offered a quick reassuring smile. "Midnight Requisition is real. We just need to meet with your mysterious *lawyer*, and it'll all have been worth it."

Maggie attempted a smile, although hers was less confident than her brother's. "I trust your judgement, Drew," she announced timidly.

They raced through the streets of Boston and headed out of the city. Drew slowed the car and scanned his mirrors for signs of anyone following them.

"I think we lost them," he announced and finally released a sigh of relief.

A car came at them and veered into their lane. Drew and Maggie screamed as he swerved to avoid hitting the oncoming car. Drew drove at high speeds half on the side of the road while attempting to keep control of the car. The car that nearly hit them spun around and raced after them. Maggie looked out the rear window then eyed Drew.

"They're following us," she gasped.

"Why do these guys want you so badly?" Drew practically shouted. "Did you tell anyone else about Midnight Requisition?"

"No, of course not. I was supposed to be safe," she replied while alternating looking behind and in front of them. "What could they possibly gain by coming after me?"

Drew suddenly looked at her and raised his brows. "Maggie," he announced with some alarm. "What if they're not after you?"

The pursuing car raced alongside them. Drew attempted to speed up to get away from the car chasing them. They heard a pop. The car suddenly swerved.

"They shot out the front tire," Drew cried out. "Hang on, Maggie!"

Drew attempted to keep the car going straight without slowing despite the flat, front tire. The car alongside them picked up speed, pulled a little ahead of them, and rammed into their front fender. Drew's car swerved sharply to the right, hit the guardrail, and sailed over the small cliff. The car rolled down the embankment several times before striking the bottom. Smoke billowed from the hood and eventually caught fire. The car on the road stopped a moment then raced away.

Chapter 11

Present day. One week later. Rayner Roderick worked on a computer within the massive office space of one of the larger buildings in town. The office floor contained multiple cubicles and nearly a dozen men and women milling around, hanging over cubicle walls while talking to one another. The office personnel were obviously enjoying their work break while their computer systems were down.

"If the system stays down, maybe they'll send us home early," one of the men announced seeming a little too enthusiastic.

"I wouldn't mind a few hours of peace and quiet before the kids get home," a woman responded.

One of the men hung over the cubicle wall where Rayner sat behind the monitor and watched him work on the computer. His focus was amazing despite the employees' low chatter in the background. The screen seemed to change every second as Rayner's fingers rapidly struck keys while he stared at the monitor.

"How can you even see what it says?" the man hanging over the cubicle asked.

"I don't have to see it," Rayner replied with little emotion as he concentrated on his work. "I know what it says."

"So what does it say?" the man asked.

Rayner struck several keys while sitting back in his chair. Every computer monitor within the room came back to life. Rayner turned in his chair and raised his brows at the man hovering over him.

"It says I'm a genius," Rayner proudly announced then grinned.

The man rolled his eyes and groaned. "Yippee for you," he muttered.

Every employee groaned when they saw their computers were once again working. A neatly dressed man in his mid to late thirties walked through the cubicles while laughing cheerfully and motioned to the workers.

"Everyone back to work," their boss announced and approached Rayner, who collected his small tools and placed them in his case. The boss, Daniel Townsend, paused before Rayner while laughing and eagerly extended his hand. "Excellent work, Rayner!"

Daniel was a tall, lean man with a headful of thick, light brown hair. Although his suit gave him the appearance of an athletic build, he actually lacked muscle and possibly spent too much time sitting in front of a computer.

Rayner shook Daniel's hand in their usual greeting then grinned. "It was actually a simple computer glitch," he informed him. "Since Davenport has me on retainer, I'd like to debug the system sometime next week and see if I can fix the root cause of your problems."

"Of course," Daniel announced cheerfully. "Anything you need. Since you started tending to our computers almost a year ago, production has been up with less equipment downtime. You make me look good in front of Davenport."

"I'm sure you don't need my help for that," Rayner replied. "This is one of the more efficient offices I've been to in years."

"I appreciate that," Daniel remarked cheerfully. "The key to that? A small town environment. These people all know one another. They're friends and neighbors. If one succeeds; they all succeed."

"I've noticed that about this town," Rayner replied. "I've never lived in a small town before. It's so quiet, and the people are extremely friendly." He leaned on the desk and shook his head. "I was only here a month before just about everyone knew my name. I'll admit; it was sort of spooky at first. In the city, you're practically invisible."

"They'd be nice to you regardless," Daniel informed him, "but it doesn't hurt that Davenport holds you in such high regard. He brags about you to all the right people. He likes smart men on his team." Daniel then laughed. "And he's convinced you're the smartest man in any room."

"Yes, it's a gift," Rayner remarked then muttered while frowning, "and a curse." He sighed deeply. "Honestly, I'd rather be taller."

Daniel leaned against the cubicle wall and casually rested his arm on top. "Are you attending Davenport's party this weekend?"

"Is that this weekend?" Rayner asked then shook his head and groaned. "I swear; he has formal functions every other week."

"Yeah, as the richest man in town, that's his job," Daniel teased. "I don't know what you're complaining about. You're single. There are always a dozen or more gorgeous women at his parties."

"None of them are local," Rayner remarked.

"Yeah, I said they were gorgeous," Daniel teased with a hint of a smile. "He's not going to invite a bunch of farm girls and fishermen's daughters to his high-brow functions. Women at his parties are a little more, well, sophisticated."

"And one hundred percent eye candy," Rayner commented then gave him a curious look. "What does he do? Import them from the city?"

"He has businesses all over including Portland and Boston," Daniel replied. "Who knows where they're from? I just enjoy the company."

"While I'll agree that they're attentive, they're not exactly intellectually challenging," Rayner informed him in a serious tone. "I couldn't have one decent conversation at the last party."

"Some women are just meant to be admired. Like a fine painting," Daniel remarked then chuckled. "You sometimes have to choose between beauty and brains. Personally, I'll take beauty any day."

"I've encountered some beautiful women around town with more than enough intellect to hold my attention," Rayner remarked with little hesitation. "I'm guessing I lack the rustic, lumberjack appeal because I can't get even one of them to show any interest in me."

"That's because you're living in a small town filled with strapping farm boys and fishermen," Daniel teased then shook his head as his eyes widened dramatically. "Have you seen some of those good ole' boys? Never spent a day in the gym, yet they have six-pack abs and biceps to spare. Your typical small town beauty has her eyes on those boys. Around here, the only beautiful women going for us business types are attending Davenport's parties."

"I choose not to believe that," Rayner scoffed although his look nearly betrayed him. "There has to be small town girls who like clean-cut men in suits."

"You may have to go a little older and divorced," Daniel informed him. "Some woman who's fed up with the fisherman's son fairy tale."

"There aren't many divorced women in this town either," Rayner reminded him then appeared disgusted. "Where do I meet these women? I've been to nearly every business in this town, and I don't meet single women my age. Is there some law that says a woman in this town must marry by the time she's twenty-one?"

"Trust me," Daniel remarked while adding a throaty laugh. "These good ole' boys start dating the best ones during high school and waste little time putting a ring on her finger." Daniel playfully pouted. "Give the women at Davenport's parties another chance. If you just put in a little effort, they're surprisingly easy to engage in conversation and perfect for a one-night-stand."

Rayner drew a deep breath and stared at Daniel a long moment. "Casual dating is not really my thing, Daniel." He then tensed and gently cleared his throat. "Did you ever consider that the gorgeous women attending his parties are 'hired' to be there?"

"I've been with a few of them," Daniel insisted while grinning. "I've never been asked for a dime."

"I didn't say you were the one footing the bill," Rayner remarked and raised his brow in suggestion.

Daniel sank into thought while staring at Rayner. "You honestly think--?" He suddenly straightened and shook his head. "No, Davenport wouldn't--" Daniel drifted off into his own thoughts as if reconsidering the unthinkable.

"Yeah, let that sink in for a minute," Rayner announced then sighed with defeat. "Ten months I've been in this town, and I've only been on two dates. Where are the single women hiding?"

"Have you tried the tavern on a Friday night?" Daniel asked, finally returning to life, although with a little less enthusiasm.

"You mean pickup truck central?" Rayner teased then immediately shook his head. "I know I wouldn't fit in with that crowd. They'd chew me up and spit me out. I went in there once the first month I moved here. It was very uncomfortable, and I don't just mean because of the country music. Talk about sticking out like a sore thumb--"

"I'll tell you what," Daniel announced resuming his cheerful demeanor. "Why don't you come to the tavern with me and a few of the guys this Friday? Between us, we know plenty of single women in the place. Maybe you'll find one more your type. Can't hurt, right?"

"Well, at least with a group of guys, it won't be as uncomfortable," Rayner agreed while giving it some thought. His cell phone chirped from its muffled location. As he removed his cell phone from his jacket pocket, he nodded. "I'll meet you there this Friday."

"Eight o'clock," Daniel announced.

Rayner looked at the caller ID and immediately raised his brows with enthusiasm. "Oh, I have to take this." He eagerly answered the phone. "Rayner Roderick." He listened a moment to the person on the other end then nodded. "Absolutely. I have just enough time between jobs now." He listened another moment. "I'll be there in ten minutes." Rayner disconnected the call and couldn't contain his enthusiasm. "Speaking of unattainable gorgeous women." Rayner grinned at Daniel and waved his cell phone. "Scorpio Wayland. Have you seen her? I don't know if she's an angel or the devil himself, but I'd give my soul for a shot with that one."

Daniel's smile immediately faded as he vigorously shook his head. "You may want to steer clear of Scorpio," he announced in a stern tone.

Rayner stared at him and appeared surprised. "Why's that?"

"She dated the heartthrob of our little town, so she can clearly have any man she wants," Daniel began then immediately tensed and shook his head. "You'll never compete with that man's heroic greatness. He died tragically saving her life after brutally killing four armed intruders. We're talking decapitated and disemboweled."

"Don't you think that was exaggerated?" Rayner asked while raising a skeptical brow.

"I don't know, and I don't care," Daniel informed him. "After what happened at the hotel, he was dubbed a legend and the town's biggest badass. No man will ever be able to live up to that. She's unattainable." He then shook his head and seemed to relive some silent horror. "All of that aside, Scorpio's tragic story only gets worse. Days after her boyfriend's murder, five more men break into that horror hotel of hers, and they were slain by her new bodyguards."

"I remember hearing about that incident shortly after I'd moved here," Rayner remarked then shuttered at the thought. "Chilling. I was at her house the afternoon before that happened."

"But her history of woe and despair doesn't end with that little horror tale," Daniel continued. "Last week they found her brother dead. He was killed over six months earlier execution style and set ablaze in Virginia." He shook his head as his eyes widened. "Trust me; you'll want to stay far away from that girl. You'll undoubtedly live longer."

"I know I don't stand a chance with her," Rayner replied with a defeated sigh. "She's completely out of my league. Besides, she's only about twenty-five. A little young for me."

"Twenty-five," Daniel announced then laughed. "Try twenty-two. She's mature beyond her years. And to answer your question, she is the devil. A beautiful devil luring men to their deaths."

Rayner replaced his phone to his jacket pocket and grabbed his bag. "Well, at least a man can safely fantasize about her," he announced cheerfully while grinning. "If you'll excuse me; I have a date with the devil, and I don't want to keep her waiting."

"It's your funeral, man," Daniel announced while sighing. "Just remember, I warned you not to be tempted by the siren's call."

"Last time I was there, she was wearing a nearly see-through tank top," Rayner casually informed him.

Daniel paused to consider the comment. "Well, we all gotta die sometime," he announced then grinned. "Good luck."

Chapter 12

Scorpio leaned against the kitchen island counter and watched while Rayner fiddled with the alarm alongside the back door. He appeared puzzled and punched in several codes. Scorpio listened to the machine beep as it flashed messages and different colored lights indicating it was armed then disarmed. Rayner finally straightened seeming puzzled and looked at Scorpio.

"Who's been messing with this?" he finally asked.

"Messing with it?" she remarked and straightened. "No one that I'm aware. I mean, Maverick attempted to fix it when it was malfunctioning."

"Well, he screwed up something," Rayner insisted then returned to the alarm panel. "It's on remote access."

"What does that mean?"

"That means it's set to operate remotely from another location," Rayner informed her while pressing buttons. He then turned to face her. "Can I see your cell phone?"

"I don't have much use for my cell phone," she remarked then fidgeted with some embarrassment. "It's in the study. I only carry it when I intend to leave the hotel." She snorted a laugh at her own expense. "Which is hardly ever anymore. I'll get it for you."

"I'll come with you to the study," he replied. "I'd like to look at the control panel anyway."

"Yeah, sure," she remarked. "The study is this way, but I'm sure you remember that."

Rayner followed her from the kitchen and marveled at the updated and refurbished rooms. "You've remodeled quite a bit in the last few months."

"Yeah," she replied with a little added cheerfulness in her tone. "Maverick and Stone are incredibly handy. I had some help from that guy you suggested too. He's really great with older homes."

"He's had a lot of experience."

Rayner paused within the hallway, stared at the wall beneath the stairs, and then tapped on it. Scorpio turned and looked back at him with some surprise.

"What are you doing?" she asked.

He suddenly grinned and pointed at the wall. "You had him do it, didn't you?"

"Do what?"

"Create a secret passageway," Rayner announced then laughed while looking at the wall. "There was a closet here."

She stared at him with some surprise then snorted a laugh. "You have a good memory," Scorpio remarked.

"Yeah, one of my many curses," he informed her then scanned the wall for the trigger.

"It's not polite to poke around a lady's secret passageways without permission," she informed him.

Rayner eyed her then laughed. "Sorry," he announced. "Another nasty habit of mine. I'm perpetually nosy."

"It's okay," she remarked. "It's more of a hidden compartment than a passageway." She smiled slyly. "Ironically, I still keep the vacuum sweeper in there."

Scorpio headed for the office. Rayner joined her near the study doorway.

"I always wanted to be a detective," he announced with great pleasure. "I consider myself to be great at problem-solving, but I'm far too squeamish."

Scorpio eyed him almost mockingly and nodded. "Uh, huh," she remarked. "Then you probably won't want to hear that there was a dead guy right where you're standing."

She headed into the study. Rayner immediately looked down to the hardwood floor beneath his feet. The wooden floorboards were a shade lighter where he stood, having been refinished in order to remove the blood. Rayner gasped and jumped from the spot. He looked around then hurried into the study behind her. Rayner crossed the study and approached the armoire while Scorpio removed her cell phone from the desktop. She handed him the cell phone. He took the phone, immediately entered her password, and searched the installed applications.

"How did you know my password?" she asked while eyeing him suspiciously.

He didn't bother looking up from her phone and pointed to a scrap of paper taped to the desk blotter. It contained her password.

"Incidentally, you shouldn't use your birth date for your pin," he remarked then came to a password-protected screen. He typed onto the screen then groaned and eyed her. "Nor Calvin for every password."

"I don't use Calvin for all my passwords," she insisted. "You just remembered that from the last time."

Rayner cast a look at her then stepped behind the desk to her open laptop. He moved the curser and brought up the password to gain access to her computer. Before he could start typing, she slammed the lid shut nearly clipping his fingers. He jumped back with surprise although hiding his grin.

"Fine," she huffed. "I'll change my passwords. My God. You're almost as annoying as my brother."

He hesitated before returning his attention to her cell phone. His mood turned less jovial. "I'm sorry about your brother," Rayner announced timidly.

She frowned and collapsed into the chair behind the desk. "Yeah, me too."

He hesitated then returned to his work on her cell phone. She studied him a moment while he worked then shifted uncomfortably.

"My grandfather is offering a ten thousand dollar reward to anyone who can identify his killer," she informed him while lazily leaning back.

Rayner looked at her with some surprise. "If I knew anything about his death, I'd hand over that information for free," he informed her.

"You said you wanted to be a detective," she remarked. "Here's your chance."

"I'm pretty sure I'd throw up if I even read the police report," he remarked then eyed her. "No disrespect. I know you've suffered your share of unpleasantness."

"What a nice way of saying my life is a complete shithole," she muttered and played with a pen on the desk.

"I didn't mean--"

Scorpio offered a tiny smile. "I know," she announced. "You were being polite. I'm the one with the issues."

He resumed fiddling with her phone possibly to hide his embarrassment. She again studied his profile as he worked, although not seeming nearly as engrossed as he had originally been. He seemed distracted. She was good at making people uncomfortable with the horror show that was her life. His silence piqued her curiosity.

"You're probably the first person who hasn't asked me about what happened either of those nights," she remarked without taking her eyes off him.

He didn't bother looking at her. "Probably because it'll make me nauseous."

"It's nice."

Rayner cast a look at her with bewilderment. "Being made nauseous?"

"No, not being treated like a lab experiment or Typhoid Mary." She cast the pen across the desk with disgust and leaned her head back in the chair. "Rome is falling, and all I can do is sit and watch it happen."

He set her phone on the desk while studying her. "Well, Cassandra, at least we can fix your alarm system. Maybe you'll feel a little safer."

She remained reclined in the chair and stared at him. "I don't care about my safety," she informed him softly and with little emotion. "I want the head of the beast delivered to me on a silver platter."

Rayner stared at her, unable to take his eyes off her. She stared back without a word. Her eyes suddenly strayed past him to the security monitors. She flew forward in her seat startling him.

"What the hell--?"

Rayner turned and looked at the monitors as well. Davenport and two of his men stood on the front porch speaking to Stone, who stood rigid in the doorway with his arms across his chest and an emotionless expression on his face.

"What's he doing here?" she snarled leaping from her chair.

"Carson Davenport?" Rayner questioned and looked back at her, but he was too late, she was already bolting across the room. Rayner hurried after her.

Scorpio darted up the foyer steps and approached the open front door where Stone kept Davenport and his men just outside. Davenport appeared relieved when he saw her.

"Scorpio, my dear," Davenport announced almost cheerfully. "Can you call off your guard dog?"

"Can I help you?" she announced bluntly and took the same stance as Stone.

Davenport seemed surprised by her tone but managed a smile regardless. "I thought we were passed all the hostility," he announced and attempted to remain polite. "I wanted to express my condolences about your brother. I'd been out of town the last few weeks and hadn't had a chance to stop by. Did you receive the flowers?"

"Yes, the flowers were lovely," she remarked while attempting to control her emotions.

"I heard your grandfather has offered a reward to find the person responsible for your brother's death," Davenport announced. "I've sent word to all my contacts in law enforcement within Virginia, and I've hired a few private detectives to check into the murder as well." His look was sincere. "I intend to do everything within my power to help find the person responsible and bring closure to your family. You may not have known, but your grandfather and I were good friends many years back. We'd even bought this hotel together back in the day. I always regretted letting him buy me out." He inhaled deeply and looked around while smiling. "I'm so glad you're trying to get her up and running again. I hated seeing your grandfather let her sit and rot the way he had. I thought for sure your uncle would do right by her, but he didn't have your passion."

"Yeah, him dying didn't help either," Scorpio scoffed.

"That was unfortunate," Davenport replied. "Would you mind if I had a look around? I'd love to see the restorations you've made. I hear you've been putting a lot of time and money into the old girl."

"Yes, she would mind," her grandfather snarled from behind them.

Davenport and his men turned to see Newman slam his car door shut. None of them had even heard him drive up the long driveway in his fancy black car. He approached the porch while glaring at Davenport.

"Newman," Davenport announced enthusiastically. "Your granddaughter and I were just talking about you."

"What the hell are you doing here?" her grandfather bellowed in anger. "I don't want you hanging around the hotel, and I certainly don't want you anywhere near my granddaughter."

"What's gotten into you?" Davenport suddenly demanded. "I can't talk to Scorpio?"

"No, she's off-limits," Newman scoffed as he walked past them and stood alongside Stone while directly in front of Scorpio, blocking her view of Davenport.

"Off-limits?" Davenport proclaimed. "What the hell is that supposed to mean?"

"It means I don't want my granddaughter having an *accident*," her grandfather lashed out.

"I realize there have been a lot of accidents in your family history, Newman, but none of them had anything to do with me," Davenport launched. "I'm appalled and offended by the accusation."

"If the accusation fits--" Newman snarled back.

"This has got to stop," Davenport snapped and threw his arms in the air. "You can't go around accusing me of killing people." He then pointed a warning finger at him. "Keep it up, and I'll have your ass in court for slander."

Her grandfather punched Davenport in the mouth, surprising him. As Davenport's men were about to lunge forward to intervene, Stone stepped forward and intended to respond with his own hostility. Davenport held his hand up and stopped his men from lunging forward.

"Sue me for that too," Newman shouted while pointing a warning finger at him. "I'd love to get you into court and swear under oath everything I know about you."

Davenport wiped the blood from the corner of his mouth then looked at Scorpio. "Sorry for any inconvenience," he announced then motioned to his men.

Davenport headed from the porch and back for his car. Scorpio watched Davenport and his men drive away then turned to her grandfather.

"Someone's in a mood today," she boldly announced.

"I don't know how," Newman launched while pointing at the black sedan as it headed down the driveway, "but that man is knee-high in this shit with your brother's murder. I just don't know how to prove it."

Her grandfather turned and saw Rayner within the doorway behind them. Newman's look turned hostile. "What the hell are you doing here?"

Rayner stared at him with surprise by the hostility directed at him. "I'm servicing Ms. Wayland's security system."

"No, you're not," Newman shouted. "I know you work for Davenport. Get the hell out of here!"

"Grandpa!" she scolded.

"Haven't you learned anything after all this?" her grandfather demanded. "Carson Davenport hired that man--" He pointed demandingly at Rayner. "He wants you to trust him so he can infiltrate your home."

"Rayner is not the enemy," Scorpio insisted. "Of course he does some work for Davenport. Davenport owns half the businesses in town."

Newman glared at Rayner. "What's the percent?" he demanded. "Ninety percent of your work is for Davenport, right? You attend his parties and hang out with his hired henchmen."

"Well, I, uh--" Rayner fumbled. "I do work for him, but I don't work *for* him."

"Get out of here," Newman again shouted while pointing off the porch. "Get out of here and stay away from my granddaughter!"

Scorpio groaned and looked at Rayner. "You should probably go while I defuse this situation."

"My tools are in the kitchen," Rayner remarked in a timid tone. "I'll show myself out."

"It's okay," she replied. "I'll go with you."

As Rayner entered the house, Scorpio glared at her grandfather and followed the meek man inside.

Newman cast an impatient look at Stone. "Keep an eye on her," he ordered.

Stone folded his arms across his chest and stared down her grandfather. "With all due respect, sir," Stone announced. "I don't work for you. You either dial that explosive temper down a notch, or I'll be asking *you* to leave." He then smirked. "Or are we going to have a problem?"

Newman stared at Stone with some surprise.

Chapter 13

The local tavern looked more like a rustic hunting cabin that had seen better days than it did a bar. It was Friday night, and there were more than thirty pickup trucks parked outside. Country music could be heard blaring from within the building. The tavern was filled with local men and women of all ages, although most were in their twenties and thirties. A few married couples visited the tavern, but on weekends, it was mostly single, small town boys and girls. Nearly every table was filled, as were all the seats at the bar, which also contained many single men standing around while drinking and socializing. Scorpio sat at one of the round tables in the middle of the action with Trudy, Maverick, and Stone. She fidgeted uncomfortably while casting looks around the crowded barroom.

"Was coming here really necessary?" Scorpio asked her friends.

"You wanted to talk to Kane's friends," Trudy remarked then looked around. "Well, these are Kane's friends." She hesitated and then indicated the table with four men. "And potential killers."

Scorpio eyed the table across the room. Two of the men worked at Davenport's mansion. Schmidt and Blain were in their late twenties and seemed to share the same physical attributes as most of the men working at the mansion. All muscle and no brains. Neither man was necessarily unattractive, but they almost certainly lacked as much charm as intellect. The third man was Daniel from Davenport's office building, and the fourth man was Rayner, who appeared to be having a good time with his questionable co-workers. An excessively attractive, redheaded waitress paraded around the bar and flaunted her cleavage in men's faces while taking their orders.

"You remember Amber from high school," Trudy remarked to Scorpio.

Scorpio stared at the woman and couldn't believe her eyes. "That's Amber?" she practically gasped. "I had gym class with her. She barely made a 'B' cup. What's with the double 'Ds'?"

"Apparently, she was seeing some rich guy last year," Trudy announced while raising her brows suggestively. "He paid for her new boobs. Since she joined the 'D' club, she's been very popular with Davenport's hired goons."

Stone gave the waitress a quick once over then grinned. "I can't imagine why."

"According to my mother she and one of Davenport's henchmen are in an 'off and on again' relationship," Trudy announced. "You remember Rico, right?"

"Yeah," Scorpio muttered while making a face. "I remember Rico. He was one of the bastards giving Cal a hard time."

"Sounds like a fine suspect," Stone remarked.

"So what's the plan then?" Maverick asked while casually looking around. "Which one of these good ole' boys has the most information on your brother?"

Scorpio drew a deep breath and sighed. "Amber," she replied.

Maverick and Stone both looked across the bar and watched Amber flirt her way across the room while taking drink orders. Stone eyed Maverick and raised his hands in the air already admitting defeat.

"This one's all on you, man," Stone announced.

"Me?" Maverick playfully demanded. "Why is it on me?" His eyes narrowed. "It's because I'm devilishly handsome, isn't it? Why are you always holding my good looks over me? It wasn't my fault I was born this way."

"Face it; you're not that handsome," Stone scoffed then leaned on the table while staring down his friend. "There's no scenario where this black man hitting on the most popular girl in the bar doesn't end with a bunch of good ole' boys stomping on my ass."

"And yet I don't see it ending much better for me," Maverick deducted while cleverly raising his brows. "Even more so, because I can't afford to have my face ruined. Yours is pretty much a total loss already."

Stone leaned back in his chair and chuckled. "Oh, I'm so going to kill you in your sleep."

Trudy appeared to have enough of the bickering duo and eyed Scorpio. "They're all yours," she boldly announced. "I'm going to talk to Tony, the bartender. Kane spent a lot of time here, so he must have interacted with Tony. Tony always had a thing for me. Being hit on has to be better than listening to these two lug heads all night."

Both men watched Trudy walk away as their mouths hung open.

"Did she just call us lug heads?" Maverick demanded then shook his head. "And I was going to allow her the honor of my overnight company." He frowned. "Well, she can kiss that goodbye."

"What if she begged?" Stone teased, although he kept a straight face.

Maverick took a moment to think about the comment then offered a tiny grin. "I'd reconsider if she begged," he casually replied.

Scorpio groaned with irritation. "You guys dragged me out here," she snapped hotly. "One of you had better man-up and make the moves on Amber because I didn't come out here for my health."

"You know you want her," Stone announced to Maverick while grinning as he cast a peek at the large breasted woman.

Maverick grinned boyishly and nodded. "Yeah, I do kind of want her."

"And I kind of want a drink," Scorpio muttered, unable to handle either of her friends anymore.

Lack of a sexual partner had soured Scorpio on all thoughts of intercourse. She didn't want to hear about it or even think about it ever again. As Amber approached their table, Maverick struck his sexiest casual pose and cast his eyes upon the gorgeous woman. Stone had a hard time keeping a straight face and went to great lengths hiding his grin.

"What can I get you guys?" Amber announced then saw Scorpio and immediately beamed with delight. "Scorpio! Hey, you haven't been here since never! How are you?"

Scorpio managed a smile and shrugged. "Surviving, I suppose," she replied.

"Maybe it's more of a girls' night," Stone muttered to Maverick, although Scorpio overheard but refrained from glaring at them.

"Trudy insisted I crawl out of my cave and socialize, so bring me a pitcher of something strong," Scorpio joked although she was mostly serious. "If I leave here sober, I'm not tipping."

Amber let out a shrill laugh and touched Scorpio's shoulder. "I'm glad to see you haven't changed!" She then eyed Maverick and Stone with increasing interest. "And who are your handsome friends? Are these the bodyguards we've been hearing about?"

"A mild exaggeration," Scorpio corrected and kept from laughing. "This is Maverick, my new general manager, and that's Stone, Head of Operations."

Both men politely nodded. Amber's smile increased as she gave them lustful once-overs. "What can I get for you handsome hunks?"

"We'll have a pitcher of whatever beer you have on draft," Maverick announced while maintaining his charming smile. "Perhaps while Scorpio is on her quest to get drunk, you could join us for a drink on your break."

Amber eyed both men and returned the smile. "That's the best offer I've had all night."

She made a flirty turn and walked away. Stone grinned and slapped Maverick on the back. "Even after that lengthy dry spell, you've still got it."

Maverick glared at Stone and didn't seem pleased. "That's not funny."

Stone chuckled. Apparently, he thought it was. Nearly an hour later, Scorpio was already working on her third drink from the pitcher containing the colorful, fruity drink. Trudy was still involved in her in-depth conversation with Tony at the bar and hadn't been back to help Scorpio with the pitcher. Scorpio was well on her way to getting plastered before Amber finally joined them at their table. Maverick pulled the chair out between him and Stone, which Amber eagerly accepted. She sat between them and immediately leaned on Stone's shoulder and took a swig of beer from his glass.

"So tell me, Stone," Amber announced while taking in a sweeping eyeful of the large man. "What exactly is the *head* of operations?" Her hand found its way to his leg and caressed his thigh while working her way higher.

Maverick stared at the back of Amber's head with complete surprise, realizing he'd been cast aside for the larger, more muscular man. Scorpio chuckled into her glass and mocked Maverick with her drunken smile.

"It's, well, a fancy term for groundskeeper," Stone replied while staring at the gorgeous woman and her partially exposed 'D' cups.

As her hand moved higher, Stone jumped with surprise then grinned uncontrollably. He shifted in his chair so no one would see where her hand had disappeared.

"Groundskeeper, huh?" she cooed. "So that means you're good at spreading and nailing things?"

Stone groaned and nodded, obviously enjoying more than the play on words. "Oh, yeah," he announced then grinned. "Real good."

"I'll bet you have some pretty big tools for the job too," she announced while sinking against him as her hand caressed parts unseen.

Maverick sank back in his chair, folded his arms across his chest, and eyed Scorpio. "I think I'm going to be violently ill," he scoffed.

Scorpio maintained her grin and laughed. "Somebody's getting some," she sang softly, "and it ain't you."

Maverick refilled her glass with the colorful drink and offered a cheap smile. "Drink up, my pretty," he announced. "Another drink or two, and *you'll* be hitting on me."

Only a few minutes later, Amber and Stone kissed passionately while she ran her hands along his chest and shoulders like a wild woman. She finally broke off the kiss and looked at her watch.

"Oh, my break's over," she announced and sprang up from the table. She smiled seductively at Stone. "I get off at two. What time can you get me off?"

"Oh, uh, I," he stammered. "After I drop my friends off at the hotel, I'll come back for you," Stone announced while grinning uncontrollably.

Her eyes suddenly lit up. "Oh, that's right," she chirped. "You live at the hotel, don't you? This could be an interesting night."

"Oh, definitely," he replied.

Amber kissed him quickly but passionately then hurried back to her customers.

Stone rolled his eyes, sank back in his chair, and groaned with ecstasy. "I'm actually starting to like this town."

"My feelings are mixed," Maverick sulked.

Chapter 14

Rayner sat at the table across the room from Scorpio and gazed at her with a drunken, lovesick look in his eyes. He had his chin in his hand and a permanent smile on his face while staring at her. Daniel waved his hand in front of Rayner's face. When he didn't react, he followed his friend's gaze to the table with Scorpio, who was laughing with her tall, attractive male friends.

Daniel seemed almost alarmed and shook his head. "Oh, no," he announced boldly. "Get that thought from your head. You're not making a fool of yourself by going over there especially in your condition."

"What condition?" Rayner asked in a drunken tone without even looking at Daniel as he continued to smile at Scorpio across the room. "I'm fine."

"You're drunk out of your mind," Daniel insisted and forced him to meet his gaze.

Rayner sat up straight and attempted a sober appearance. "I don't know what you're talking about," he replied. "I'm perfectly fine. Besides, I already told you she's too young and out of my league. I wouldn't dream of making a fool of myself in front of her." His eyes again fell upon Scorpio. His smile returned, and he sighed dreamily. "I can almost see her little horns pushing the halo from her head."

Daniel groaned and shook his head. "I'm taking you home," he insisted. "You've had too much. I know you're going to do something stupid."

Blain and Schmidt noted Rayner's gaze and snickered to themselves.

"Going after that one?" Schmidt remarked. "Yeah, that would be pretty stupid."

"Listen to the guys," Daniel announced. "I'm going to get you some coffee so that you can get your head on straight." He eyed the other guys. "Keep an eye on Romeo."

"You've got it," Blain announced.

Daniel headed for the bar and made his way through the crowd. Blain leaned closer to Rayner.

"You should go over there and talk to her," Blain announced slyly.

Rayner straightened and looked at the man alongside him. "No, I wouldn't know what to say."

"You'll think of something," Blain continued. "You were at her house installing her security system. You must have talked about something."

"We did," Rayner replied and again looked at Scorpio. He smiled dreamily. "She really opened up to me. She's so pretty."

"So," Blain announced in a firm tone, "go over there and talk to her. You'd better hurry too before Daniel tries to take you home. Who knows when you'll have an opportunity like this again? She never goes out."

"Yeah," Schmidt chimed in. "She's had a few drinks, she's laughing, and she's in a good mood. You should totally talk to her."

"What's the worst that could happen?" Blain remarked while holding back his devious snicker.

"You think so?" Rayner asked.

Both men managed innocent looks and nodded. Rayner stumbled to his feet, put on his best sober appearance, and headed across the crowded barroom. Both men laughed at Rayner's expense.

"She's going to kill him," Blain chuckled through his hand over his mouth.

"Oh, yeah," Schmidt replied. "She's chewing him up and spitting him out."

Rayner approached Scorpio's table and the vacant seat alongside her. Trudy still hadn't returned, and Scorpio was on her second pitcher of drinks.

"Hey, Scorpio," Rayner announced and managed a nearly sober appearance.

She looked up and immediately recognized him despite her drunken condition. A humored smile crossed her face. "*Rayner Roderick*," she announced with emphasis on each 'R' while giggling.

"Any problems with the security system?" he asked while hiding his drunken state as he clung to the back of the vacant chair for support. "We never really got to test it the other day."

Scorpio's look turned serious despite her being drunk. "I'm sorry about my grandfather being such a miserable jerk," she informed him. "He's usually a nicer jerk."

"It's okay," Rayner replied. "I understand. Your family has been severely tested lately."

She groaned and half flopped on the table. "You can say that again." Scorpio refilled her glass, attempting not to spill any of the fruity content. She then eyed him and grinned. "Thankfully, in times like this, there's alcohol."

"My friends are cutting me off," he informed her while frowning. "They think I'm plastered." He waved his hand and nearly lost his balance. "I'm fine."

"Not me," she announced boldly with a serious look on her face. "I'm plastered. I have every reason to be drunk and none to be sober."

Rayner chuckled and flopped into the empty chair alongside her. At that point, it was either sit or fall. "That pretty much sums it up."

She pushed the filled glass in front of him and filled another for herself. "Drink up, *Rayner Roderick*," she announced while again emphasizing each 'R'.

Rayner accepted the glass then started laughing. Scorpio laughed along with him. Stone and Maverick watched the drunken couple laugh over nothing in particular then exchanged looks.

"Is this what I'm like when I'm drunk?" Maverick finally asked.

"Nah," Stone replied and sipped his beer. "You're just an ass."

Maverick stared at him while frowning. "At least I have being drunk as an excuse," he muttered.

§

It was nearly one-thirty in the morning, and the crowd at the tavern was now thinning. Scorpio and Rayner were half falling on the table drunk and laughing. Trudy sat alongside Maverick and watched the drunken couple with her brows knitted in bewilderment.

"This is just sad," Trudy muttered then eyed Stone as he repeatedly checked his watch. "Have a hot date?"

"As a matter-of-fact, I do," he announced and clapped his hands together causing everyone to jump. "The bus leaves in five minutes. Anyone who wants a ride home needs to get their asses in the car."

Trudy eyed Maverick, who appeared disgusted. "Did I miss something?"

"Stone's getting laid tonight," Maverick casually remarked while reclined in his chair. "He's picking up Amber at two when she gets off."

"Amber?" Trudy remarked then groaned and shook her head. "That girl has zero morals." She then stood while sighing with boredom. "I've had enough of this place anyway." Trudy patted Scorpio on the head. "Come along my drunken friend. Time to put you to bed."

Scorpio groaned and stood on command. She was clearly unsteady on her feet forcing Trudy to catch her. Rayner watched her with bewilderment.

"Are we going somewhere?" he asked.

"Yeah," Scorpio informed him. "We're going home. You heard the man. Get your bus in the ass. The car leaves in five minutes."

"Oh, okay," Rayner replied and stood as well.

Maverick placed a hand on Rayner's shoulder and forced him back into his seat, which wasn't difficult in his condition. "You're not invited."

He checked his pockets then looked at Maverick, who attempted to help Trudy keep Scorpio on her feet. "I gave my car keys to Daniel."

"Then find Daniel to give you a ride home," Maverick snapped with little concern.

Rayner stood with some unsteadiness, looked around the less crowded barroom, and seemed confused. "Where the hell is Daniel?"

"Oh, for Pete's sake," Scorpio scoffed and broke free from her friends, nearly falling in her condition. "We can take *Rayner Roderick* home."

"Yeah, I probably shouldn't drive anyway," Rayner remarked and felt his pockets. "Now where the hell are my house keys?" He considered the comment then frowned. "I think they're with my car keys." He again looked around. "Where are my car keys?"

"There are more than enough spare bedrooms in the hotel," Stone finally blurted out becoming frustrated. "Can we just go? I have important things to do tonight."

Scorpio leaned on Rayner's shoulder and giggled in his ear. "Stone's getting laid tonight."

"That's not why he invited me back to the hotel, is it?" Rayner suddenly asked and stared at her with wide eyes. "I'm not that drunk."

"That's okay," Scorpio teased then giggled. "I don't think you're his type."

He stared at her and appeared almost offended. "What is it with me?" Rayner suddenly demanded. "No one in this town wants me."

Scorpio threw her arms around his neck and sank against him while grinning. "I want you," she announced while giggling. "You're cute; like a Muppet."

Rayner stared at her with surprise then grinned at the comment. Stone groaned and shook his head at the drunken couple. Maverick frowned and pulled Scorpio away from Rayner before he could latch onto her.

"That's enough you two," Maverick insisted.

Scorpio caught onto Maverick for balance. She threw her arms around his neck, stared at him a moment, and then grinned drunkenly.

"You're one hell of a handsome man, you know that?" she announced and patted his face.

Maverick stared at her a moment then grinned deviously. "I should probably ride in the back with Scorpio," he suddenly announced.

"The hell you will," Trudy launched while glaring at him as she pulled Scorpio away from Maverick.

Scorpio nearly fell against Trudy. She looked at her friend and smiled. "I love you."

Trudy frowned and passed her back to Maverick. "She's all yours."

§

Once they'd returned to the hotel, Trudy assisted Scorpio from the old-fashioned elevator and into the second floor corridor while Maverick kept Rayner from following. Scorpio danced seductively in the hallway attempting to entice the men while Rayner and Maverick watched with increasing interest. Trudy tried to rein her in, but she wasn't making it easy. Rayner attempted to leave the elevator and follow his dancing devil. Maverick stopped him.

"I don't think so," Maverick announced firmly. "You're sleeping on the third floor in the brother's bedroom. We're keeping the two of you far apart just in case."

"In case of what?" Scorpio asked and looked back at the elevator as Maverick closed the gate.

"In case this one gets any ideas," Maverick remarked while raising his brows. "Trust me; he's safer on the third floor where he's less likely to wander."

The elevator disappeared up to the third floor. Scorpio leaned heavily on Trudy's shoulder and laughed.

"You and Maverick are hooking up, aren't you?" Scorpio announced with humor.

"Doubtful," Trudy remarked then actually gave the comment some consideration. After a moment, she seemed to toss the idea from her head, managed a smile, and guided Scorpio to her room.

"I miss Cal," Scorpio pouted while leaning on her friend as they headed down the hall.

"I know you do," Trudy gently replied, although she obviously didn't want to get on the subject while Scorpio was drunk. It would only cause tremendous mood swings.

"We had great drunken sex," she announced while grinning. "Like two wild animals." Scorpio scratched at the air and added sound effects like that of a cat.

Trudy laughed and patted Scorpio's arm. "I wouldn't mind a night like that myself."

Scorpio eyed her friend and giggled. "You're hooking up with Maverick, aren't you?"

"Stop giving me ideas," Trudy remarked and again considered the comment.

Chapter 15

That night in her dreams, Scorpio relived her most erotic sexual encounters with Cal. She enjoyed every moment; every touch and every caress. As her naked body pressed against his, he kissed her passionately while his firmly caressing hands made her entire body ache for him. His kiss and touch electrified her senses until she couldn't take anymore. She needed him so badly and wanted to feel his hard body. She pinned him to the bed and aggressively had her way with him. Her screams of ecstasy were matched by his loud groans of pleasure. When it seemed as if she couldn't take anymore, he tossed her onto her back and made wild love to her. She never needed him or wanted him more than that moment, and he'd done everything right. Once their lovemaking was over, he gathered her in his arms and nuzzled her as she fell asleep.

The morning sun entered the bedroom through the partially open curtains and shined on Scorpio's face. She groaned lowly from the sun invading her sexual dreams and making her aware of her pounding head. As she opened her eyes, she wondered why her curtains were open. Had she forgotten to close them last night? She strained to look at the unfamiliar bedroom. Scorpio glanced across the walls and realized she was in her brother's bedroom. How the hell did she get into Kane's room? She felt a man's naked body pressed against her from behind as a hand caressed her hip beneath the covers. Scorpio gasped with alarm and pulled away from the man. She sat up in the bed while holding the sheets to her naked body. Rayner nuzzled the pillow and looked at her through partially open eyes.

"Morning," he announced pleasantly.

Scorpio placed her hand to her aching head, groaned, and shut her eyes. She couldn't believe Trudy would let this happen. Scorpio again looked around the room and started putting the pieces together.

"Oh, God," she gasped.

Rayner hadn't snuck into her room; she ventured into his room! He propped himself on his elbow and looked at her with concern.

"Are you okay?" Rayner asked then managed a slight chuckle. "I guess we're both a little hungover after all that drinking. To be honest; I don't even know how I got in this room." He then reconsidered and looked around. "Actually, I don't even know where I am."

"Please tell me nothing happened," she begged while covering her eyes.

He stared at her with surprise as his expression dropped. "You don't remember?"

"I'm not sure what I remember," she muttered, although that wasn't true. She didn't want to remember, because what was replaying in her mind was almost embarrassing.

"I just about passed out before you crawled into bed with me," he informed her then grinned as he recalled the events of the night. "My head is still spinning. What a wild night. I never knew women could be that aggressive in bed."

Scorpio cast a look at him then covered her eyes again and groaned. Rayner fell silent while staring at her. What had actually happened then seemed to dawn on him.

"Oh, you thought I was someone else," he remarked with concern. "You thought I was Maverick."

"What?" she suddenly gasped and glared at him with annoyance. "No, of course not! I thought you were Cal, my dead boyfriend!"

Rayner fidgeted and ran his fingers through his mussed hair while deep in thought. He suddenly looked at her. "Okay, let's get something straight," he announced firmly. "You jumped on me. I was just as drunk as you were, so don't try to blame me for any of this."

Scorpio rolled her eyes and grabbed his discarded shirt. She slipped into it without offering him even the slightest peek at her naked body. "I'm not blaming you," she scoffed with annoyance. "I know it was my own fault, but that doesn't mean I have to like it."

"I knew it had to be too good to be true," Rayner groaned while holding his head. "The best sex of my life was obviously a mistake."

"Okay," Scorpio snarled. "Can we stop talking about it already? Let me just find my clothes and then you can get dressed and go home."

He stared at her with surprise at the comment. "So that's it?" he demanded. "You violate me then throw me out without as much as a cup of coffee? Hey, I have feelings too."

She snatched her tank top and shorts from the floor and glared at him. "Do you want a cup of coffee?"

"No," Rayner scoffed then frowned. "I'm used to women treating me like shit, but that usually happens before sex." He then considered the comment. "Most times *instead* of sex."

"I'm sorry, Rayner," she announced and sat on the edge of the bed. "I really am. This is all my fault, and I don't blame you for any of it."

"And?" he asked while cleverly raising his brows as if waiting for the rest.

"And what?"

He groaned and shook his head. "You could at least tell me the sex was good," Rayner snapped.

"Yes, the sex was good," she practically cried out. "Are you happy?"

"Not really," he replied then sighed, "but I guess it'll have to do." He eyed her with a curious look. "Of course, if you'd consider 'morning after' sex, that'd make everything right."

Scorpio didn't bother looking at him as she stood. "Okay, this conversation is officially over," she growled then headed for the bathroom door with her clothes. She then turned and glared at him. "If you ever discuss what happened last night with anyone, there's a good chance I'll kill you." She entered the bathroom and slammed the door.

§

Maverick and Trudy sat at the island counter huddled over cups of coffee looking exhausted. Stone appeared on the back stairs with a lively spring to his step, which immediately infuriated the weary man and woman.

"Good morning," Stone announced cheerfully. "What a beautiful morning!"

"We get it," Maverick muttered with irritation. "You got laid last night. Goody for you."

"I didn't get laid last night," Stone informed them then grinned uncontrollably. "That little vixen violated me three ways from Sunday."

"Yes," Trudy snapped while glaring at him. "We heard. With all the screaming and thumping, I'm surprised someone didn't land in the hospital."

Stone poured a cup of coffee then eyed the weary couple. "What are you talking about? How could you have heard us?" he demanded. "We never made it out of the tavern parking lot."

Trudy and Maverick stared at him with shared looks of surprise. "What?" Maverick questioned.

"We went at it in the back of her car in the tavern parking lot," Stone informed them. "I didn't bring her back here. She went home right afterward."

"Then who was driving the headboard through the wall?" Trudy practically demanded.

Rayner entered the kitchen through the hallway entrance and hesitated when he saw the others. He fidgeted slightly. "Uh, morning," he announced timidly. "Could someone give me a ride to the tavern for my car?"

All three looked at Rayner, who appeared to be in a slightly bad mood.

"Uh, yeah, sure," Stone replied while staring at him with a strange look.

Maverick and Trudy could only stare at him in silence with their mouths hanging open. Neither seemed sure how to respond as they put the pieces together.

"No way," Maverick gasped and shook his head. "It couldn't be."

"What did Scorpio have to say this morning?" Trudy asked with a curious look, obviously fishing for information about his night.

"She's not talking to me," Rayner informed Trudy, "and there's a slight chance she's planning on killing me so I'd like to get out of here as soon as possible."

Stone folded his arms across his chest while coming to his own conclusions and stared at Rayner. "I'm wondering if I should kill you myself," he scoffed with anger. "What did you do?"

"Did you sneak into her bedroom? You bastard," Trudy gasped.

"No," Rayner announced defensively. "I swear, it was the other way around, but don't tell her I said anything." He frowned in response. "She threatened to kill me if I told anyone about last night."

"She came on to you?" Maverick asked with surprise, unable to look away.

"It was sort of a mutual drunken thing," Rayner replied while avoiding eye contact.

Scorpio appeared at the bottom of the back kitchen stairs and glared at Rayner with a look of betrayal. She couldn't believe he blurted out what had happened to her friends after agreeing to keep it between them.

"You bastard!" Scorpio suddenly cried out. "You just promised you wouldn't say anything!"

"Oh, please," Trudy scoffed while rolling her eyes and had to look away. "We heard you two going at it for nearly an hour last night."

Scorpio immediately turned red then headed back up the stairs without a word.

Chapter 16

Scorpio held her head while leaning across the kitchen table. Her head was pounding, the walls were breathing, and she couldn't remove the images of her wild night with Rayner from her mind. The first two she could deal with; the last was making her insane. Somehow, she felt as if she'd cheated on Cal. She knew she'd eventually date someone again, but to have a cheap one-night-stand, particularly with a geeky computer nerd like Rayner, was too much to rationalize right now. Trudy poured more coffee for Maverick and Stone, who had just returned from taking Rayner home. Although neither man said anything, she felt as if she were secretly being judged or even condemned for cheating on their friend. Would they bail on her over it? Would they think less of her now? She needed to say something, but discussing what happened between her and Rayner wasn't an option.

"So," Scorpio groaned as she straightened at the table. "Besides never drinking again, did we learn anything useful last night?"

Trudy joined them at the table and sipped her coffee. "Tony said your brother was enthusiastic about something two nights before he pulled up stakes and left town," she announced. "But the last time he saw him, he seemed off. Almost paranoid."

"Paranoid? Kane?" Scorpio held back her laugh. "When wasn't Kane paranoid?" she remarked then turned serious. "Did he elaborate?"

"It was crowded that night, so Tony didn't have time to get into a conversation with him," Trudy informed her. "But he did say your brother really wanted to talk to someone about what he'd learned."

"Did he see him talking to anyone else after that?" Maverick asked.

"I asked," Trudy replied. "He talked to a lot of people, but I sort of doubt he shared anything personal with any of them. They weren't the sort of people he discussed personal matters with. More of casual conversations." She then remembered something. "Although he did say Amber had been flirting with him. Rico, who was her boyfriend at the time, tried to pick a fight. Supposedly, Kane wanted nothing to do with Rico and left the bar around midnight."

"Yeah, I've seen Rico," Maverick announced. "He's a powerhouse."

"And Kane left the bar alone?" Scorpio asked.

Trudy nodded.

Scorpio straightened in her chair. "He didn't get home until after two in the morning, but he left the tavern alone by midnight," she remarked while in thought. "So where was he from midnight until two?"

"Did you actually hear him come home?" Stone asked. "I sometimes watch sports highlights after a night out before going to bed."

"No, I heard his car pull up around two in the morning," Scorpio insisted. "He didn't go to his room until a little after three. He must have been tired because he took the elevator. I've told him not to use the elevator in the middle of the night because it's noisy and wakes me."

Maverick turned to Stone. "Did you get anything at all off Amber?" he asked.

"Besides STDs," Trudy muttered.

Maverick held his hand up in a high-five to Trudy while keeping his attention on Stone. Trudy laughed and slapped his hand.

"Hey, I did what was asked of me," Stone insisted while glaring at Maverick. "Don't blame me because she wasn't attracted to you."

"Fight nice," Scorpio moaned, again flopping on the table. "My head can't handle much more of this."

"I did have a little back seat talk with Amber before we parted ways," Stone informed them. "Where Kane was concerned, she was very accommodating."

Scorpio managed to lift her head from the table and eyed Stone. "How on earth did you work my brother into after sex talk?" she asked with surprise.

"I mentioned knowing she and Kane had dated and hoped that wouldn't make things awkward between you and her," Stone remarked. "Women like sensitive men who consider their feelings."

"What did she say?" Scorpio asked with renewed interest as she straightened. "Did he talk to her that night? Did he meet her after he supposedly left the bar?"

"No, she didn't see him after he left," Stone continued. "She said he was preoccupied with something called Midnight Requisition."

"Midnight Requisition?" Trudy suddenly announced then looked at Scorpio, who had immediately perked up. "You mentioned that a while back."

"I found an empty folder on the desk in his room," Scorpio insisted. "The only thing on it was a 'confidential' stamp and a label on the tab with Midnight Requisition on it. Did she say what it meant?"

Stone shook his head. "That was as much as she knew," he replied. "I could go for the long con and see what else she knows. Although it might be fun, I doubt I'd learn much from her."

"We need to find out what Midnight Requisition is," Maverick suddenly announced. "Where did Kane get that folder? What was in the folder? What does Midnight Requisition even mean?"

"I could be mistaken," Stone announced, "but I think it's military slang for 'borrowing' something that's not necessarily authorized."

"Kane did love his war games," Scorpio remarked then sneered. "Some foolish belief that he'd gain insight into the life of our father."

"Could it have anything to do with your father?" Trudy asked.

"Our father died before we were born," Scorpio reminded her. "I don't see how it could. Kane always did have an unrealistic approach to our father's death. He refused to believe he was dead." She rolled her eyes and mimicked her brother. "His untimely death was far too convenient."

"What did happen to your father?" Stone asked.

"My grandmother told us the story once or twice," Scorpio replied. "Supposedly, he was murdered in front of my mother. Although, I think Kane made up his own version of what really happened."

"I know this is a long shot," Maverick announced. "But what if your brother was investigating your father's death and stumbled upon something more sinister?" He eyed those at the table. "Where did he get that file? Was it important? Who knew he had it?"

"Well, obviously Amber knew something about it," Stone replied. "He spoke to her in the bar that night. There's no telling how many ears heard him mention it."

"If I could get into his desktop computer," Scorpio huffed, "maybe there's something in there."

"You know who might be able to hack that computer?" Stone announced then grinned at Scorpio.

She glared back at him. "No way," she scoffed. "That isn't happening."

"I'm not suggesting you sleep with him," Stone remarked, although his smile was suggesting it.

"Again," Maverick muttered while smiling slyly.

At least she knew they weren't upset that she'd slept with another man since Cal's death. She almost would have preferred them being upset over teasing her about it.

"It's his job," Stone continued. "Just ask him to come out and look at it."

"I don't think I can look him in the eyes right now," Scorpio insisted. "It's too embarrassing."

"I honestly don't get the hang-up with women and sex," Stone announced while shaking his head. "You both obviously had a good time."

"From what I heard, it was wild kingdom up there," Trudy remarked.

"Why does it have to be awkward?" Stone insisted. "Why not just say 'hey, that was fun' and move on?"

Scorpio again flopped on the table and groaned. "I don't want to see him ever again," she moaned. "I remember too much of last night. My memory of Cal's been tainted. Every time I close my eyes I see Rayner Roderick looking at me like a lovesick puppy." She rolled her eyes shut and groaned while burying her face into the table.

"You want to know what's on Kane's computer?" Maverick demanded. "You have to overcome your guilt and look that computer geek in the face."

Scorpio lifted her head and glared at Maverick. His sly smile returned.

"I hate you," she scoffed.

"I hate to make your life even more miserable," Trudy announced while eyeing Scorpio then cringed, "but maybe it wouldn't be such a bad idea to bury the hatchet with Davenport."

"Bury the hatchet *in* Davenport?" she asked while straightening with renewed enthusiasm. "Because that I can do. If you're suggesting I make nice with him, that's *not* happening."

"She has a point," Maverick announced. "The enemy wants to be your friend. You should play along and see what you can learn."

"What if I learn the enemy wants to kill me?" she demanded. "How will that help then?"

"We'd know we were on the right track," Stone casually replied.

"If I extended an olive branch to Davenport, my grandfather would probably kill me himself," she insisted. "They had a major falling-out years ago, and he seems convinced Davenport had something to do with Kane's murder. You heard him threaten Davenport."

Stone nodded. "Yes, I did," he replied. "But your grandfather doesn't need to know everything you do. Invite the guy to the hotel. Show him the renovations he so eagerly wanted to see. Engage in small talk. We'll be right beside you. Nothing will happen."

"Facing Rayner Roderick doesn't sound nearly as bad anymore," she muttered.

"You're not in this alone," Trudy boldly announced. "I had a thing for your brother for years. If I can help find his killer, I'm willing to take one for the team."

Maverick and Stone eyed her at the same time.

"Come again?" Maverick questioned.

Trudy straightened proudly in her chair. "Rico's always had a thing for me," she announced. "I'll go out with him if it helps find your brother's killer."

"By go out you mean--?" Stone asked while raising his brows.

"Yes," Trudy replied. "I'll sleep with him if I have to." She then eyed Scorpio. "If our sacrifice helps find Kane's killer, there's no reason to feel ashamed."

Scorpio nodded then offered a smile. "You're right, Trudy," she replied. "I need to face Rayner and ask him for his help. I owe my brother that much, but I don't want you offering yourself to Rico. It's not necessary. We'll work with our current plan and see what happens."

Chapter 17

Scorpio collapsed into the office chair and stared at the phone on the desk. Maverick sat on the desk and grinned almost boyishly while giving her his undivided attention. Trudy cast herself into the chair before the desk and wore a devious smile that matched Maverick's grin. Scorpio eyed both and was immediately irritated. They were enjoying her torture just a little too much.

"I can't call him with the two of you leering over me," she announced and pointed to the door. "Out!"

"Oh, come on," Trudy pouted. "We wanted to hear the morning after talk."

Scorpio folded her arms across her chest and leaned back in the chair. "Well, I'm not making the call with either of you here."

They appeared disappointed and left the room, leaving the door open behind them. They obviously intended to eavesdrop on the conversation.

"Shut the door behind you," Scorpio impatiently called after them.

Maverick returned and shut the door. Scorpio shook her head then drew a deep, nervous breath. She removed Rayner's card from her desk and picked up the phone. She grimaced with each number she pressed then shut her eyes and listened to the phone ring, hoping she'd get his voicemail. The phone was answered on the second ring.

"Hello, Scorpio?" Rayner eagerly announced from the other end.

She jumped with surprise. He must have seen the hotel name on his cell phone's caller ID. She was taken aback and didn't know what to say.

"Uh, yeah," she announced and gently cleared her throat. "I, uh, know we got off on the wrong foot this morning, and I wanted to--"

"No, no," he announced eagerly over the phone. "It was all my fault."

"Stop apologizing," she announced with a groan then ran her fingers through her hair. "It was more my fault than yours. Can we just forget about last night and pretend it didn't happen?"

"Uh, yeah," he replied with less enthusiasm. "Sure, if that's what you want."

"Yes, it is," she announced then held her breath while cringing. "You're, uh, also the only one I know who can figure out what's wrong with my computer. Could I make an appointment to have you look at it?"

"Actually, I have time before my next appointment," he announced over the phone almost a little too eagerly. "I'll come right over."

"I don't want to put you out--"

"No, I have time now," he replied. "Otherwise, I may not get to you until next week."

"Well, okay then," she remarked.

"I'll be there in ten minutes."

"Okay, see you then." Scorpio hung up the phone and shook her head. "Convenient how he always has time before his next appointment."

The office door opened. Trudy poked her head in and giggled. "Is he coming out now?"

"You should know," Scorpio scoffed. "You were obviously listening."

"Yeah, your lovesick little puppy has got it bad," Trudy teased. "Let's face it; you brought him home now you have to keep him."

"I made it perfectly clear I need his assistance with a computer issue," Scorpio informed her friend. "He knows it's business and not a booty call."

Maverick appeared in the office doorway with a bewildered look on his face. "Your computer geek is pulling up the driveway."

Scorpio appeared stunned and looked at the security monitors. She could see Rayner's car pulling up to the hotel. She sprang to her feet.

"What the hell was he doing?" Scorpio launched hotly. "Was he sitting at the bottom of the driveway waiting for me to call?"

"Make sure you set him straight on that booty call thing," Trudy teased and left the office with Maverick, who was grinning at the comment like a schoolboy hearing a dirty joke for the first time.

Scorpio groaned and headed into the hallway after them. She passed them and continued for the front door.

"I don't know which of you is worse," Scorpio scoffed under her breath.

As she headed up the foyer steps, Maverick casually leaned against the staircase banister and grinned.

"Isn't that computer in your brother's bedroom?" Maverick asked then shook his head while attempting a serious look that failed. "That's going to be awkward."

Scorpio spun around and stared at Maverick, but he was already herding Trudy toward the lounge and shut the door behind them. She frowned and shook her head. Scorpio jumped when she heard the knock on the door only inches from her. She drew a deep breath, collected herself, and opened the door. Rayner stood in the doorway, smiled innocently, and fidgeted slightly.

"Good afternoon, Scorpio," he announced politely. "So where's the computer?"

Scorpio felt her heart leap into her throat. She fidgeted slightly. "It's, uh, actually my brother's computer. You know where it is. The third floor at the end of the hall. Maybe you could show yourself upstairs."

"You didn't even tell me what's wrong with it," he remarked with noted surprise by her reaction. "It'd be best if you went along."

Scorpio forced a smile although she actually wanted to hit him. "Yes, of course," she replied and headed for the grand stairs.

"Your brother's room?" he announced while following her and appeared to tense slightly. "Is that the room I, uh, slept in last night?"

"Yes, that's why I wanted you to show yourself to the room," she remarked without looking at him.

"We're both mature, consenting adults," he informed her. "I think we can handle being in the same room together without feeling awkward."

"Speak for yourself," she muttered.

They headed up the grand stairs to the third floor. Rayner took in the staircase and marveled at the view over the railing to the foyer below.

"I can't get over the restorations to this staircase," he remarked with amazement. "Looks like it would be found in a medieval castle."

"I loved this staircase the moment I saw it as a little girl," she informed him.

"The hotel has been in your family that long?" he asked with surprise.

"My grandfather owned it," she announced then hesitated. "He and Carson Davenport bought the place and ran it back when they were best friends. It sat vacant for years before my uncle insisted on buying it from my grandfather." She sighed and looked around as they continued up to the third floor. "He never got around to renovating it."

"I'd heard about your mother and uncle," Rayner replied in a gentle tone.

"I suppose everyone in town has," she remarked with little emotion. "Naturally, Davenport wanted to buy the hotel back, but my uncle refused to sell it. After my uncle died, he tried to buy it from my grandparents, but it had been left to my brother and me and sat vacant until my brother and I were given our trust funds. Kane didn't want any part of this old place. My grandfather even offered to buy it back, since he didn't want it going for sale or auction." She cast a look at Rayner. "Obviously, he didn't want Davenport getting his hands on it, but I decided I wanted to keep it. Cal and I thought we could bring her back to life." She glanced at Rayner as he walked up the steps alongside her. "You know the rest of the story."

Chapter 18

Scorpio led Rayner down the third floor hallway to the end of the hall and paused before Kane's closed bedroom door. She hesitated before opening the door then stepped inside and immediately felt uncomfortable being there with him. Rayner didn't even react. He approached the desk and sat before the computer, immediately turning it on. Scorpio remained in the doorway and rubbed her chilled arms. She glanced at the neatly made bed and was reminded of her wild night of passion with Rayner. She frowned and looked away. The images wouldn't leave her head and played out like some horrible porn flick running through her mind. Rayner cast a look at her then indicated the computer.

"What's the password?" he asked and placed his fingers to the keyboard in anticipation.

Scorpio fidgeted, knowing she was about to be called on her true reason for needing his help. "I was hoping you could figure it out," she replied.

He removed his hands from the keyboard and looked at her with surprise. "You don't have the password?" he asked. "How do you know there's something wrong with the computer if you haven't been in it?"

"Not getting in it *is* the problem," she replied.

Rayner stared at her with surprise. "You called me over here to hack into your brother's computer?"

"It's not as if he's coming back for it," she remarked in her own defense. "Certainly you do this sort of thing all the time when people die."

"Usually they have the password," he informed her. "Most times, if they don't, we do a factory reboot."

"No," she gasped and practically lunged forward then collected herself. "I need to know what's on that computer. There could be answers to his murder. Don't forensic teams recover data from computers?"

"Yeah, and they have more sophisticated equipment than what I've got," he replied.

"Are you honestly telling me that you've never hacked into a computer before?" she asked while raising a clever brow, taunting him.

"Of course I have," he replied defensively, "but it's not that simple."

Rayner searched the top of the desk then opened drawers and routed through them.

"If you're looking for a password, you won't find one," she informed him with a defeated sigh. "Kane was as clever as he was paranoid."

"What had him paranoid?" Rayner asked while continuing his search.

"Well, that sort of depended on the year," she replied with a sigh. "The last few years he lived with the belief that our father was alive. He wanted to believe that his death was some huge government cover-up. Kane refused to believe our father was just some average guy who happened to be in the wrong place at the wrong time." She rolled her eyes. "He first started with the theory that our father was some sort of spy for the CIA. I guess, in his mind, our father was just posing as a Navy SEAL when our mother met him. Then he moved on to some sort of witness protection theory."

"A young man growing up without his father is liable to fantasize his father was some glorified hero," Rayner replied then eyed the empty folder with a bewildered look then indicated it. "What's this?"

"Whatever he was researching last," Scorpio replied. "I was hoping there was some information in his computer about that."

"What's Midnight Requisition?" he asked then opened the folder, saw it was empty, and eyed her. "And why would an empty folder be marked confidential?"

"I'd like to know that too."

"So he was obsessed with whatever this was when he took off?" Rayner asked.

"Yes, very obsessed."

Rayner turned toward the computer and typed on the keyboard. She approached with a curious look and watched him type the words 'midnight requisition'.

"You can't honestly think--"

As he hit enter, the front screen disappeared. Rayner chuckled and appeared pleased with himself. Scorpio practically lunged over his shoulder and stared at the screen. Rayner immediately pulled up a window and typed into it.

"What are you doing?" she asked.

"Pulling up the last viewed files," he replied. "We can also search his internet browsing history." He studied the screen while pulling up files. "We'll be able to see everything he looked at before he took off."

"Maybe you should tell me what to do," she announced and practically stepped in front of him.

He eyed her with surprise and leaned back in his chair. "You lured me in with the promise of international intrigue, spies, and the witness protection program, and now you want to sideline me?"

"It's nothing personal, Rayner," she insisted.

"Of course it is," he snapped back while glaring at her. "The pretty girl always wants the geeky computer nerd to type her college papers then toss him aside for the jock." His eyes suddenly narrowed. "You didn't actually forgive me for last night, did you? You just played nice, so I'd unlock your brother's computer."

"It's sort of your job," Scorpio reminded him. "Fixing computers is what you do, remember?"

"No, this is just the popular girl in high school keeping the computer nerd out of her circle of friends," he boldly informed her.

"Trust me," she muttered. "You don't want to join this club."

"Just once, I'd like to decide that for myself," he insisted with some arrogance.

Scorpio groaned and sat on the edge of the desk facing him. She stared into his eyes with a serious look. "Stop romanticizing the situation," she demanded as her eyes pierced into his. "Listen carefully to what I'm saying, Rayner. People in my circle have huge targets on their backs. My boyfriend was brutally murdered. My brother was brutally murdered. Men broke into my house on two separate occasions and tried to kill me. Whatever they were looking for; they haven't found it yet. That means they're eventually coming back to finish the job. They're coming back to kill me and anyone standing next to me." She leaned closer to him and stared into his eyes with a demanding look. "Given your squeamish nature with blood, do you really want to be standing anywhere near me when that happens?"

Rayner stared back at her with some surprise by her words. He tensed slightly and straightened proudly. "Yes, I would like to be standing next to you," he announced.

She sat up straight and stared at him almost dumbfounded. "Why the hell would you want to risk your life for me?" she demanded. "You don't even know me."

Rayner drew a deep breath and didn't take his eyes off her. "Because if you're going to solve this mystery and manage to stay alive, you need me," he informed her.

"You have no idea what's even going on," she insisted firmly. "I've been living it, and even I don't know what's going on."

"That's exactly why you need me," he replied then leaned on the desk closer to her. "After your brother was killed, I overheard some of Davenport's men discussing him."

Scorpio stared at him while feeling her heart pounding. She hadn't even considered his acquaintances and how useful he might be to her. Rayner did a lot of work for Davenport. He had instant access to the information she needed, and it never occurred to her.

"I heard your brother was smart," he announced and raised his brows. "Crazy smart. They don't think like you and me, but I understand crazy smart." He then pointed to the computer monitor. "Within this computer is a trail of breadcrumbs your brother left behind. I can follow those breadcrumbs and figure out what he was thinking days and weeks prior to the time he left. I can access his credit card if he had one and numbers he called on his cell phone. I can tell you everyone he spoke with and every move he made up until the day he died." Rayner sat back in the chair and raised an arrogant brow. "Can you do any of that?"

She stared at him a long moment as if attempting to read his mind. Neither flinched.

"You're insane," she scoffed while shaking her head then drew a deep breath. "I guess that means you're in. I'll get you a target to pin to your back."

Rayner grinned and turned back to the computer. "I'm going to need a few hours and a lot of coffee."

Scorpio stood and cocked her head while offering a sly grin. "You've got it."

Chapter 19

It was nearly one o'clock in the morning. Maverick, Stone, Trudy, and Scorpio sat at the kitchen table looking weary. Each checked their watches several times. Scorpio couldn't help her distrustful nature, but she passed it off. Despite doing work for Davenport, she didn't believe Rayner actually *worked* for him as her grandfather had speculated. She had to trust he'd do right by her even if it was just because of some lovesick fantasy of his. Finding Kane's killer was important to her, and she was willing to risk just about anything at this point to find the person responsible.

"Maybe he fell asleep up there," Trudy offered. "Should we check on him?"

"After he yelled at me the last time I attempted to check on his progress?" Maverick demanded then adamantly shook his head. "He nearly bit my head off. I'm not going back up there."

Stone stood with a groan. "You can do what you want," he announced. "I'm going to bed."

"Yeah, me too," Maverick agreed with his friend and stood as well.

Trudy sighed and joined them. "I'm with him," she announced then received several looks. She immediately fidgeted. "I meant I'm going to bed." She hesitated then glared at the others. "In my own room." Trudy became slightly flustered. "Alone."

Scorpio stood and joined her friends. "I'm going to check on Rayner," she announced. "If he didn't learn anything yet, it can wait until morning."

"You know he's just trying to impress you," Trudy informed her as they headed for the back stairs. "You should give the guy credit for trying."

"He can impress me all he wants," Scorpio announced. "It won't be enough to change our relationship. Besides, I think he understands that's not happening."

All four wearily headed up the back stairs. While her friends headed into the second floor corridor, Scorpio continued upstairs to the third floor. Her brother's room was closer to the kitchen stairs, so it was a shorter walk. She stepped into the open doorway and saw Rayner alternating between Kane's desktop computer and his own laptop. He seemed wide-awake, after drinking nearly a pot of coffee, and completely engrossed in his work.

"If you're not finding anything--"

He didn't bother looking up, and her presence didn't disrupt his work. "I'm finding plenty," he informed her, catching her attention.

Scorpio entered the room and sat on the edge of the bed closest to the desk. "What did you find?"

"Let's just say I would have loved to have known your brother," Rayner informed her without looking away from either monitor. "He was beyond crazy smart. He was evil villain genius."

She raised her brows and glared almost sarcastically. "Okay, my brother was not a genius," she bluntly informed him. "He was always losing his keys; he continually forgot my birthday--"

Rayner hesitated and looked at her for the first time. "I thought you were twins."

"We are," she scoffed.

He laughed and returned to his work.

"Kane barely graduated high school and would have dropped out of college if my grandparents had let him," she added then laughed. "Trust me; he wasn't a genius."

"He hacked into the secured server of a Navy Admiral and downloaded hundreds of confidential files," Rayner informed her as he pulled up several screens revealing documents with most of the words blackened. "He has software and programs so sophisticated; I can only guess he was using it to pair his cell phone to phones of others." Rayner then nodded to a thick, black, fireproof locked box on the bed. It was about the size of a shoebox. "Then there's that."

Scorpio glanced at the unfamiliar locked box with a digital code on it and moved closer to it so she could examine it. "Where did you find this?"

"Within a hidden compartment in his closet," Rayner replied without taking his eyes off the computer while he worked. "Look inside and tell me your brother wasn't evil villain genius."

"It's locked," she informed him then pushed several buttons on the numbered panel.

"I assure you; he didn't use his birthday," Rayner announced mocking her.

She sneered back at him. "You've obviously been in the box," she remarked. "What's the code?"

"Zero, six, zero, three," he replied. "The day your mother died."

Scorpio gave him a strange look then punched in the code and opened the locked box. She stared at the contents with surprise bordering on horror as she removed several passports and driver's licenses. Each one had her brother's photo but with different last names.

"What the hell is this?" she gasped.

"Either your brother was secretly a spy, or he anticipated trouble in a big way," Rayner informed her.

She set aside the passports and sorted through several deeds for houses. "He's been buying up homes?" Her eyes suddenly narrowed with bewilderment as she read some of them. "He owned property in Colorado, Florida, and Virginia?" Her expression suddenly dropped as she looked at Rayner's profile. "He owned a home in Virginia?"

"I researched their locations," he informed her. "Some are in the middle of nowhere."

"What does that mean?"

"It means they're safe houses," Rayner replied while briefly glancing back at her. "He bought them all under a corporation name, so they couldn't easily be traced back to him. His corporation also has credit cards, cell phones, and several bank accounts."

She stared at Rayner with disbelief. "We received a sizable inheritance from my uncle's estate as well as my mother's work and personal life insurance policies, but it wouldn't be enough to finance all of this."

"Yeah, I'm guessing all those stocks his corporation owns helped finance most of that," Rayner replied matter-of-factly then flashed a devious smile. "I told you; evil villain genius. I also found a copy of his Will in the computer. Are you aware he left everything to you?"

"A lawyer called after his death, but I didn't get back to him yet," she replied. "I figured he didn't have anything worth willing to anyone. My grandfather was going to take care of that for me, but now that I know this, maybe I should visit him myself."

"I think you should too," Rayner replied.

"I assumed he blew most of his inheritance," Scorpio remarked. "He was living here rent free. The only thing he owned or cared about was that damned sports car of his. Ironic, he died in his car, and it was destroyed with him." She replaced the items to the locked box and shut it. "It's probably best if this is returned where you found it until I can figure out what to do about it."

"Yes, we need to learn a lot more before you show that to anyone," Rayner announced then hesitated and finally turned to face her. "I don't want to upset you, but I think this should stay between us."

"Who was I going to tell anyway?" she remarked.

"I mean just between us," he again stated and pointed his finger between them.

She stared at him a moment with surprise. "You mean keep Maverick and Stone out of the loop? Why wouldn't I tell them?"

Rayner drew a deep breath and rolled his chair closer to her on the bed. He stared into her eyes with a strange seriousness. "They're your boyfriend's childhood friends, right?"

She nodded.

"Did they ever show you a picture of them with Cal?" Rayner asked.

Scorpio stared at him but didn't respond.

"Two men from your boyfriend's past, yet he never once mentioned them to you," Rayner continued. "Why would Cal not mention them? They show up just in time to save you from some men who tried to kill you, securing their place in your home and in your circle. Hell, they are your circle." He raised his brows demandingly. "Do you have any evidence to support they even actually knew Cal?"

"We've talked about Cal," she insisted feeling slightly irritated that he was insinuating the worst of her new friends. "They've told me personal things about him they wouldn't otherwise have known. They also knew things about me. Personal things they couldn't have known."

"I'm just asking you to think like a woman who's been nearly killed twice," Rayner insisted. "Once upon a time, Cal worked for Davenport. It's possible Maverick and Stone aren't who they say they are."

"I know they seem suspicious," she informed him, "but we've had long discussions. With everything that has happened, I think I can trust them."

Rayner returned to his laptop and pressed a button. He rolled away allowing her to see the screen. She stared at images of Maverick and Stone in police mugshots with different names.

"I need more time and the privacy of my own office in order to dig up more information on them," he announced then frowned. "The two of them have been pacing this hall all evening."

Scorpio stared at their images and the different names beneath their mugshots. She was feeling betrayed and confused. Anger soon set in.

"I'm sorry, Scorpio," Rayner informed her while offering a sympathetic look. "I really am, but this doesn't mean they're out to harm you. I'd like to get more information first. Just keep everything I've told you between us. I'd feel better about your safety."

She tore her eyes away from the computer screen and nodded. "Yeah, I'll do that," she muttered and stood. Scorpio immediately started pacing the room. "Did you find anything about Midnight Requisition?"

"Not yet," he replied. "There's nothing in the computer. You said he had a laptop. Whatever he had on it was probably on his laptop."

She tensed and eyed Rayner. "There wasn't any mention of his laptop in the car with him." Her eyes suddenly lit up. "Maybe he left it at one of his homes in Virginia. We should go there."

"I think you should hold off on that for now," Rayner informed her while offering a concerned look. "Let me see who we can trust first. If someone is after that file, they could make their move if we produce the laptop. We need to know who we can trust."

She immediately nodded. "Yes, you're absolutely right," Scorpio announced.

She grabbed the small but heavy locked box, hurried to the closet, and returned it to its secured location, once more keeping it hidden. She returned to the bedroom and fidgeted with nervous anxiety.

"Maybe you should pack it in and call it a night," Scorpio suggested.

"I thought I'd just crash in your brother's bed," he replied, "if that's okay with you."

"I'm not sure that's a good idea," she informed him and sat back on the bed near the foot end. "Are you sure it's safe to stay here?"

Rayner stood, approached the door, and shut it. She tensed slightly while watching him, uncertain what he was up to. Rayner approached the bed, sat on it, and then felt behind the bedpost. He turned off the light, surprising her. Scorpio stared at the bedroom door with astonishment. There was an illuminated red line across the door.

"What's that?" she practically gasped.

Rayner approached the door and opened it, disrupting the red light. The alarm clock suddenly flashed and the bed vibrated. Scorpio jumped off the bed and stared at it. She looked at Rayner as he shut everything off.

He smirked at her. "Evil villain genius," Rayner replied a little too proudly.

Scorpio looked around the room then met Rayner's gaze. "No wonder he was always awake when I came to his room," she announced. "He had an advance warning system. Why was he so paranoid?"

"I'm hoping Midnight Requisition will give us the answers," Rayner replied.

Scorpio shook her head in disbelief. "What the hell was Kane into?" she demanded.

"Find out, and we may figure out why he was killed," Rayner replied.

Chapter 20

Early the following morning, Scorpio headed into the kitchen through the main hallway entrance and found Trudy and Maverick sitting at the island counter laughing over coffee. Scorpio paused in the doorway, since they didn't hear or see her, and eyed the couple. She wondered if something was going on between them. It was understandable. Maverick was a handsome, charming man, and Trudy was beautiful and sexually available. Although, after Rayner's bombshell last night, Scorpio was feeling slightly tense regarding her two new friends. There were too many questions, but she couldn't ask just yet. She needed to give Rayner time to snoop a little first.

If Maverick and Stone were double agents working for Davenport, there could be another bloody incident similar to the last one. She wasn't ready to kill either of her new friends, and she certainly didn't want to die trusting them. When it didn't seem as if she was about to interrupt anything embarrassing, she approached them and turned the kettle on for hot tea. Maverick and Trudy shifted uncomfortably, almost as if they had been caught doing something dirty, telling Scorpio there was something going on between them even if it was only in the flirting stages.

"Good morning," Scorpio announced cheerfully.

"Morning," both replied in response.

"Any news from our resident computer geek?" Maverick asked, immediately causing Scorpio to tense.

He could have simply been curious since they were working on getting answers, but it made her suspicious all the same.

"No, he was packing it in when I checked on him last night," Scorpio replied. "I should probably see if he's up and in need of coffee."

"Don't bother," Maverick replied and held up a note. "He left before I was up, but he did leave a note. He was all excited about something and will call you later."

Scorpio approached and took the note from him. If he had discovered something that had him fired up, it seemed strange he didn't stop and see her before leaving. Stone entered through the exterior kitchen door, indicating he had gone somewhere since they typically parked near the kitchen entrance.

"You must have left early this morning," Trudy remarked to Stone. "If I had known you were going out, I would have asked you to pick up some coffee creamer."

Stone removed a carton of creamer from his plastic bag, grinned, and set it on the island counter.

Trudy groaned and immediately reached for it. "Oh, thank you!" She added some creamer to her coffee.

"It's not even seven o'clock," Scorpio announced while eying him. "Where did you find an open store?"

"The convenient store out on the highway," Stone replied. "Rayner used all of the creamer last night in that pot of coffee he drank." Stone poured a cup of coffee then eyed the others. "His car was gone this morning when I left. Where'd he go so early? I thought he'd sleep until noon."

"You mean he left before you did?" Scorpio asked with surprise. "You must have left around six. What the hell time did he leave?"

"Must've been around sunrise," Stone replied then shook his head. "I hope he found something good."

Scorpio shifted uncomfortably and approached the wall phone. "I should call him and see what got him up and out so early." She picked up the phone and dialed the number she remembered from yesterday. The phone immediately went to voicemail. "Voicemail," she announced then hung up. "That means he's on his phone, right?"

"Or he's out of range," Trudy responded. "If you tried calling me right now, it would go to voicemail, since there's no reception on your little cliff-side resort."

"I hope if he learned something, he didn't act without telling us," Scorpio muttered and sank into thought. She didn't want to be suspicious of her friends, but his leaving without talking to her seemed out of character.

§

It was nearly three o'clock in the afternoon, and Scorpio still hadn't heard from Rayner. She even called his cell phone several times, getting the voicemail each time before it even rang. She left two messages, but she still hadn't heard back from him. She hung up the hall phone and turned to Trudy, who stood alongside her.

"Still nothing?" Trudy asked.

"No, nothing," she replied as her anxiety spiked. "It's Sunday. There's hardly anything open on a Sunday around here. Where could he be?"

"Want me to drive around town and look for his car?" her friend asked.

"You have to think about heading back to the city soon," Scorpio reminded her. "You have work on Monday."

"I know," Trudy replied and became tense. "But I hate to leave without knowing if he's okay. I sort of feel we're responsible. We asked him to help. What if he followed some lead and something happened? I couldn't live with that sort of guilt."

"Yeah, me either," Scorpio muttered then eyed her friend. "Why don't you drive around town and look for him? I'll drive to the edge of town past Davenport's mansion and look for his car there."

"If something happened to him," Trudy boldly informed her, "there's no way Davenport would leave his car just sitting around in his driveway. They'd hide it in one of their many garages."

"Of course you're right," Scorpio announced with a frown. "I'll have to put plan 'B' into effect."

"Which plan is that?"

"The one where I invite Davenport to the hotel and see what he knows," Scorpio replied.

"Not without me," Maverick announced as he approached from the kitchen area. "You're not going to his mansion by yourself. I'll go with you."

"Where are we going?" Stone asked and joined them in the hallway.

"We're just going to drive around town and look for Rayner's car," Trudy insisted.

"Then let's go," Stone replied.

"You go with Trudy," Maverick announced then looked back at Scorpio. "I'll go with Scorpio."

"Are you sure you wouldn't prefer to go with Trudy?" Stone asked while raising his brow and grinned.

"What's with you people?" Trudy demanded. "There's nothing going on between us."

§

Rayner slowly opened his eyes and looked around the unfamiliar cave from where he had been unconscious on the cold, wet floor. The cave was dimly lit, damp, and desolate. He sat up and immediately felt pain in his wrist as well as resistance. He looked at his left hand and saw the handcuff attached to his wrist. The other end was attached to a rusted pipe in the solid cave wall. He quickly stood and immediately felt dizzy as pain radiated through his head. He didn't let that interfere with his agenda and pulled against the pipe within the stone. It didn't budge.

"Hello?" he called out. "Anyone there?" There was no response, but he did hear the sound of water. "I must be near the ocean."

The sound of water got louder. A gush of water entered the cave and touched his feet before rolling back out. He jumped with surprise. As the water rushed back in, it was higher now. His eyes widened with alarm as he looked around the mostly damp cave.

"This whole cave is going to flood," he gasped. "I was left here to drown."

He struggled to pull the pipe from the stone wall, but it wouldn't budge. Despite the nearly deafening sound of the ocean as it got louder, he could hear music coming from somewhere. He listened a moment then realized it was coming from above him. He looked up to the cave ceiling above him and sank into thought.

Rayner's eyes suddenly widened as he listened to the familiar, classical music. "I know where I am," he gasped then touched the pipe.

The music could be felt vibrating through the pipe, indicating the pipe led to the building on the bluff above him. He clutched the handcuff around his wrist with his free hand and banged on the pipe, sending an S.O.S. through the pipe. It almost seemed ridiculous considering how loud the music had to be coming from the building above him. Whoever was in the building would never hear him banging on the pipe. He looked at the water now covering his feet and rising.

"I suddenly feel very foolish," Rayner announced. "What the hell were you thinking?"

He continued pounding on the pipe with the other half of the handcuff attached to his wrist.

Chapter 21

Maverick drove Scorpio's jeep along the coast while they checked out several of Davenport's businesses for signs of Rayner or his car. The office building just on the edge of town was closed for the weekend, so there were no cars in the lot, and the place seemed quiet. Scorpio remained alert in the passenger seat, insisting Maverick drive since she felt she was more observant than he was.

"Are we being a little shortsighted here?" Maverick asked while glancing at her several times as he drove her car slower than the speed limit. "Maybe Rayner's enthusiasm had nothing to do with Davenport. What if Davenport has nothing to do with any of this?"

"Davenport is the only person of interest I have, Maverick," she explained now feeling frustrated.

Rayner's words from last night seemed to echo through her mind. She cast a look at her friend's profile and just couldn't imagine he wasn't anything but truthful with her. If he hadn't been Cal's childhood friend, she'd feel betrayed beyond comprehension. With Kane and Cal gone, Maverick and Stone were the closest things she had to a support system. Sure, Trudy came home to visit on occasion, but she'd be gone after today, and it'd be back to the "Three Musketeers". She needed to believe Maverick and Stone were her allies otherwise she'd be devastated.

Still, there was that tiny part of her that couldn't help feeling suspicious. Call it residual paranoia passed along from sharing a womb with Kane. Did Rayner actually leave her that note? Where did Maverick find the note? Her friends had access to Rayner. It was possible he didn't even leave of his own free will. Would Rayner really pick up and leave without telling her? He was such a little, lovesick puppy yesterday. If he found something of extreme interest, he'd want to share it with her, she was certain. He'd want to ride in on his white horse, draw his sword, and reveal he was her knight in shining armor. Ironically, she could almost envision it playing out exactly like that.

Scorpio again glanced at Maverick and took in his handsome profile. He was suave, sophisticated, and the most charming man she'd ever met. He talked her into helping with the hotel. He talked her into letting them stay with her and fix the place. Her thoughts strayed to the image of his mugshot. How many women from his past thought the same thing about him? Was he nothing more than a good-looking conman? Was he playing her in some elaborate long con? What would he possibly want? He certainly wasn't attempting to get into her bed. He never came on to her and rarely made any inappropriate remarks up until the 'Rayner' incident. That was the making of a loyal friend, wasn't it?

Scorpio felt defeated as she looked out the side window to the country club located along the coast. Her eyes suddenly lit up.

"There," she cried out while pointing to the mostly crowded parking lot. "That's his car; I'm almost positive."

Maverick turned into the nearly filled parking lot. The country club was located on the outskirts of town and bordered with the slightly larger neighboring town. It was a magnificent two-story building nestled on prime oceanfront property. Although it didn't have a beach, the view from the cliff was spectacular, especially to those playing golf. The 18-hole championship golf course drew in members on the warm, sunny afternoon, explaining the crowded parking lot and fleet of golf carts careening alongside the fairway. Maverick drove up to the familiar car, allowing Scorpio to confirm it was indeed Rayner's car.

"This guy must be making good money if he can afford this place," Maverick announced.

"I doubt he's making that kind of money," Scorpio informed him. "If anything, he's fixing their computer system or checking out their security, but that doesn't explain why he's not answering his phone."

Maverick parked her jeep, and both got out. Scorpio removed her cell phone and pressed in Rayner's number as they approached his car. They heard a faint chirping sound. Both looked around. It came from his car. They approached the car and looked inside. Rayner's cell phone was plugged into the charger and hung from the dashboard.

"Well, that explains why he's not answering his phone," Maverick remarked.

"Why isn't it on him?" Scorpio practically demanded while casting a curious look at her friend. "He always has it in his jacket pocket."

"Maybe he forgot it," Maverick replied. "Maybe the battery was dead. He spent the night in Kane's room. He probably didn't have time to charge it, which might also explain why it goes right to voicemail."

Scorpio peered into the car through the window and saw his toolkit on the passenger side seat. She immediately straightened and looked at Maverick.

"His toolkit is in the car," she announced with concern. "He can't possibly be working on something without his toolkit."

"Maybe he's having lunch with Davenport," Maverick suggested. "Want to go inside and ask? Lord knows they won't let us past the front door without a membership or a member present."

Scorpio pulled on the car door. It opened, indicating it had been unlocked. She looked inside the car, saw the keys in the ignition, and then glared at Maverick as she shut the door.

"He wouldn't leave his tools in the car with the door unlocked and the keys in the ignition," she announced. "Something's happened to him."

Maverick held his breath and glanced around. He then looked back at her and nodded in agreement. "Okay, what now? They won't let us in there," he reminded her. "The most we can do is ask at the front desk, but if something has happened to him, the receptionist isn't going to know anything. She probably won't even know he was there."

"I happen to know a member," she informed him and again removed her cell phone. She pressed a single button, placed the phone to her ear, and waited. "Grandpa? I need a big favor," she announced into the phone. "Can you come to the country club right away?"

"Do you honestly think your grandfather is going to--?"

"Thanks," she announced into the phone and disconnected the call. "He's in the club's smoking lounge. He wants us to meet him in the lobby."

Maverick stared at her with surprise then followed her to the building. "I'll call Stone. We're going to need them to help look around the property and ask about Rayner. With all these people around, maybe someone has seen him."

Chapter 22

Scorpio and her grandfather stood before the mildly stuck-up, middle-aged country club manager. He reeked of expensive cologne, and his suit was from some posh suit designer from Boston. It was apparent he was attempting to impress the club's clientele, who were far wealthier than he was. Maverick stood behind them by a few feet, feeling out of place among the well-dressed crowd. Scorpio's grandfather was dressed in his finest golf wear looking like a handsome throwback from the sixties. He argued with the neatly dressed manager, who obviously spent more time on his clothes and hair than Scorpio had on hers.

"You can't miss him," her grandfather insisted and held his hand up to chin level. "He's about yay high. If he had a bowtie, he'd pass for a chemistry teacher."

"I'm sorry, Mr. Wayland," the manager insisted. Despite his obvious snob appeal, he was slightly intimidated by her grandfather. Most people were. "We haven't seen him. He didn't arrive with any of our guests, and he didn't have reservations for the dining room or on the golf course. We know who's here every minute of every day."

The manager's cell phone beeped in his hand. He glanced at the text but kept his attention on Newman. "You've already checked the dining room for Mr. Roderick. I assure you; he isn't here."

"Okay, so you know who's here every minute of every day," her grandfather boldly announced then raised his brows. "Is Carson Davenport here?"

"Of course he's here, sir," the manager replied. "He's always here on Sunday. He's somewhere around the eighth hole."

Newman looked at Scorpio and nodded. "I knew it," he announced and appeared ready to explode. "I think you're right about Rayner being in trouble."

The manager's cell phone beeped again. He seemed to tense and eyed Newman. "I'm sorry," he announced. "I have to take care of a water pipe issue in the kitchen. If you'd like, you can wait for Mr. Davenport in the lounge, but it'll probably be a while before he returns to the clubhouse."

"What's wrong with the pipes?" Maverick asked, finally coming to life.

"Nothing that concerns the members," the manager replied. "Just an annoying pinging."

"Pinging?" her grandfather asked with a bewildered look and suddenly seemed interested.

"Yeah, it started about twenty minutes ago," the manager replied. "I'm sure it's nothing serious."

Maverick immediately stepped forward. "I know a lot about plumbing," he announced and laid on the charm. "Mind if I have a listen?"

The manager sighed then nodded. "Sure," he replied. "Follow me."

They followed the manager down the long corridor and eventually into the massive kitchen. Several dishwashers stood around while arguing over the pinging pipe, which could be heard echoing throughout the kitchen. Maverick, Newman, and Scorpio stopped to listen.

"Is that--?" Scorpio suddenly asked.

Maverick immediately groaned in agreement. "It's an S.O.S.," he cried out with enthusiasm then turned to the manager. "Is there a basement? Where do the water pipes come together?"

"Of course there's a basement," he replied and pointed to the nearby door. "What do you mean an S.O.S.?"

"Weren't you ever a Boy Scout?" Newman practically demanded then waved off the pompous manager in mild disgust. "Of course you weren't."

Maverick, Newman, and Scorpio ran for the basement door and hurried down the stairs. The pinging sound was getting louder. They looked around and found a trap door in the floor. Maverick opened it and looked into the tunnel more than halfway filled with water. He swiftly climbed down the vertical ladder. Scorpio attempted to follow him, but her grandfather stopped her.

"You should wait here," he announced.

She ignored him and climbed down the ladder after Maverick. Newman groaned then removed his expensive shoes and wallet. He grabbed a flashlight from a nearby bench and followed her. Scorpio hurried through the waist high, ocean water behind Maverick.

"Rayner!" Maverick called out. "Rayner!"

The tunnel was getting dimmer the further they went. Scorpio removed her cell phone and fiddled with an app turning on a light. The cell phone was fading in and out from being wet.

"Over here," Rayner called out.

Scorpio shined her cell phone across the tunnel. They caught a brief glimpse of Rayner in the waist deep water just before her cell phone died. The light from a flashlight just behind Scorpio lit the tunnel. Newman shined his light on Rayner.

"What the hell are you doing down here?" Newman demanded to Rayner and pointed behind them. "Didn't you see the ladder back there?"

"I'm handcuffed to a pipe," he shouted back with increasing hostility.

"I saw some tools in the basement," Maverick announced then hurried back for the ladder.

Panic swept over Scorpio only a brief moment as she envisioned Maverick betraying her and locking them all in the tunnel to drown. She cast the thought aside, not having time to entertain such nonsense, and continued through the deep water toward Rayner with her grandfather following.

"How did you get handcuffed to a pipe down here?" Newman suddenly demanded.

Scorpio and Rayner glared at him and raised their brows. Newman saw their looks and appeared horrified.

"You mean someone cuffed you to the pipe and left you down here?" her grandfather gasped. "In another twenty minutes, that would have been very unhealthy."

"I think they were going for fatal," Rayner responded while panting with exhaustion.

Maverick returned with a bolt cutter. He followed Rayner's wrist to the chain connecting the cuffs, placed the bolt cutter to the chain, and easily snapped it.

Rayner pulled his hand free and eyed the cuff still dangling from his red, bruised wrist. "Well, this has been one of the worst days of my life."

"Stick around," Scorpio muttered, knowing from experience that it would only get worse, then directed him toward the ladder down the tunnel.

§

Rayner sat on a bench toward the back of the kitchen while drying his hair with a fluffy, white towel lent to him from the country club shower room. He was given a white chef's outfit so he could change out of his drenched clothes. The sheriff stood in front of Rayner and jotted notes on his tablet. Sheriff Horton shook his head then eyed the broken handcuff within the evidence bag.

"That's messed up," the sheriff remarked almost as if he didn't believe any of it. "Let me recap what you told me. You left your house this morning around eight o'clock and met your friend, Daniel, for breakfast at the diner. You stopped by Carson Davenport's mansion around ten o'clock, did a system upgrade on his home computer, and returned to your office around noon."

"I walked through the door, and someone must have hit me on the head," Rayner informed him. "I don't remember anything until I woke up in that cave, which I'm guessing was around three o'clock."

"So sometime between noon and three, someone knocked you out and brought you here where they handcuffed you to a pipe in the tunnel," Sheriff Horton announced. "Leaving you to drown."

"That's how it looks," Rayner replied.

The sheriff turned to the manager with a strange look. "And your security cameras didn't get any of that on tape?" he demanded.

"We don't have cameras in the parking lot, Sheriff," the manager informed him. "I swear; there's no way anyone brought an unconscious man past the front desk, through the entire club, and across the kitchen without someone noticing. That's our busiest time."

"The parking lot was pretty full," Newman added. "The golf course was packed."

"There has to be another way into the tunnel," Scorpio announced.

Her grandfather snapped his fingers. "Down on the beach," he replied. "Someone could have parked along that abandoned stretch of road and carried him across the beach to the tunnel. That beach is garbage. Full of rocks."

"That would explain why no one saw anything," the sheriff replied with a sigh. "Any evidence of footprints or tire tracks will be washed away with the high tide. That stretch of beach will be covered until tonight. With the morning tide, we won't be able to take a look until tomorrow afternoon. I doubt we'll find anything."

One of the bus boys approached them and handed Rayner his freshly cleaned clothes that were neatly folded. He thanked the young man.

"Are you sure you don't want to go to the hospital and get checked out?" Sheriff Horton asked. "At the very least, have Doc look at you."

"No, I'm fine," Rayner replied and gingerly touched the back of his head. "My head's just a little bruised along with my ego."

"Concussions can be serious," the sheriff informed him. "You probably shouldn't be alone tonight. You may want to consider staying with some friends, especially considering someone broke into your house."

"Are you going to look into that?" Newman practically demanded.

"Two of my men are heading over there now," Sheriff Horton replied with mild irritation.

"I suppose I could crash on Daniel's sofa," Rayner replied and again touched the back of his head.

Scorpio groaned. "Don't be stupid," she huffed. "There are dozens of empty beds at the hotel, and I can attest for the security system." She eyed him and smirked knowingly.

"I won't argue with you," Rayner replied.

As he stood, Scorpio linked her arm onto his. "Come on," she announced. "Let's get you home."

Her grandfather and Maverick exchanged looks then followed them from the kitchen.

Chapter 23

Rayner sat on the back patio at the hotel with his friend, Daniel. The patio itself had been partially restored, but the decorative half wall was slightly crumbling and needed attention soon before it collapsed completely. Beyond the patio had once been a garden filled with beautiful flowers, but they had been choked out by weeds more than a decade ago. A few crumbling statues and marble benches were all that remained of the garden's past beauty. It had only been a couple of hours after Rayner's near-death experience when Daniel had heard about it and sought out his friend. The two men were given some privacy, although Scorpio and her friends remained in the kitchen and kept an eye on them.

"I can't believe someone tried to kill you," Daniel gasped then shook his head as his eyes narrowed. "Just to steal your laptop?"

"You can't imagine how valuable that laptop was," Rayner remarked with a defeated sigh.

"Wasn't it insured?"

"Yeah, sure, but it wasn't the monetary value," Rayner corrected. "Valuable in the other sense. My life was on that laptop. Research, programs, tons and tons of information." He shook his head. "It's going to take me months to reinstall everything."

"So if they were willing to kill you for whatever information was on that laptop, it's over, right?" Daniel asked with increasing optimism for his friend. "They have it now, so you're no longer in any danger."

"They have it, but they'll never be able to access it," Rayner replied. "I have passwords, face recognition, and security up the ass on it. Too many invalid entries and it cleanses the files."

"A self-destruct?" Daniel grinned at the thought and shook his head. "You're like a spy or something, I swear." His look again turned serious. "Why were you targeted in the first place? What do you think they were looking for on your computer?"

"I'm still trying to put that together," Rayner informed him. "Did I inadvertently say something I shouldn't have? Maybe I know more than I even know. Someone could have overheard our conversation at breakfast. Maybe I said something in front of Davenport or his mansion employees. I honestly don't know."

"But you and I didn't really discuss anything. Well, practically nothing," Daniel reminded him. "The only person we saw this morning that would be connected to Davenport was his wife, Celine."

Rayner appeared curious and stared at his friend. "We didn't see Celine at the diner," he corrected.

"Of course we did," Daniel insisted. "She stopped in to talk with her cousin at the counter while we were paying for breakfast."

"You paid for breakfast," Rayner reminded him. "I left the tip then waited for you outside."

"Oh," Daniel remarked. "That's probably why you don't remember seeing her." He waved him off. "It was just Celine. She's often in her own little world. I doubt she even noticed either of us. She certainly didn't acknowledge me, that's for sure."

He considered the comment then sighed with defeat. "You're probably right. After what happened today, I think we need to just take things easy for a while," Rayner remarked. "Just forget what I told you."

"Consider it forgotten," Daniel announced then looked at his watch. He grinned and stood. "Well, I'd better go. I have to get ready for my date."

Rayner stared at him with surprise. "You're still going out with Amber?" he suddenly asked. "I thought we just discussed that."

"We did," Daniel replied then flashed a smile. "But if you think for a minute I'm cancelling my date with Amber, you're insane. I have my shot at a sure thing. If I can keep from screwing up, I'm golden."

Rayner shook his head and groaned. "I'd prefer you didn't go out with her," he balked. "I told you Rico's been working on getting her back. You don't want to get in the middle of that."

"Sure I do," Daniel chuckled almost deviously. "They're not together yet."

"Just don't ask her any questions about what we discussed," Rayner insisted. "Be smart."

"I'll do you one better," Daniel announced then grinned. "I'll be horny."

Daniel slapped him on the back and headed for his car, which was parked alongside the hotel. Scorpio walked onto the patio as Daniel left and approached Rayner. She nodded after Daniel.

"Your friend could have stayed for dinner," she informed him. "We have plenty. Stone bought enough steak to feed half the town. I think he forgot Trudy was heading home before dinner."

"That's okay," Rayner informed her. "Daniel has a date tonight."

"Oh?"

"With the ever popular Amber," he replied and withheld his laugh.

Scorpio collapsed in the nearby chair and managed her own laugh. "She certainly makes the rounds. Stone had a 'date' with her Friday night as well."

"I don't think Daniel cares," Rayner teased.

She stared at him with a stern look. "I couldn't help overhear some of what you said to your friend," Scorpio announced in a scolding tone. "You discussed something with him about what you found. You realize that could be what almost got you killed."

"Yes, I'm aware of my error," Rayner replied with a defeated sigh. "I couldn't help myself. Daniel said something at the diner that nearly knocked me from my seat."

"What's that?"

"Midnight Requisition," Rayner informed her.

"What?" she practically gasped with surprise and immediately sat forward.

"Daniel said he overheard Rico on his cell phone several months ago," Rayner remarked. "Rico referenced Midnight Requisition."

"To whom?"

"Unknown," Rayner responded, "but he swore he heard something that sounded an awful lot like a professional hit. It's possible this was brought up before your brother's murder. Amber was dating Rico around that time."

"And he just happens to have a date with her tonight?" Scorpio questioned.

"He thought he could get some information out of her," Rayner replied, "but I told him not to say anything to her."

"Yes, we don't need anyone else nearly drowning handcuffed to a pipe," she scoffed.

He eyed her with surprise. "I'm sensing some hostility," Rayner remarked.

"You're damned right you're sensing hostility," she snapped. "You had no business discussing what we talked about last night with anyone. If I can't trust anyone, neither can you. Honestly, you're closer to the problem than I am."

"Davenport?"

"Yes, Davenport."

"I don't know that he's the one, Scorpio," Rayner insisted. "There's nothing pointing to him in all this."

She drew a deep breath and attempted to control her rising temper. "What had you fired up this morning?" she asked while resisting picking a fight. "Why did you run out so early in the morning without saying anything to me?"

"Back when the hotel was actually a hotel--"

"When my grandfather and Davenport owned it?" she asked.

"Yes," he replied. "Quite a few influential people stayed here during off-season. There were parties. Apparently, your brother found an old guest list and kept it for some reason. There were some pretty famous or shall I say infamous names on that list. Mafia sort of infamous. Along with those influential and famous people were other guests with just initials."

"Is that supposed to mean something?"

"Not by itself, but I caught a peek at Davenport's party list. His list has a handful of guests with only initials as well," Rayner announced. "I dug a little and discovered the guests with initials are hired escorts."

"Hookers?" she asked with surprise. "Are you suggesting my grandfather hired hookers to entertain parties back in the day?"

"I'm not suggesting he did," Rayner replied, "but I'm suggesting someone did. Davenport has attractive, friendly women at all his parties. Seems to me he's not a stranger to the concept of pleasing his guests."

"My grandfather may have found out," Scorpio announced suddenly putting it together as her enthusiasm increased. "They had some sort of falling-out. Maybe that's what it was about. He could have found out Davenport was bringing prostitutes to the hotel."

"It's possible."

"When did you see this list for Davenport's parties?" she asked.

He shifted uncomfortably. "When I upgraded Davenport's home computer today," Rayner replied. "I did a little poking around in his files."

She stared at him with surprise. "And you wonder why someone tried to kill you?" she launched as her anger resurfaced. "Not a smart move. He probably found out you were poking around. Do you have any idea how close you came to dying today?"

"I'm pretty sure I do," Rayner replied while staring at her, surprised by her rising temper. "Why are you getting so upset about it? I told you there's nothing to support Davenport was involved in your brother's death. I came close to proving that today."

"You came close to dying today!"

"Yes, I realize this," he replied and continued to stare at her. "Why are you so upset?"

"What part of you almost dying aren't you understanding?" she lashed out.

"The part where it was me and not you," he replied simply.

"I didn't ask you to risk your life for me," she announced with increasing anger. "I'm not a target at the moment. You purposely put yourself in danger. If you had died, I'd feel responsible."

"Until we know who to trust, you could be in more danger than you know," Rayner informed her. "I don't want to see anything happen to you."

"I'm not your responsibility," she insisted. "I can take care of myself."

"And so could Cal and Kane," he snapped back. "Sometimes that's not enough."

Scorpio glared at him wanting to hit him for commenting on Cal and Kane's abilities to take care of themselves, but he wasn't wrong. She attempted to remain calm and drew a deep breath.

"You did your part, Rayner," she announced. "You should probably go back to your own work and steer clear of me and my problems."

"I can help you," he insisted turning defensive. "Whether you realize it or not, you need me."

"It's over," she informed him while leaning back in her chair and sighing. "All that information you found was on your laptop. It's gone. Even if whoever stole it can't access it, some of what you found would be difficult to find again. You may never find it again. We only have what's left on Kane's computer, which is less significant without what you found piecing it together." She immediately tensed and sank into her own world. "We should backup Kane's computer files and hide it somewhere."

"I already did that," Rayner informed her. "I hid it in that box we'd found." He removed his keys from his pocket and indicated one of the car keys. He pulled it apart to reveal a hidden flash drive. "And this is the information from my laptop."

Scorpio stared at the cleverly hidden flash drive within the exterior of a realistic looking car key. "That's ingenious," she remarked while sitting forward.

"No, that's full-blown paranoia," he replied. "But you've heard the saying."

"Which saying?"

"It's not paranoia if they really *are* trying to kill you," Rayner replied. "Well, we've concluded that I'm not paranoid."

Chapter 24

The front door to Daniel's quaint little home opened to reveal Daniel and Amber kissing and aggressively groping each other as they fell against the doorframe. Amber was already working on his pants while the door was still open. Without breaking off the kiss or curbing her aggression, Daniel attempted to close the front door of his house. He almost had the door closed when it was shoved open, tossing them into the dimly lit living room. Amber screamed with surprise as she fell to the floor. Daniel hit the sofa then turned toward the doorway. An intimidating man thick with muscles stood directly in front of him and punched him in the face then in the abdomen. Daniel clutched himself and doubled over from the hard hit. Big Bob, as he was known to most, wasn't the smartest of men, but he wasn't hired for his intelligence or his diplomacy.

A second, well-built man entered the darkened living room, grabbed Amber by her arm, and pulled her to her feet. He used enough force that she was nearly airborne. Despite not being as thick as Big Bob, Rico was an intimidating powerhouse all the same. He had a steely gaze that put instant fear into most who knew him. He was almost as handsome as he was intimidating. His thick, jet-black hair was slicked back without a hair out of place, and his perfectly bronzed skin was flawless. Although most women would agree that he was handsome, most were frightened away by his aggressive nature and his less than

compassionate demeanor.   Amber screamed as he pulled her
roughly to his side.   His dark eyes pierced through hers with
anger.

"If you want to be with me, your days of whoring around
are over," Rico snarled while staring Amber down.   "What's it
going to be?"

Amber stared at him with fear only a moment then
immediately ran her hands along his chest.   "Of course I want
to be with you, Rico," she announced and rubbed her body
against his.   "It's always been you."

He kissed her passionately then pulled away just as abruptly
and again stared into her eyes.   "If I catch you with another
man again, I'm putting you both in the ground," he informed
her.   "Do you understand?"

She nodded and continued to caress his chest.

"Go wait in the car," he ordered.

Amber cast a look at Daniel, shrugged with little reaction,
and then left.

Rico turned to Daniel where Big Bob stood over him and
pointed a warning finger at him.   "You're a major
disappointment, Daniel," he growled.   "If it were any other
man, I'd break bones.   You're lucky I like you."

Rico took a step toward him and punched him in the
crotch.   Daniel clutched himself and fell to his knees in agony.
Rico nodded to Big Bob, who left the house.

"Be smart," Rico informed Daniel.   "Don't ever look at
Amber again."

Rico left the house and shut the door behind him, leaving
Daniel alone on his knees in the darkened living room.   Daniel
gasped several times and endured the pain, not bothering to
stand.   He heard a floorboard creak.   Daniel immediately lifted
his head and looked behind him.   Someone dressed in black
stood in the darkness.   He was struck on the head with a small
baton.   Daniel collapsed to the floor.

Just outside Daniel's house, Big Bob leaned against the
driver's side of the expensive town car while it rocked.   Male
grunts and female moans could clearly be heard through the
partially open windows.   It was obvious Rico didn't care who
heard them, although there was no one outside at ten o'clock on
a Sunday night.   Big Bob smoked a cigarette and remained

unaffected by the sounds coming from the back seat of the car. The faint sound of glass breaking was heard from inside the still dimly lit house. Big Bob eyed the nearly dark house a moment then cast his cigarette aside and approached the front door. He pushed open the door and peered into the darkened living room.

A framed photo lay on the floor, the glass broken and scattered. A dull scraping sound was heard. Big Bob saw Daniel's shoes as he was dragged around the corner into the kitchen. Big Bob appeared bewildered and removed his semiautomatic from his hidden shoulder holster. He approached the kitchen while carefully stepping around the broken picture frame. He entered the kitchen with his gun aimed and saw a man dressed in black dragging Daniel toward the back kitchen door.

"Hold it right there," Big Bob yelled out.

The man released Daniel, allowing him to drop the rest of the way to the floor, and straightened while staring at the gun aimed at him.

"Daniel," Big Bob called to the unconscious man. "Daniel, wake up!"

Big Bob took a step closer while keeping his weapon on the masked man. He paused by Daniel's feet and looked at him while tapping his foot with his own. The intruder bolted out the kitchen door.

"Come back here," Big Bob cried out and ran for the door just past the unconscious man.

As Big Bob stepped into the kitchen doorway with his gun aimed, the intruder lunged from the side and struck Big Bob on the side of the head with a hammer. Big Bob immediately collapsed to the floor. The intruder leaped to Big Bob's side and pounded on his head with the hammer, leaving bloody streaks with each blow. He took the gun from Big Bob's hand, placed it down his own pants, and then returned to Daniel's unconscious body. He hoisted Daniel up over his shoulders in a fireman's carry and hurried him through the doorway before Rico would realize Big Bob was missing.

§

Scorpio entered Kane's bedroom through the open door.

Instead of being in bed, she saw Rayner sitting before her brother's computer while working feverishly, each finger striking the keyboard with purpose. She leaned in the doorway with her arms across her chest and glared at him.

"You're supposed to be resting," she reminded him.

"And you were going to bed," he countered without looking at her.

She entered the room and sat on the edge of the bed not far from where he worked on the computer.

"Do you always have that serious look of mayhem on your face when you work?" she asked.

"Pretty much," he replied then glanced at her and offered a sly smile. "If a man's not passionate about his work, he'll never know success."

"If a man doesn't get enough sleep, his brain turns to mush, and he's completely useless," she informed him then grinned slyly.

"Well, I'm supposed to limit my sleep due to the possible concussion," Rayner announced then looked back at her. "So that doesn't give me many options, does it?"

She stared at him but couldn't come up with a counter-response, which was unusual for her.

He grinned pleased with himself. "That silenced you awfully fast," Rayner teased then returned to the computer monitor. "I'm trying to find more information on your roommates, but it's proving difficult."

"I'll admit; I'm having a tough time getting those mugshots from my mind," she announced while staring at his profile. "The fake names are a bit troubling too, but I can't bring myself to doubt them."

Rayner groaned and spun the chair to face her. "Smart women don't blindly trust men with mugshots, Scorpio," he insisted. "You've survived two murder attempts. You need to be suspicious when suspicion is called for."

"I'd like to remind you that the only reason I survived that second time was because of the two men you think I should suspect of wrongdoing," she informed him. "Do you honestly think they planned the entire incident just to gain my trust? Do you think they hired five men to attack me so that they could swoop in and save the day? Killing five men seems a bit severe to gain someone's trust. I mean, couldn't they have accomplished the same thing with one or two guys? Couldn't they have just chased them off?" She defiantly shook her head. "I assure you; they didn't set it up, which means they came to my rescue."

"Even so," Rayner announced. "That doesn't mean they didn't come here for the long con."

"And what's the long con?" she asked. "What do they want? I'm not sitting on piles of cash. Most of what I have is invested in this hotel. Do they want the hotel? Look around. It needs more work than I can afford. Face it, Rayner. There's nothing here they could possibly want that they couldn't have already taken."

"What about Midnight Requisition?" he asked boldly. "We don't even know what that is. Maybe they're here for that. What if they're just waiting to see if you find it? If something's valuable enough, a wealthy person can afford to sit and wait forever."

"You really are paranoid," she scoffed then laughed. "You're right; you and Kane would have gotten along." She finally straightened and sighed. "Give up the search for their past identity. Find out about Midnight Requisition. I want to know why someone killed my brother. That's all I'm worried about right now."

"I have one more avenue to explore," Rayner announced and returned to the computer. He began typing. "If I can't find anything on Maverick and Stone, I may want to consider the backdoor approach."

"What's the backdoor approach?"

Before Rayner could even respond, she saw Cal's image flash on the computer screen. He too was in a mugshot taken by the same sheriff's department also with a fake name listed. Scorpio stared at Cal's picture with horror on her face. She wasn't sure if she was angrier with Cal or Rayner at that moment.

"Stop it," she practically cried out and shot up from the bed.

Rayner looked back at her with surprise and the anger on her face directed at him.

"Leave Cal out of this!"

"You don't want to know--?"

"No, I don't want to know!"

Rayner pressed a button, and the image disappeared. He slowly stood from his chair and stared at her. "I'm sorry, Scorpio," he gently announced. "I'm always searching for facts. I guess I forgot the human factor in that equation."

"Just leave my friends alone," she stated firmly while holding back her tears and attempted to wipe them away before he could see signs of weakness. "If you insist on helping, find out who killed Kane. I'm not ready to deal with the rest right now."

He nodded. "Yes, of course," Rayner replied timidly. "I'm sorry. I wasn't thinking."

Rayner no sooner returned to his seat when his cell phone beeped. He glanced at his phone and his expression immediately dropped.

"Oh no," he gasped in horror.

Scorpio turned and looked at the image on his cell phone. They both stared at a photo of a bound and gagged Daniel tied to a chair. He was bruised and bloodied. Scorpio read the accompanying text with it.

"Turn over the access codes for the laptop, or your friend dies," Scorpio read aloud then gasped and looked at Rayner. "What do we do?"

"Even if I could bypass the facial recognition on my laptop remotely, he's probably already attempted to access it too many times," Rayner informed her and stared at her with a serious, concerning look. "The hard drive will have been wiped clean. Tell him the truth or let him find out for himself; either way ends the same for Daniel."

"So we should call the sheriff," she announced and hurried for the bedside phone.

"Notify the sheriff, but I'm afraid he'll be dead long before Sheriff Horton can do anything," Rayner replied while staring at the cell phone screen. "There are some things visible in the background. If we can enlarge the image, we may be able to figure out where he's being held and help the sheriff find him sooner." He immediately downloaded the image to Kane's desktop computer and worked on enlarging the image. "After you call the sheriff, wake your friends."

Scorpio nodded and ran for the bedside phone.

Chapter 25

The sheriff's cruiser pulled up to the open junkyard gate and slowly entered the dark, narrow aisle between the wrecked cars. Sheriff Horton angled the spotlight while the deputy held his cell phone to his ear. Deputy Gaines was about as thin as a man could be without being malnourished. Due to his thin frame, his facial features were slightly pointy from his nose and cheekbones to his chin. He wasn't an unattractive man but by no means considered handsome either. What he lost in looks, he made up with his compassionate nature. He was easy to approach and sometimes gave up a little too much information just for the asking. Despite being in his mid-thirties, Deputy Gaines sought the approval of others and wanted everyone to like him.

"We're at the junkyard," Deputy Gaines announced into the phone. "Everything is dark here. Any idea what we're looking for?"

"Some sort of gray bus or vehicle with a worn number imprinted on the side," Scorpio announced through the phone. "Stone and Maverick are checking the bus terminal on the edge of town."

The squad car drove slowly through the junkyard while the sheriff shined the spotlight around. They saw a gray bus up ahead.

"Over there," Sheriff Horton announced while pointing and headed toward the bus.

"We spotted an old bus," Deputy Gaines informed her. "Stand by."

The squad car pulled up to the gray bus with the spotlight shining on it. The deputy and sheriff got out of their car, drew their weapons, and cautiously approached it. Deputy Gaines forced the side door open and stood aside while the sheriff shined his flashlight inside and aimed his weapon. When nothing moved, Sheriff Horton hurried onto the bus with the flashlight leading the way. They searched the rusted bus, but it was empty. The sheriff looked at his deputy and shook his head. The deputy returned to his cell phone.

"Negative on the bus in the junkyard, Scorpio," he announced. "Any word from the guys?"

"They haven't found anything yet," she replied. "Rayner wants to know what he should do."

Deputy Gaines looked back at the sheriff. "Negative on the bus station as well," he announced. "Rayner wants to know what he should do."

Sheriff Horton groaned as they left the bus and looked around the mostly dark junkyard. "Tell him to give the guy what he wants," the sheriff replied. "We need to buy more time if we're going to find Daniel."

§

Scorpio paced Kane's bedroom with the cordless phone to her ear while listening to the sheriff's instructions. She frowned at what he had to say and then nodded.

"Okay, Deputy Gaines," she announced with a defeated sigh. "I'll tell him." She disconnected the phone and looked at Rayner, who stared at her while frowning.

"He wants me to give him the password, doesn't he?" Rayner muttered.

She nodded and cast the phone onto the bed with disgust. "He's hoping it'll buy them more time to find Daniel," Scorpio repeated Sheriff Horton's words.

"Except the passwords aren't going to help if the hard drive has already been wiped clean," Rayner reminded her.

"You said the computer requires facial recognition," Scorpio reminded him. "Maybe we could agree to meet him to unlock the computer in exchange for Daniel."

"So instead of him killing Daniel, he'll kill Daniel *and* me," Rayner announced while leaning back in his chair. "Yeah, that sounds like a solid plan."

Rayner reluctantly started typing on his cell phone while Scorpio studied the enlarged picture on the computer screen. It looked more like a gray blob than anything now.

"Is there any way we can see the numbers on the bus better?" she asked.

"No, I lose resolution as I enlarge it," he announced and worked on his text message to the kidnapper.

Scorpio squinted then suddenly straightened with a look of astonishment on her face. "That's not a bus," she gasped. "It's a train."

"A train?" Rayner asked and looked back at the picture. "That doesn't look like a train."

"A trolley train," she corrected with enthusiasm and spun to face him. "They're at the shipping yard by the docks!" Scorpio grabbed the cordless phone from the bed and immediately dialed the sheriff's number. "Deputy Gaines, the shipping yard! The picture was taken near the old trolley!" She listened to the man on the other end and nodded. "I'll tell him." Scorpio disconnected the call and looked at Rayner. "The sheriff said to start the text messages in ten minutes. It'll be a distraction once they reach the old shipping yard."

§

Sheriff Horton and Deputy Gaines hurried along the dimly lit shipping yard not far from the docks. There were dozens of old boats in dry dock at the yard. Some were in excellent shape while others were rotting in place. Both men had their weapons drawn while hastily making their way through the yard. Maverick and Stone hurried to join them.

The sheriff looked at them with surprise. "How did the two of you get here so fast?"

"We were already on our way back from the highway," Stone replied. "Want us to slip around back so our guy can't make a run for it?"

"You're with me," the sheriff announced to Stone then nodded Maverick with his deputy. "You go with my deputy around the back way."

Stone and Sheriff Horton approached the trolley among the ships. As they got closer, they could see Daniel's back to them where he remained seated and tied to the chair. Maverick and the deputy approached from the opposite direction. Stone kept watch among the dark ships for signs of the kidnapper, but it was more likely he was inside the old trolley, hopefully texting with Rayner. They made their way closer while circling Daniel, where he sat slumped in the chair. As they approached, they saw the blood streaking the side of his head. It wasn't until they got closer that they saw the blood saturating the front of his shirt as well. The sheriff stared at the deep slit across Daniel's throat. He attempted to control his anger as he removed his cell phone and called Scorpio. Sheriff Horton motioned his stunned deputy to check the area.

§

Scorpio continued to pace the bedroom while watching Rayner text with the kidnapper. The cordless phone rang in her hand nearly startling her. She saw the sheriff's number on the caller ID and immediately answered it.

"Hey, Sheriff," Scorpio announced to the sheriff while running her fingers through her hair. "Rayner is texting with him now."

"Well, you can tell him to stop," Sheriff Horton gruffly remarked over the phone. "Don't give him anything. Daniel is dead."

Scorpio had a blank stare as her heart pounded at the sheriff's words. Rayner looked up at her. His expression immediately dropped.

"Is he dead?" he gasped.

"Thanks, Sheriff," she whispered and disconnected the call. She looked at Rayner, met his gaze, and frowned her response. "Tell the bastard they found Daniel dead, and he can go fuck himself."

Rayner appeared unable to move a moment then texted the kidnapper. Once his message was sent, Rayner tossed his phone aside with disgust and sat back in his chair. He covered his eyes and groaned loudly.

"This is my fault," he remarked under his breath. "They couldn't get to me, so they went after Daniel."

"It's not your fault, Rayner," she insisted then drew a deep breath. "It's my fault. I should never have asked you to help me. I should have let the police handle it."

Rayner leaned forward, hunching over, and clasped his hands between his knees. "I'm smarter than this guy," he muttered. "I can figure out where I screwed up. I just need to remember every detail about everyone I interacted with today. Something I said somewhere was overheard by someone. Daniel said Celine was in the diner at the counter while he was paying the bill." He shook his head. "Maybe she overheard our conversation. Maybe I shouldn't have dismissed her so easily."

Scorpio crouched before Rayner and placed her hands on his, forcing him to meet her gaze. "How do you know it was something you said?" she asked. "If you talked to someone, who's to say they didn't talk to someone else? Davenport has employees and friends everywhere in this town."

"We keep circling back to Davenport, but we don't know that this has anything to do with him." He shook his head. "I need to review my entire day in detail," Rayner informed her then sighed. "The answer has to be there somewhere." He abruptly stood and appeared unable to control his anxiety. "I need to be alone."

Before Scorpio could straighten to leave the room, Rayner hurried out the door. She watched him leave but knew better than to follow. If he needed to be alone, she needed to give him that time. The portable phone rang in her hand. Scorpio pressed the button and collapsed in the chair before her brother's computer.

"Yeah, Maverick," she sighed into the phone, although she really didn't feel like talking.

"I just thought you'd like to know," Maverick announced in a dull tone. "Daniel's been dead for quite some time. It's possible he was already dead before Rayner received the text message."

"That doesn't make any sense," she practically gasped while sitting forward. "Why kill him? He didn't get what he wanted."

"I know," Maverick replied. "Seems strange. What if Daniel's murder had nothing to do with Rayner's laptop? What if the killer wanted us to think that was the motive to cover up the real one?"

"Obviously, the killer has Rayner's laptop, or he wouldn't have sent the text asking for the password," Scorpio remarked. "Otherwise, how would he know it was missing?"

"Are you okay there alone with Rayner?" Maverick asked. "Stone and I want to hang out until the coroner arrives and see what we can learn."

"Yeah, Rayner and I are fine," she replied. "Take your time. If you're going to be really late, we'll talk in the morning."

"See you then."

Scorpio disconnected the phone then sank into thought. Why would he wonder if she'd be okay alone with Rayner? Did Maverick suddenly not trust him?

"Damn it, Kane," she muttered. "What did you get me into?"

Chapter 26

It was early the following morning. Scorpio hurried along the grand hallway to the sound of someone urgently knocking on the front door. It was only seven in the morning, so the fact that someone was at her front door was almost concerning. As she ran up the foyer steps, Maverick hurried down the grand staircase.

"What's going on?" Maverick wearily asked. "Who's here so early in the morning?"

"I'll let you know in a minute," she replied and paused before the door. She peered out the peek hole and looked back at Maverick with an annoyed sneer on her face. "It's Davenport."

She punched in the alarm system code then unlocked the door and opened it. Davenport stood in the doorway with a strange look on his face.

"Sorry to disturb you so early in the morning, Scorpio," he announced and peered past her. "Is Rayner here?"

She fumbled slightly at the question. Why would Davenport believe Rayner was at the hotel so early in the morning? What was going on? Did everyone in town think she was secretly dating Rayner?

"Actually, I don't know that that's any of your business," she announced while taking the defensive approach. "If you want to talk to Rayner, call him on his cell phone."

"I tried, but it went straight to voicemail," Davenport announced. "So he's either on his phone, which is doubtful considering the time, or he's somewhere without reception, which tells me he's here."

"I'm sure if you leave him a voicemail, he'll get back to you--"

"I know he was attacked yesterday afternoon," Davenport boldly announced. "I also know they found Daniel murdered at the shipping yard."

"I'm glad you're up on town politics," Scorpio remarked with irritation. "He doesn't need you harassing him right now. I'll tell him you were looking for him, and he'll get back to you when he's up to it."

She attempted to shut the door. Davenport placed his hand to the door and stopped her from closing it. Maverick hurried up the foyer steps, prepared to intervene. Davenport stared into her eyes.

"They found one of my associates murdered at Daniel's house last night," Davenport informed her. His concern was evident by the way he looked at her.

"What happened?" Scorpio asked with surprise while reluctantly opening the door.

Davenport entered the foyer and shook his head. "I guess there was a minor scuffle between Daniel and Rico last night," he announced. "Over a woman, of course."

"Which woman?" Scorpio asked.

"Amber," he replied. "Which other woman? You know Rico's history with Amber."

"I can't say I'm current on town gossip," Scorpio responded and headed down the foyer steps.

Davenport and Maverick walked with her down the grand hallway to the kitchen. "According to Rico, he and Bob went to Daniel's house last night and interrupted his date with Amber. While Rico and Amber were talking in the driveway, Bob slipped away unnoticed. He sometimes paces while smoking, so Rico didn't think much about it. When they were ready to leave, Bob was gone. Rico tried calling Bob, but he wasn't answering his cell phone."

All three entered the kitchen while Davenport continued with his story.

"It was a long night, and Rico was eager to get Amber home," Davenport informed them. "He assumed Bob walked to the bowling alley down the road and left him a voicemail to call him if he needed a ride." Davenport collapsed at the island counter and shook his head. "Apparently, after the police found Daniel murdered last night, they went back to his house to investigate the abduction and found Bob murdered just outside the kitchen door."

Maverick poured coffee for himself and their guest then leaned against the island counter from the other side while Scorpio sat in the chair alongside Davenport.

"The sheriff took Rico in for questioning early this morning, but released him after Amber collaborated his alibi," Davenport announced. "She was with him right up until the time the police showed up."

"Sounds like Bob saw something he shouldn't have involving Daniel's abduction," Maverick remarked.

"The sheriff thinks so too," Davenport reported.

"Rayner doesn't know anything about what happened," Scorpio insisted and eyed him suspiciously. "Why is it so important you see him?"

"Rico said Daniel and Rayner had been spending a lot of time together the past few months," Davenport replied. "Word had gotten around about what happened to Rayner at the country club, and there was rumor it involved his stolen laptop. I want to know what happened to my employees, and I was hoping Rayner could shed some light on it."

"Rayner already told the police everything he knows about his attack," she insisted while eying him suspiciously. "He has no clue what someone would be looking for on his laptop. He spoke to Daniel yesterday morning before his computer was stolen. The diner was crowded. Anyone could have overheard something and gotten ideas. Who and why are a mystery to us all." Scorpio tensed slightly while remembering something Rayner had said. "Maybe you could ask your wife if she remembered anyone suspicious at the diner. Daniel said she was at the counter while he was leaving."

"Celine was at the diner yesterday morning?" Davenport asked with surprise. "She was supposed to be at the spa all morning."

"I guess she saw her cousin there and stopped to talk with her," Scorpio remarked.

"Her cousin?" He then considered the comment, tensed slightly, and nodded. "Yes, I suppose her cousin could have been at the diner."

Scorpio and Maverick exchanged looks across the island counter. Davenport seemed unusually bothered that his wife was talking to her cousin. Davenport was quick to change the subject.

"I'm convinced more now than ever that what happened here nine months ago is somehow connected to recent events," Davenport informed her. "Things like this don't happen in our town. One incident perhaps, but there have been too many coincidences lately." Davenport stared at her with a serious look and raised his brows in gesture. "I hate to say it, but I'm concerned your brother's murder may be a direct result to what's happening here."

Scorpio shifted uncomfortably. "I've entertained that thought myself," she replied.

"The detectives I'd hired in Virginia haven't come up with anything yet," Davenport informed her. "Your brother seemed to be covering his tracks involving his travel plans." He then shifted in his chair. "I'm worried that all of this has something to do with me."

"With you?" Maverick asked with great interest. It was the opening they had been looking for. "Why would you suspect what happened here at the hotel and what happened with Scorpio's brother has anything to do with you?"

"Cal used to work for me," Davenport informed him. "Daniel worked for me. Bob worked for me. Rayner works for me. There's a pattern. It's possible Kane had a connection to what's happened. Why the sudden trip to Virginia? Why hadn't anyone heard from him during the time leading up to his death?" He raised his brows as he shifted slightly in his chair. "I heard it looked like a professional hit. There are too many coincidences happening."

"I won't disagree with you on that," Scorpio muttered under her breath.

Davenport leaned across the counter toward Maverick while shifting looks at Scorpio alongside him.

"Your brother was living with you here at the hotel. Men break into the hotel. A month later, your brother is killed. A few days after Rayner does work at the hotel, he's almost killed, and his laptop is stolen. His friend is then kidnapped by someone wanting access to the stolen laptop. It's obvious Rayner stumbled upon something while he was here, possibly the same thing that got Kane killed. Perhaps he doesn't even know what he'd found. That's why it's important I talk to him."

"Which obviously means there's something in this hotel connecting everything to you," Rayner announced as he appeared at the bottom of the back stairs.

All three looked at Rayner with surprise. He approached the island counter and glared at Davenport.

"You were co-owner of this hotel," Rayner continued. "Perhaps there's something relevant from back then that explains why people are dying now."

"The hotel hasn't been operational in nearly twenty-five years," Davenport insisted. "I don't know how anything that happened that long ago could have any bearing on what's happening today."

"It would if Kane found something he shouldn't have," Rayner replied then tossed several papers onto the island counter. "There's a copy of the guest list for one of the off-season parties held here when you and Scorpio's grandfather owned the place." Rayner raised his brows while folding his arms across his chest. "With a little digging, I discovered that list is the 'who's who' of the mafia underground. What was it? Prostitutes? Drugs? Something worse?"

Davenport picked up the first paper and glanced over the list of names then frowned and looked back at Rayner. "Not something either Newman or I was proud of," Davenport announced then sighed. "We were approached about holding a private party in the off-season, and it sounded like a great way to make some money in an otherwise dead time of year. It seemed almost too good to be true. They brought in all their own workers to cater and clean the hotel. We didn't even have to be present."

"What could possibly go wrong," Maverick muttered sarcastically while shrugging.

"Did my grandfather know anything about the parties at the time?" Scorpio asked, feeling unusually tense for asking, but she needed to know.

"Your grandfather was just as shocked as I was when we discovered what the weekend parties really were and who was actually attending them," he informed her. "We couldn't allow that sort of element into our quiet little town. It's like a cancer. Eventually, it would have spread."

"So why didn't you just stop booking them during the off-season," Rayner asked.

"You can't tell people with that sort of reputation their money is no longer welcomed. Our only solution was for one of us to buy out the other and keep the doors shut long enough for certain kingpins to find another place to hold their illegal parties," Davenport announced then frowned. "I reluctantly let your grandfather buy me out. At the time, he had more money than I did, and I feared more for my reputation that someone was going to find out the things that went on in this hotel. I couldn't risk it like he could."

Chapter 27

Scorpio and Davenport had an unusually lengthy discussion about the hotel despite her feelings for the man. He was telling her things she wanted to know without even asking. Offering him a cup of coffee seemed like a small price to pay for the first-rate information. They remained in the kitchen for over an hour discussing the hotel, and it's sorted past.

"I always loved this place and regretted having to sell it," Davenport announced. "That's why I attempted to buy it back over the years." He then looked at Scorpio. "Your grandfather would never allow me to obtain this place. I think he still secretly blames me for having to shut the place down because he loved the hotel just as much as I did." Davenport tensed while staring at Scorpio. "Even though your grandfather hates me because of our fallout, I don't want you to think he sanctioned anything that happened during those parties. We were both being used."

"What exactly happened during those parties?" Maverick finally asked with a curious tilt of his head.

The question was one Scorpio had wanted to ask as well. She thought she knew everything about the hotel's history, but she wasn't sure she wanted those memories tainted by horror stories.

"Everything from mild to wild," Davenport informed him while shaking his head. "The biggest draw was illegal gambling, prostitution, and drug use."

"Sounds like a Tuesday night in Hollywood," Maverick muttered. "I can't imagine shutting a place down to keep that out."

"That was the mild," Davenport announced then drew a deep breath. "The wild was more of a nightmare."

"What happened?" Rayner asked and rejoined them at the island counter after pouring another cup of coffee.

Davenport tensed and eyed the three surrounding him. "I need you to promise what I'm about to tell you never leaves the three of us."

"Four," Stone announced and approached from the main kitchen door, "but don't let that stop you now. Maverick will catch me up later."

Stone joined them at the island counter and listened intently with the others.

"They had an illegal fight club," Davenport announced and immediately shuttered. "Two men fighting to the death for sport."

Scorpio held back her surprised gasp.

"What did they do with the bodies?" Stone asked while staring at Davenport with horror on his face. "Please tell me they're not in some pit in the basement."

"That may have been preferable," Davenport muttered. "They brought their own disposal system with them."

"Disposal system?" Scorpio gasped now unable to control her emotions. "What kind of disposal system?"

"An acid bath or the ever popular feeding of the alligators," Davenport replied.

All four stared at Davenport in stunned silence.

"Understand, everything was designed for gambling purposes," he continued. "They'd make side bets on how long the acid would take to destroy the body. What body part the alligator would eat first." Davenport made a face and shook his head. "I wish I had been prepared for the horrors before I stumbled upon them." He eyed Scorpio. "Fortunately for your grandfather, he never witnessed any of that firsthand. He didn't want to know. He just wanted to call the police regarding the clearly visible illegal activity. After I told him what I'd seen, we knew we couldn't call the police. We'd be painting a bullseye on our backs if we had." He nodded with conviction. "We made the right decision by dissolving our partnership and shutting down the hotel."

"Where did all of this take place?" Scorpio choked on her question.

"The fight club took place in the basement," he replied. "I believe your uncle stored some furniture down there after he bought the place." Davenport's look turned sympathetic. "Don't worry, Scorpio. There's absolutely no residue of any of what I'm telling you left behind. Our 'guests' made certain of that. And your grandfather and I inspected the hotel thoroughly afterward."

"How did Kane get ahold of the guest list?" Rayner asked with a curious look. "How's it possible he would have discovered any of this?"

"I don't know," Davenport replied. "If he made any contacts outside of our town, there's no telling who he spoke to and what they told him. Anyone could have become nervous and started poking around."

"There hasn't been anyone inside the hotel since it was shut down twenty-five years ago," Scorpio insisted. "That leaves a very short list."

"I wouldn't be so confident with that statement," Davenport informed her. "There are people around town who know what went on in this hotel. Anyone your brother may have had contact with prior to his death could be part of our little community as well. I have tons of people working for me in recent years who weren't local."

Scorpio was again reminded of Maverick and Stone's mugshots. She then considered Cal's mugshot and a chill raced down her spine. Who knew about the hotel's past? How far back was it known? She suddenly wondered if there was anyone above suspicion.

"Who else in town knew what went on in this hotel?" Stone practically demanded. "Do you know anyone specific? Or are you just speculating?"

"I hate to name names," Davenport announced.

"Name them," Stone scoffed while turning angry and flaunting his intimidating, large frame.

"The sheriff for starters," Davenport replied. "He didn't condone it, but as a deputy at the time there was nothing he could do about it. The old sheriff didn't want to cause waves with the *wrong* people."

"Anyone else?" Rayner asked.

"A few older men who've since passed on were aware of what happened here," Davenport informed him. "I can't guarantee they never told their spouses or children the stories. All things considered, the rumors never really got around." He then turned to Rayner. "If you find anything about this hotel or those parties, please let me know. You may not understand their significance, but I will. If what happened to Cal, Kane, and my men has anything to do with what happened here when I owned the hotel, I can help piece it together. I want to right a wrong from all those decades ago."

Rayner nodded. "If I find anything, I'll let you know," he replied. "After what happened yesterday, you'll understand that you won't be the only one I share that information with. Right now; I don't trust anyone." He then eyed Scorpio with a serious look. "And neither should you."

She received his meaning and shuttered at the thought. Maybe it was time to investigate her friends and, as much as she hated to admit it, maybe she needed to let Rayner dig up information on Cal as well.

Chapter 28

A few hours later, Scorpio, Maverick, and Rayner walked through the main room of the basement, which was mostly used for storage since her uncle bought the hotel from her grandfather. All three looked around the massive, slightly cluttered area strewn with cobwebs. Scorpio rubbed her chilled arms despite not finding anything disturbing.

"He said they wiped everything clean," Maverick insisted. "What did you really expect to find?"

"Nothing the way it is," she replied then eyed Maverick. "That's why we're going to clear out this room."

"Excuse me?" Maverick remarked with some surprise as he stared at her. "There's several dozen pieces of furniture in here. Where would you like to go with it?"

"There's another storage area just across the hall," she informed him. "I want to see the room gutted and cleaned. That's the only way we're going to know if there's anything left behind."

"I'd think Davenport would have made certain there wasn't," Rayner informed her. "They wouldn't have left anything incriminating behind."

"I also don't trust Davenport enough to take his word on anything," she replied simply while casting a glance at him. "I want to see the room for myself. None of this furniture is excessively heavy. It won't take more than a few hours to clear it."

Scorpio grabbed a box on the floor near her and left the room with it. Maverick shook his head while looking around the moderately cluttered room.

"Stone picked a good time to run to the tavern to pick up lunch," Maverick announced with a groan. "I wasn't built for hauling furniture."

"Quit your complaining," Rayner scoffed and grabbed one end of many piled mattresses. "Grab an end and let's start moving these."

"God," Maverick scoffed and grabbed the other end of the mattress. "She says jump, and you say how high. You are so whipped."

"The willingness to help a woman who asks is not the definition of being whipped," Rayner informed him with some irritation. "It's called being gentlemanly. You should try it sometime."

As they carried the mattress toward the doorway, Maverick stared at Rayner a moment in silence before speaking. "You're not her type, you know," he finally remarked showing little emotion.

"And I suppose you are," Rayner scoffed.

"Closer to it than you," Maverick replied.

"Are you suggesting she has a thing for men who've been arrested?" Rayner snapped.

Maverick dropped his end of the mattress nearly causing Rayner to fall with it. Rayner released the mattress and locked eyes with Maverick, who stared at him with a stunned look on his face.

"What are you talking about?" Maverick suddenly demanded and let the mattress fall to the floor.

Rayner casually placed his hands in his pockets and stared back at the suddenly not so charming conman. "Someone's out to get Scorpio. Did you honestly think I wouldn't check into all her known associates?"

"You had me checked out?" Maverick practically gasped while glaring at him.

"You, Stone, and Cal," Rayner informed him. "I've seen your mugshots and, quite frankly, I wasn't sure what to do with the information."

"Confronting a man about his questionable past while alone with him isn't exactly smart," Maverick informed him while offering an unsettling smirk.

There was a tense, silent moment as they exchanged stares.

"Fortunately for you, I'm not some sociopath," Maverick announced and allowed the mood to lighten.

"No, stupid would be confronting you and your friend while you're together," Rayner replied while raising an arrogant brow. "Smart is waiting to get you alone while the bigger, stronger man is out of the house."

Maverick snorted a laugh and smirked. "Yeah, well, I still think it was a pretty stupid move on your part," he announced. "I'd like to say our being arrested was a huge misunderstanding, but the three of us weren't exactly choirboys."

Scorpio stood in the doorway and stared at Maverick. "What's going on?" she suddenly asked and eyed both men as she leaned against the doorframe. "Is there something I should know about?"

"Maverick was just about to inform us about his life before he became a choirboy," Rayner announced as he leaned against a dusty dresser.

Scorpio stared at Maverick. "What about your past?" she demanded. "What haven't you told me?"

Maverick drew a deep breath then sighed while running his fingers through his hair. "It didn't seem important at the time," he announced. "I certainly didn't think Stone and I would still be here all these months later. Once we made ourselves at home, it made telling you the truth a little more difficult." He fidgeted slightly and stared into her eyes. "Stone, Cal, and I were, well, mischievous."

"That's not very forward," Rayner announced while glaring at him.

Maverick fidgeted while keeping his attention on Scorpio. "We were conmen and cat burglars."

Scorpio felt her heart nearly pound through her chest. She wouldn't have believed it if someone had told her, but she was hearing it from the man she'd spent the last nine months trusting with her life.

"You mean, you came here to steal from me?" she gasped with horror and felt instantly betrayed.

"No, nothing like that," Maverick insisted in a defensive tone. "Quite the opposite. Cal was our friend. Someone killed him, and the woman he loved was in trouble." His look softened and seemed sympathetic. "We came here to make sure you were safe. When we realized you were still in danger, we couldn't leave." Maverick drew a deep breath and sighed. "When Cal told us he'd quit working for Davenport because he'd fallen in love, we stayed out of his life. We didn't want to ruin the only positive thing he had going for him. After we heard what had happened, we questioned if his past hadn't caught up with him, in which case you could have still been in danger."

"You did that for him?" she asked.

"Of course. He was our friend. When Cal went straight, it actually inspired us to turn our lives around as well. We haven't had so much as a parking ticket between the two of us since you and Cal started dating. We just thought if we cleaned up our act, we could be a part of Cal's new life. It's a bit of a boring life in quaint little nowhere, but Stone and I have been adjusting to this new life. You've been a positive influence on us as you had Cal." Maverick frowned and rubbed the back of his neck. "I guess it was a little too good to be true. You'd eventually find out and kick us to the curb."

Scorpio drew a deep breath and groaned softly. "No one's kicking you to the curb," she reluctantly remarked. "I just wanted to know the truth. I needed to know I could trust you."

Maverick stared at her a moment then looked at Rayner, who smirked. "You mean you two plotted this little confrontation?" He looked back at Scorpio with surprise. "You already knew we'd been arrested."

"I told her the moment I found the mugshots," Rayner informed him. "I didn't share her faith or trust in you. Honestly, I still don't."

"After everything that's happened in the last twenty-four hours," Scorpio announced, "I had to be sure."

"Divide and conquer aside," Maverick announced and managed a slight chuckle while eyeing both. "You took a big risk. What if I had been behind what was happening? I could have killed you both."

Rayner removed his hand from his pocket and revealed a small caliber semiautomatic. "I'm a genius," he reminded him. "I always have a plan."

Maverick casually removed his 9mm semiautomatic from the back of his pants and flashed it. "Yeah, but mine is bigger," he announced while smirking, "and I'm willing to bet I'm a better shot."

Scorpio finally straightened and revealed the shotgun in her hand that had been hidden behind the doorframe. "Yeah, but mine is point and shoot. No aiming required."

"Okay," Maverick replied while nodding as he stared at the shotgun in Scorpio's hand. "You would have won. Are we okay?"

"Yeah, we're okay," Scorpio replied while offering a tiny smile.

"Are we still moving furniture?" he then asked.

"Oh, yeah, I still want this room cleared," she announced firmly. "Let's go, boys. Enough slacking off." Scorpio flicked her wrist and made a whip cracking sound. She chuckled and walked past them.

Maverick frowned. "I guess she heard that part of the conversation too."

"She's sneakier than you'd think," Rayner remarked and again picked up the mattress. "Let's go."

§

Stone entered the tavern that afternoon and approached the bar and the part-time bartender. The tavern was mostly empty during weekday afternoons. The bartender approached and grinned.

"Take-out, right?"

Stone nodded and smiled. "After how many months, you finally remember," he teased.

"I'll get that from the kitchen for you," the bartender announced. "Give me a minute."

Stone nodded and leaned against the bar. He casually looked around while waiting for the bartender to return.

Amber sat in a corner booth by herself with a beer in front of her. She looked almost sedate and more than likely drunk. Stone glanced at his watch. It was only noon and a little early for her to be drinking let alone be drunk. Once the bartender returned with his large take-out bag, Stone paid him and headed for the door. He cast a look at Amber, who looked back at him. Stone offered a tiny, pleasant smile but continued on his way. He left the tavern and approached his car practically by itself in the parking lot. He heard the tavern door open as he paused before his car.

Stone looked back and saw Amber leaving the tavern in a hurry. He brushed it off, got into his car, and turned the key in the ignition. The passenger side door opened. Amber jumped inside, nearly crushing his take-out bag. He stared at her.

"Uh, hey, Amber," he announced with some surprise although attempting to act casual.

She sank into the seat and clutched her chilled arms without looking at him. Amber stared at the windshield, although it was obvious she was somewhere else.

"Can I, uh, give you a lift somewhere?" Stone asked without taking his eyes off the drunken woman.

"Your place," she announced.

Rico's car pulled into the parking lot. Amber gasped and sank all the way down in the seat so he wouldn't see her. She finally looked at Stone and appeared frightened.

"Hurry, before he sees me," she gasped.

Stone backed away from the tavern and headed from the parking lot while casting glances at the obviously distraught, drunken woman.

"You and your boyfriend having a fight?" Stone asked while casting glances at her as he drove.

"No, not exactly," she replied and slowly sat up on the seat. She checked the side mirror then looked out the back window to make sure they weren't being followed. She looked at Stone with fear in her eyes. "I need somewhere to hide, and I need someone I can trust. Will you help me?"

Stone stared at her a moment then returned his eyes to the road and nodded. "Yeah, I'll help you," he replied.

"Whatever is going on, you'll be safe at the hotel. Plenty of places to hide there."

Chapter 29

Scorpio, Rayner, and Maverick entered the kitchen a little after noon knowing Stone should have been back with lunch by then. They paused when they saw Stone sharing his food with Amber, who sat huddled in a ball on the island counter chair. Stone put on a broad, false smile while looking at his friends.

"Look who I ran into at the tavern," Stone announced in a fake cheerful tone. "Rico's girlfriend."

Amber saw Rayner, gasped with horror, and leaped from the chair. She darted behind Stone, who looked behind him to see where she'd gone.

"You didn't tell me he was here," Amber gasped while clinging to Stone's shirt. "I have to get out of here. He works for Davenport. He'll tell him I'm here!"

Rayner stared at the sliver of the woman hiding behind Stone and appeared surprised by her reaction. "You're hiding from Davenport?"

"Quick, get me out of here," Amber gasped while clutching Stone's arm.

"Amber," Scorpio announced and stepped in front of Rayner. "Relax. It's okay. He's not going to tell Davenport you're here." She eyed the woman suspiciously. "What's going on? Did something happen?"

Amber slowly moved from behind Stone and stared at Rayner with a look of distrust. "He can't be trusted," she insisted.

"I've been saying that all along," Maverick muttered. "They wouldn't listen to me either."

"You're not helping," Stone scoffed then gently guided Amber to her chair. "You never mind about Rayner. I assure you, I can handle him. You were starting to tell me about last night."

Scorpio attempted to keep herself from leaping forward at the comment. "Last night?" she announced a little more eagerly than she'd anticipated. "What happened last night?"

Amber sat on the chair, placed her arms insecurely around her knees, and held them tight against her chest while staring at Scorpio. "Rico and I found Big Bob dead in Daniel's house." She shivered and appeared traumatized. "Someone had bashed his head in." She rubbed her cheek against her knee while trembling. "Really bashed in."

"She's going into shock," Rayner suddenly announced with concern.

Stone removed his jacket and placed it over her shoulders. "She's not in shock; she's drunk." He clutched her shoulders and forced her to meet his gaze. "You're safe, Amber. Tell us what happened."

She drew a deep, shaken breath and looked back at Scorpio, focusing on her for some reason. "I had been out on a date with Daniel. Rico followed us back to his place. He wanted me to be his girl again." Her eyes widened. "I've learned not to say no to Rico. He's unstable. He told me to wait in the car, but I just went outside. I didn't know what he intended to do to Daniel. I just wanted to make sure he didn't get carried away."

"You thought he might kill Daniel?" Maverick asked.

Amber looked at Maverick and shivered slightly. "I don't know that he'd kill anyone," she insisted, "but I was concerned for Daniel." Her eyes shifted from Maverick back to Scorpio. "He was in a foul mood, so I thought I'd better get him into a good mood as soon as possible. While we were messing around in the back of his car, Big Bob must have wandered off. Rico was ready to go, but Big Bob was gone. Since he had the car keys, Rico had to find him, which made him angry again. When he went back inside the house, I knew I had to make sure he didn't run into Daniel, or he'd beat him again. Maybe even hurt him pretty bad. We didn't find either of them. When we entered the kitchen, we found Big Bob dead in the kitchen doorway. There was a bloodied hammer next to him. Someone used the hammer on his head."

"Sheriff Horton said you two left without finding Bob," Maverick remarked.

"Do you think Rico was going to admit he found Big Bob dead?" She vigorously shook her head. "No, he grabbed his keys, grabbed me by the arm, and practically dragged me out of the house. I wanted to scream, but he told me if I made a sound, he'd hurt me. I knew he meant it too."

"You can go to the sheriff and tell him what really happened," Scorpio insisted.

"Rico didn't kill Big Bob," she insisted while vigorously shaking her head. "What good would it do crossing Rico over something so trivial? Besides, Sheriff Horton does whatever Davenport tells him to do."

"What?" Rayner gasped.

"Davenport has Sheriff Horton by the balls," she insisted. "You can't trust anyone in this town. Either they're in Davenport's hip pocket, or they think he's a great guy."

"I don't understand why you're afraid to go home," Stone announced. "You haven't done anything to cross Rico. What has you so frightened?"

"That was just the beginning of my nightmare," she informed him while casting glances at those in the room. "Naturally, Rico expected me to stay over. We were heading into the staff wing of Davenport's mansion when we ran into him. After he told Davenport what happened at Daniel's house, we learned that the sheriff found Daniel dead at the shipping yard. I knew Rico didn't kill him, but I was terrified anyway." She shuttered. "Despite everything we witnessed, Rico expected me to make him look good by keeping half the house awake with loud sex." She rolled her eyes and grimaced. "He wanted me to perform like a show pony even though I couldn't get that image of Big Bob out of my head. Since I couldn't sleep and I needed to get out of the room before Rico rolled over for round two, I went to the library. Davenport has this great big library."

"It's gorgeous," Rayner agreed.

"I can watch television in there and not disturb anyone," she continued.

Rayner appeared slightly embarrassed, having mistaken her library comment for that of a book lover.

"That's when Sheriff Horton showed up and told Davenport that he'd found Big Bob dead in Daniel's house," she continued. "They got into a nasty argument about it. I pretended to be asleep on the library sofa in case they happened to see me from the hallway. I heard the sheriff saying he had to take Rico to the station to make it look good. Davenport was hurling threats at him involving some incident a few years back. I think it had to do with the sheriff shooting that kid robbing the liquor store. It sounded almost as if the kid was innocent and they planted the gun on him."

Scorpio stared at her with astonishment. "I remember when that happened," she gasped. "Deputy Larson backed his version of the story."

"Somehow Davenport must have found out it was a lie, because he was using that against him," Amber insisted. "When they took Rico to the station, Davenport went along with him. I was later forced to sign a paper that said we didn't see Big Bob, and Rico drove me to the mansion. Sheriff Horton never even asked me what I saw. I was just told to sign the paper and never mention that we found Big Bob dead."

"There's still no proof either of them had anything to do with Daniel or Bob's murders," Maverick informed them with little reaction.

"Oh, it gets worse," Amber informed them, catching their attention. "After Davenport went with Rico to the sheriff's office, I was the only one awake in the main house. I wanted to go home, but I didn't have a ride. I could have walked, but if Rico got back and found out I was gone, he'd be mad. I needed a drink, so I went to the game room, where there's a fully stocked bar. I poured myself a drink and sat on the sofa. It was cold in the game room, so I slipped into a jacket I found on the arm of the chair. There was something bulky in the pocket, so I removed it. I found a wad of cash. All one hundred dollar bills. I counted it." Her eyes widened. "It was ten thousand dollars."

Stone shut his eyes and muttered, "Please tell me you didn't take it."

She looked at him with surprise. "Of course I didn't take it," Amber gasped. "Do you think I'm stupid? I may not know what Davenport is into, but I know it wouldn't be good for my health to take money from him. There were also pictures in the same pocket along with a thumb drive."

"Please tell me you took the thumb drive," Rayner muttered while staring at her.

She frowned and removed the thumb drive from her cleavage. Rayner practically lunged for her. She sprang from her chair and again darted behind Stone.

"He can't be trusted," she cried out. "He'll erase what's on here."

Scorpio pushed Rayner back and approached Amber hiding behind Stone. She met her gaze with a sympathetic look. "You had a thing for my brother once upon a time," Scorpio announced gently.

Amber nodded. "I liked Kane," she replied. "If he'd been interested in me, I never would have ended up with someone like Rico."

"Kane found something that may have gotten him killed," Scorpio gently informed Amber. "That flash drive could tell us who killed Kane and why. Rayner has to pull up the files on it."

"He'll erase what's on here," she insisted. "Kane's killer will get off, and they'll come after me."

"He won't erase anything on that flash drive," Scorpio insisted.

"How can you be so sure?" Amber asked. "What's going to stop him?"

Scorpio reached beneath Maverick's jacket from behind, removed his semiautomatic from his pants holster, and aimed it at Rayner's head without even looking at him. Her eyes never left Amber.

"I will."

Rayner stared at the gun aimed at his face as his eyes widened. "Uh, this isn't funny," he announced.

"I'm not joking," Scorpio scoffed without looking back at him despite the gun aimed at him. Her eyes pleaded with Amber. "You can trust me. Do it for Kane."

Amber nodded and handed Scorpio the flash drive. Scorpio lowered the gun from Rayner's head, allowing him to resume breathing. She then placed the flash drive down the front of her shirt and returned the gun to Maverick, who grinned and replaced it to the holster down the back of his pants. Scorpio continued to stare at Amber as she slowly moved from behind Stone and returned to her seat.

"What was on the photos you'd found?" Scorpio asked with a curious tilt of her head.

"They were dirty pictures of some guy and girl having sex," Amber replied. "I recognized the red fainting couch from Davenport's library."

"The antique velvet Victorian chaise lounge?" Rayner suddenly asked.

She glanced at him and nodded. "It's popular for doing the nasty," Amber replied. "You can get into lots of positions. Rico drags me in there for quickies all the time."

Rayner frowned at the comment. "It used to be good for lounging while reading," he muttered then shook his head. "I guess I'm never sitting in that chair again."

"Did you recognize anyone in the picture?" Stone asked while ignoring Rayner.

"I've seen the girl before," she replied. "Rico would drag me to Davenport's parties. She was one of the escorts he hired to make his rich friends feel attractive."

"You mean prostitute," Maverick corrected her while smirking.

Amber gave him a surprised look. "No, they were escorts," she firmly insisted. "I talked to them several times. They never asked anyone for money. Rico told me they were just escorts. You know, arm candy. Women who make rich guys feel attractive by flirting with them. No money was exchanging hands. I would have picked up on that in conversations."

"You never heard the conversations because Davenport paid the women a flat fee," Rayner informed her and shook his head. "I told Daniel they were hookers. No one believes me."

"Sounds like Davenport pays his hookers to show his male guests a good time so he can catch them on tape and blackmail them later," Stone announced.

Amber stared at them with surprise. "Is that what was happening?" she announced then shook her head as her eyes widened with realization. "I honestly thought they just enjoyed themselves at parties. Rico and I were always sneaking off for quickies during Davenport's boring parties." She then frowned her distaste. "Of course, he'd insist I make a lot of noise to stroke his ego."

"If Davenport was blackmailing his wealthy guests and finds out you know about it, you won't be safe," Scorpio informed Amber.

She shivered and nodded with a look of fear still in her eyes. "That's why I was hanging out in the tavern drinking," Amber replied. "I didn't know what to do. I don't think that sofa is visible on the security cameras, so he wouldn't have seen me take the flash drive, but once he realizes it's missing, he's liable to put it together."

"Until we can figure out what's on the flash drive and who we can trust with the information, I think you should stay here and remain hidden," Scorpio informed the frightened young woman.

"I was thinking the same thing," Amber replied while looking around with concern. "What's to stop him from sending his men to come for me?"

"First he has to figure out you're here," Maverick announced. "And then he has to get past our security system unnoticed."

Stone then smiled deviously. "And then he has to get past us."

Amber took Stone's arm, pulled it against her chest, and clung to it. "I trust you to protect me," she replied. "You're built like a brick shithouse."

Stone smirked and eyed his friends. "You've gotta love a small town compliment."

"Well, she's not wrong," Maverick announced. "You're built like a house, and you're full of shit."

Stone sneered at his friend. "And you would know all about that."

"Rayner and I are going into the study so that he can check out the flash drive on my laptop," Scorpio announced then eyed Maverick. "Make sure all the doors are locked and set the alarm." She then looked at Stone. "Take Amber to Kane's room and keep an eye on her."

"Set your cell phones to walkie-talkie mode using the wireless router," Rayner announced. "If we see anything on the security monitors, we'll alert you."

Maverick and Stone nodded.

Chapter 30

Rayner sat behind the desk in the office and plugged the flash drive into Scorpio's laptop. He downloaded the files from the flash drive to her hard drive to make certain they had another copy then read through the files while Scorpio hovered over his shoulder and watched. She studied the files with a curious look.

"They're all names with dates," Scorpio remarked. "I don't recognize any of the names."

"Well, the only way we're going to know what's in the files is by opening them," Rayner informed her and opened the first file at the top of the list.

They stared at the photo files within the named file. Rayner was about to open one of the pictures when he hesitated. Scorpio eyed his profile with some surprise.

"What's wrong?" she asked while studying him. "Aren't you going to open it?"

"I have a pretty good idea what I'm going to see," he informed her without looking back. "Are you sure you want to see them?"

"I can handle a few dirty pictures, Rayner," she scolded while raising a cocky brow.

Rayner opened the first file. When she saw Sheriff Horton in a compromising position with a woman from Davenport's party, Scorpio gasped and immediately looked away.

"Oh, my God," she cried out while turning her back to the computer and the graphic image of the sheriff's manly parts. "Make it go away!"

Rayner closed the file and cast a look at her. "I thought you said--?"

She swatted his shoulder with annoyance. "I didn't think I'd be seeing the sheriff having sex with a woman," she cried out then looked at the name on the file. "Why is it named that?"

"I guess they're code names," Rayner replied.

"You better look through them without me," Scorpio announced and vigorously shook her head. "I can't risk seeing someone naked that I can't unsee. I mean; what if my brother is in there? I'll absolutely die!"

Scorpio moved around the desk and sat on the edge facing Rayner. He returned to the laptop and started opening files. As he opened each file, he made faces. She watched the faces he made and cringed in time with him.

"Are they that bad?" she asked.

"I've never seen so many unattractive, naked men in my life," he replied. "So many old men too. And women complain about their sagging breasts." He hesitated and tilted his head while staring at the screen. "I hope I can do that when I'm that old. How does an old guy bend that way?" He switched pictures and gasped. "That looks painful." He groaned and shut the lid. "I think I've seen enough." Rayner sat back in the chair and was finally able to look Scorpio in the eyes. "We can safely assume Davenport has been blackmailing married men with dirty pictures."

"Are you sure there wasn't anything else more incriminating than married men with hookers?"

"You're more than welcome to browse through them and find out," he announced while raising a skeptical brow. "There are only five hundred pictures in those fifty files."

"Can't you just make them into thumbnails?" she suggested. "That way we can see what they are without seeing all the graphic detail."

Rayner drew a deep breath and opened the laptop lid. "Considering I'm not being paid, you're asking an awful lot from me." He then considered the comment. "Maverick is right. I'm whipped," he muttered while he fiddled with the files.

"What happened to wanting answers?" she prodded while raising a curious brow and a slightly humored smile. "I thought you just wanted to help."

"I do," he eagerly replied then frowned and looked back at the computer. "It's complicated."

"Would you like if I compensated you for your time?" she asked.

"It's not about the money," he informed her without looking up from the laptop. "I owe it to Daniel to see this through."

"That's commendable," she replied and straightened. "Although, I wasn't offering monetary compensation."

His eyes shot up from the laptop and met her gaze.

She stared back at him and immediately gasped. "I wasn't offering that either."

Rayner's eyes returned to the laptop. "I assure you; I don't know what you're talking about," he announced with little emotion.

She laughed at the embarrassed and moderately flustered look on his face. Rayner returned his attention back to the computer.

"All dirty pictures," he announced. "Even if we could nail Davenport with blackmail, there's nothing to indicate he was behind killing anyone."

"Nothing about Midnight Requisition?"

"No, nothing at all." He again shut the laptop lid and casually leaned back in the chair. "I don't doubt Amber is frightened of Rico and Davenport, but I can't imagine either of them would kill her because of these files. It doesn't prove anything. Even those being blackmailed probably wouldn't kill someone over infidelity. Well, except maybe the wives if they found out."

"So all of that was for nothing?"

"I wouldn't say nothing," he replied. "We know Davenport is a dirty blackmailer even if we can't prove it. If he's into one thing, he could be into other things. We'll just have to keep digging."

"Maybe you don't think Rico would kill Amber over blackmail files, but I do," Scorpio informed him. "I think he'd kill her for breathing on his car wrong or making him look bad."

"Yes, she needs to get away from him, but she has to leave willingly," Rayner reminded her. "Probably leave the state just to be safe. No matter how frightened she is, I don't see that happening."

"We'll have to keep her hidden here until we can figure something out," Scorpio informed him. "I don't know what that is, but we have to try to keep her away from him for her own good."

"One thing blackmailers understand is blackmail," Rayner replied simply. "We can threaten Davenport with exposure if anything happens to Amber. He may be able to keep Rico's temper in check."

"I'm not sure I like stooping to his level," she remarked. "We'll keep that as our backup plan."

Chapter 31

Stone played solitaire on Kane's desktop computer while Amber relaxed on his bed and flipped through the television channels. She cast the remote aside and appeared bored. Amber glanced at Stone's profile, studied him a moment, and then grinned.

"I'm bored," she cooed sweetly. "Want to come over here and entertain me?"

Stone looked back at the woman on the bed with surprise. She raised her brows seductively and patted the bed alongside her.

"Do you really think this is the time and place for that?" he asked in disbelief.

She stretched her body seductively across the bed and clawed at the sheets like a cat asking for a belly rub. Her sly smile answered his question.

"There's never a bad time for a good time," Amber insisted then winked at him. "And you, sir, are a good time. I only got a teaser the other night. Now I want the full Stone experience."

His brows rose at the comment. "I honestly don't know how to refuse that."

"So don't," she insisted while easily slipping out of her shirt and casting it aside.

He stared at the woman caressing the bed and then the lacy bra containing her ample breasts. Stone felt the desk for his phone without taking his eyes off Amber moving seductively along the bed while caressing her own body. He pressed a button on his cell phone.

"Hey, uh, how are we looking? Any concerns?" he asked using the cell phone in walkie-talkie mode. "Any sign of hostiles?"

"No, we're clear for the moment," Maverick responded through Stone's phone. "Doors and windows are secure, and the alarm system is activated."

Stone strummed his fingers on the desk while continuing to watch Amber who slipped the bra strap off her left shoulder in a small striptease.

"Why are you asking?" Maverick practically demanded. There was a moment of hesitation. "What's going on up there?"

"Nothing," Stone responded a little too quickly into the phone. "Absolutely nothing."

Stone placed the phone face down on the desk and lunged for the door. He shut and locked it before Maverick would consider checking on them.

"You didn't have to shut the door," Amber cooed. "I don't mind if your friend watches."

"I mind," Stone announced then tore off his shirt as he rushed for the bed.

§

An hour later, Stone trotted down the grand staircase and swung around the banister with a lively gait. As he turned down the grand hallway, Scorpio leaned in the office doorway with her arms folded across her chest while glaring at him. Maverick and Rayner stood behind her and shook their heads while giving him a shameful look.

"What?" he asked innocently.

"You know what," Scorpio demanded. "You took advantage of that vulnerable girl."

"Vulnerable?" Stone practically gasped. "No, no. I didn't take advantage of her. If anything, she took advantage of me. She's some sort of seductress."

"She's been through enough," Maverick informed him. "How could you exploit her like that?"

"Exploit her?" he cried out. "She's a sexual ticking time bomb. She has either the healthiest sexual appetite or a very serious psychosis. Honestly, I was lucky to get out of there with my life." He then turned serious. "Do we have any cucumbers?"

Maverick and Scorpio moaned and threw their hands in the air with disgust. Rayner eyed all three while attempting to understand what just happened.

"She wants it sliced for her eyes," Stone snarled then shook his head in disgust. "Come on, people. Get your minds from the gutter."

Rayner's eyes suddenly widened. "Oh," he muttered finally getting it.

There was a knock on the front door. All four looked toward the foyer and appeared momentarily frozen while staring at the door. Maverick ran back into the office to check the security monitor.

"It's Rico," he called back then hurried into the hall. He grabbed Rayner by the arm and pulled him toward the elevator. "Go keep an eye on our guest."

Rayner did as he was told and shut the elevator gate behind him. Once the elevator was nearly to the third floor, Scorpio and Stone approached the front door. Maverick slipped into the nearby hall bathroom and remained mostly hidden in the doorway. Stone stood alongside the front door with his hand on his semiautomatic hidden in his shoulder holster beneath his jacket. Scorpio entered the code into the alarm then unlocked the door and opened it only a foot or two, keeping Stone hidden behind the open door. She eyed Rico and one of his hired henchman buddies, who stood behind him. Scorpio was pretty sure Rico's muscular reinforcement was a man named Muddy or something close to that. Muddy seemed appropriate for the moderately hulking man with large muscles. He looked a bit grimy, in her opinion.

"Rico?" she asked with some surprise then looked around, catching a glimpse of the bulge beneath Muddy's left arm, indicating he was carrying a concealed weapon. "Davenport isn't with you?"

"No," he announced abruptly while glaring at her. "I'm looking for Amber."

Scorpio raised her brows and gave him a bewildered look. "Amber? Why would she be here?"

"She was at the tavern when your bodyguard came for take-out," Rico informed her. "Then she was gone. I know she came back here with him."

"Well, I'm telling you she's not here," Scorpio casually informed him while attempting to assess if Rico was also carrying a weapon. She didn't see one, but she was sure he was. "And I think I'd know."

"I know she's here," he insisted, "and I think *I'd* know. I know she was fucking Stone. She's fucked every black man who's ever set foot in this town. Bring her to me."

As Scorpio glared at him, her eyes narrowed in anger. "First off," she snarled, "I don't take orders from you. Secondly, fuck you!" She pointed to his car in the driveway. "Get the fuck off my property before I shoot you in your favorite body parts!"

Rico thrust his shoulder against the door, striking Scorpio while throwing open the door. He bolted past her. Stone's fist struck him square in the mouth, knocking him back a step and stopping him from making it past the threshold. His accompanying goon took a step for the doorway. Stone pulled his weapon and aimed it at Muddy's face, stopping his approach. Scorpio clutched her shoulder while straightening. For a usually charming, light-hearted man, Stone was frightening at that moment. His eyes were locked on the hired henchman, and the gun was steady in his hand.

"You *don't* want to do that," Stone snarled.

Muddy backed away and held his hands up to prevent any misunderstandings. Rico moved to his feet while holding his bleeding mouth. Stone turned the gun on him as he straightened. Rico spit out a tooth then glared at Stone despite the gun now aimed at his face.

"She can't hide in there forever," Rico announced. "You can't keep her from me. She'll come back to me eventually. She always comes back to me. If you know what's best, you'll send her out. I know she's conned you into letting her stay with you, so I'll give you this one out of respect to our profession." He shifted a look at Scorpio then back at Stone. "If you insist on keeping her from me, you and your friends will be the ones who'll need protecting."

"Did you just threaten to harm my friends?" Stone suddenly demanded with a wild look in his eyes. "Make my day. Cross the threshold. Let's see how many holes I can put in you before you reach me."

Rico took a step back while holding his hands in the air as well. "We'll be leaving now," he announced then eyed both. "See you around."

Scorpio slammed the door and turned the lock. She drew a deep breath as Stone lowered his weapon. She spun toward him with hostility.

"What the hell was that?" she suddenly cried out. "What were you thinking?"

"What?" he launched back with surprise. "I was protecting you."

"You were provoking him," Scorpio shouted. "You wanted to shoot him!"

"You're damned right, I wanted to shoot him," Stone shouted back with an unpredictable look in his eyes. "You wanted the head of the beast on a silver platter, remember? Those were your words. That's what I intended to do. With him out of the way; it's over."

"Davenport will find another Rico," she shouted back. Scorpio drew a deep breath and attempted to calm down. "We'll need to avoid going to town for a few weeks until this blows over. We can't be looking over our shoulders every time we go into town."

"I can handle Rico," Stone insisted.

"Yes, I'm sure you could, but he's *not* going to be alone," she snapped back.

"I'm sorry," he replied gently. "I wasn't thinking. I just wanted to end this for you."

"I know," Scorpio replied with a defeated sigh. "Let's just lock the hotel down and try to have a somewhat enjoyable evening."

Maverick leaned against the doorframe in the hall bathroom and glared at her. "You want to move the rest of that furniture, don't you?"

She looked back at Maverick with surprise. "Of course I do," she announced. "Don't you?"

Chapter 32

Now that the room was empty with the exception of a few piles of swept dirt, the massive, dimly lit basement room appeared larger than most banquet halls. The floor and walls were dreary gray block stone, giving the room an almost medieval appeal. Amber swept the floor while the four stood within the center of the room and looked around as if attempting to unlock some secret contained within the walls. Scorpio studied every corner looking for something that would confirm what Davenport had told them.

"Well, your room is empty," Maverick announced while appearing exhausted then looked at his watch to reveal it was after midnight. "I don't know what you expected to find, but there's nothing here."

Scorpio continued to look around and shook her head. "I don't know either," she replied.

"So why did we clear this entire room of its junk?" Stone practically demanded. "You already knew the room had been thoroughly cleaned. I don't know what you possibly thought you'd find down here."

"Something," she replied feeling almost foolish. "Anything, I suppose. I'm running out of theories."

"And I don't know why you dragged me down here either," Amber announced while setting the broom aside. She eyed the empty room and rubbed her chilled arms. "This place gives me the creeps. Like a medieval torture chamber."

"In a way, I suppose you're right," Rayner informed Amber then walked the room while examining it more closely. "Same concept."

Stone leaned closer to Scorpio. "He's your little lapdog, isn't he?" he muttered.

"No, he just sees the bigger picture," she insisted then glanced at Amber in order to respond to her question. "We dragged you down here because we didn't want to leave you alone upstairs. There's not much chance of Rico getting past our security system undetected, but after the day I had, I wasn't taking any chances."

"Well, I hope you're happy," Amber announced and sighed. "I'm officially sober."

"Good, I'm glad to hear. I'd prefer if you stayed that way until we can figure out what to do with that information you found," Scorpio informed her.

Amber groaned and cast her back against the nearby wall. "I haven't been sober in years," she remarked while huffing. "This sucks."

"One hell of a hangover, huh?" Maverick teased, withholding his laugh.

"Actually, I don't get hungover," she informed him. "I just have a better time when I'm drunk."

"You need to join us in reality for a while, Amber" Scorpio insisted. "There's a time for fun and games, but this isn't one of them."

Amber groaned and pouted like a little girl. "You're far too serious when I'm sober," she announced. "Can I go to bed now?"

"There's nothing down here," Maverick insisted looking ragged himself. "I'd like to get a few hours' sleep before you decide we need to dig a moat to go with your new torture chamber."

"Fine," Scorpio moaned and waved them off. "Go to bed, you wimps."

"I should probably stay with Amber," Stone insisted a little too eagerly but managed his serious expression. "Someone should keep an eye on her."

Amber immediately pounced alongside Stone, linked onto his arm, and ran her hand along his broad chest while grinning.

"Maybe we could have a small nightcap before bed," she cooed sweetly.

"No nightcaps," Scorpio announced while glaring at Amber then Stone.

Amber huffed with annoyance, took Stone's hand, and dragged him toward the doorway. "Let's go before she implements a no sex rule."

Stone's grin said it all, and she didn't have to drag him too hard. All three watched them leave.

Maverick shook his head while wearily running his fingers through his hair. "I'm glad they're on the third floor, or we'd never get any sleep tonight," he muttered under his breath. "I'm going to make rounds, check the doors, and peek at the security cameras before going to bed." He eyed Scorpio and Rayner. "Enjoy your empty basement."

Once Maverick left the room, Rayner leaned against the nearby wall and stared at Scorpio. "So now that Stone and Amber are occupying my bed, where does that leave me?" he asked. "Am I being sent home?"

"Wouldn't you rather go home?" she asked.

"Safety in numbers," he announced without hesitation. "Someone did knock me on the head in my own home and tried to kill me."

"As crazy as it sounds, I guess you are safer here. You can sleep in Stone's room," she casually replied then scanned the room determined to find something.

"Stone's room. Right," Rayner replied with a defeated sigh. "That would be logical, I suppose."

Scorpio paused and cast a look back at Rayner, who attempted to hide his disappointment. "You didn't honestly think that put you in my room, did you?" she asked while raising an arrogant brow.

He immediately straightened. "No, of course not. Why would I think that?" Rayner walked the length of the room while looking around.

"I don't pretend to know how men think," Scorpio replied as she looked more closely at the floor. "Although Kane believed I should have been able to read his mind. He believed twins were connected beyond the womb."

"There have been some studies proving there is a strange connection between twins," Rayner informed her as he too studied the stone floor while walking it. "An ESP sort of phenomenon."

"No one could read Kane's mind," Scorpio scoffed. "Not even Kane. When we were younger, he used to con me into doing all sorts of things."

"Was he actually conning you, or were you competing against him?"

"There was a lot of competition between us as well," she reluctantly admitted then rolled her eyes at the comment. "The trouble he got me into. I'm sometimes surprised I'm alive."

"I don't have any siblings," Rayner reported. "What was it like having a twin?"

"Hell," she replied. "Pure hell."

Rayner laughed without looking at her. "I'm sure you don't mean that."

"Oh, I mean that," she announced then turned to face him, although he continued to scan the floor. "He wanted to take karate lessons, so naturally I had to keep up with him. The bastard would sneak attack me whenever the mood would strike him. While I was sleeping, while I was reading. He even jumped out at me from the back seat of the car. That time, he nearly killed us both."

"Now I'm sort of glad I didn't have a brother," Rayner teased while chuckling.

"So, naturally, I had to get him back, which only ever escalated things," she remarked. "To make matters worse, we'd come out here and play in the hotel since it was abandoned. We broke too many things at home. You've never seen my grandparent's home. They're super rich with antiques everywhere. Roughhousing was strictly forbidden. At least here, we couldn't really damage much." She looked around and folded her arms across her chest. "I fell in love with this place. It was always special to me."

"Because you and your brother used to play here," Rayner deducted while grinning.

"No," she snapped back and glared at him. "It had nothing to do with that. I could always see the beauty beyond the decay. Grandma would show me pictures of the place when it was operational. It was breathtaking."

"Just admit it, Scorpio," Rayner groaned while staring at her. "This was your childhood with your brother. You had fun times here. You and your brother were close no matter how many times he tried to scare you."

"He didn't scare me," she corrected. "He just liked to provoke me into fighting with him. I would hardly call them fun times."

"So why did you come out here to play with him?" he asked while grinning slyly.

Scorpio considered the question then laughed. "Because I wanted to beat his ass," she announced while hiding her smile. "He needed his ego deflated once in a while to keep him grounded." She then frowned. "I suppose all that ended when I fell in love with Cal. I didn't have time for Kane anymore. I was too busy being an adult." Scorpio sighed and ran trembling fingers through her hair. "Now I've lost both of them."

Rayner approached her while she held back her emotions and gently pulled her into his arms. She attempted to push him away, resisting his security, but reluctantly gave in and let him hold her.

"We have to find that bastard," she whispered.

"We will, Scorpio," Rayner announced gently near her ear. "I promise."

She fought her tears a moment then pulled back just enough to meet his gaze. Scorpio smiled and gently touched his face.

"Thank you," she whispered.

She kissed him briefly but warmly on the lips then pulled away, leaving him moderately stunned and rendered motionless. She ran her hands along her chilled shoulders and shivered while looking around the basement.

"Amber was right. This place does look like a medieval torture chamber," she announced. "Kane would have loved it." She then eyed Rayner, who continued to stare at her still unable to move after the quick kiss. "Let's get out of here."

Chapter 33

Early the following morning, Scorpio woke to the sound of a car horn honking long and repeatedly. She jumped from her bed, feeling her heart pounding from being woken so abruptly and attempted to process the information before reacting. She heard the horn again. It was coming from out front.

"What the hell--?"

She ran across the hall to the opposite side of the hotel, entered Maverick's room without knocking, and headed to the balcony door. Maverick was already jumping out of bed and pulling his pants up as she peered through the part in the curtains. She saw Rico standing alongside a red Porsche convertible.

"Who the hell is out there?" Maverick demanded and hurried to the balcony doors to join her.

"Who do you think?"

Maverick looked to the driveway below and groaned. "What the hell does he think he's doing?"

"Who knows," she moaned.

They heard someone on the stairs. Maverick ran to the bedroom doorway and peered into the hallway. He groaned and looked back into the room.

"Might be a good time to call the police," Maverick casually informed her. "I just saw Stone running for the stairs with the shotgun."

Scorpio groaned and ran to the bedroom door to join Maverick. Rayner met them in the hallway.

"Stone just ran into his bedroom and took off with a shotgun," Rayner announced. "What the hell is going on here? Is Rico looking to get shot?"

"I'm concerned we're about to find out," Scorpio announced and hurried after Maverick for the stairs.

All three ran down the grand stairs after Stone, who was halfway to the foyer door while pumping the shotgun. All three stopped in their tracks at the sound and refused to move. As Stone punched the disarming code onto the security panel, Scorpio knew she had to stop him.

"Stone, shooting him isn't going to help," she insisted while hurrying toward him and the door. "You're only going to get yourself arrested."

"I don't intend to shoot him," Stone informed her above the blaring car horn as he unlocked the door. "I'm just going to blow a hole in the car."

Scorpio threw her body in front of the door, preventing him from opening it. Stone impatiently glared at her. "You realize I can easily move you."

"And you realize I might hurt you if you attempt it," she remarked while glaring back.

Stone stared at her almost humored and raised his brow. "I'm willing to risk it."

"We'll call the police," she insisted. "Let the sheriff remove him."

"You heard Amber, and you've seen the pictures," Stone remarked. "Sheriff Horton is in Davenport's hip pocket. Even if he does chase Rico away, he'll just keep coming back. We need to send a message loud and clear. Blowing a hole in the engine of a Porsche will do the trick."

"Don't do this, Stone," she practically begged while pleading with her eyes. "It's not going to help. We don't need more violence right now."

Stone gave her an arrogant look. "You'll be sure to let me know when we do need more violence, won't you?" he demanded while smirking.

Her eyes narrowed as she glared at him. "That's not funny," she scoffed at his hidden dig.

"It is a little."

Rico continued to honk the horn. Stone groaned and fought the urge to open the door. He slammed the shotgun into Scorpio's hands and walked away from her.

"What the hell is he trying to prove?" Stone demanded while throwing his arms in the air. "What does he think that's going to accomplish?"

Amber hurried down the stairs and looked at them. "What's happening?" she gasped. "Did I see a Porsche outside? Who's out there?"

"Who do you think?" Maverick scoffed.

Amber ran to the door, opened it, and looked out. Everyone jumped.

"Don't get too close," Scorpio cried out and lunged for the door to keep her from opening it any wider.

Before Scorpio reached her or the door, Amber ran from the hotel. All four stared after her with equally stunned looks on their faces. Scorpio bolted out the door with the shotgun in her hand and Stone on her heels. Rayner and Maverick ran for the door. They stopped on the porch and watched Amber run up to the red car, which she immediately started caressing. She looked at Rico, who grinned.

"You bought a Porsche?" she squawked nearly giddy with delight, unable to take her eyes off the car. She appeared ready to make love to the car.

Rico nodded and held up the keys. "I know you always wanted one," he announced while grinning. "Want to take *your* new car for a spin?"

Amber squealed with delight and snatched the keys. Rico suavely opened the door for her. She jumped into the car and started it as Rico headed for the passenger side. He looked at the others on the porch and grinned deviously. Rico jumped in the car and waved at them as Amber backed up then spun the car around and raced down the driveway.

Stone shook his head in disbelief. "She went back with him over a car."

"Well, it was a nice car," Maverick insisted then shook his head, somehow not surprised. He patted Stone on the back and headed into the hotel.

"She has to realize her life is in danger, right?" Stone practically demanded.

"I'm guessing she wasn't thinking about that," Scorpio remarked and headed for the front door.

"If they don't suspect she took the flash drive, she could be okay," Rayner replied and followed Scorpio.

Stone stared at the empty driveway and listened to the sports car racing along the back road despite being out of sight. "That's one confused girl," he muttered more to himself. "Mistaking sex and material things for love."

"He has to know she took the flash drive," Maverick announced and entered the foyer behind Scorpio and Rayner. "Why else would he be so hell-bent on getting her back in such a hurry?"

Stone entered the foyer and shut the door behind him. He didn't wait for an answer as he frowned and headed for the stairs.

"I have a theory," Rayner replied while taking a deep breath. "It's a little thin though."

"What's your theory?" Scorpio asked.

"Davenport is having one of his high profile parties tonight," Rayner informed her. "According to Amber, Rico has one hell of an ego. He wouldn't want to be seen alone at one of Davenport's parties. He'll want his arm candy, particularly arm candy that's willing to pull off sexual stunts in public to benefit his ego."

"So even if they suspect she found something, Rico won't harm her until after the party?" Scorpio questioned with a curious look.

"That's just my theory," Rayner replied.

Stone stopped short of the stairs and returned to them with renewed interest. He paused before Rayner and stared at him. "Are you invited to these parties?"

"Davenport enjoys showing me off to his high society friends," Rayner replied. "I've been to a few, but I can't say I care for them. Daniel was always trying to get me to go, so he'd have a wingman."

Scorpio eyed Stone with a curious look. "What are you thinking?"

"I'm thinking that Rayner needs to attend that party," Stone informed her then smiled slyly and pushed her closer to him. "With a date."

She remained skeptical and glared at Stone, taking note of the grin on his face. "How's my going with Rayner to Davenport's party going to help Amber?"

Maverick eyed his friend and grinned. "Are you thinking what I hope you're thinking?"

"Party crashing?"

Maverick groaned with delight. "I love crashing mansion parties," he announced. "The champagne goes down *so* easy."

"Davenport would invite you, if I asked," Rayner informed them.

Both men eyed him as if they'd been insulted. "Where's the fun in that?"

Chapter 34

For a mansion, Davenport's ballroom was smaller than Scorpio had thought it would be, but it was one of the few homes in their town large enough to have a ballroom at all. There were possibly one hundred guests in attendance, which still seemed smaller than Scorpio thought for the parties she'd heard so much about. Scorpio was linked onto Rayner's arm as he guided her into the ballroom among the wealthy, well-dressed men and women. Scorpio wasn't a stranger to formal parties, since she grew up in a fairly wealthy household, although it had been some time since she'd attended such a party. She wore her black evening dress from the last party she attended, which was her and Kane's high school graduation party. Both had refused a formal party for their college graduation. They'd opted for a cruise with their grandparents instead.

Rayner looked at home and handsome in his expensive, black suit. Scorpio was actually surprised at his expensive taste in suits, considering she hadn't really seen him dressed up since he'd moved to their town. She couldn't help but admire how adult he had been regarding dressing up and wearing a tie. Cal didn't like dressing up, and he adamantly refused to wear a tie. Even Kane handled dressing up better than Cal had, probably because Kane was forced to wear suits growing up just as Scorpio was forced to wear dresses and high heels. It always made her grandmother happy to see them dressed up, so they did it without complaint.

Davenport saw them, appeared almost stunned to see Scorpio, and hurried his attractive wife across the room to greet them. He shook Rayner's hand and immediately eyed Scorpio in her dress.

"I can't believe you actually got a Wayland to attend one of my parties," Davenport announced to Rayner with enthusiasm. "Scorpio, you remember my wife, Celine."

Scorpio managed a polite smile and nodded at the attractive woman in the revealing dress. Her cleavage stood out, catching the attention of every man in the room. Davenport motioned to the neatly dressed waiter with a tray of filled champagne glasses. As the man approached, Davenport handed both a filled glass.

"I have so many people I'd love to introduce you to," Davenport informed Scorpio. "My parties are the 'who's who' of influential people from the city."

She casually looked around then smiled at Davenport. "I recognize a lot of the people here from my grandfather's last big party."

"Well, we used to run in the same circles," Davenport reminded her.

Rayner's cell phone vibrated in his inner jacket pocket. He removed his phone, looked at the caller ID, and smiled with embarrassment. "Sorry, I have to take this," he announced. "I'll only be a minute."

He stepped away to answer his call. Davenport was being flagged down from across the room. He nudged Celine.

"Darling, will you entertain Scorpio?" he asked. "I'm being paged."

As Davenport darted away, his blonde, trophy wife attempted a smile at Scorpio. "How did you get roped into one of these boring parties?" she asked with little emotion.

Scorpio eyed the woman only a few years older than herself and shrugged. "Rayner asked nicely," she replied. "He's been so helpful with my security system; I couldn't possibly refuse accompanying him when he asked."

"Yeah, he's not so bad," Celine replied although she appeared bored. "He at least has a personality. Most of these rich guys are boring." She rolled her eyes. "Don't even get me started on their wives--"

Scorpio glanced around the crowded ballroom and noted many younger women all dressed daringly seductive. Obviously, they were the hired escorts Rayner had mentioned.

"So many older guys with young wives," Scorpio remarked then eyed Celine and fidgeted. "No offense."

Celine waved her off with little emotion. "No need to apologize," she announced. "I'm used to it." She raised her brow and leaned closer to Scorpio. "And those women aren't the wives. They're hired escorts."

"Escorts?" Scorpio asked while playing dumb.

"Young, attractive women to stroke the massive egos of wealthy men," Celine replied. "If you ask me, I think some of them are making a few extra bucks on the side catering to those egos."

"Really?" Scorpio squawked in fake surprise.

"I wouldn't doubt Rico has something to do with that," Celine continued while curling her upper lip at the mention of his name. "He's such a sleaze." She nodded across the room and indicated Rico with Amber.

Scorpio glanced at the neatly dressed couple. Amber wore a form-fitting dress that revealed plenty of cleavage and more than enough leg to catch attention. Rico's hand periodically caressed Amber's backside as he socialized.

"In an hour or two, his little girlfriend will be bombed out of her mind, and then he'll take her to some nearby room where he'll screw her brains out," Celine reported with distaste. "He wants everyone to know how much of a *man* he is, and then all the envious men will congratulate him on another successful lay."

"And this happens at every party?" Scorpio asked with surprise.

"Twice a month every month since I've been with Davenport," Celine replied. "That's why Amber is always drunk. She needs the booze in order to perform for him. If she managed to stay sober long enough, she'd dump him as she does every time she's sober."

"You don't care for Rico, do you?" Scorpio teased while grinning.

"Not at all," Celine replied dryly. "Rico is as repulsive as a man can get."

Either Celine was an excellent liar or the rumors she was having an affair with Rico weren't true. Amber saw Scorpio across the room and immediately smiled and waved. She said something to Rico and attempted to walk away, but he caught her around the waist, keeping her against him. When he whispered something in her ear, she frowned.

"I'll admit; I don't have much respect for the man myself," Scorpio announced.

Rayner found a secluded corner where he could talk on his cell phone. He seemed preoccupied with the caller. "Just stick to the plan," Rayner growled into the phone. "Don't touch anything but what we discussed." He disconnected his call and scanned the room for Scorpio. His expression dropped when he saw Scorpio heading across the room to intercept Rico and Amber. "Ah, Scorpio. Don't do it."

§

Maverick and Stone stood in Davenport's dimly lit study before the open wall safe. Both men were dressed in black suits with black shirts and matching ties. If their little side trip was discovered, they could easily blend in with the rest of the party crowd as long as they were dressed the part. Stone removed several expensive pieces of jewelry and grinned like a schoolboy. Maverick frowned and replaced his phone.

"Rayner isn't any fun," Maverick informed him then glared at Stone and shook his head. "He was very insistent that we only take what we came for."

Stone frowned and held the amazingly expensive, gold Rolex watch to his wrist. "But this would look so good on me," he announced with enthusiasm.

"Put it back," Maverick groaned. "We promised on Cal's grave that we'd never go back to that lifestyle. Scorpio is depending on us."

Stone removed a hefty diamond necklace and held it up. "Yeah, but Scorpio's never had a necklace like this before. She might reconsider with this bobble around her neck."

Maverick considered the comment a moment then frowned and waved him off. "No, not happening," he announced. "No more screwing around. Let's just get what we came for and get out of here."

"Rayner isn't the only one who's not any fun," Stone muttered and replaced the necklace to the wall safe.

§

Scorpio approached Rico and Amber where they stood with a few other well-dressed henchmen on Davenport's payroll. Rayner caught her wrist and slowed her approach.

"Let it go, Scorpio," he attempted to whisper in her ear while holding her back.

Amber smiled eagerly upon seeing her while Rico's grin mocked Scorpio. Rico silenced Amber before she could open her mouth.

"Well, hello, Scorpio," Rico announced while chuckling. "What brings you here?"

Scorpio stared into Rico's eyes and showed no fear despite Rayner fidgeting alongside her. It was clear Rayner was debating how much of a beating he was about to take for whatever Scorpio intended to say. Rico stared back at her while grinning. She didn't look away as her eyes pierced through him. Rico tensed slightly from her silent rage and looked at Rayner in order to regain control of the situation.

"I don't know, Rayner," Rico remarked boldly. "According to Cal, she's quite the vixen in bed. She may be too much woman for you to handle."

Scorpio twitched at the mention of Cal, particularly regarding their love life. Rayner immediately stepped in front of her and faced Rico.

"Mind your manners, Rico," Rayner scoffed while maintaining his authoritative demeanor despite that Rico could easily crush him. "I wouldn't want to tell Davenport about your little side ventures."

Rico shifted his glare at Rayner and attempted to stare him down. Rayner didn't flinch, although it was obvious he feared being hit by the muscular man. Rico chuckled and turned to Amber.

"Come along, Amber," Rico announced then shifted a sly look at Scorpio. "My neck needs some massaging. Let's go to the library."

Rico took two steps toward the ballroom door, but Amber didn't follow. She stared at Scorpio a moment as if she wanted to say something.

"You don't have to go with him, Amber," Scorpio firmly insisted. "You can come home with us. You don't have to put up with this Neanderthal."

Rico grabbed Amber by the arm, forcing her to look back at him. He then smiled at Scorpio. "She'll always choose me over anyone else."

Amber smiled timidly at Scorpio and allowed Rico to pull her from the ballroom. Scorpio took a step after them. Rayner stepped into her path facing her.

"Let it go," he announced firmly. "You have to trust me. I know what I'm doing."

Scorpio fidgeted and ran trembling fingers through her hair. "I just want to wipe that smile from his smug face," she muttered.

"I know," Rayner replied with a sigh, "but I don't feel like picking your broken body off the floor."

She eyed him then frowned. "I'm not made of porcelain," Scorpio informed him. "He can't break me."

"I'll just disagree with you on that one," Rayner remarked then offered a timid smile and extended his hand. "How about a dance instead?"

She rolled her eyes and groaned. "I hardly feel like dancing."

"Do it out of pity," he replied. "I've never danced with anyone at one of these parties. This will probably be my only chance."

Scorpio sighed and placed her hand in his. He smiled warmly and led her to the dance floor. Rayner twirled her in a circle and then into his arms. She was slightly surprised by his suave move and had to smile as they slow danced. He held her left hand to his chest as they danced a little closer than acceptable. She managed a smile and marveled at his dancing skills.

"You're a better dancer than I thought," she remarked. "I thought you said you never danced."

"I said I never danced at one of Davenport's parties," he corrected. "I actually took ballroom dancing in high school."

"Well, aren't you full of surprises," she announced and grinned. "That must have been a fun."

"Not really," he replied and smirked almost painfully. "It was an all-guys school."

Scorpio stared at him a moment, noted his teasing smile, and then laughed.

Chapter 35

The following evening, Amber and Rico sat at the corner table in the tavern along with three of Davenport's men. They all laughed while drinking. Despite that Amber was drunk to the point of passing out, she continued to drink. She laughed while clinging to Rico, who more or less had to hold her up. He leaned closer to her and whispered something in her ear. She grinned and nodded. Rico stood and practically pulled Amber to her feet. Maverick and Scorpio sat at the bar closest to the wall and sipped their drinks while watching Rico just about carry Amber toward the back. There was an exterior door in the hallway beyond the bathrooms, which led out back. It was one of Amber's favorite 'quickie' locations. Scorpio shifted uncomfortably and leaned closer to Maverick while watching Rico with the drunken woman.

"This isn't good. We don't actually know he might kill her, but I can't shake the feeling that her life is in danger," Scorpio whispered and nervously glanced at her watch. "I barely slept last night after the party fearing for her life as it was. If he manages to get her out back, there's no telling what might happen."

"We've done everything we can," Maverick insisted without looking at her. "She chose an insane killer over rational thinking because of a car. It's not as if we can remove her against her will. She's entitled to make her own decisions no matter how stupid or irrational they are."

"Well, this one will end up getting her killed," Scorpio scoffed.

"I'm sure it briefly crossed her mind at some point," Maverick remarked while attempting to act natural and sipped his beer. "Now we have to let it play out and hope everything comes together."

"Where are they?" Scorpio muttered and again looked at her watch.

"Stop fidgeting," Maverick demanded while casting a look at her.

"I can't help it."

"There's only so much we can do, and we're already doing it," Maverick insisted. "Just try to relax."

Two state troopers entered the tavern and looked around. Although the tavern was only partially filled for a weekday evening, everyone looked at the men, including Rico, who had Amber just about to the bathroom hallway. The state troopers pointed in their direction. Rather than run, Rico held his hands in the air, remaining calm and relaxed as they approached. He apparently knew the drill too well.

"I haven't done anything wrong," he announced as the men hurried for them.

Amber had to cling to the wall to keep from falling down after Rico had abruptly released her. The troopers approached Amber, ignoring Rico.

"Amber Roth?" the first trooper announced.

She nodded while attempting to focus on the two uniformed men.

"You're under arrest," the trooper continued while the second trooper attempted to handcuff her.

Despite her drunken condition, she resisted the handcuffs and immediately protested. "What's this about? Get your hands off me!"

The officer nearly had her wrist cuffed when she slapped him. He didn't even flinch from the rather light hit. She was too drunk to do any real damage. He swiftly cuffed her hands behind her back.

"That's striking an officer," the state trooper informed her with little emotion.

The entire tavern fell silent and stared at the unfolding scene. They seemed stunned at what they were witnessing. Rico slowly lowered his hands and stared at both men with surprise and dismay.

"What's the charge?" Rico demanded.

"We received an anonymous tip about a stolen necklace," the first trooper announced. "We searched Miss Roth's house and found the necklace in question."

As they attempted to remove the drunken, handcuffed woman, Rico stopped them.

"What stolen necklace?" he demanded.

"Bridget Hamler reported her diamond necklace had been stolen three months ago," the officer informed him. "It's estimated value was a quarter million dollars. Miss Roth attended the same party where Mrs. Hamler last reported having the necklace."

"Party? What party?" Rico demanded. "The only party Amber would have attended--" He suddenly silenced and seemed to be putting it together.

"An anonymous caller reported seeing the necklace in Miss Roth's apartment," the trooper announced. "Don't worry; we had a court order for the search."

"I work for Mr. Davenport," Rico boldly announced. "He won't be pleased when he hears you've arrested Amber. He's friends with Mrs. Hamler. I'm sure she'll drop--"

"Charges will be filed," the trooper insisted. "Mrs. Hamler's insurance company already paid the claim, and they have a zero tolerance policy."

"What does that mean?" Rico demanded.

"It means your girlfriend is going to jail for grand theft," the officer announced. "With a good lawyer, she'll probably be out in eighteen months."

"Eighteen months?" Amber suddenly squawked. "I didn't steal any necklace!"

As they removed her, Rico could do little more than watch and frown. Rico removed his cell phone, placed it to his ear, and continued down the hallway for the back. Rayner and Stone entered the tavern as the troopers removed Amber. They watched with surprise as they headed toward the bar to join their friends.

"Looks like we missed the excitement," Stone remarked with little emotion.

"What took them so long?" Rayner muttered.

"It's a small county," Maverick informed him. "Finding a judge to issue a warrant takes time."

"I feel a little bad for her," Stone announced while frowning then sighed. "It seems a bit cruel to lock her up for something she didn't do."

"I suppose women's lockup is better than being killed at the hands of a man like Rico," Maverick assured him.

"I doubt it'll come to that," Rayner casually informed them. "If Davenport and Rico are out of the picture, I'm sure some new evidence will surface, and she'll be cleared of all charges." He cleverly raised his brows. "In this day of computers, there's no telling what can happen."

Stone chuckled and held his fist to Rayner for a fist bump. He eyed Stone's fist a moment as if unclear what to do then figured it out and gave him a fist bump. Scorpio leaned on the bar in order to speak privately to her friends.

"I can't believe you pulled it off," she remarked with surprise. "How did you know about that necklace?"

"You can thank my eidetic memory," Rayner replied. "I remembered the party when Mrs. Hamler wore that expensive necklace. I also remembered that it was reported stolen a few days later. After I hacked into the insurance company's computer, I was able to read the entire report. That's where the guys came in."

"We've been in this business long enough to know when someone is lying on an insurance claim," Maverick informed Scorpio while grinning.

"I'd rather you didn't tell me much about your past life," Scorpio muttered.

"It was just a matter of going through that flash drive to find the right blackmail victim," Rayner announced. "Mr. Hamler was one of Davenport's 'clients'. We realized Hamler stole his wife's necklace so he could pay off Davenport. The insurance company would cover the cost of the necklace and everyone was happy."

"It's only logical that something that valuable is too hot to sell right away," Stone added while leaning back in his chair. "If he had taken the necklace, he'd sit on it for a while before trying to sell it."

"We're talking a needle in a haystack here," Scorpio insisted. "How were you so certain Hamler gave it to Davenport? What were the chances of actually finding it in his safe in the first place?"

Stone and Maverick exchanged casual looks then shrugged and smiled at her.

"We're good," Maverick insisted.

Scorpio's eyes narrowed as she stared at them. "You knew it was there," she scoffed with disappointment. "You were in Davenport's safe before you knew the necklace was reported stolen, weren't you?"

"You can't prove that," Stone informed her as he let out a throaty laugh.

"I don't have to prove it," she snarled while glaring at them. "How could you?"

Both men frowned and shrugged. "We didn't take anything," Maverick insisted. "Sometimes, we just like to keep our skills sharp."

Scorpio rolled her eyes and looked away. "You two are unbelievable."

"Your disappointment in us is really your own fault," Stone informed her.

She glared at him with surprise to the accusation. "How do you figure?"

"You ask questions when you don't really want the answers," Maverick casually replied.

Scorpio's eyes narrowed as she stared at her friends. Both men fidgeted.

"We're going to play a few rounds of pool," Stone announced and practically pulled Maverick from his chair, keeping their distance from Scorpio. "Give you a chance to keep your inner volcano in check."

Maverick snickered at the comment. She shook her head as they hurried across the room then leaned on the bar near Rayner.

"I want to be proud of them, but at the same time I'd like to wring their necks," Scorpio scoffed.

"There's a good chance we saved a woman's life tonight," Rayner informed her and offered a smile. "Let's just be happy with that for now."

Chapter 36

After a brief celebratory drink at the tavern, all four returned to the hotel, having driven in two separate vehicles due to their little escapade to frame Amber. Their celebration was short lived when they saw the sheriff and deputy's cars parked in front of the hotel with their lights flashing, lighting up the moderately dark hotel. When she saw her grandfather's car beyond the police vehicles, Scorpio threw her jeep into park and jumped from it. She ran to the front porch where her grandfather sat on one of the rocking chairs while holding a bloodied cloth to his mouth. She stared at him with horror. Someone had beaten him up! His cheek was red, and his lip was cracked and swollen.

"Grandpa," she gasped and hurried to his side. "What happened?"

"I heard about the trouble with Rico yesterday," he announced. "When you didn't answer my calls, I came out to make sure you were okay." He shook his head and looked at the blood on the cloth with disgust. "A couple of men were coming out of the hotel. I don't know what I was thinking when I yelled 'hey, what are you doing?' Naturally, they jumped me."

"Are you okay?" she asked while visually assessing his facial injuries.

"I've lived through worse," he informed her and stood from the rocking chair. "You really need to get more comfortable chairs on your porch."

"Grandpa," she groaned while glaring at him. "Don't change the subject."

He managed a smile, although it must have been painful, and placed his hands on her shoulders while looking into her eyes.

"I'm fine, Scorpio," he announced seeming touched by her concern. "Don't you worry about your old grandpa. He got in a few shots of his own."

She managed a laugh. "Kane would have been proud of you."

Her grandfather attempted a smile but couldn't quite manage it with his swollen, cut lip. Mentioning Kane obviously upset him, perhaps more so in his current condition. Sheriff Horton and Deputy Gaines left the hotel and stepped onto the porch. The deputy wrote on his tablet while the sheriff did most of the talking. Maverick, Stone, and Rayner joined them on the porch as well.

"Well," Sheriff Horton announced to Scorpio, "they were obviously looking for something. Judging by the cables in the office, I'm guessing they stole your laptop."

Rayner gently cleared his throat and revealed the bag he held. "Actually, I took that with me tonight," he informed the sheriff. "Scorpio let me borrow her laptop to do some of my work."

"I guess that was fortunate," Sheriff Horton informed them, "because the office was trashed."

"Great," she muttered then looked at her grandfather. "Were they Davenport's men?"

"Hard to say," Newman replied. "They were wearing masks, and I'm pretty sure they were wearing leather gloves. Their fists were surprisingly soft and supple when they greeted my face." He drew a deep breath and delicately dabbed the corner of his mouth. "There weren't any cars in the driveway when I pulled up. If it hadn't been for the front door being partially open, I probably would have turned around and gone back home when I didn't see your jeep here."

"Only one bedrooms had been touched, so I'm guessing your grandfather interrupted whoever broke into the hotel," the sheriff remarked. "I know why you would want to accuse Davenport, but we don't have any evidence to back that up."

"Of course we do," Rayner announced, surprising Sheriff Horton. "There are security cameras positioned all over the estate grounds. All we have to do is view the video and see if we recognize any of them."

"Security cameras?" the sheriff asked with surprise. "I didn't realize you'd installed security cameras."

Rayner suspiciously eyed the sheriff then managed a tiny smile. "That's the whole point, Sheriff," he announced. "You don't want the bad guys to know all your secrets. That's how you catch them in the act."

Her grandfather suddenly chuckled while eyeing Sheriff Horton. "This should be entertaining," Newman announced. "Let's have a look at that security video."

Everyone followed Rayner into the hotel and down the grand hallway to the office. Scorpio's heart sank when she saw the condition of the office. Papers and objects were carelessly tossed around, fragile ceramic trinkets were broken on the floor, and her lovely armoire and antique desk had been savagely broken into. Apparently, when the intruders discovered the security monitors hidden within the armoire, they smashed the system as well as the cameras.

"Oh, that's great," Stone scoffed. "They destroyed it so we couldn't see them."

Sheriff Horton shook his head. "Yeah, these guys were professionals."

Rayner removed the console panel and poked around a moment. He removed part of the system, cleared a spot on the desk, and set it down. Everyone watched as he removed wires from his bag and connected them to the disconnected computer part.

"What is that?" the deputy asked.

"Think of it as an airplane's black box," Rayner replied. "This is the brains of the security system. It wasn't damaged. I'm careful to hide a backup deep inside my systems to prevent someone from doing what our intruders just did. Sure, they ruined the system and made a mess, but they didn't destroy the part that will incriminate them."

Maverick chuckled while eyeing the deputy. "The man's a genius," he announced proudly.

Rayner hooked the device to the laptop from his bag and pressed in a code. "I have to manually pull up each camera since I'm only working with one monitor. We'll start with the front door camera then try the back door. More than likely, they entered through the front door since Mr. Wayland said the door was open when he arrived."

On the computer screen, they saw a man dressed entirely in black, who was also wearing a black mask, slip from the woods. He reached the porch. Everyone watched his every movement with anticipation, hoping they'd catch a glimpse of something to indicate who he was. He looked at the camera and sprayed the lens. The video was now black.

Rayner straightened. "How did he know that was there?" he gasped with surprise. "That camera is practically hidden. He couldn't have seen it."

"I'll tell you how he knew it was there," Newman scoffed with annoyance as he straightened. "You installed similar systems in Davenport's home and businesses. He knew where to look and what to look for." Her grandfather shook his head. "We know it was Davenport's men, but we don't have a shred of proof to back it up."

"Which bedroom did they ransack?" Scorpio asked while frowning. "I'm guessing it was mine since it was my office they trashed."

"Whichever bedroom is on the third floor near the back stairs," the deputy replied.

Scorpio and her friends looked at the deputy. Her grandfather appeared equally surprised.

"That was Kane's room, wasn't it?" her grandfather gasped then glared at the sheriff. "I told you Kane's murder wasn't a coincidence. Someone is targeting my family!"

"I'll admit; that is a little too coincidental," Sheriff Horton reluctantly agreed. "We'll take another look around. It's possible they found what they were looking for, in which case, they probably won't be back."

"I'm going with you," Newman insisted to the sheriff. "If you find something, I want to know."

The deputy, sheriff, and Newman left the office to check on Kane's ransacked bedroom.

Scorpio frowned and eyed Rayner. "Well, so much for that state-of-the-art security system," she huffed. "Defeated by a man in a mask. How did they get past the alarm system?"

"I don't know," he replied with a defeated sigh. "I'll have to have a look at it. It may tie in with the break-in at my house. Maybe they found a way to override it when they'd gone through my things."

"Will you be able to tell by looking at the system?" Maverick asked.

"Not if they got their hands on the codes," Rayner informed him then sighed with defeat. "I should take this drive back to my place and hook it up to multiple screens. Maybe I can find one camera they didn't anticipate or a different angle where we see them before they disabled the camera." He shook his head in disgust. "I have to believe I'm smarter than anyone on Davenport's payroll."

"You *are* on Davenport's payroll," Maverick firmly reminded him.

"I don't think you should go back to your place tonight," Scorpio informed Rayner. "I think that would be unwise. You should stay here with us. Security breach aside, it's still safer here."

"I won't argue that," he replied. "But first thing tomorrow, I need to watch everything that recorded last night. I can scan a few feeds on the laptop, but it'll take a while to get through the footage even knowing the approximate time of the breach."

"We should probably see how badly Kane's room has been trashed," Stone announced with a defeated sigh. "It may not be habitable."

"He could sleep in the room Trudy uses," Maverick suggested.

"No, you never know when she'll show up unexpectedly. We'll do a spit and shine on one of the guest rooms near ours," Scorpio informed them. "We should all be in close contact with one another anyway."

Maverick groaned at the comment. "That means we have to clean a bathroom too," he announced. "Stone and I already share one."

"We'll clean the room connected to my bathroom so that he can share mine," she suggested to her friends. "That way we'll only have to do a little light cleaning and change the bedsheets."

"I like that idea better," Maverick announced with a little more enthusiasm.

Chapter 37

After Sheriff Horton and Deputy Gaines had left the hotel nearly an hour later, Scorpio stood by the partially opened basement door and stared at it. Rayner approached from the laundry room where he had found a fresh set of sheets to make his newly appointed bed. He eyed her then the basement door with a curious look.

"Is something wrong?" he asked.

She indicated the door with some concern. "We closed that door when we were finished down there, didn't we?" she asked. "I never leave that door open."

"I guess the sheriff and deputy went down there to check for more intruders," Rayner replied. "You don't think the intruders went into the basement, do you?"

"Only one way to find out." She opened the door the rest of the way and headed down the steps.

Rayner set his sheets on the counter and hurried after her. "Maybe we shouldn't go down there without the shotgun," he announced only a few steps behind her.

"You're right, it was probably just the sheriff checking that the place was clear," she informed him. "I just want to make sure we're secure."

"Yeah, which means we should have brought the shotgun," Rayner reiterated.

They entered the large, empty room within the basement and looked around. It was obvious nothing had been disturbed, since there was nothing in the room. Scorpio ran her fingers through her hair and groaned. She was letting her imagination get the better of her. She feared she was turning into her brother. Maybe it was a twin thing.

"I'm being paranoid," she remarked then sighed. "I guess I'm just tired. It's been a long day."

When she looked up, she saw Rayner walking across the empty room with a fast gait and purpose. She gave him a strange look and followed him.

"What are you doing?" she asked, bewildered to his sudden interest in nothing.

Rayner picked up a small, gold object within a pile of swept debris and held it in his hand. Scorpio stared at the gold cufflink with a look of bewilderment.

"Is that a cufflink?" she asked.

He held it between his fingers, studied it a moment, and then eyed her. "A very expensive one," he replied and indicated the small diamond in the center of the black onyx." It contained the initials J.R. "Do you know a J.R.?"

She shook her head. "Certainly no one on Davenport's payroll," Scorpio remarked.

"This isn't the average man's cufflink," Rayner informed her. "That's a quarter karat diamond. Looks like it's been laying around a while. It's covered in dirt."

"Amber swept," Scorpio reminded him. "We would have found it then, wouldn't we?"

"It could have been covered within the pile of dirt," he replied. "But why did I just notice it now? How long did we pace this room trying to find answers?"

"Long enough," she muttered. "Perhaps we kicked it around without realizing it. There's quite a bit of dirt and debris still on the floor."

"Scorpio," her grandfather called out. "Are you down here?"

Rayner placed the cufflink in his pocket as her grandfather entered the room. He paused within the doorway and stared at the empty, stone room with a strange look on his face. He looked back at his granddaughter.

"With everything you have to renovate upstairs, don't tell me you're considering utilizing this space," he announced with concern. "You can't afford to heat the basement in the winter, believe me."

She eyed him with surprise. "Didn't you use to?" Scorpio asked.

He stared at her with a puzzled look. "Use to what?" Newman asked.

"Heat the basement in the winter."

"Are you kidding?" he replied and chuckled. "Honey, I barely heated the main hotel in the winter. There wasn't much point. We were closed during the winter months. You know that. I kept just enough heat in this place to keep the pipes from freezing."

"Davenport claims you and he rented the hotel out for parties in the off-season," she remarked.

Her grandfather immediately frowned and became irritated. "I don't want you talking to Davenport," he snarled hotly. "I don't know what he told you, but renting out this place for those low-life parties was all his idea." He shook his head in disgust. "Him and his low-life thug friends. I can't believe I actually trusted him back then. The weekend parties he allowed during off-season were degrading to our reputation, and I put an end to them as well as our partnership when I found out the sort of depraved things happening here practically under my nose."

"He mentioned the parties and the questionable clientele," she announced.

Newman frowned and shook his head. "He shouldn't have told you any of that," he announced with obvious disgust. "I don't want your plans for the hotel to be tainted with its past. This place has stood empty far too long. I suppose he mentioned the prostitutes, huh?"

"Prostitutes?" Rayner practically gasped then shook his head. "He mentioned a lot worse than that."

Her grandfather eyed Rayner and appeared bewildered. "What do you mean?"

Scorpio stared at him with surprise. "You aren't aware the things that happened in this room?"

"In this room?" he asked then looked around. "It's a basement. It's used to store things that we were too lazy to haul away." Newman's eyes suddenly widened. "What did he tell you happened in this room? Is there something I should know about?"

Scorpio was stunned that her grandfather was clueless about the basement when Davenport insisted he knew what went on. Had Davenport been playing her? Had the violence really happened? Or was he just making it up in hopes to get her to sell? She wasn't sure what to think now.

"He said they had street fights down here," she informed him. "Illegal gambling."

"I knew there was illegal gambling," Newman remarked, "but I thought that was held in the banquet hall upstairs. I never knew there was street fighting held down here." He groaned and shook his head. "Although, I guess I shouldn't be surprised. Actually, nothing would surprise me at this point. I'm just glad I dissolved my partnership with that bastard before anything really bad happened."

Rayner was about to open his mouth when Scorpio caught his hand, silencing him.

"You made the right call," she informed her grandfather. "I'm sorry Davenport lied to you."

"Well, in his defense," Newman announced boldly, "he didn't know what was really going on until near the end. I think he suspected, but he looked the other way because it was good money. At least enough to pay for the upkeep over the winter months. Still not worth risking our reputations over, though."

"You're absolutely right," she announced.

"I'm heading out," her grandfather informed her. "Your grandma was worried sick after I called her earlier. I'd better get home and let her tell me what I did wrong tonight."

Scorpio smiled warmly and kissed her grandfather on the cheek. "Thanks for everything, Grandpa," she announced. "Don't listen to Grandma. I think you were very brave tonight."

He laughed and nodded. "Brave is facing your grandmother," he teased then left the room.

"Why didn't you tell him what Davenport said really happened down here?" Rayner asked.

"Because he's already upset with what he believes he knows about the off-season parties," she replied. "What's the point to upsetting him further?"

"Well, none, I suppose."

"Honestly, if he found out the horrible things that had happened under his watch, he may withdraw support to reopening the place," Scorpio announced. "Besides, have we considered that maybe Davenport lied about what happened down here?"

"Why would he lie?"

"He wanted to buy the hotel back since he'd sold it to my grandfather," she replied. "If I thought horrendous things had happened here, it could sway me to sell."

"If you didn't sell after the horrible things that happened while you were here, I doubt you're going to let the hotel's past sway you," Rayner remarked.

"Stubbornness runs in our family," she announced with a chuckle.

Chapter 38

Scorpio tossed beneath the covers on her bed unable to sleep then stared at the clock. It was almost three in the morning. She groaned and threw the covers off her. It was useless sleeping anymore these days. She wondered if she'd ever get a full night's sleep again. It seemed since Cal's death she hadn't slept through the night without bouts of lying awake and staring at his empty pillow. As stupid as it sounded, she was going to take a long, hot bath, think about Cal, and hope she managed to drown herself. She cursed herself for allowing such thoughts even cross her mind. Losing Cal was bad enough, but since Kane's murder, she'd been feeling less than whole. There was that twin curse thing again.

As she padded into the bathroom in her bare feet, she couldn't help but reminisce about everything she'd lost during her lifetime. Her short life had been filled with death and disappointment. She'd lost so many people she loved; some even before she knew them. She then noticed that the bathroom door connecting to Rayner's new room was partially open and his bedroom light was on. Scorpio poked her head into his room just because she was the curious type. Actually, nosy was more accurate. Rayner sat up in bed busily working on the laptop he borrowed from her office. He stopped typing and immediately looked up when he saw the bathroom door open.

"I'm sorry," he announced timidly. "Did my typing wake you?"

"No, of course not," she replied. "I couldn't sleep and thought I'd take a bath and hopefully drown. What are you still doing up?"

"What was that last comment?"

"What are you still doing up?" she repeated.

"No, the other last comment."

"Just a joke in poor taste," she replied and managed to wave it off.

"Yes, it was in poor taste," he agreed in a low tone. "I couldn't sleep either. After we found that cufflink, my brain refused to shut down. All these weird thoughts were racing through my head."

She leaned in the doorway while folding her arms across her chest. "Such as?"

"Our mysterious J.R.," he announced while raising a clever brow. "Who is this wealthy man with such expensive cufflinks? Was he in the basement recently or decades ago?"

"Not exactly storming the trenches with excitement, Rayner," she remarked. "I don't know why any of that couldn't wait until morning."

"I may have hit the jackpot on this one," he informed her. "Our J.R. is obviously someone with a lot of money."

"Obviously."

"If the cufflink had been in the basement for decades, that means he attended the off-season parties," Rayner continued. "Someone like that is possibly connected to Davenport either through friendship or his little side business, so I cross-referenced some of Davenport's current party lists."

Scorpio became interested particularly by the sly grin on Rayner's face. "If you tell me you didn't find anything, I'll probably kill you."

"I found a J.R.," he announced while chuckling.

"Now we have to figure out if it's the same J.R.," Scorpio remarked.

"Already checked into that," he added while grinning. "I found a picture of J.R. taken a few decades ago from some fancy fundraiser." He turned the laptop toward her.

She hurried to the bed, sat on the edge, and stared at the man who was possibly in his late thirties or early forties at the time the picture was taken.

"So how do you know this is him?"

He enlarged the picture to reveal the cufflinks. They matched the one they found.

Scorpio laughed and patted Rayner's face. "You evil genius!"

"Thank you." He turned the laptop to face him and continued typing. "He apparently owns a large shipping company not far from here. They had a website and contact information. With your permission, I'd like to contact him and tell him we think we found a cufflink he may have lost several years back."

"Several years," she teased. "That's a stretch. Yeah, by all means, contact him. If we can get him out here, that cufflink puts him in the basement. We can play up the 'full disclosure' angle by pretending we heard all about it from others and see what he'll tell us about the death games."

"Sounds like a job for Maverick," Rayner remarked. "He seems to have a gift for getting people to talk."

"Probably because he speaks their language," Scorpio remarked. "A devious mind and all that." She moved off the bed. "I'm sure you're in need of some sleep, so I'll get out of your hair."

"I doubt I'm sleeping anymore tonight," he replied dryly then sighed. "I was about to see what movies I could find online."

"You have an account for online movies?" she asked with surprise.

"No, I just put in your password and pulled up yours," Rayner remarked.

Scorpio groaned then shook her head while smiling. "Find something good, and I'll watch with you."

He eyed her then smiled. "It's a date."

She raised her brow and folded her arms across her chest. "No, it's not."

§

Early the next morning, Scorpio woke to sunlight poking in through the curtains. She struggled to open her eyes even though the temptation to sleep all morning was strong. She saw Rayner holding her while she snuggled against him beneath the covers and immediately remembered they had been watching a movie together last night. Although nothing had happened and both remained fully dressed, her mind immediately strayed to their drunken night of passion. She had been wild and aggressive while he eagerly tried to please her. She remembered clearly the look on his face, his loving caresses, and the amazing passion he'd shown for her. For a moment, her body ached for him. She could almost feel his hands intimately caressing her and his attempts to kiss every part of her body while she was insistent on ravishing him.

Cal had been her first, and he showed her a world of mind-blowing sex. Sex with Cal was great, and they were mutually energetic in bed, but after her drunken night with Rayner, she wondered if there wasn't a more passionate side. Something less wild and more intimate. She was never given the opportunity to take her time and explore Cal's body just as he had never explored hers. It was all about keeping with the fast, energetic pace. She found herself thinking back more and more to her encounter with Rayner.

What would he have shown her if she had let him? She felt his warm body against hers while they slept cuddled together and his morning enthusiasm pressed against her hip. She wanted him to slowly and passionately make love to her. Scorpio's hand slid down his body, wanting to caress him awake. Her hand suddenly stopped and rational thinking quickly set in. If she had sex with Rayner, she'd have to concede to a relationship with him. He'd be relentless in his pursuit. She doubted her ability to have a casual fling, and he'd be heartbroken if she attempted to resume a non-physical friendship. She enjoyed having him around as a friend and didn't want to risk losing that.

Risking everything over her impulsive, sexual desire wasn't an option. Instead, she remained nestled in his arms and let that be enough. When Rayner woke, she shut her eyes and pretended to be asleep. He nuzzled her, and she could almost feel his smile upon her. His hand lightly caressed her cheek, and she felt his lips gently kiss her forehead. That's when she realized, for his sake, she'd made the right decision. She couldn't risk breaking his heart over her selfish desires. He nuzzled against her, held her a little closer, and drifted back to sleep.

Chapter 39

Scorpio hurried along the grand hallway for the foyer door. It was nearly noon and a few hours after they had gotten a response from Rayner's cufflink email to J.R. Rayner was only a few steps behind her, attempting to keep her from acting impulsively.

"Remember," he scolded. "Act casual. If Davenport's been blackmailing this man, he's going to be selective about what he says in front of us."

"I know; I know," she insisted as she hurried for the front door.

She turned off the alarm and was about to unlock the door when she hesitated and looked through the peek hole. She hated that she had to be so paranoid, but it was becoming the new theme for the lives of her and her friends. Granted, Maverick and Stone were always on the paranoid side, considering their former profession and associations. Scorpio suddenly hesitated and looked at Rayner, who now joined her in the foyer.

"That's not him," she insisted.

"Who is it?" Rayner asked with surprise. "Someone you know?"

"I don't know who he is," she announced, "but it's not him."

Rayner moved her aside then unlocked and opened the door to reveal a neatly dressed man in his mid-thirties wearing an expensive suit. Obviously, it wasn't the man they were expecting. He would have to be in his sixties by now. Rayner attempted to hide his surprise.

"May I help you?" Rayner asked while giving the man a curious look.

"Are you Rayner Roderick?" the man close to him in age asked. "I'm Jerome Roth. We corresponded about a cufflink you'd found."

"Uh, yes," Rayner replied. "But I was expecting someone, uh, well, older."

"Oh, you thought I was my father," he announced while grinning then added a laugh and shook his head. "I'm Jerome Roth, Junior."

Rayner and Scorpio both nodded with understanding and some disappointment. Rayner stepped aside and allowed him to enter.

"I'm sorry for the misunderstanding," Rayner announced. "Won't you come in?"

"Thank you," Jerome replied and marveled while looking around the foyer. "This old hotel is a work of art." He glanced at Rayner and Scorpio as the door shut. "Are you the new owners?"

"Ms. Wayland is the owner," he informed Jerome. "I'm in charge of security."

Scorpio hid her smile and had to keep from laughing. Rayner wasn't her first choice for the position. She was of the old school opinion where the head of security was a beefy bouncer with more muscle than brains.

"We were actually hoping to meet your father," Rayner announced in a casual tone. "We haven't met many people who'd attended the infamous off-season parties here at the hotel. Scorpio is fascinated with the hotel's history. She's been attempting to compile a photo history throughout the years." Rayner eyed the man and grinned. "We heard the off-season parties were a sight to behold, and it only seemed fitting to include them in her photo storybook."

"I'm sorry I can't help you out with that," Jerome replied while showing less enthusiasm than Rayner. "My father disappeared after attending one of those historical, weekend parties. Afterward, my mother insisted we didn't speak about his visit to the hotel. When we contacted the police about his disappearance, she told them he'd driven to a business meeting, but she was vague on the details."

"Why didn't she want you mentioning the weekend party?" Scorpio asked.

Jerome stared at her a moment then raised his brows. "Didn't anyone tell you what sort of parties they held here during off-season?" He shook his head in disgust. "They were a politician's wet dreams." His disgust turned to anger. "My mother knew my father came out here for sex, drugs, and illegal gambling, but she didn't dare say anything because the host was connected."

"Who was the host?" Rayner asked.

"Some slime ball named Jacob," Jerome replied. "I honestly don't know if he's still alive today. It just seemed best not to discuss the hotel, Jacob, or my father's disappearance." He eyed them suspiciously. "So you only found the one cufflink?"

"Yes," Rayner replied then removed the freshly cleaned cufflink from his pocket and handed it to Jerome.

Jerome held the cufflink and studied it a moment. "He called them his lucky cufflinks," he remarked. "It was the only pair he took with him that weekend."

"So he had them when he disappeared?" Scorpio asked sounding a little surprised.

"More than likely," Jerome replied. "It's possible someone stole them. The weekend guest list was mostly rich men like my father, but a lot of them were from the seedy underworld. I suspect he was murdered by one of them. I heard rumors that he wasn't the first to disappear from this place, and he certainly wasn't the last."

"Where had you heard that?" Rayner suddenly asked appearing curious.

"A friend of my father's used to come here for the off-season parties too," he replied then drew a deep, slightly shaken breath. "He wasn't able to attend the weekend my father disappeared. He blamed himself for not having his back. After that, he never returned for another party."

"Had he ever mentioned the death fights?" Scorpio asked almost delicately.

He stared at her an uncomfortable moment then frowned and nodded. "Yeah, he mentioned them," Jerome replied, although his distaste was evident.

"So it's true then?" she asked with surprise. "They actually existed?"

He nodded. "That would be one way to dispose of a body," Jerome informed her. "Supposedly, there's a dumping ground not far from here, where the host would dispose of the bodies. My father's friend and I searched for it once, but we couldn't find it."

"The bluffs are another convenient way to dispose of a body," Scorpio remarked.

"Not really," Jerome replied.

"The tide would eventually wash the bodies back to shore," Rayner informed Scorpio. "With the typical flow of the current, I'm guessing they'd drift to shore somewhere near the marina."

"They'd be easily spotted," Jerome added. "Since my father was never found, they didn't go with the bluffs." He looked at his watch. "I really have to go." He then eyed Scorpio. "You seem like a nice woman. Take my suggestion. Pretend you never heard of the off-season parties. You'll live longer."

They watched him leave then shut the door behind him. Rayner placed his hands in his pockets and leaned against the door.

"The more I think about it," he announced with a disgusted sigh, "the more I fear that cufflink surfaced after Amber swept."

"You don't think it was there the entire time?" she asked with surprise.

"At this point, there's no way to be sure," he informed her then sighed. "We need to explore that basement with a magnifying glass."

"Do you mean that literally or metaphorically?" Scorpio asked.

"Literally."

She sighed deeply and scratched her head. "I'll go find my magnifying glass."

§

Scorpio and Rayner walked the large, stone room the better part of an hour. Both carried flashlights and checked every crack in every stone. Scorpio was becoming disgusted, but Rayner seemed to have the patience of a saint.

"Maybe we have this wrong," Scorpio announced. "If this was the main gathering room, they'd dispose of evidence elsewhere away from prying eyes." She then became excited. "There's an old, wood burning furnace down the hall. Maybe they disposed of the evidence in that relic."

"No," Rayner informed her. "I already checked into that monstrosity. That thing stopped working before your family even owned the place."

"Okay, genius," she announced while impatiently glaring at him. "Why don't you think of something you haven't thought of before?"

He stared at her with a moderately insulted look.

She eyed him and immediately felt bad. "I didn't mean that," she quickly covered. "You've come up with more ideas than I have."

"No, you're right," he announced. "I am a genius. I need to think of something I hadn't thought of before."

He hurried for his bag, replaced the flashlight, and removed another light. He put on a pair of yellow glasses and turned off the light. Scorpio cried out with surprise. Rayner shined the black light across the floor while walking it. His light hit something, revealing a large stain.

Scorpio suddenly gasped. "Is that blood?"

"I'm guessing it was blood," he announced. "Unless they were using this area for a bathroom."

"Makes sense," she replied. "That area would probably contain the fighting ring. Blood would cover that area if the matches were to the death."

He continued looking around and found a place where there were stains on the wall and floor. "And this would be a great place for the alligator cage we heard about. It would explain the blood on the floor and wall." Rayner suddenly hesitated. "Where did we find the cufflink?"

"Across the room," she announced.

He hurried across the room and shined the light in the area where they'd originally found the cufflink. There were stains on the floor leading up to the wall with some stains on the wall itself.

"Give me your flashlight," he announced.

She handed him her flashlight. "Should I turn on the lights?"

"No, that would be counterproductive," he replied and shined the light against the floor where a majority of the stain remained. She could see the light filter back into the room through cracks in the stone. Rayner stared at the returning light on the wall. "There's something behind this wall. We need to look for an opening." He returned her flashlight to her. "Now we'll need the lights."

Once Scorpio turned on the lights, they began tapping the stone and pushing on it. The lower portion of the wall finally opened, startling both. They stared into the dark area within the stone wall, which was only a four-by-four space. Both crouched before the entrance for a better look. Rayner shined his flashlight into the opening and discovered a large manhole. The vertical shaft contained metal rungs leading downward. Rayner moved to his knees, leaned in as far as safely possible, and shined the light down the opening. He only saw the vertical concrete access hole. It was a long drop to the unseen bottom.

"We're not going to know what's down there unless we climb down," he informed her while sitting back on his feet. "Looks like it used to be a well of some sort."

"A little tight for a well."

"Indoor outhouse?"

She made a face then crawled past him on all fours and tugged on the first metal rung. Rayner studied her backside not far from his face. When she crawled back out, Rayner immediately looked away, fidgeted, and ran his fingers through his hair.

"Kane should have some climbing gear in a gray bag in the storage room near the basement elevator," she informed him.

"The rungs seem secure, but I don't know how far of a fall it is to the bottom."

"Especially if you fall into an old pile of shit," he remarked. "This really sounds like a job for Maverick. He was a cat burglar, right? He should be great at climbing."

She stared at Rayner a moment and considered the comment. "I'll ask him to do it if you promise not to mention the outhouse theory."

"Deal."

§

Half an hour later, Maverick had been fitted with Kane's climbing harness while Stone and Rayner held the rope. Maverick climbed the rungs into the vertical access and was almost about to disappear from their view when he looked back at them.

"I don't know what you're worried about," Maverick announced. "The rungs seem secure."

"Just being cautious," Scorpio replied while kneeling alongside the opening then handed him the flashlight.

He climbed down several rungs then shined the light below. "Still too dark," Maverick announced. "It must be pretty deep."

Rayner and Stone exchanged looks.

"Is it possible it's an old tunnel leading to the ocean?" Stone asked. "We're snug against the ocean, and the cliff isn't all that high."

"Like a secret passageway?" Rayner asked and entertained the thought. "It's possible."

"This hotel has been around forever," Scorpio informed him. "We're talking Colonial old."

"I'm nearly at the bottom," Maverick announced while carefully scaling the rungs. He shined the light beneath him. "I see something, but it's still too dark." Maverick stepped down from the last rung and heard something crunch beneath his feet. "Like kindling or something," he called up to them while shining the flashlight around his feet.

There were clumps of dark material, which was all he could see, but the sound of the ocean seemed to echo. He shined his light around and saw a tunnel at least six feet high by four feet wide.

"There's a tunnel down here," he called up with enthusiasm. "I hear the ocean. It must come out on the beach below the bluffs."

Maverick stepped off the mass of dark material and slipped on the mobile pile, falling onto his backside. His flashlight fell from his hand. He groaned, reclaimed his light, and then shined it alongside him to aid in standing. He saw a skeleton face staring back at him. Maverick cried out with horror and surprise.

"What is it?" Scorpio yelled down with concern. "Are you okay?"

"It's a dead guy!" He shined his light around him and remained horrified at the massive piles of bones. "Several dead guys!"

Ten minutes later, Scorpio and Rayner were at the bottom of the vertical access in the tunnel and shined their flashlights at the piles of bones. There was no telling how many men were among the bones, but Scorpio was sure it was at least a dozen. What clothing remained were obviously expensive suits. Stone remained at the top of the ladder, in case they needed someone to call for help if they couldn't climb back out. Scorpio crouched down and examined the men's suit jackets, feeling the pockets. She removed a wallet. Rayner and Maverick shined their lights on it. Scorpio revealed the man's ID and frowned.

"It's Jerome Roth, Sr.," she muttered.

"I think it's time to call someone," Rayner announced while straightening.

"Not Sheriff Horton," Maverick muttered.

"No, I'm thinking the FBI," Rayner replied.

Chapter 40

It was just about dark when there was a knock on the front door. Scorpio hurried up the foyer steps, looked through the peek hole, and then unlocked the door. Her grandfather stood in the doorway with a strange look on his face. His concern for her was evident.

"What's wrong, honey?" Newman asked. "You sounded upset on the phone."

Scorpio hurried him inside and immediately locked the door behind him. She turned to face her grandfather with a look that obviously concerned him. Her friends purposely stayed away to allow her some privacy with her grandfather to discuss the delicate subject of what they'd found.

"We found something disturbing this afternoon," she informed him, "and I thought you'd want to be here when the FBI arrives."

He stared at her with an astonished look. "The FBI?" he practically gasped. "What's going on? What have those idiots gotten you into?"

"They're not idiots, Grandpa," she insisted, "and I asked them to help me; not the other way around."

"You found something about Kane's murder, didn't you?" he gasped then became impatient as his look narrowed. "Was it Davenport?"

"No, this isn't about Kane," she replied with a serious expression. "We found bodies in the basement."

He stared at her a moment as if unable to comprehend what she'd said. "Bodies? Whose bodies?" Newman demanded. "Where in the basement?"

"Back from the off-season weekend parties," she informed him and showed him the wallet.

He opened it and stared at the ID. Horror crossed his face, and he looked back at her. "I'd heard of this guy. Some big shot around these parts," Newman informed her. "Davenport knew him and his family."

"We left everything the way we found it," she announced, "but I'm guessing there are at least a dozen bodies."

"I don't understand how that's possible," her grandfather insisted. "After I found out about the illegal activity going on here, Davenport and I thoroughly inspected the hotel, including the basement. After your uncle bought the place, he and I went through it and even cleared some things out. We stored a whole bunch of old furniture in the basement. Why didn't we find any bodies?"

"They were dumped in a secret pit," she explained.

"A pit?" he demanded. "What sort of pit?"

"I don't know," she replied. "An old one. There's a tunnel that leads to the beach. Maybe it was used by pirates. That tunnel is as old as the hotel."

"If I never knew about some secret pit and hidden tunnel, how on earth did those bastards from the off-season parties know about it?" her grandfather scoffed.

"Maybe they knew more about the hotel than you did," she replied.

"Davenport must have found it," Newman announced. "It has to be him."

Scorpio tensed and attempted to redirect her grandfather's hostility before he started another rant. "I know the FBI will want to question you since you were Davenport's partner. I just wanted you to have all your facts straight before they arrived. Anything you have on Davenport's involvement in the off-season parties--"

Newman managed a warm smile and gently caressed her shoulders while staring into her eyes. "Honey, don't worry about your old grandpa," he insisted. "I can handle a few questions about the off-season weekends. Unlike Davenport, I wasn't even here while they were going on. Your grandmother and I would take your mother and uncle on cruises and to tropical islands over most of the winters just as we did when you were kids. You know how much I hate Maine in the winter."

"I can't tell you how relieved I am to hear that," she announced and breathed a sigh of relief. The last thing she wanted was to cause problems for her grandfather. "I was worried you'd be over the same barrel as Davenport, and it'd be my fault."

"Honestly, my bigger concern is that he wasn't involved," Newman remarked.

She stared at him with surprise by the comment. "What do you mean?"

"Well, if Davenport didn't kill those people that means someone from the off-season party did," he informed her. "Talk about your evil men. I certainly don't want any of them stopping by unexpectedly. It's bad enough Davenport allowed that influence into our town in the first place."

"Even if someone like that was involved, they wouldn't have any reason to come after us here at the hotel," Scorpio insisted.

"Considering you're not witnesses, no, they wouldn't have any grievances with you," Newman agreed. "If Davenport knows something, he may have a higher authority to answer to though." He looked around and appeared curious. "Where are your friends, Abbott and Costello?"

"You mean Maverick and Stone?" she muttered not humored by the comment.

"Yeah," her grandfather replied with a serious look. "Isn't that what I said?"

As she glared at him, he grinned and chuckled.

"They're in the kitchen," she announced. "Giving us some privacy."

"Privacy is over," Newman replied and then eyed the closed sitting room door. "Aren't you going to offer your old grandpa a drink?" He headed for the sitting room. "I need something strong if I'm going to deal with the FBI and their tiny microscopes up my posterior."

"That's locked," she informed him.

Her grandfather stopped, turned to face her, and walked back to join her while giving her a curious look. "You still haven't been back in there?" he asked with surprise.

She fidgeted, rubbed her shoulders, and avoided looking at him. "I choose not to," she replied.

He shook his head while offering a sympathetic look. "Scorpio, honey, it's been almost a year."

"Nine months," she interjected a little too quickly and hoped he hadn't picked up on her defensiveness.

"Yeah, and that's almost a year. It's just a room," Newman informed her. "There's nothing to fear within that room."

"I'm not afraid to go in there," she insisted.

His look turned stern. "It's also not a shrine," he remarked.

"The game room bar is stocked if you need a drink," she informed him. "I'll get the guys from the kitchen, and we'll join you in the game room until the feds arrive."

"Healthy young men not drinking at a moment like this," her grandfather grumbled and shook his head. "There's something not right with those men." He headed for the game room with a defeated look upon his face. "I'd better call your grandmother and tell her I'm going to be a while. She's probably freaking out by now."

As her grandfather headed into the game room, Scorpio continued along the hall toward the kitchen. She entered the kitchen and found her three friends sitting at the island counter drinking coffee and eating muffins.

Scorpio eyed the muffins with a disapproving glare. "Those were for tomorrow morning," she informed them.

"We were starving tonight," Maverick insisted. "Someone wouldn't let us leave to pick up dinner."

"I made you dinner," she protested.

"Tomato soup and crackers isn't dinner," Stone protested and sharply raised a dark brow. "We're grown men. Grown men need meat."

"How did your grandfather take the news?" Rayner asked and appeared sympathetic.

"Rather well, actually," Scorpio informed them and sighed. "He said he was never here during the off-season parties. In fact, my whole family spent most of each winter at some tropical destination, so he's pretty much in the clear. Although, he'd rather wait for the FBI in one of the few rooms that has a bar."

"A man after my own heart," Stone announced and sprang from his chair.

Maverick reluctantly stood and groaned. "I don't like drinking before dealing with law enforcement," he remarked while frowning. "I like to have my wits about me when being interrogated."

"That's because you can't control your mouth when you drink," Stone retorted.

All four headed down the grand hallway.

Newman bolted into the hallway from the game room and eyed them with a strange look on his face. Something had him upset. His eyes then shifted to Rayner, and he immediately turned hostile.

"You," her grandfather announced in anger while pointing a demanding finger at him. "You worked for Davenport. I think you have some explaining to do."

"What?" Rayner asked with surprise. "What are you talking about?"

Newman motioned them into the game room. All four hurried after him. Her grandfather pointed to a small, barely visible camera in the far corner, which would allow a view of the bar and the game room entrance.

"Who are you spying on?" Newman demanded while casting his hateful glare upon Rayner. "Or should I ask who are you spying for?"

Rayner stared at the camera as he approached and took a closer look at it. He immediately shook his head while appearing stunned. "I didn't put that there," he insisted. He then looked at Scorpio and turned defensive. "That's not mine."

Stone approached the camera and easily pulled it off the wall since he was the tallest in the group. He looked at it then handed it to Rayner.

"It has a microphone on it," Stone informed them. "If that's not yours that means someone else has been spying on us."

"And listening to our conversations," Maverick announced with near horror on his face.

Scorpio's expression suddenly dropped. "The office," she gasped and ran from the room.

The four men ran after her and into the office. They looked around the room but didn't find any hidden cameras on the walls. Their relief only lasted a moment when Rayner looked at the nearby bookshelf, and his expression dropped. Everyone realized what he'd found.

"Oh, no," Rayner gasped and removed the camera. He swiftly disabled it and looked at Scorpio. "Whoever planted this here probably heard our phone call to the FBI. If it's Davenport, he's aware that they're coming."

"He's going to escape," Scorpio gasped.

"Call Deputy Gaines," Newman announced to Scorpio. "Have him check Davenport's house, see if he's still there, and tell him to keep an eye on him until the feds arrive." He then looked at the three men and pointed almost demandingly. "You three, come with me. We're going to check the doors and windows then search for any more spy cams."

Chapter 41

The official-looking, black SUV pulled up to the front of the hotel and parked near the other cars. Only the front porch light remained lit for the fed's arrival. Two men in standard, fed-issued black suits got out of the car and looked around as they approached the porch. Both men seemed to have matching haircuts and showed the same non-reaction to being called out at night.

"What's the history of this hotel?" the first agent asked while eying his partner.

"Only the rumors provided by the current owner," his partner replied. "Illegal parties thrown for the most corrupt men of wealth and power."

"Leaving behind a dozen or more skeletal remains in a basement pit," the first agent scoffed then shook his head. "Those must have been some parties."

"If we're lucky, forensics may find some evidence pointing to one of our favorite mob bosses," his partner commented while studying the old hotel as they approached.

"I think you're asking too much," the first agent remarked then eyed the building as well. "We're probably looking for a ninety-year-old Norman Bates."

"Go ahead and joke," the second agent remarked, "but if it's true they found the decades-old remains of J.R. there could be some pretty serious consequences for your Norman Bates.

J.R.'s sister was married to one of the most ruthless east coast crime bosses. If someone killed J.R. and tossed his body into a pit, there's going to be hell to pay even twenty years after the fact. With those boys; there's no statute of limitations on an eye-for-an-eye."

The sound of parting air was heard, startling both men who knew exactly what they were hearing. As they reached for their hidden weapons, the first agent watched his partner fall before his hand even reached his gun. The remaining man drew his weapon, crouched down, and looked around, although uncertain from which direction the shot came. The sound of parting air was barely heard as he took a bullet to his chest and collapsed not far from his partner.

§

Scorpio entered the grand hallway and looked around. The first floor seemed unusually quiet despite her friends supposedly roaming around somewhere. Her grandfather and friends were still off on their mission to secure the doors and seek out anymore hidden cameras. Scorpio heard the grandfather clock on the staircase landing chime ten o'clock in unison with the one within the locked front sitting room. She wondered what was taking the feds so long. Even though they may not consider a mass murder over two decades old a priority, she still thought they'd be at the hotel by now. She headed for the foyer and nearly collided with her grandfather as he came out of the lounge across the hall from the sitting room. Scorpio jumped with surprise and placed her hand on her chest.

"I'm sorry, honey," he announced and offered a mildly reassuring smile. "I didn't mean to scare you. You can relax now. The feds are here. I saw their car out front through the lounge window."

"Thank God," she announced and was about to continue for the foyer steps when her grandfather gently took her arm stopping her. She gave him a bewildered look.

"I know you're stubborn, and I realize you get that from me," he announced in a serious tone while searching her eyes, "but you can also be a little naïve and trusting. You get that from your grandmother." He drew a deep breath and frowned. "Please listen to me when I tell you, even beg you; don't trust Rayner."

She groaned and attempted to avoid the conversation. "I think you're worrying over nothing."

"Don't dismiss me so easily," he remarked as gently as possible. "I've been around. I know people. Your new friend works for Davenport. You told me Davenport paid for the security system that Rayner installed. How much more of a warning sign do you need?" He shook his head and frowned his disapproval. "The guy can't be trusted. I can almost guarantee you Davenport is on the other end of those cameras. You have to see the connection."

"I realize you think I'm too trusting," she replied while staring back at him. "But I'm not nearly as trusting as you think. I'm also not some helpless little girl. I can take care of myself."

"I know you can," he replied then hesitated, "but so could your brother. Being able to take care of yourself isn't always enough. It's who you surround yourself with that truly matters."

She fidgeted at the comment. What he said made perfect sense, and she knew she should listen to the words he had to offer. Her grandfather was betrayed by Davenport. He learned a hard lesson and didn't want her to trust the wrong people. Perhaps he was right, but she wasn't ready to give up on her friends just yet.

"Sorry," Newman announced delicately. "I didn't mean to upset you about your brother." He drew a deep breath and attempted to change the subject. "What did Deputy Gaines say?"

"I couldn't get ahold of him," she replied. "The sheriff is on duty tonight."

His eyes suddenly lifted with concern as he stared at her. "What did you tell him?" her grandfather asked. "He's a little protective of Davenport. I don't know that I trust him."

"Protective?" she cried out with humor then laughed. "That's putting it mildly. Davenport's been blackmailing him into doing his bidding."

"Blackmail?"

"It's a long story," she replied and waved him off. "I'll tell you all the sorted details another time. I need to greet the feds."

"I know Deputy Gaines' home phone number," her grandfather insisted. "You greet your feds, and I'll call Gaines at home."

"If you insist," she replied.

As Scorpio headed for the foyer, her grandfather hurried for the hall phone. Scorpio unlocked and opened the front door to see the fed's black SUV parked out front with the headlights on, which were practically blinding her. Since she didn't see them anywhere, they were obviously still within their vehicle. Were they talking or attempting to case the place in the dark? She clung to her chilled arms and stared at the vehicle a moment, expecting them to get out when they saw her, but the car doors didn't open, and the lights remained on. Scorpio stepped onto the porch and stared a moment longer. She considered approaching their vehicle, but something made her decide against it. She wasn't sure why she was getting such a concerning vibe at that moment, but something didn't feel right. Let them come to her. Someone grabbed her arm from behind, startling her. Scorpio spun around and saw her grandfather looking fearful.

"I don't think those are the feds," he insisted with concern. "Get back inside."

"What?" she practically gasped as he attempted to pull her back into the hotel.

"The phone line is dead. I don't think it's a coincidence," he announced and continued to pull her toward the door.

The sound of parting air immediately alerted them. Her grandfather shoved her into the hotel doorway, cried out, and bolted in behind her. He slammed the door shut and clutched his bleeding arm.

"Grandpa," she gasped while staring at the blood seeping between his fingers.

"Don't worry about me," he ordered and endured the pain. "Last time I saw Stone, he was in the kitchen. Find him." Before she could protest, he forced her to meet his gaze. His look was concerned and demanding. "Stay away from the windows and turn out the lights in the kitchen. If they see you, they can shoot you through the glass."

"Your arm--"

"We'll take care of that later," he insisted. "Close the doors to the other rooms, so they can't shoot through the windows. We're safer here in the grand hallway where they can't see us. I'll go upstairs and warn Maverick on the second floor."

"Where's Rayner?"

"He's on third," her grandfather reported. "If he's not involved, he's safe up there. You and Stone meet me back here in the grand hallway in ten minutes. Got it?"

She nodded and hurried down the hallway toward the kitchen, pausing to shut each open door along the way. Despite his bleeding arm, her grandfather hurried up the grand staircase for the second floor. For an older man, he was surprisingly athletic and in amazing shape.

§

Scorpio finally reached the eerily silent kitchen and looked around. To her surprise, Stone wasn't there. Her eyes then fell upon the open back door. She nervously looked around as her heart pounded. Stone wouldn't have gone outside, would he? Not under the circumstances. Did that mean someone got inside? She silently crossed the kitchen and removed the snub-nosed revolver hidden in the holster in the small of her back. She wasn't one for carrying guns, but after their call to the FBI, she decided to be prepared. She cautiously approached the back door and the back stairs. With the stairs being enclosed, anyone could be hiding on the steps waiting for her. She threw herself alongside the open back door and aimed the revolver up the stairs.

When she didn't see anyone on the stairs, she concentrated on the open door alongside her. The back lights were out, which meant Stone didn't go outside at least not willingly. She turned on all the outside lights with one flick of the many switches. The entire back patio lit up as well as the surrounding grounds. Scorpio crouched low and peered out the doorway with her gun aimed. With the lights on, she was able to see almost the entire rear hotel grounds. Everything was unusually quiet. She didn't see anyone, although that didn't mean they weren't out there. She feared she'd find Stone wounded or worse outside, but thankfully that wasn't the case. That still didn't explain where he was, why the door was open, or if someone was possibly already in the hotel.

She shut the door and swiftly locked it. It didn't take a genius to figure out that the door hadn't been broken down. All the locks still worked, and the frame hadn't been splintered, which meant either someone opened the door from the inside or someone on the outside had access. She stared at the alarm system on the wall and considered her options. Rayner had fixed the alarm after the last break-in, but how did the intruders get past his alarm in the first place? They would have had seconds to disarm the alarm before it went off, sending a call to the local sheriff's office. Something didn't add up.

She then realized that the same message was seen on the alarm, announcing it had been disarmed. Disarmed? She remembered Rayner telling her someone had disarmed the alarm remotely, but it had to be a malfunction since only she had access to that on her cell phone. Well, her and Rayner. Was it possible someone hacked the alarm and remotely disarmed it? She didn't want to entertain the other thought where her grandfather was right about Rayner. A chilling thought then occurred to her. Anyone with access to her cell phone could have control over the system as well, which meant anyone inside the hotel could have used her cell phone to disable the alarm remotely. Stone and Maverick again raised suspicion. Scorpio pressed the panic button on the alarm, which would immediately send a message to the sheriff's office, notifying them of trouble at the hotel. Even if Sheriff Horton was on Davenport's payroll, the call would be logged, and he'd have to respond.

To her surprise and possible horror, nothing happened. Scorpio stared at the alarm display. It didn't even indicate she'd manually set off the alarm. It had been disabled! Her thoughts were suddenly all over the place. Why didn't the alarm work? Rayner had fixed it. How could the intruders know to disarm the alarm? They'd need an inside source. Had her grandfather been right? Was Rayner the only common denominator regarding the failed alarm system? She didn't want to suspect Rayner, but she was suddenly alone and afraid. Trust was a luxury she no longer had.

"Stone," Scorpio softly called out while keeping her back to the wall and the gun in her hand. There was no response. "Stone?"

When he didn't answer the second time, she knew he wasn't within earshot of the kitchen. A few less pleasant thoughts crossed her mind as well, but she brushed them aside for the moment. She promised her grandfather she'd meet him and the others in the grand hallway in ten minutes, but she couldn't simply walk away without attempting to find Stone. Her grandfather said he left Stone in the kitchen, but several minutes had passed by the time he told her that. Stone could have headed upstairs, in which case, she'd run into her grandfather and Maverick while looking for Stone. She was a bit concerned about leaving the first floor unattended, but there were other entry points to the hotel, and they certainly couldn't cover them all. If intruders wanted in, they were coming in. Scorpio headed up the back stairs while keeping her gun securely in her hand and close to her body.

Chapter 42

Scorpio silently walked along the second floor hallway while keeping her back to the wall and the gun clutched in her hand close to her chest. She listened for sounds of her grandfather, Stone, or Maverick, but she didn't hear anything. The small hotel was still fairly large, but sound had a way of traveling. She should have heard something. The lack of sound frightened her more than her own imagination. A familiar floorboard creaked, alerting Scorpio to someone not far from the grand stairs. Scorpio hurried past the bedrooms with closed doors then hesitated before Stone's open bedroom door. Despite that the room was dark; she remained alert to possible intruders. She darted past the open doorway, threw her back against the opposite side, and felt inside the inner wall for the light switch.

When the bedroom light came on, she waited a second before leaping into the doorway while crouched halfway to the floor with her gun aimed. The room was empty. She heard the faint sound of a floorboard creaking near her. Scorpio spun while remaining in her crouched position and aimed the gun down the hall. Her grandfather jumped with surprise and immediately held his hands in the air.

"Jesus, Scorpio," he cried out. "It's just me. Put that thing away before you hurt someone!"

She lowered her gun and straightened while her grandfather relaxed and placed his bloodied hand to his chest.

"You nearly gave me a heart attack," he announced while breathing heavily.

A man appeared in the hallway behind her grandfather with a gun in his hand. She saw the man raise the gun, prepared to shoot her grandfather in the back.

"Down!" she shouted.

Her grandfather jumped with alarm and turned rather than duck. When he saw the man with the gun, he frantically waved his hands while stepping between her and the gunman.

"No, not her!"

Scorpio didn't have a clean shot or any shot. She was left stunned that her grandfather was prepared to take the bullet he thought was meant for her. When she heard a gun fire, her heart pounded with a fear she remembered all too well. Her grandfather suddenly tensed. The armed intruder stood frozen a moment, spit up blood, and collapsed to the floor at her grandfather's feet. Newman stared with shock at the dead man before him. Scorpio and her grandfather both looked further down the hall and saw Maverick standing in one of the bedroom doorways with his own semiautomatic.

Maverick lowered his weapon and eyed her grandfather with concern. "Are you okay?"

Newman stared at Maverick almost unable to answer and again placed his hand to his chest. "Maybe," Newman replied while clutching his shirt, bloodying it with his hand. "Ask me again when my heart starts back up."

Scorpio was relieved Maverick had stepped in when he did and saved her grandfather's life. She hurried to join them just down the hall knowing they could still be in danger.

"Stone wasn't in the kitchen, and the back door was open," she informed them while nervously looking around. "Someone tampered with the alarm."

Her grandfather's eyes narrowed as if silently reminding her what he'd said earlier. She ignored his look and took the dead man's gun containing a silencer. She handed her revolver to her grandfather. He stared with horror at the revolver she'd forced into his hand.

"You know I can't shoot worth a shit," Newman insisted. "I'm a worse shot than you are."

Maverick eyed Scorpio and raised his brows with a surprised look. "I hope that was a joke," he announced.

"God, she's an awful shot," her grandfather remarked while making a face.

"We need to find Stone and Rayner," Scorpio announced while ignoring the comments on her shooting skills. She was too concerned for her friends. "We don't know if there are more armed men in the house."

Maverick hurried past Scorpio while glaring at her. "Don't be shooting anyone too close to me, okay?" he boldly announced. "If I'm going to die, I'd prefer it wasn't you who killed me."

She sneered at him then followed him down the hall to the back stairs. Her grandfather hurried after her obviously still tense about the gun in his hand.

"Why don't we take the grand stairs to the third floor?" Newman asked. "They're closer."

"Because they're open and exposed," she informed him. "A shooter could pick us off from either floor. We'd be sitting ducks."

Her grandfather stared at her with some surprise as he hurried after them. "How do you know this stuff?" Newman asked.

"From hours and hours of horror movies Kane made me watch growing up," she replied without looking back at him.

§

Rayner removed the spy camera from alongside a framed picture on the bedside table inside Kane's room. The room had been moderately organized after whoever broke in had torn through it, but there was a large empty spot on the desk where the monitor used to be. Since it had been smashed, they removed it.   The computer tower had been stolen, so there were cords and wires scattered along the desk among the mildly dusty spot where it had once sat.   Rayner studied the spy cam a moment then eyed the framed picture of a black sports car on the nightstand.   Scorpio had mentioned her brother's love for his cherished Chevy Camaro.   As he stared at the picture of the car in a spot reserved for most men's love interest, something suddenly troubled him.   He picked up the framed photo and looked at the words scribbled in yellow permanent marker across the bottom of the picture.

"Midnight Ride," Rayner remarked softly to himself although aloud.   "Coincidence?"

He turned over the picture and removed the back.   There was a five by seven manila envelope behind the photo.   He heard an old floorboard creak near the bedroom.   Rayner put the frame back together and placed the photo back on the nightstand.   He turned toward the open doorway, uncertain who to expect, when he saw an intruder with a gun.   That the weapon contained a silencer was enough to convey he was a professional.   Rayner's expression suddenly dropped at the sight of the unfamiliar man with the intimidating weapon in his hand.   As the man aimed the gun at him, Rayner leaped for the door, throwing his body into it, and slammed it against the man.   The armed intruder was tossed into the hallway, and the gun flew from his hand.   Rayner hesitated, uncertain if he should lock himself in the bedroom or go for the discarded weapon.

The sound of footfalls on the back stairs was both a relief and concerning.   There was no telling who was on the steps and what would happen to them if they suddenly appeared in the hallway with the armed intruder.   As the fallen man scrambled across the floor for the gun, Rayner made his decision and leaped on top of him, tackling him the rest of the way to the floor.   The man punched Rayner several times.   The computer genius had limited fighting skills and could barely defend himself against the man's hard fists striking him in the ribs and then in the face.   Despite being punched several times, Rayner still attempted to keep him from reaching the gun.   His plan seemed to end there.   The man punched him in the mouth, sending him across the floor.

Once the man had successfully knocked Rayner off him, he leaped for the gun while moving to his knees and aimed it toward the stairs, preparing to ambush the first person he saw. Maverick appeared in the corridor from the back stairs and saw the man with the gun aimed at him. As the nearly silent shots were fired, Maverick leaped across the hall. Several shots splintered the wall where his head should have been. Scorpio held her ground just inside the stairwell then poked it out, catching the man's attention. As he turned toward her with the gun aimed, the sound of a shotgun being pumped echoed through the hallway with its terrifying sound.

Everyone including Rayner, who remained on the floor, looked down the hall in the direction of the main stairs and saw Stone holding the shotgun. He had fresh blood streaking the side of his face from a laceration on his temple, which only seemed to increase his bad disposition. The intruder was moderately stunned to see the man holding the shotgun and attempted to aim his weapon at Stone. Stone unloaded both barrels into the man, buckshot tearing into his chest and sending him airborne before striking the floor. Rayner covered his face as blood sprayed across him, the floor, and the wall. Scorpio let out a startled scream and had to turn away at the gruesomeness of the kill.

Stone immediately lowered the shotgun while maintaining his stern look. "There were four of them," he shouted down the hall. "I took a tumble with one of them down the basement steps. He broke my fall and his neck."

"I took one out on second," Maverick informed him. "So that leaves just one."

Stone pumped the shotgun then cracked his neck. "Time to clean house."

Scorpio hurried down the hall for Rayner while avoiding the mess left behind from the butchered man on the floor. Rayner remained sitting on the floor while staring at the bloodied remains of the intruder not far from him. He hadn't taken his eyes off the dead man and was possibly in shock. Scorpio extended her hand to Rayner, who had been spattered with the dead man's blood. He snapped out of his trance, eyed her, and then accepted her hand, allowing her to help him to his feet.

"You take front," Maverick announced to Stone. "I'll take back."

"Meet you on first," Stone growled.

Rayner, Scorpio, and Newman watched the men hurry down the hall in opposite directions. They were off on some covert mission like a couple of rogue mercenaries.

Her grandfather placed his hands on his hips while shooting looks after each man. "Who the hell are those guys?" he cried out.

"Damned if I know," Scorpio casually replied and raised her weapon. "I'm going to run interference for Stone on the staircase."

"You can't hit shit," her grandfather reminded her. "Maybe you should sit this one out."

"I don't need to hit shit," she replied. "I just need to get close enough to be a distraction."

"I'm uncomfortable with you--" her grandfather began, but she was already running for the grand stairs.

Rayner eyed Newman and indicated the gun in his hand. "If you aren't going to use that, I'll take it."

"Do you know how to shoot a gun?"

"I suppose we'll find out," Rayner replied.

Newman groaned with defeat and handed him the revolver. Rayner hurried after Scorpio.

§

The sheriff's cruiser with its blue and red lights flashing pulled up to the hotel alongside the fed's black SUV. Sheriff Horton got out of his vehicle, removed his flashlight, and approached the unfamiliar car with its headlights on. He paused before the driver's side and shined his light through the side window. The front was empty. He then shined his light into the back and saw the two federal agents lying in the back seat as if they'd been carelessly tossed on top of each other. The sheriff stared at the two dead men with a look of horror on his face.

"Oh, shit!"

He leaped backward, dropping the flashlight, and immediately drew his weapon. He scanned the area surrounding him with his gun aimed. When he didn't see anyone, he caught his breath, picked up the flashlight, and turned toward the hotel. He came face-to-face with Rico.

"Rico," he gasped with surprise but didn't aim his weapon. His eyes narrowed with bewilderment. "What are you doing here? What happened to the feds?"

"Did you remove all the evidence from the pit through the cave entrance?" Rico demanded showing little emotion.

"Yeah, the pit is empty," Sheriff Horton nervously informed him and again looked at the dead feds in the car behind him. "Is that what happened here? You initiated a bloodbath at the hotel as a diversion while I removed the evidence? That wasn't part of the deal."

"You have bigger problems. They're about two minutes away from discovering your involvement in everything," Rico announced with little emotion. "The boss is no longer in need of your services." Rico raised a semiautomatic containing a silencer and aimed it at the sheriff.

Sheriff Horton then saw the gun in Rico's hand. He was about to cry out a protest when Rico shot him twice in the chest. The sheriff fell against the SUV then slid down the driver's side door to the ground. Rico looked back at the hotel when he heard the front door open then hurried toward the woods alongside the driveway. Stone saw someone moving in the darkness and stepped onto the porch with the shotgun in his hands. He witnessed a man running into the woods and aimed his weapon, but it was too late. He cursed while lowering the shotgun. He didn't dare follow for fear of being ambushed. The last intruder had gotten away.

Chapter 43

Three days later. Deputy Gaines sat on the front porch with Scorpio, Maverick, and Stone. The four sipped iced tea on the warm, lazy afternoon. Since the murder of not only Sheriff Horton but also two federal agents, there hadn't been any peace in the last three days at the hotel or in town. The deputy had been particularly stressed with the added bonus of mourning the loss of their sheriff and having to fill his position temporarily. While the town screamed for answers, he helplessly had none to offer.

"I'm not sad to see the parade of medical examiners, cadaver dogs, and feds finally leaving our town," Deputy Gaines announced, seeming glad he could relax after everything that had happened. "It's been a rough week."

"It's only been three days," Scorpio corrected.

Deputy Gaines looked at her and tilted his head. "Really?" he asked seeming genuinely surprised. "Seems like a week to me. I can't believe Carson Davenport was behind this entire mess." The deputy's eyes widened dramatically. "And all the evidence you found on that flash drive linked to the current stuff like blackmail, prostitution, and corruption." He shook his head. "Blackmailing the sheriff into doing his dirty work for him is what really has me shocked."

"I can't believe he was blackmailing some of those heavy hitters for decades," Maverick interjected as he gently rocked in the porch chair. "With the corrupt backgrounds of some of those guys, you'd think one of them would have had him whacked a long time ago."

"And they still haven't found him?" Scorpio asked the deputy.

He shook his head. "Nope," Deputy Gaines replied. "Carson Davenport is officially MIA. Probably on a plane to some foreign country without extradition. I doubt we'll ever see him again."

"Rico had no trouble stepping into the role as commander-in-chief to Davenport's business affairs," Stone remarked and managed an uneasy laugh from where he sat on the porch railing. "I can't believe they didn't find one shred of evidence on him."

"My grandfather doesn't think we're in any danger from Rico," Scorpio informed the guys. "Rico got exactly what he wanted out of the deal, so he's quite happy with how things worked out."

"The dead men in your hotel aside," Deputy Gaines announced, "I can't believe the feds didn't find those bodies in the pit."

"More than a dozen skeletal remains just up and moved," Maverick muttered then shook his head. "Seems strange to sacrifice a bunch of lives just to remove some decades old bodies. I don't understand the significance."

"I'm guessing it had more to do with *who* the dead men were," Scorpio informed him then shook her head. "We know the off-season parties attracted a lot of heavy hitters. Davenport must have feared the families would come after him once their bodies were discovered."

"Maybe the bodies disappearing is for the best. There would have been some pretty pissed off mafia types buzzing around our sleepy, little town. That could have been bad for all of us." He then considered something else. "But since the bodies were removed, that has to mean Davenport killed those men himself," Deputy Gaines remarked then squinted with confusion. "Does that sound right?"

"As good an explanation as we're going to get," Scorpio replied then sighed. "I'm just relieved my grandfather was cleared of any wrongdoing. I was afraid Davenport would manage to drag him down with him on that one."

"It's a known fact around town that your family never stuck around for winter," Deputy Gaines remarked. "Well, not your grandparents. Your uncle stuck around for winters after he graduated college."

"Kane and I braved the winters after college too," Scorpio informed him. "Imagine living in Maine your entire life and not seeing snow until age eighteen."

"Yeah, rich people are messed up," Stone muttered then laughed when he received a glare from Scorpio.

Maverick eyed Deputy Gaines while raising a curious brow along with a strange smirk. "So are you officially the new sheriff?"

"Acting sheriff," Gaines replied. "We'll have to see if they make it permanent. After everything that's happened, I'm not sure I want the job." He stood and politely nodded to Scorpio. "Thanks for the iced tea and all your patience with the investigation. I appreciate that you didn't make me look foolish in front of the feds or the media."

"Trust me," Stone announced while hiding his smile. "None of us wanted any part of the feds and their investigation." He then muttered under his breath, "Or the media circus."

Deputy Gaines nodded politely then headed down the steps and to his police cruiser. As he drove away, Maverick's grin cheapened.

"Oh, the trouble we could get into in a town where Deputy Gaines is in charge--"

Scorpio cast a threatening glare at him. "You will behave," she announced sternly. "Don't think I won't throw you under the bus at the first sniff of a crime spree."

"I know," Maverick moaned while rolling his eyes. "You don't have to turn all motherly on us."

"We're not plotting anything," Stone remarked with a sincere tone she almost believed. "We have it good here.

We're treated with respect. It's a good gig, and we're starting to actually like you."

She gave Stone a look then smirked. She wasn't sure if she should be humored or offended by the comment. Rayner's car pulled up the driveway.

Maverick rolled his eyes and stood. "Speaking of lost, little lovesick puppies--"

"No one was speaking of them," Scorpio muttered while glaring at Maverick. "Be nice."

He groaned and pouted like a schoolboy. "Can't you send him packing already?" Maverick demanded while making a face. "You're never going to get rid of him if you don't shake him loose."

"Maybe I don't want to shake him loose," Scorpio insisted while glaring at her friend.

"So you want to sleep with him?" Maverick asked and appeared curious.

"I didn't say that."

"If you don't want to sleep with him, what's the point of keeping him around?" Maverick demanded.

"I don't want to sleep with you, and I keep you around," she scoffed.

Stone chuckled and held his fist to her. Scorpio smirked and bumped his fist with hers. Maverick wasn't humored by the comment or his friend's humor at it.

"That's different. Rayner is only really good with computers and annoying people," Maverick remarked.

"He doesn't annoy me," she corrected. "I like having him around."

"Until he fixes all the security cameras and door locks," Stone announced while grinning. "Then she can shake him loose."

"You're both horrible," she informed them.

"What about your grandfather's concerns?" Maverick remarked with genuine interest. "What if Rayner had a part in Davenport's scheme all along? How do we know he wasn't masterminding it all?"

"Be serious," Stone groaned. "The only thing Rayner is scheming is a way to get in Scorpio's pants."

She glared at him.

Stone caught her look, raised his brows, and smiled boyishly. "Excuse me," he announced seeming almost ashamed. "Get *back* into Scorpio's pants."

"If you two can't behave, maybe you should go play pool or fix lunch," she scoffed. "Anything. Just go."

Stone stood and joined Maverick. "I think you're right," Stone announced while eyeing his friend. "She does want to sleep with him."

Maverick nodded and headed into the house with Stone following. Rayner got out of his car with his briefcase and toolkit and approached the porch.

"What are the flying monkeys up to today?" Rayner asked while eyeing the door.

She snorted a laugh. "The usual."

"Oh," Rayner replied and smirked. "Tormenting me behind my back."

"Yeah, something like that," she replied then entered the hotel with him.

"You won't believe what a little fed told me," Rayner announced as they entered the foyer.

"What's that?"

"They found your brother's computer tower at Davenport's house," he announced cheerfully. "All the information is still on it. He didn't have time to find someone to wipe it clean, I suppose. He certainly couldn't ask me. Apparently, I'm meddlesome."

"Yes, that you are," she agreed and walked past him into the hallway.

Rayner hurried after her toward the office. "You can have it back after they've finished their investigation," he informed her.

"I'm not sure what I need it for," she insisted with little care. "We already sorted through all the information on it, right?"

"I searched the most important files," he informed her. "There could be something in some of the other files that seemed less important."

She turned to face him by the office doorway and cleverly raised her brows. "Is this some sort of devious plot to pad your bill?" Scorpio asked. "Or a desperate attempt to hang around?"

He considered the questions. "Yes," Rayner replied then grinned.

She laughed and entered the office with him following almost certainly like a lost, lovesick puppy. Rayner set his briefcase and toolkit on the desk and looked over the new system inside the armoire.

"Looks good," he announced. "I'll need a couple of hours to hook up everything."

"So you're staying for lunch?"

"I was anticipating staying straight through to dinner," he casually replied, hiding his grin from her.

Scorpio eyed him then laughed. She didn't care what Maverick and Stone said. She thought Rayner was entertaining.

Chapter 44

It took Rayner nearly an hour to hook up all the connecting wires and figure out what went wrong when some of the monitors didn't work properly. He finally removed his brand new laptop from his briefcase and attached it to the monitors. He punched in a code and hit enter. As the computer flashed several screens, he stepped back to watch a moment then finally turned to face Scorpio, who remained comfortably seated behind the desk while watching him. She wore a tiny smile on her face. Scorpio enjoyed watching Rayner work. His genius with computers entertained her. Kane was quite the computer geek himself. However, there were many profanities used when he attempted to accomplish tasks. Rayner just seemed to know what he was doing and did it. He noticed the way she watched him and seemed pleased by it, which made Scorpio self-conscious about the way she had been staring. She immediately fidgeted and attempted to seem less interested.

"That's going to take an hour or longer to transfer the data to the new system," he informed her.

"Then that's lunch, I guess," she announced and was about to stand when he stopped her.

"There's something I wanted to discuss with you but didn't have the chance the last few days, you know, with everything going on around here," Rayner informed her.

She stared at him a moment and felt a slight pang. She didn't know what he was going to say, but she was almost certain he intended to blindside her with something she wasn't ready to answer.

"Okay," she announced with some concern.

Rayner shut the office door and returned to his briefcase. She watched him a moment with some confusion. Now she wasn't sure what he was up to. He removed a five by seven manila envelope from his briefcase and gave her a serious look as he sat on the edge of the desk.

"You know that car picture on your brother's nightstand?" he asked.

"You mean the framed eight by ten glossy photo of his black 1967 Chevy Camaro 396 Big Block muscle car?" she teased then laughed.

"Yeah, that one," Rayner replied while giving her a strange look not getting the joke.

"I vaguely recall that photo," she remarked with humor.

"On the photo were the words 'Midnight Ride'," Rayner informed her.

She gave him a curious look. "I knew there was something written on the photo," she admitted, "but I didn't remember the exact words."

"Yeah, his handwriting pretty much sucks," Rayner remarked. "Midnight Ride stuck in my head, so I took the back off the frame." He drew a deep breath and handed her the envelope. "I found this hidden inside."

Scorpio uncertainly accepted the envelope and anxiously opened it. She removed a red greeting card envelope and saw her mother's name neatly printed on it. Scorpio tensed, eyed Rayner, and then removed the greeting card from the envelope. It was a sappy love card with red roses on the front. She opened the card, and a note fell out. The card was signed 'I love you' with a heart drawn with an entangled tail, but there was no name. She picked up the folded paper and carefully opened it. The letter was also written in neat print, obviously written carefully and with great thought.

"My dearest Maggie," Scorpio read softly aloud. "My past has finally caught up with me, and I regret doing this in a letter. I know you won't approve, but I must confront my demons for us to live a life free from those who wish me, and possibly us, harm. I've accepted one last mission in order to balance the books. If I'm successful, we'll never have to worry about looking over our shoulders ever again. I can't risk your life because of my past. I will make this right; I promise. My last mission, Midnight Requisition, will make everything right. If anything happens, please know that I will always love you. Love always." Scorpio drew a deep breath and looked at Rayner while indicating the note. "Signed only with a heart like the card."

"He was careful not to put his name on much," Rayner remarked.

"So Midnight Requisition was some secret military mission," Scorpio announced with a bit of confusion. "The one that got my father killed, I assume."

"Sounds that way," Rayner replied while studying her. "Are you okay?"

She looked at him with some surprise. "Yeah, sure," Scorpio announced. "Why wouldn't I be?"

He shrugged while shifting uncomfortably. "Your father's last words to your mother," Rayner replied. "I guess I thought it would bother you a little."

"I didn't know my father," she informed him. "I only knew my mother through photos and stories from my grandparents. I'm not Kane. I don't let these things eat me up inside like he did."

She handed him the card with the note. As he accepted it, she saw him shift a photo within the envelope. "What's that?" Scorpio suddenly demanded.

"Oh, it's just a photo," he replied. "I didn't think you'd want to see it."

She held her hand out with an annoyed look on her face. He removed the photo and handed it to her while frowning. She looked at the photo obviously printed on a computer printer. It was a picture of Kane sitting against their mother's headstone. He'd taken the picture himself with his cell phone using a selfie stick. Scorpio made a face and extended the photo to him.

"As you probably guessed, Kane was a slightly disturbed person," she remarked. "We used to visit her grave once a month when we were younger. We'd put flowers on it and sometimes drawings we'd colored for her. By the time I was fourteen or fifteen, I stopped going. I didn't see the point. Kane would still go. He'd sometimes send me pictures of him with 'our mother'. I suppose he was trying to guilt me into going with him."

Rayner hesitated then looked at the picture again. His brows suddenly knitted. "Huh?" he announced, catching her attention.

"What?"

"Just the same heart from the letter," Rayner announced and shook his head. "I guess your grandparents knew it was symbolic and had it added to her headstone."

Scorpio gave him a strange look and removed the picture from him. She studied it more closely. At the bottom of the headstone was an elegantly carved heart. Although it looked professional, it was obviously hand etched. She removed the letter and compared the two hearts. They each contained the same entangled tail at the bottom. Her eyes met Rayner's.

"That heart wasn't there before," she insisted.

"Are you sure?"

"I visited her grave every month for years," she informed him. "I'm telling you; that heart wasn't there."

"Do you think Kane carved it into the headstone?" Rayner asked.

"You never know," she replied although unconvinced then shook her head while staring into his eyes. "Kane put this picture in with the letter from my father to my mother. Was it a romantic gesture? Or did he put this photo in here to acknowledge the newly added heart?"

"Newly added by who?" Rayner asked.

"What if Kane was right," she announced while staring at him. "What if my father never actually died?"

Rayner stiffened while returning the stare. "Then your brother would probably go to Virginia," he announced. "Where people knew his father so he could search for answers."

"What if Kane's death had nothing to do with this whole Davenport business?" Scorpio demanded. "What if Kane went to Virginia and poked around about Midnight Requisition? We know it's a top secret something or other. My father's last mission. The mission that was supposed to put his past behind him once and for all. If Kane ran into the wrong people, that could be what got him killed."

"Midnight Requisition?"

"Yes."

"Before you get any crazy ideas about going to Virginia to follow in your brother's footsteps," Rayner announced, "maybe I can poke around a little with my laptop and find out more about this mission."

"I'd be eternally grateful."

He eyed her with a curious look and immediately raised his brows. "How grateful?"

She frowned her irritation. "Not that grateful."

"I was thinking apple pie grateful," he announced. "Get your mind out of the gutter."

Scorpio managed a laugh. "I think I can manage that," she teased.

§

Maverick and Stone appeared bored while standing before the kitchen door with Scorpio while Rayner showed them how to set the new alarm system.

"Yeah, we get it," Maverick muttered. "It works just like the old one. Can we go now?"

"Go?" Scorpio asked with surprise. "I thought we were having dinner together."

"Our first night of freedom," Stone announced and grinned. "We thought we'd have dinner at the tavern and then hustle locals at pool for a few hours."

"You could have told me before I thawed out all that chicken for dinner," she insisted.

"We didn't decide we were going out until Rayner said he'd have the new system working tonight," Stone informed her. "We didn't want to leave until we were sure it was up and running."

"Maybe even running properly," Maverick muttered catching a glare from Rayner.

"I'm telling you," Rayner snarled. "There was nothing wrong with the old system. Davenport somehow managed to bypass it."

"I thought you were a genius," Maverick demanded. "How does something like that happen to your self-proclaimed perfect system?"

"I don't know," Rayner snapped back. "He had access to my cell phone after he conked me on the head. You remember? Right before he tried to kill me. He could have wielded his way around and transferred remote access to his own computer or cell phone. It's not like pressing a button, but a smart person can figure it out."

"Okay," Scorpio blurted out. "Let's not fight about this." She groaned and eyed her friends. "Next time give me a head's up on dinner."

"You and the boy wonder are welcome to join us," Maverick informed her.

"Thanks, but no thanks," she replied. "Trudy is getting in late, and I'll need to be available to let her in. Her key and code no longer work, and I promised her she could stay here. She gets along better with her parents when they're not under the same roof during her visits."

Maverick suddenly became interested. "Trudy's coming for a visit?"

Stone placed his hand on Maverick's shoulder and held him back. "No, we're going out tonight," he insisted. "We've been cooped up for too long now. You can woo Trudy all weekend."

"I'm not wooing her," he insisted, sounding almost offended by the comment. "She just has this fantastic gift for making everything sound sexual."

"I think that's more in your interpretation that makes things sound sexual," Scorpio informed him, "but don't let me ruin your fantasy."

"Yeah, too late," Maverick muttered.

Scorpio watched both men leave through the back kitchen door then turned to face Rayner with a stern, serious look. "They hate my cooking, don't they?"

Rayner managed a weak smile. "That's subjective," he gently replied.

She stared at him with horror. "Oh, my God! You hate my cooking too!"

"I didn't say that," he announced defensively then grimaced. "It's just, well, if the poor bird had to die for our dinner, it deserves a little more respect."

She stared at him a moment as her eyes narrowed. "That's in poor taste."

"That's the point I was trying to make."

Scorpio suddenly gasped at the insult. "And after I made you apple pie."

Rayner gently cleared his throat and shifted uncomfortably. "Stone admitted he made the pie."

She frowned and pouted. "I can't help it if I was never good in the kitchen," Scorpio remarked. "Kane was practically a chef at five years old. I couldn't get out from under his cooking shadow."

"Why don't I show you how to make a tasty chicken dinner?"

"You cook too?" she practically demanded.

"It prevents starvation," he replied.

"I must be the only person on the planet who can't cook," she muttered.

Chapter 45

Scorpio and Rayner sat on a blanket spread out on the game room floor while sipping wine and watching a movie on the large screen television. Their empty dinner plates were behind them on the coffee table and wouldn't make it to the kitchen until after the movie.

"That was a great meal," Scorpio announced. "If I knew that sandwich press worked that good, I would have used it before."

"It's an indoor grill," he informed her.

"Kane bought it," she remarked and shrugged to the comment. "He did most of the cooking when he lived here. I wasn't allowed in the kitchen. Cal used to tell me to let Kane earn his keep." She suddenly frowned. "I suppose he hated my cooking too."

"No one expects you to be good at everything," Rayner teased.

She frowned and was no longer interested in the movie. "Everyone has something they're good at, I suppose," she remarked while drifting off into her own thoughts.

He studied her expression and appeared curious. "You haven't found your niche?"

She laughed at the question while fidgeting. "My talents are the useless kind," Scorpio replied. "I was pretty good at gymnastics and even better at climbing. I have great balance and freakishly amazing hearing." She sighed then frowned. "I wanted to be a cheerleader in school, but my dancing skills lacked." She forced a smile then laughed. "But I was a superstar with a baton, so I got to be a majorette."

"Oh," he announced then grimaced. "The cheerleader's sad cousin."

"Yeah," she muttered. "My life has always drifted that way. Wanting to be a cheerleader but ending up a majorette. Wanting to date a football player but going to the prom with the lead trumpet player." She drifted off into her own world. "When Cal came along, I finally thought I had it all. All the women in town wanted him, but he wanted me. My dream of restoring this old place was finally becoming a reality." She eyed him and smiled slyly. "And the best part? My 'better than me at everything' brother was going to be working for me."

"You still have the hotel," he remarked in an attempt to cheer her up.

"After everything that's happened here," she announced while looking around, "this place is tainted. Davenport ruined the hotel for me."

"You don't have to let him win," Rayner informed her. "This hotel can still be everything you wanted it to be. Maverick and Stone aren't Cal and Kane, but they're devoted little parasites."

She managed a tiny smile at the comment. "I appreciate what you're trying to do, Rayner, but I don't know that I'll ever feel the same way about this place again."

He shifted uncomfortably catching her attention.

She eyed him with a curious look. "Something on your mind?"

"Maybe you can't move on, because you're unwilling to let go of the past," Rayner remarked.

"Meaning what?" Scorpio asked and immediately became suspicious of the comment. "You think I need to start dating again?"

"No, I didn't say that," Rayner replied then shook his head. "You seem to think I have only one thing on my mind. You're obsessing over our one-time indiscretion. You need to let that go."

"That's because I know it's always in the back of your mind," she informed him. "It's hard for me to move on when I know you're living in that moment every time we're together."

He stared at her a moment and appeared puzzled. "You know," he announced. "I never bring that up, but you bring it up a lot. Seems like you're the one living in that moment. You're the one unable to let it go."

She shifted uncomfortably as the image again played out in her mind. He wasn't wrong, but despite what he said, she knew he was thinking it too. He had to be.

"I know you don't want to hear it," he announced, "but you're never going to fully heal until you open that front sitting room and stop treating it like a shrine."

"Why does everyone assume I'm treating that room like a shrine?" she practically demanded.

"Because it's been locked since the forensic clean-up crew left," he insisted. "Maverick told me about your obsession with that room remaining locked and sealed. No one shall enter, and all that crap. It's not healthy."

"God, you sound like my grandfather," she moaned then glared at him. "It's not a shrine to my dead boyfriend. Think of it as therapy."

"Therapy?" he asked with surprise. "Locking away bad memories isn't part of any therapy I know."

"You don't understand," she huffed.

"So make me understand."

Scorpio groaned and ran her fingers through her hair before finally looking at him. "Imagine hate and anger as a monster," she announced. "That room is its cage."

"So you're locking away hate and anger?"

"Pretty much," she replied. "If I go into that room, I'm going to feel hate and anger." She hesitated and held her breath. "I sometimes resent Cal for dying. That entire night plays out in my mind on an endless loop of fear, pain, hate, and anger. By keeping the door locked, I can keep the monster at bay." She shifted uncomfortably and met his gaze with a strange but serious look. "If I open that door, my monster might escape."

"I understand," Rayner gently replied then shook his head. "But eventually you'll need to face that monster and learn to control those feelings."

"Eventually isn't today," she informed him.

"When is eventually?"

"When and if that day comes; I'll know it," Scorpio insisted and straightened proudly. "Until then, the door will stay locked."

Rayner nodded. "I get it," he replied. "You'll know when you're ready." He then smiled. "Me; I'm ready for apple pie."

He stood and collected the dirty dishes from the coffee table. Scorpio was about to stand when he stopped her and offered a tender smile.

"I'll get it," he announced.

"Are you sure?"

He nodded cheerfully then left the room. Scorpio sat on the floor and stared at the television although she didn't watch the movie. She finally got up and left the game room. Instead of heading for the kitchen, she approached the front sitting room. Scorpio stared at the closed door a long moment. She drew a deep breath and reached for the doorknob. As she looked down at her hand, she saw it was covered in blood. Scorpio pulled her hand back, clutched it a moment, and then looked at it. She knew the blood was all in her mind. Haunting words from the past chilled her as she listened to the last words she and Cal had ever spoken. She shivered a moment then headed down the hall for the kitchen.

Scorpio entered the kitchen as Rayner was adding a scoop of ice cream to each slice of pie. He glanced up as she approached and offered a smile.

"I said I'd bring it to you," he announced.

Her expression didn't change as she approached him behind the island counter. Her look puzzled him.

"Is everything okay?" he asked.

Scorpio didn't respond. She placed her hands firmly on his face and kissed him passionately and with aggression. Rayner immediately grabbed her around the waist and pulled her against him while eagerly returning the kiss. As she broke off the kiss, he met her gaze while grinning almost boyishly.

"You don't know how relieved I am that you made the first move," he announced while releasing a tiny laugh. "There's absolutely no pressure--"

She kissed him again, silencing him. As he returned the kiss, she ran her hands firmly along his body. He responded by eagerly doing the same, although his hands lovingly caressed her while she practically pawed at him. He had a difficult time keeping up with her aggression. Rayner finally broke off the kiss while panting heavily with anticipation.

"Perhaps we should go upstairs--"

There was a knock on the kitchen door startling both. Rayner jumped away from Scorpio as if he'd been caught doing something reprehensible. Scorpio fidgeted while running trembling fingers through her hair.

"That's probably Trudy," she announced and avoided looking at Rayner as she approached the door.

"She has great timing," Rayner muttered and practically collapsed on the island counter with a groan.

§

Scorpio and Trudy sat on the floor eating apple pie and laughing at the movie. Rayner sat on the opposite side of the blanket casting looks at Scorpio. He seemed preoccupied and hadn't even touched his apple pie with melted ice cream on it. When the movie ended, Scorpio turned to collect his plate and gave him a bewildered look.

"You didn't touch your pie," she announced then grinned teasingly. "You do remember I didn't bake it."

"Yeah, I, uh, just wasn't hungry," he replied then tensed slightly. "I should probably head home. It's getting late, and I'm sure you two have some catching up to do."

"Actually," Trudy announced, "it's been a long day, and I'm exhausted." She collected her dirty plate and looked at Scorpio who also stood. "Am I booked in my usual, ocean view room?"

"Yeah, right next to Maverick," Scorpio announced then gently cleared her throat. "You may want to lock your door in case Maverick decides to take up sleepwalking. Unless you want him accidentally showing up in your bed."

Trudy considered the comment then grinned. "I could do worse," she announced then frowned. "Come to think of it, I have." Trudy laughed then smiled at Rayner. "It was nice seeing you again, Rayner."

As Trudy left the game room, Rayner again fidgeted. "I'll, uh, clean up the few dishes before I go, if you're tired--"

"It's late, Rayner," she informed him. "You don't have to drive back home if you don't want to. You're more than welcome to stay."

Rayner stared at her a moment and appeared to have something on his mind. Scorpio was relieved when he chose to keep it to himself. He offered a tiny smile.

"Yeah, it is late," he replied. "I'll get to the dishes in the morning." A grin crossed his face. "I can show you how to make a killer omelet."

"You can make a killer omelet," she announced while raising a brow. "I'll be satisfied eating it."

§

In the middle of the night, Scorpio tossed beneath the covers on her bed, rolled onto her back, and stared at the ceiling fan lazily spinning. She tried falling asleep to one of her most stimulating sexual fantasies with Cal, but her drunken fling with Rayner kept creeping back into her mind. She almost hated him for ruining her fondest sexual memories even though it wasn't his fault. She didn't want to admit it, but she enjoyed the way Rayner attempted to slow her down. Given the chance, she didn't doubt he'd make one hell of a lover. Scorpio nuzzled the pillow then immediately cursed herself for allowing Rayner again to enter her thoughts. She couldn't believe she kissed him like that in the kitchen. She couldn't believe how incredibly great it felt. Her body ached. What was that feeling? That's right. That's how it felt to be alive.

She tossed the covers off her and got out of bed, although she didn't know what to do once she stood in the dimly lit room. Scorpio paced the room a moment. Her thoughts again strayed to the scene in the kitchen. Shortly after, they strayed to Kane's bedroom and the way Rayner's hands caressed her body. She could almost feel his hands on her bare skin, and it was making her insane. She paced for a moment longer and decided a hot bath was all she needed. She entered the bathroom, removed her scented candles from the window ledge, and placed them along the broad edge of the tub. As she lit the candles, many erotic memories of her and Cal in the tub flooded her mind. She reached for the hot water lever and hesitated. Her thoughts returned to Rayner caressing her body during their drunken escapade.

Scorpio groaned and straightened near the tub. She cursed under her breath then eyed the large standing shower. What she needed more was a cold shower. If it worked for men, why wouldn't it work for her? She took a step toward the shower then eyed the partially open connector door to Rayner's room. She'd almost forgotten he was in there. She approached the door to close and lock it then hesitated as her hand touched the knob. She gently pushed the door open just enough to peer into the dimly lit bedroom. When she saw Rayner sitting up in bed with the glow of his laptop lighting his face, she shouldn't have been surprised. He glanced up when he saw the door move.

"Couldn't sleep either?" Rayner asked while offering a weary grin.

Scorpio stared at him a moment within the glow of the computer screen. Rayner wasn't the ruggedly handsome, powerhouse of a man Cal was, but he had an almost innocent, boy-next-door appeal about him. In one sweeping eyeful, her heart seemingly skipped a beat, and she was immediately reminded of their night together. She cursed herself for thinking such thoughts and leaned her back against the doorframe with her hands behind her. Scorpio instantly realized she was subconsciously posing somewhat seductively and immediately straightened.

"I, uh, no," she replied while attempting to erase all the devious thoughts from her mind. "I couldn't sleep either. I thought I'd take a shower."

"Thanks for the warning," he teased while grinning.

She stared at him a moment longer then drew a deep breath and turned toward the bathroom with her hand on the doorknob. Scorpio felt her heart pounding as she pushed the door open a little further rather than closing it. She took a deep breath as she headed into the candlelit bathroom and opened the frosted glass shower door. She turned on the hot water then heard the door creak. Her heart was pounding as she looked back. Rayner stood on the other side of the open doorway and fidgeted slightly.

"You, uh, forgot to close the door," he gently announced without taking his eyes off her.

She turned back to the shower and removed her sleep tank top to expose her naked upper body. "No, I didn't."

Scorpio refused to look back as she tossed her top aside and slipped out of her sleep shorts. Without a word, she stepped into the shower and closed the door behind her. Scorpio stood beneath the hot spray of water facing the showerhead and allowed the water to saturate her body. She shut her eyes and held her breath as she heard the shower door open. She refused to turn around. Rayner's arms warmly slipped around her as he pressed against her from behind. She longed for the way his body felt against hers. Despite her pounding heart, she felt relief. Scorpio placed her hands on his as he caressed her abdomen. She resisted her sexual aggression, forcing him to make each move in his own time, allowing him the chance to slowly caress her body the way he wanted to.

Chapter 46

Scorpio woke the following morning to sunlight attempting to flood her bedroom. She stirred in Rayner's arms as he held her close to him while they slept. Admittedly, Scorpio didn't get much sleep, and she couldn't even blame Rayner. Once she succumb to the temptation and Rayner accepted her offer, she felt a sudden release of pent up sexual frustration. Each time she rolled over and saw him there, she couldn't resist pawing at him like some nymphomaniac. Each time, he eagerly gave in to her every whim. She watched him while he slept despite the sunlight flooding the room. She knew she'd exhausted him with her sexual cravings.

As she watched him sleep, something stirred inside her. This time, it wasn't her animalistic desires. She smiled and gently touched his face. He woke, nuzzled her, and smiled despite his weariness.

"If we're going for another round, I'd like to take a quick shower first," he announced almost too pleasantly considering how she'd tortured him last night. "You could join me. I'll wash your back."

She cupped his face in her hand and kissed him with warmth and tenderness. He attempted to prolong the kiss, but she managed to pull away. He stared at her with a tiny smile on his face.

"So was that yes to the shower?" he teased.

Scorpio held her breath and sat up in bed while holding the sheets to her naked body. She ran her fingers through her hair and avoided looking at him. Rayner studied her a moment then groaned and sat up.

"Oh, that's not good," he muttered and scratched his head through his mussed hair. Rayner sighed deeply. "Let me have it. I can take it."

"I don't want you to get the wrong idea about last night," she announced and was unable to look at him.

"It's a little late for that," he remarked with a chuckle. "You can't return something after you've worn it out. Six times, to be precise."

"Five," she corrected and cast a look at him.

"I'm counting that little thing you did in your sleep," he insisted.

She groaned and placed her hand to her head. "Fine," she retorted. "Six."

He held his breath a moment while staring at her. "So what are you not saying here?" he finally asked. "Are you kicking me to the curb?"

She drew a deep breath then sighed and finally turned to face him. "You want sex, right?"

"A bit of a loaded question, but I'll play along," he remarked and placed his hands insecurely across his sheet-covered lap. "Yes, I want to have sex with you."

"I love Cal," she informed him with little emotion. "Just because he's gone, that doesn't change anything. I don't want to replace him."

The way he watched her told her what was going through his head. She stared at him a moment and held her breath before continuing.

"If you want to be friends, I'm okay with that," Scorpio announced. "If you want to be friends with benefits, I'll also agree to that, because quite frankly, celibacy sucks." She stared at him while raising her brows. "If you want a relationship beyond that, it's not happening."

There was a tense moment as they stared at each other without comment. Rayner finally drew a deep breath and seemed compelled to respond.

"I can make friends with benefits work, although it's not exactly what I had in mind," he informed her.

"That's all I can offer for now."

"So I can stay?" he hesitantly asked while raising a curious brow.

"I didn't say no to that shower," she replied.

Rayner grinned. "And we're back to a good morning," he teased.

§

Rayner and Scorpio entered the kitchen through the main door. Stone, Maverick, and Trudy sat at the island counter and looked up as they entered. Both men began applauding them while Trudy hid her smile and had to look away. Scorpio rolled her eyes and ignored them while Rayner appeared instantly embarrassed.

"Pulled an all-nighter, huh?" Maverick teased and playfully punched Rayner in the arm. "Respect, man."

Stone chuckled and shook his head at Scorpio. "The words coming out of your mouth, girl," he announced. "Listening through the walls was better than watching porn."

"Are you kidding?" Maverick teased. "I had to turn on porn just to drown them out."

"All right," Scorpio groaned and walked past Trudy to the coffeepot.

Trudy leaned back as she passed and muttered, "I want all the erotic details."

"Enough with the wise remarks, all of you," Scorpio scoffed. "We have some actual work to do today."

Both men stood but couldn't stop grinning. Trudy's sly smile didn't help any either. Stone considered something then paused and looked back at Scorpio.

"Oh, your grandmother called about twenty minutes ago," Stone informed her. "She wanted you to call her back when you had a chance."

"Is everything okay?"

"She sounded okay."

"Oh, that's right," Scorpio announced then nodded with understanding. "My grandfather is spending the day at the country club at some annual golf tournament, so she's probably bored." She glanced at Trudy. "What time are you going to your parents' house? I'll call her back after you leave."

"Actually, I'm leaving right after breakfast," Trudy informed her. "I got a strange phone call from my mother this morning."

"Oh?" Scorpio asked after taking a sip of coffee. "Something interesting happen?"

"You could say that," Trudy remarked. "Her friend, who does some gardening work at Davenport's mansion, said a strange man showed up early this morning while she was working. Shortly after he left, Celine got into a terrible fight with Rico. My mother's friend couldn't hear most of what they were saying, but Celine told Rico he had to move out of the mansion by the end of the week. She then packed a bag and left for the beach house."

"Disagreement on how to run Davenport's affairs?" Rayner offered.

Maverick snorted a laugh and mocked Rayner. "More like troubles with their own affair."

"I highly doubt that," Rayner informed Maverick. "Celine is into wealthy, sophisticated men. Rico is nothing more than eye candy with a bad disposition. She'd never get involved with someone like him."

"I'm going to agree with Rayner on that one," Trudy replied. "Rico has a superiority complex and is abusive toward women. Celine wouldn't let him treat her the way he treated Amber."

"Which is probably why she threw him out," Stone added. "I wouldn't doubt there was a lot of tension between them after Davenport took off."

"That being said," Trudy announced, "my mother's friend is convinced Celine was having an affair with someone. Strange that this guy shows up at the mansion out of the blue after Davenport is out of the picture. He may be the one she's been seeing on the side." She sank into thought. "I just wish we knew who he was."

"Time will tell," Scorpio informed her with little interest. "I'm sure she'll be spending more time with this mystery man once the dust settles."

"You mean once she officially has her hands on Davenport's estate," Maverick teased.

Scorpio gave him an oddly innocent look. "Isn't that what I said?"

§

Scorpio collapsed behind the desk in the office with the cordless phone in her hand, propped her feet up, and dialed her grandmother's phone number. She decided to make herself comfortable since she was in for a long conversation. Anytime her grandmother was left alone, she would call Scorpio for one of their 'marathon talks'. She was certain her grandmother heard some good gossip recently too, with everything going on in their town. Undoubtedly, Deputy Gaines would be at the top of the gossip grapevine. Maybe she even had some insight into the mysterious man who showed up at Davenport's mansion. When her grandmother answered the phone, Scorpio smiled even though the older woman couldn't see it.

"Hey, Grandma," she announced cheerfully into the phone. "Today's the golf tournament, huh? Are you a golf widow for the day?"

"Oh, Scorpio," her grandmother practically gasped into the phone. "You wouldn't believe the phone call I had this morning."

Scorpio's feet hit the floor, and she sat forward in her chair. "What sort of phone call?" she practically demanded. "The good kind or the bad kind?"

"I'm not entirely sure," Patricia remarked from the other end. "This man called and left a message on the machine. He said he was a private detective investigating Kane's murder. Honestly, I have no idea what he was rambling about. He wanted to come here and talk to your grandfather and me this evening. He said something about not being able to get ahold of Carson Davenport." There was a strange pause. "I didn't call him back, because I don't know what he's talking about. Do you?"

"He must be one of the detectives Davenport supposedly hired to investigate Kane's death," Scorpio informed her then shook her head. "Honestly, I thought all that talk was bullshit, but maybe he actually did hire private detectives for some strange reason."

"I suppose it's possible he had nothing to do with your brother's death," her grandmother remarked. "Since he knew that for a fact, he probably wanted to find out who did, so he wouldn't be suspected."

"What's his number?" Scorpio asked. "I'll call him back for you."

"It's on the machine," she replied. "You know I don't know how to work that thing."

"So how do you know he called?"

"The phone rang while I was home," her grandmother replied. "I didn't recognize the area code, so I didn't pick it up. I heard the message while he was leaving it, but I didn't know that I should talk to him without talking to you or your grandfather first. I really don't want to be here alone with some stranger."

"Okay," Scorpio announced and sighed. "I'll come over and get the guy's number from the machine. We'll call him and see what this is about. You won't be alone with him, I promise."

"Can't you check the messages through your phone?" Patricia asked. "Your grandfather always checks it from his phone."

"No, Grandma," she replied. "I don't have access to your answering machine. I haven't even figured out how to do that with my own answering machine." Scorpio suddenly hesitated and straightened in her chair. "What did the man say about Davenport?"

"I don't really remember the details," her grandmother replied. "Just that he had called there and didn't get ahold of him." Patricia snorted a laugh. "No kidding. Some detective. Doesn't even know his client is wanted for murder and running from the law."

Scorpio remained preoccupied then suddenly perked up. "Grandma, make sure all the doors and windows are locked," she announced with concern. "I'm coming over there. I want you to stay with me until Grandpa gets back tonight."

"Stay with you?" she asked. "Why?"

"There's no telling what Rico will do with the private investigator's information," Scorpio insisted. "I'd rather you weren't alone right now."

"Well, okay," Patricia replied with some hesitance, "but your grandfather isn't getting home until late, so I'll probably need to spend the night at your place. I'll throw a bag together. Is it cooler up there?"

"Grandma," Scorpio announced firmly. "Check the doors and windows first. We'll worry about an overnight bag when I get there."

"Yes, dear," she replied. "I'll see you in thirty minutes or so."

"More like ten minutes," she insisted. "I'm heading over now."

Chapter 47

Patricia locked the front door then walked down the hallway of the Wayland mansion-like home. She entered the study and checked the French doors, which were already locked, and then headed to the next room over. The French doors in the dining room were also locked. She returned to the hallway and headed toward the kitchen. She crossed the large, elegant kitchen and locked the back door then approached the back stairs while talking to herself.

"I'm probably going to need a sweater," she announced as she headed up the stairs. "That old place is always a little on the drafty side. My nightgown and housecoat." Patricia then sank into thought as she walked up the steps. "What on earth did I do with that travel bag?" She paused at the top of the steps and hesitated a moment. "That's right. Kane borrowed it because his old one was too small." It then occurred to her. "I'll just use his."

Patricia opened the bedroom door closest to the back stairs and entered Kane's childhood bedroom. The room hadn't been touched since Kane had left for college. It still resembled a teenage boy's bedroom with posters of girls in bikinis, except the scantily dressed women were leaning against muscle cars. She opened the closet door and immediately spotted the smaller travel bag in front. When she removed the bag, she saw a shoebox on the floor neatly placed among other shoeboxes. The tiny picture of women's dress shoes on the end of the box caught her attention. She squinted at the strange box that seemed out of place and immediately appeared curious. What was Kane doing with a woman's shoebox? She was about to reach for the box when she heard a floorboard creak somewhere in the house.

Despite the house settling throughout the years, Patricia was familiar with all of its particular creaks. This one was from a floorboard that only creaked when someone stepped on it. Although Scorpio had a key to her grandmother's home from when she lived there, it would be impossible for her to be at the house already. The golf tournament had just started, so Newman would only be on the front nine. He certainly wouldn't be home so early. Patricia tensed and heard another creak, confirming there was someone in the house. For a moment, the older woman was unable to move. She glanced into the closet and saw Kane's old baseball bat. She grabbed the bat.

Another floorboard creaked now closer. Patricia held back her gasp, stepped inside the closet, and quietly closed the louver doors behind her. She clung to the baseball bat holding it the way she remembered Newman teaching Kane to hold it as a boy. She held her breath as she caught a peek through the louvers of someone entering the bedroom. Patricia strained to peer through the tiny slats and get a look at who it was. Perhaps it was Scorpio, and she was just being a paranoid, old woman. When she saw a man dressed in black walking across the bedroom, she didn't have to see his face to know he wasn't an invited guest. He approached the dressers and quietly opened each drawer.

Reality dawned on Patricia. The intruder was looking for something, and if he didn't find what he was looking for in the dresser drawers, he would eventually look in the closet. Patricia's only hope was Scorpio arriving and scaring him off, but the frightening reality would be the man would hear Scorpio and ambush her. Her granddaughter could end up being the victim instead of her. Patricia nervously gripped the bat. The intruder finished searching the drawers and took a moment to search under the bed. She was able to see his face for the first time. He wore a black mask, making him that much more menacing. The intruder finally turned and approached the closet.

She trembled while watching him approach. She shut her eyes and drew a deep breath. The louver doors were pulled open. Patricia screamed while swinging the bat at the startled man. The bat struck him alongside the head, causing him to stumble but not fall. She swung again. He caught the bat, surprising her, and yanked it from her hand. Patricia screamed, ran from Kane's bedroom, and bolted down the second floor hallway for the main stairs. She looked back and saw the man was directly behind her with the baseball bat in his hands. He swung the bat, striking her in the shoulder. She was thrown off balance and hit the banister near the stairs while clutching her injured shoulder.

Before she could bolt from his path, the intruder shoved her toward the stairs. Patricia screamed as she tumbled down the broad staircase, thumping against each step before finally striking the bottom. She didn't move, and her eyes were closed as blood trickled from her temple.

§

Scorpio and Rayner approached the front door to her grandparent's large, elegant home just on the edge of town. She removed her keys and unlocked the door then eyed Rayner with a stern look.

"No matter how many times she asks," Scorpio announced firmly, "just say no to tea. We'll be here all afternoon otherwise."

"Got it," he replied.

Scorpio opened the door and entered the large foyer. Both immediately froze when they saw Patricia on the floor at the bottom of the staircase with blood streaking down the side of her face. Scorpio gasped with horror as they both leaped for the fallen woman's side.

"Grandma," Scorpio cried out and touched her outstretched hand.

Rayner placed his fingers to her neck then removed his cell phone from his jacket pocket. "She's alive," he announced. "I'll call an ambulance."

As Rayner straightened, the masked intruder stepped out of the front room behind him with the baseball bat and swung for his head. Scorpio saw the man first.

"Rayner!"

He turned just in time to see the bat coming for his head and ducked, avoiding being hit. As he attempted to bolt away, the man swung again, striking him in the upper arm rather than the head. Rayner fell against the hall table, which broke his fall, but the delicate, antique table also broke beneath his weight. Both Rayner and the table crashed to the floor. He looked up in time to see the intruder about to cave in his head with the bat. Rayner defensively held his arm up to his face, which was all he could do from his defenseless position. The man was suddenly struck in the side by a woman's booted foot.

The intruder stumbled back a step and turned to see Scorpio standing before him. He attempted to raise the bat. She karate kicked him under the arm, forcing him to drop the bat. The bat fell toward the floor. Scorpio caught it in mid-air and rammed the handle into his abdomen. As he doubled over, she twirled the bat in her hand, so she was holding it correctly, and swung for him. The intruder saw the swinging bat and lunged forward, tackling Scorpio in the midsection with his shoulder. He knocked her backward and into the banister. Scorpio was momentarily stunned by the hard hit from her attacker and the railing behind her. The intruder placed a gloved hand on her throat and squeezed, choking her. She gasped and wheezed from the pressure of his gloved hand.

The fear in Scorpio's eyes suddenly vanished as she clutched his wrist. Her eyes immediately narrowed revealing a rarely seen rage as she slammed her free palm into his nose. There was a chilling crunch. He released her and clutched his broken, bleeding nose. She kicked for his side, but he recovered from his ordeal and grabbed her ankle, attempting to throw her backward and off balance. She went with the toss, throwing her free leg into the air and connecting her foot with his jaw, sending him to the floor. Scorpio hit the floor as well, rolled with it, and then sprang to her feet in an attack position.

Rayner slowly stumbled to his feet and helplessly watched the attack unfold, except the attack was coming from Scorpio rather than the intruder. The intruder returned to his feet revealing a switchblade knife in his hand. He lunged for Scorpio and attempted to stab her. She bolted from his path and kicked out, striking him in the back, increasing his forward momentum. He lost his balance, and his arm slipped through the rung on the staircase railing. Scorpio kicked his trapped arm, easily snapping it with a loud crunch. The man cried out and pulled his broken arm free. Despite his injury, he wasn't going to let her win. He took the knife into his left hand and spun to face her, slashing at her with the switchblade. She jumped onto the railing and stood on the slanted banister with amazing balance. The intruder spun with surprise.

Scorpio leaped off the railing, caught him around the neck with her legs, and flipped him through the air with her as they both dropped to the floor. The horrific crunching sound of the man's neck breaking was enough to alarm Rayner. He took a step back and stared with horror at the dead man partially on top of Scorpio. Scorpio sneered as she kicked the man off her pinned leg. She sprang to her feet and stared without remorse at the dead man on the floor. As she panted heavily, her eyes met Rayner's terrified expression. He stared at her with wide eyes and his mouth hanging open. Scorpio felt the rage drain from her body as she ran trembling fingers through her hair. As rational thinking returned, she was reminded of her grandmother and darted for the motionless woman at the bottom of the steps. She fell to her knees and immediately clutched her grandmother's hand while glaring at Rayner.

"Where's my ambulance?" she cried out.

Rayner looked around, grabbed his discarded cell phone, and pressed a single button. Scorpio clung to her grandmother's hand.

"It's going to be okay, Grandma," she whispered as tears of concern filled her eyes. "An ambulance is on its way. Just hang on."

Her grandmother moaned and opened her eyes, although she didn't move. "Oh, Scorpio," she gasped. "I had the worst dream."

Chapter 48

Scorpio sat at her grandmother's bedside within the hospital emergency room. Since it was a small county hospital, they had tiny emergency rooms with actual doors rather than just privacy curtains separating patients. Scorpio held her grandmother's hand and stared at the IV line stuck in it. There were lines, tubes, and monitors attached to the now frail looking woman. Scorpio had never seen her lively grandmother looking so feeble before and could only imagine the horror she'd been through before their arrival. Rayner entered the room while replacing his cell phone to his pocket.

"Someone at the country club is heading onto the fairway to find your grandfather and tell him what happened," Rayner announced.

Scorpio briefly glanced at Rayner and saw the strange look on his face as he stared at her. She could almost see the fear in his eyes, and it wasn't over her grandmother's condition. He was fearful of *her*.

"He's going to be out of his mind," Scorpio remarked timidly.

"Did the doctor stop in yet?" Rayner asked.

"Yeah, he was here," she replied while staring at her unconscious grandmother. "She has a concussion and a few broken bones, but they say she's going to be fine."

"But she's still unconscious."

"She's been in and out," Scorpio informed him. "She keeps asking me if I want ice cream."

"I suppose her brain is a little scrambled right now," he replied then held his breath. "I'm sure it's just temporary." Rayner seemed unusually tense within the hospital room. "I, uh, finally got ahold of that private detective who'd left the message on your grandmother's machine."

She looked up at him with surprise then interest. "What did he say?"

"He flew in from Virginia last night," Rayner informed her. "Apparently, whatever he'd found must have been important enough to warrant flying all the way here to relay the message personally."

"I guess so," she replied and remained curious. "You'd think he could just do it over the phone."

"I thought that too. He said after he couldn't reach anyone, he stopped by Davenport's mansion and finally spoke with Rico," he announced then frowned. "He then reported that he no longer needed to talk with your grandparents. Apparently, Rico paid him his commission and sent him on his way."

Scorpio was concerned by the comment while staring at him. "No," she gasped then attempted to keep her voice and frustration down. "We need to know what he found out about Kane, and we certainly can't ask Rico. He's not going to tell us anything."

"I thought you might feel that way," he replied, "so I asked him to meet with us. Although he was apprehensive, he agreed. He said he was stopping at the tavern for a drink and something to eat before heading back to the airport, so I sent Maverick and Stone to join him."

"Good thinking," Scorpio remarked with relief then sank into thought. "What could he possibly have learned that he jumped on a plane to hand-deliver the information?"

Rayner shook his head, unable to answer her question. Patricia opened her eyes, appearing slightly groggy, and looked at Scorpio. Scorpio sat forward and immediately smiled.

"Hey, Grandma," she whispered in a forced cheerful tone to hide her concern. "How are you feeling?"

Her grandmother stared at her a moment and appeared bewildered. "Why do you keep asking me that?"

"Because you keep fading out on me," Scorpio replied. "How about staying awake a while?"

"Is it too much to ask to take a nap around here?" Patricia responded and shut her eyes.

"Grandma," Scorpio announced loudly.

She woke the woman, who again looked at her. A smile crossed Patricia's face. "Hey, honey," she announced cheerfully. "Did I fall asleep on the sofa?"

"Grandma, I need you to stay awake for me," Scorpio announced. "You had an accident."

She stared at her granddaughter with surprise. "I did?" Patricia asked. "When did that happen?"

"An hour or so ago," Scorpio replied.

"What happened?"

"You, uh, fell down the stairs," she informed her while fidgeting.

Patricia stared at her with a bewildered look. "The hell I did," she announced with annoyance. "I think I'd remember something like that."

"You may have been pushed," Scorpio then added while cringing. She wasn't sure if the woman could handle being reminded of her trauma just yet.

Her grandmother's eyes suddenly widened with horror, and she immediately jumped. "Where is he?" she gasped in alarm. "Where's the man in the mask?" She clutched Scorpio's hand with amazing strength considering her condition. "I'm scared he's going to hurt you. Call the police."

Scorpio placed her hand on her grandmother's face and stared into her eyes attempting to keep her calm. "It's okay," she announced gently. "You're at the hospital. He's no longer a threat."

"We're safe?" Patricia gasped.

"Yes, we're safe," she replied. "Try to relax. No one's going to hurt either of us."

"It was Kane," her grandmother announced startling Scorpio.

"What was Kane?"

"Kane," she replied. "He saved my life. He attacked the man with his baseball bat. I must have fallen down the stairs. Kane saved my life."

Scorpio fought her tears and attempted a smile. "That sounds like Kane."

Her grandmother smiled eagerly while looking around. "Where is he?" she asked. "I'd like to see him. I miss that boy something awful."

"Me too, Grandma," she whispered while maintaining her smile.

"Why do I hurt?" Patricia asked while grimacing and attempted to touch her side.

"You fell down the steps."

She eyed Scorpio with annoyance. "The hell I did," she boldly announced.

Scorpio managed a smile. "You're going to be confused for a while," she remarked. "But the doctor said you're going to be fine. You have a broken arm, a few fractured ribs, and a sprained ankle."

"That doesn't sound pleasant," Patricia muttered then eyed Scorpio. "Where's Kane? Is he here?" She smiled pleasantly. "I miss him something awful."

Scorpio looked back at Rayner and managed a tense smile. "This could be a long night."

Chapter 49

The tavern was slightly crowded despite being early evening. Men and women had a good time drinking and line dancing to the country music. Maverick and Stone sat across from the private detective at one of the corner tables. Josh Kerrigan was in his late forties. He was almost as tall and muscularly built as Stone. He wasn't a handsome man by any standards, but he wasn't repulsive either. His clean-shaven face, businessman haircut, and meticulous clothing suggested he took care of himself. He wasn't the stereotypical, burned out detective working for himself due to limited options. In fact, he proudly boasted his practice.

"It turns out the homicide detective investigating the murder was an old colleague of mine back in the day," the private detective informed them. "There was an anonymous tip of a burned car, the police investigated it, found a body inside, and my old buddy in homicide just happened to be nearby. The abandoned warehouse is in the middle of nowhere." Josh shook his head. "The moment I heard he was the detective in charge of the investigation; I immediately suspected the whole thing was a set-up."

"So whoever put out the hit on Kane had connections with the police?" Maverick asked.

"Not necessarily the police," Josh corrected. "Just this particular homicide detective." He leaned forward on the table and eyed both men. "If you want my opinion, I think he was the killer."

"The homicide detective?" Stone asked with surprise.

"Yes, the homicide detective," the private detective boldly replied. "I got an unofficial copy of calls he made that day prior to being called out to the scene of the eight-month-old crime. He made several phone calls to this area. They believe the receiving phone has already been destroyed and the number was disconnected. Tracing it to an actual person would be a little difficult but not impossible. I thought I'd ask the grandparents about the mysterious phone number as well as a few questions about Kane's trip to Virginia."

"And you told Rico this?" Maverick asked attempting to hide his concern.

"Yeah," Josh replied while nodding and seemed surprised by the questions. "Carson Davenport hired me, and Rico is his assistant. Why wouldn't I tell the people who hired me? You're the ones I shouldn't be telling. My fee was paid, and I was told to scrub the case. Mr. Davenport was no longer interested in pursuing it."

"Did Rico tell you why Carson Davenport wasn't available?" Stone asked.

"He said he was out of town on business," the detective replied.

"More like he fled the country to avoid being arrested," Maverick informed him. "Carson Davenport is wanted for multiple counts of murder. I wouldn't doubt he was the one who hired your homicide detective to kill Kane."

"That makes no sense," Josh remarked. "If he hired someone to kill this guy, why would he hire me to find the killer?"

"We haven't figured that one out yet," Stone informed him. "We have a lot more questions than we do answers."

The detective shook his head. "No, your man hired me to prove he *didn't* do it," Josh announced. "Only an innocent man does that. If he wanted a lackey, he could have hired any number of unaccredited private detectives in the area. I pride myself on results. He wouldn't have hired me. I'd eventually discover the connection implicating him."

"Well, he's certainly not innocent," Maverick informed him while leaning back in the chair.

"I don't know what evidence you have to support that theory, but we can talk about it after I return from the men's room," Josh informed them with great interest. "If the man I'm working for is dirty, I want to know. That could change everything. If I could figure out who killed the homicide detective, I'd be a hero. I'd have more business than I could handle."

Josh stood and was about to walk away from the table for the men's room. Maverick and Stone exchanged surprised looks and stopped him.

"Whoa, whoa, whoa," both men bellowed.

"Did you just say the homicide detective was killed?" Maverick asked with surprise.

He gave both men a strange look. "Yeah, I thought I mentioned that. He supposedly killed himself a week after the investigation, but I never bought that. Men like that don't have a conscience," Josh informed them. "If what you're saying is true, I think I can prove someone murdered the homicide detective."

The private investigator headed for the bathroom as his cell phone rang. He wasted little time answering his phone as he crossed the room.

"Josh Kerrigan, Private Detective."

"Detective?" a muffled voice on the phone announced. "We met the other day. I think I have some information on that young man who was killed."

As Josh hurried into the connecting hallway to get away from the loud music, there was excess static on the line.

"What information do you have?" Josh asked with surprise. "Who is this?"

The person on the other end responded to the question, but the man's voice was completely drowned out in static.

"Hang on," Josh announced and headed out the back door for a possible clearer connection. The static immediately cleared up. "Who is this?"

The back door closed behind him, and the loud music was finally muffled. Josh was suddenly grabbed from behind by a hand covering his mouth. Before he could even struggle against his captor, a knife was dragged along his throat. He gasped as blood poured from the gaping neck wound before he sank to the ground.

"It's not important," Rico announced while standing over the nearly dead detective. "I'll call back another time."

§

Nearly two hours later within the county hospital, Scorpio's grandmother was finally coming to her senses and was able to talk with the police. She relayed the accounts of her attack in great detail. Scorpio's anger increased as she listened to the ordeal her grandmother had suffered. She wished she could kill her attacker all over again. Despite everything Patricia was able to offer, it didn't seem to matter. The state police couldn't find a link placing the dead man on Davenport's payroll. Once Scorpio's grandfather showed up, Scorpio was relieved of duty. With her grandmother's police detail outside her hospital room and Newman inside her room, Scorpio knew her grandmother would be safe.

Rayner and Scorpio left the hospital and returned to the hotel, which was a thirty-minute drive away. Rayner was unusually quiet the entire drive home. It was already dark by the time they pulled up to the hotel. Stone's car was gone, indicating the guys were still at the tavern. Scorpio hoped they were able to get some information from the detective. Rayner followed Scorpio into the hotel through the foyer and shut the door behind them. He locked the door and punched in the alarm code. Scorpio looked at the bloodstain on her shirt and frowned.

"I should probably take a shower with my clothes on," she muttered in disgust at her condition. She cast a look at Rayner, who stared at her. Scorpio fidgeted and ran her fingers through her hair until she hit matted blood. "This afternoon, uh, got a little freaky, huh?"

He nodded while staring at her with the same strange expression. "Yeah, you could say that."

"I, uh, really don't know what came over me," she announced defensively. "My grandmother was in trouble, and I just sort of panicked and went on the defensive."

Rayner drew a deep breath and shook his head. "No, Scorpio," he announced gently. "You didn't panic, and you certainly weren't defending me, you, or your grandmother. You went into attack mode."

"I've been through a lot," she insisted. "I guess I was going to snap eventually."

"You never mentioned you were into martial arts," he remarked.

"I told you Kane and I took karate lessons when we were kids," she reminded him. "You knew that. I got lucky tonight, that's all."

"Please don't lie to me," he groaned while staring at her. "I've heard Maverick and Stone making comments here and there. At first, I just thought they were teasing you because you *couldn't* defend yourself, but that wasn't the case, was it?" Rayner took a step closer to her and stared into her eyes. "The way you reacted this afternoon was nothing short of frightening. After what I witnessed, I find it very difficult to believe you hid while the man you loved sacrificed himself to save you."

Scorpio's eyes strayed to the closed sitting room door. She couldn't seem to tear her eyes away. Rayner gently touched her face and forced her to meet his gaze.

"What really happened the night Cal died?" Rayner asked in a gentle tone.

Her entire body seemed to twitch, and her eyes again strayed to the closed sitting room door. That night came rushing back to her in a tidal wave of emotion. Unfortunately, most of it was anger and rage.

Chapter 50

Nine months earlier. Cal leaned over the pleasantly rumpled Scorpio where she lay on the massive bed after their aggressive lovemaking. The mostly tangled sheets indicated the intensity of their sexual encounter. Cal kissed her warmly then pulled away and smiled sweetly while she affectionately caressed his bare chest.

"I'm going downstairs and catch the end of the game," he announced in a tone meant to sound charming.

"You can watch it up here," she replied while continuing to caress his chest. "I promise not to roll my eyes too loudly when you yell at the players."

He chuckled at the comment and kissed her quickly on the lips. "It's late already," he informed her. "I don't want to disturb your sleep. You have to get up early. I'll be up in an hour or so."

She nodded and watched him leave the room, partially closing the door behind him. Scorpio slipped into her tank top and shorts pajama set, turned out the light, and climbed under the covers. Despite that she no longer felt tired; she seemed to fall asleep almost instantly. Scorpio hadn't been asleep too long when she heard the bedroom door creak open. She had a difficult time waking herself and even considered not commenting on the game. She rolled onto her back as her eyes opened and saw a strange man standing over her. Scorpio suddenly gasped and attempted to leap up in bed.

The man grabbed her by the throat and slammed her back onto the mattress. With his free, gloved hand, he raised a hunting knife above his head. Scorpio struggled against the hand on her throat while gasping for air then saw the knife. As he plunged downward with the knife, she caught his wrist and kept him from stabbing her. His strength and leverage was working against her. As she gasped for air beneath the crushing hand on her throat, she knew she only had seconds to react before losing the fight. She'd either pass out or lose the power struggle over the knife.

Scorpio made her decision. She released the man's hand that was choking her and drove the palm of her hand into his nose. He jerked back, releasing her throat, and involuntarily pulled the knife away from her. He stumbled back a step giving her only seconds to move. Scorpio jumped out from under the covers, rolled across the bed to the far side, and leaped to her feet, putting as much distance between her and her attacker as possible. He removed his hand from his bloodied nose, looked at her on the opposite side of the bed, and lunged across the bed for her.

Scorpio was already reaching alongside the bed and removed a hidden baseball bat. She didn't even take time to aim. She swung the bat for the lunging man and struck him in the hip, dropping him to the bed with a bounce. The intruder recovered from his position on the bed, grabbed his discarded knife, and straightened. His look was angry as bright red blood poured from his nose and his eyes pierced through hers.

"I'm going to kill you, you little bitch," he cried out then lunged for her.

Scorpio sneered with anger while swinging the bat. The bat struck the lunging man on the side of the head and projected him face first into the headboard. The crack of his neck breaking had been almost as loud as the sound of his skull splitting when the bat connected with his head. Despite her heavy breathing, Scorpio's gaze was hateful and angry. There was no remorse nor was there any fear. She snatched the phone from its cradle on the bedside table and immediately dialed the police. She hesitated with surprise when she realized there was no dial tone. Her eyes suddenly widened with the realization that this had been a carefully planned attack, and she wasn't the only one in danger.

"Cal," she suddenly gasped while dropping the phone to the bed.

She gripped her bloodied baseball bat and ran out the open bedroom door. Scorpio hurried along the second floor hallway then quickly but quietly headed down the main stairs in her bare feet. She avoided stepping on the one step she knew would creak beneath her weight while keeping her back close to the wall. She clutched the baseball bat in both hands while keeping it close to her shoulder, prepared for another confrontation. As she reached the bottom of the staircase, she was about to head for the game room where the television was located when she heard a sound coming from the study. Scorpio paused, listened a moment, and then headed for the dimly lit office. She paused alongside the doorway and peered into the room.

Two men took turns punching Cal. A third man, Argyle, stood before them and simply watched the two men beating her boyfriend. Scorpio held her breath a moment while noting the position of the three men within the room. None of them were facing the doorway and wouldn't see her. Scorpio crept into the room with the baseball bat clutched in her hands and silently approached the men hitting Cal. Cal managed to look up and saw her. His expression immediately dropped. All three men were suddenly alerted to something behind them and spun simultaneously.

"What's she doing down here?" Argyle cried out. "She was supposed to be tied up!"

Scorpio gasped, unprepared for the surprise reversal, and swung at the first man. He had enough time to dodge her swing and took the shot to his shoulder rather than his head. The second man lunged for her. Cal leaped for Argyle and tackled him onto the desk, sending objects flying across the floor. The two men wrestled across the desk while punching each other. Scorpio swung the bat at the second man. To her surprise, he caught the bat, stopping her swing. She attempted to pull the bat from him, but he refused to release it. She gripped the bat with both hands then karate kicked him sharply in the ribs. He stumbled backward pulling the bat from her hands along with his body.

Scorpio looked across the room just in time to see Argyle slash Cal across the arm with the knife. Cal jumped back with surprise by the deep cut and the stinging pain. Argyle thrust the knife forward and stabbed Cal in the abdomen, momentarily stunning him. Scorpio suddenly gasped in horror at what she'd just witnessed. The second man came at her with his ill-gained baseball bat. Scorpio kicked him in the groin, instantly dropping him to his knees. She leaped onto his shoulder, giving her aerial advantage, and spun into a roundhouse kick for Argyle, knocking him across the room. Scorpio landed a little less than gracefully. The first and second man recovered and came at Scorpio and Cal. Cal clutched his bleeding abdomen as he hurried toward Scorpio. He grabbed her arm and rushed her from the room away from the men.

They ran down the hallway toward the front foyer door. As they pulled the door open, they saw another man standing with his back to them on the other side of the door. He turned and saw them. Once Cal slammed the door, Scorpio rushed him for the front sitting room as the three men from the study entered the hallway. Scorpio and Cal ran into the sitting room and shut the door behind them. Scorpio latched the door and hurried Cal to the large side window. As she opened the window, Cal sank to his knees while blood seeped between his fingers. Scorpio kneeled alongside him and attempted to help him to his feet. Cal panted unable to catch his breath. He looked up and met her gaze.

"Go, Scorpio," he gasped softly. "Run for town and don't stop."

"Not without you," she whispered and again attempted to pull him to his feet.

"It's too late," he gasped while staring at her as he sank the rest of the way to the floor.

Scorpio stared at him with horror in her eyes and practically fell to his side. She held his head against her lap and clung to him while tears streaked her face.

"Cal, no," she gasped while holding back her sobs. "Please, stay with me."

Cal stared at her but didn't respond. He was dead. She gasped and couldn't breathe a moment, refusing to believe he was actually dead.

"Cal?"

When he didn't respond, she realized he was truly gone. Scorpio sobbed a moment, allowing her emotions to take control despite her dire situation. There was a thump against the sitting room door interrupting her grief. Scorpio's eyes suddenly lifted and narrowed as she stared at the door. She drew a deep breath and looked back at her dead lover on her lap. Scorpio lovingly fixed Cal's hair, gently laid his head on the floor, and moved to her feet in no particular hurry. There was another thump against the door. Scorpio's eyes fell upon the door again; this time with anger, hatred, and rage. She cast a look across the room at hers and Kane's samurai swords hanging on the far wall.

Chapter 51

The four intruders remained posted within the hallway outside the sitting room. Three watched while the first man slammed his shoulder repeatedly into the sturdy door. The old door was made of solid wood and was less forgiving than cheaply made newer doors. Argyle became frustrated when his man hadn't broken it down as quickly as he'd intended. He looked demandingly at the man on either side of him while the first man continued his assault on the thick door.

"You two, circle outside the house and make sure they didn't escape through one of the windows," Argyle ordered while gesturing wildly.

One man ran down the broad hallway toward the kitchen while the other ran for the front door. Both men drew their semiautomatics from hidden shoulder holsters as they hurried away. When it seemed as if the front sitting room door would never break, Argyle relayed his frustration.

"Stop screwing around," Argyle finally demanded. "Shoot the lock out."

The remaining man stopped his assault on the old door and looked at his leader with surprise. "The boss specifically said no gunfire, Argyle," the man reported. "It's not supposed to look planned."

"It's a little late for that," Argyle insisted in anger. "We're running out of time."

The first man reluctantly removed his gun containing a silencer from his shoulder holster, took a step back, and fired several nearly silent shots into the door lock. Argyle pushed him aside and easily kicked open the door. The solid door flew open and struck the opposing wall with a thunderous crack. They scanned the large sitting room and immediately noticed Cal dead on the floor. The large window near him was standing open as a gentle breeze blew the white, bloodstained sheer curtains inward.

"Son-of-a-bitch! The girlfriend must have escaped," Argyle announced with irritation then turned to the man alongside him. "Go outside and help those idiots find her. Shoot her if you have to. She can't get away!"

"But we were told--"

"The hell with what we were told," Argyle launched in anger. "It's too late. She's seen our faces. We can't let her get away."

The first man nodded and hurried from the room. Argyle again scanned the room and eyed the empty, mounted sword rack on the nearby wall. It seemed oddly out of place with no swords on it. He dismissed the sword rack. Argyle approached the open window, stepping over Scorpio's dead boyfriend, and peered outside into the darkness. The excessively large grandfather clock just on the other side of the portable bar struck midnight. The man heard the loud chiming from the clock and instinctively looked at his watch. Despite the grandfather clock's insistence on it being midnight, it was actually a little after one in the morning. He appeared bewildered and glanced at the clock. The door to the base was now open, indicating someone had possibly been hiding inside the clock. He jerked his head to the left and saw Scorpio standing only a few feet away from him. Her stare was void of expression as she held a samurai sword in each hand.

Argyle jumped with surprise to her stealthy appearance, although he didn't seem too concerned about the weapons she held. He was possibly more stunned than anything that she was able to fit inside the lower portion of the grandfather clock. With little forethought, he aimed his gun at her. She sneered as she swung the sword, striking the gun, and knocking it from his hand. Argyle gasped with surprise and jumped back a step.

Scorpio took a step toward him while twirling both swords with precision and skill. He smiled smugly almost mocking her despite the weapons in her hands.

"You'd never kill an unarmed--"

Scorpio slashed with both swords in opposite directions, her expression never changing. Argyle suddenly tensed while staring at her with a frozen look of horror on his face. Blood poured from his mouth as he managed to look down. She'd sliced an 'X' across his lower abdomen. When he coughed, the cross-section slice opened up, spilling his intestines from his body. He stared a moment as if attempting to figure out what had just happened then his eyes met hers. She showed no emotion to the carnage she'd inflicted upon the man. He wheezed then collapsed to the floor. Scorpio twirled the swords so they were pointing behind her as she casually stepped over the bloody pile of organs in her bare feet. She headed for the sitting room doorway in no particular hurry.

As she entered the hallway, she heard someone running across the front porch just outside the open door. Scorpio casually crossed the hall, stepped into the small, gated elevator, and closed the gate behind her. She pushed the second floor button. The elevator lifted, taking Scorpio to the second floor as the man from outside entered the foyer. He saw the elevator ascending to the next floor and ran up the stairs, his feet loudly thumping on each step so he could catch the elevator before whoever was using it could escape.

Only moments after the first man had thundered up the staircase, the second man ran along the first floor hallway from the kitchen, also approaching the elevator. He watched as the elevator stopped on the second floor and then ran for the grand staircase as well. He was about to head up the stairs when he heard someone running along the second floor hallway, their booted feet loudly thumping. There was an unusual silence from the floor above. The second intruder paused by the bottom of the stairs and looked up them, listening for any further sounds. He was about to head up the stairs when he saw the first man now standing at the landing with a strangely horrified, fixed stare on his face.

"Did you find them?" he called up to his partner. "Have you seen Malone?"

His partner on the landing didn't respond almost as if he were in shock. The man at the bottom of the stairs became impatient.

"Are you deaf?" he snarled. "Did you find them? Who was using the elevator?"

The man on the upstairs landing still didn't respond. Blood suddenly poured from the now visible slit across his throat. His severed head slid from his neck and rolled down the stairs, thumping against each step before striking the second man's feet. The man at the bottom of the stairs stared at the severed head of his comrade with horror and appeared almost unable to react. He finally cried out and jumped back as the headless body collapsed and tumbled down the elegant staircase. The frightened man leaped away just in time to avoid the tumbling body. He turned and ran to the sitting room doorway.

"Argyle," he cried out as he entered through the open, splintered doorway.

The man suddenly stopped when he saw the bloody heap that was once his boss in the sitting room. He leaped away from the doorway then heard someone in the first floor hallway coming from the back of the house. He hurried down the hall alongside the staircase hoping to run into his remaining teammate. A small gust of wind and a thump just behind him caught his attention. He spun around from his position just beyond the staircase. Scorpio remained in a slightly crouched position with her swords in hand, having jumped over the railing behind him. He aimed his gun at her.

As she straightened, she slashed upward with the first sword, slicing him from groin to sternum, and then slashed sideways with the second sword, slitting his throat. He barely had time to gasp as the blood poured from his neck and dripped from his groin. His eyes rolled back as he collapsed to the floor. She heard a startled gasp from the hallway. Scorpio saw the last intruder near the office doorway staring at his dead teammates with horror. His look turned angry, and he aimed his gun at her. As the gun fired, she leaped across the hall, dove into a forward roll with her swords still in her hands, and disappeared into the nearby sitting room. The remaining intruder ran down the hall for the front room, paused before the open doorway, and aimed his weapon.

From his position just inside the doorway, he scanned the empty room. His eyes fell upon the gruesome fate of his leader, but he didn't let that distract him. Scorpio seemed to have vanished. He saw several possible hiding places behind sofas and in dark corners where she could be hiding. He then eyed the splintered door alongside him and smirked. With all his weight, he shoved his shoulder against the mostly open door, sending it against the wall, crushing anyone standing behind it. To his surprise, the door struck the wall without resistance. She hadn't been hiding behind the door. He frowned and slowly stepped into the room.

"I know you're in here," he announced while cautiously scanning the room. "You're going to pay for what you did to my friends. If you're smart, you'll force me to kill you quickly, because if I get ahold of you, I'm going to kill you slowly one slice at a time."

He looked behind the sofa centered in the room then passed in front of it while scanning the rest of the furniture. A sword suddenly appeared from beneath the sofa behind him and slashed his lower calf as he passed. He cried out and clutched his bleeding calf. He immediately aimed his weapon at the sofa and fired four shots into it. Scorpio was already rolling across the floor and behind the portable bar. The man saw her out of the corner of his eye as she disappeared behind the small bar, and he fired four more shots into the heavy wood. When he heard no sound and nothing moved, he approached the bar. The bar suddenly thumped. He fired another shot into the bar. Nothing moved, and there was no sound, indicating he'd gotten her. He leaped around the bar and aimed his weapon behind it. Scorpio was crouched behind the thick portable bar unscathed from the shots that didn't penetrate the wood. She looked up at him with little emotion despite the gun aimed at her and tightly gripped her swords.

"Nine," she casually announced.

He sneered and squeezed the trigger. The gun clicked empty. His expression suddenly dropped to the meaning of her words. As he reached for another magazine from his pocket, Scorpio sprang to her feet and slashed his arm, stopping him from completing the action. He dropped his weapon and clutched his bleeding arm with surprise. She could have easily killed him but chose to disarm him instead. He stared at the emotionless woman standing before him.

"One slice at a time," she announced and raised her brows. "That was the deal, right?"

He backed away from her while staring at her swords dripping with blood. "It was nothing personal," he announced. "Just a job."

"Who hired you?" she demanded.

"It was all done anonymously," he insisted while continuing to back away from her despite his bleeding leg. "It was just a job."

"I know who hired you," she snarled back. "If you don't want to rat him out, you can give him a message from me instead." Her eyes narrowed as they pierced through his. "Never fuck with my family." She flipped the sword through the air in her right hand and caught it, changing the sword's position now holding it in a threatening manner above her head. "An eye for an eye."

He stared at her as if attempting to decipher the message when she plunged the sword through his eye and out the back of his skull. She didn't even bother pulling the sword free as he fell to the floor. Scorpio stared at the dead man on the floor for several minutes without moving. She allowed the breath she'd been holding to escape, and her expression immediately dropped. All her emotions returned in a tidal wave and flooded to the surface.

"Cal," she gasped and bolted for the nearby window where Cal remained motionless on the floor.

She fell to her knees alongside him and dropped the second, blood-covered sword. She gathered her dead boyfriend into her arms, pulled his head to her chest speckled with blood, and sobbed softly while holding him.

§

Present day. Scorpio continued to stare transfixed at the closed sitting room door while Rayner stared at her with shock and disbelief. The hotel was so quiet; all they heard was the ticking of the grandfather clock on the staircase landing. Scorpio drew a deep, shaken breath and shook them both back to reality.

"I didn't want anyone to know," she practically whispered. "I wanted people to think Cal died a hero. He was my hero. He was always my hero."

Rayner seemed unable to speak while staring at the strange expression on her face. "Maverick and Stone realized your story to the police was inaccurate," he remarked. "They knew, didn't they?"

She snorted a soft laugh but didn't bother looking away from the door. "They called me on it almost immediately. Cal had told them about me," Scorpio replied in a sedate tone. "He told them he had a kickass girlfriend. Apparently, Cal wasn't much of a fighter. His time working for Davenport proved that much." She shook her head then finally looked into Rayner's eyes. "Lying about what happened would also keep whoever hired those men from seeking revenge on me for what I'd done." Scorpio looked down at her trembling hands. She could still see the blood on them even though they were clean. "That night frightened me." She met his gaze with tears in her eyes. "Not just because of the horror of losing Cal, but because of what I'd done without mercy."

"You were in survival mode," Rayner informed her. "It's a natural reaction. Fight or flight. You chose fight. Instincts kick in."

She shook her head. "No," Scorpio insisted. "It wasn't survival instinct. You said so yourself. This was much worse. It's as if it wasn't even me. It didn't feel like me. I didn't go into survival mode; I went into predator mode."

"You're being too hard on yourself, Scorpio," he gently informed her. "You were just pushed beyond reasonable limits. Anyone would crack under that pressure."

"No, you don't understand. All the play fighting Kane and I had done as kids, it played out before me. I was aware of sounds. I heard everything. My senses were on fire. I could almost feel every move those men made, and I was able to stay one step ahead of them. When it was all over, I had no remorse. None." She looked back at the door. "I don't want to go back into that room. I told you there was a monster behind that door, and that monster is me."

Chapter 52

Two hours later, Scorpio nervously paced the hallway while Rayner sat on one of the bottom steps and watched her. A car's headlights hit the windows in the foyer, indicating Stone and Maverick had returned. Scorpio ran to the main entrance, hastily disarmed the alarm, and unlocked the door. As she opened the door, Stone and Maverick walked up the porch steps with matching defeated looks upon their faces. Scorpio stared at them with concern.

"What the hell happened?" she gasped. "Did someone kill that detective right there at the tavern?"

"That's about the size of it," Maverick muttered with disgust.

"The man got up to go the bathroom, got a call on his cell phone, and never came back," Stone informed her.

"Next thing we know, one of the waitresses comes from the back hallway screaming," Maverick announced. "As soon as she said she found a dead man out back, we knew it was our guy."

"I can't believe it," Scorpio remarked while shaking her head. "What did Deputy Gaines have to say?"

"You mean after he screamed like a little girl?" Maverick scoffed.

"He didn't--"

"Yeah, he kind of did," Stone agreed while nodding. "He was calling the city detective to the scene. I'm pretty sure he went outside the throw up after that."

"The man only had contact with Scorpio's grandmother, Rico, and us," Rayner remarked. "Scorpio's grandmother is nearly killed, and the detective is murdered less than twenty-four hours after arriving in a town where he doesn't even know anyone. They have to see the connection."

"Don't count on it," Maverick replied with little emotion. "Deputy Gaines didn't want to even discuss the possibility that Rico had something to do with the private detective's murder. He's leaving it up to the city detectives."

"If you ask me, Deputy Gaines is scared of Rico," Stone remarked, "and I can't say I exactly blame him. I'm sure the man is a cold-blooded killer."

"I think we're in for a long day with the city detective tomorrow," Scorpio announced in a defeated tone while scratching her head. "I'm going to bed and hopefully forget this day ever happened."

§

Scorpio turned over in bed unable to sleep and reached for Rayner. He wasn't there. She looked around the dimly lit room and saw the bathroom door was open, but the light was off. She heard a strange tapping sound. It took a moment or two for her to figure out it was the sound of fingers striking a laptop keyboard. Scorpio crawled out of bed in her sleep shorts and tank top and padded into the dimly lit bathroom. She could see there was a light on in the connecting room despite that the bathroom door was partially closed. Scorpio pushed open the door and saw Rayner, fully dressed, sitting on the bed with his new laptop. He was so absorbed in his work; he didn't initially notice her in the bathroom doorway.

When he finally saw her, Rayner jumped with surprise then offered a timid smile. "I was trying not to wake you," he announced.

"You didn't," she replied then approached the bed and crawled into it with him. She nuzzled against his shoulder and stared at the laptop screen. "Couldn't you sleep?"

"Actually, I was sleeping soundly when my brain woke me up," he remarked. "Too many things started just popping in there."

"Anything I'd be interested in?" she asked.

"If you like riddles with no answers, yeah, sure," he replied.

"It's three o'clock in the morning," she responded. "I don't do riddles until well after eight o'clock." Scorpio considered his question then groaned. "Now you've piqued my curious nature. What are you working on? What's the riddle?"

"Why was a private detective from Virginia murdered so far from his investigation?"

"He must have told Rico something," Scorpio replied. "Whatever it was, Rico must have felt threatened and killed him before he could tell anyone else."

"Which was almost Maverick and Stone," Rayner reminded her. "So that has to mean Kane's hit was ordered by Davenport, right?"

"I think we covered that already," she replied and hid her weary smile.

"Yes, but why would Davenport hire a detective to find out who put the hit on Kane if he was, in fact, the one who ordered the hit?" Rayner practically demanded. "Why purposely attract attention to yourself if you're the killer? Had he done nothing, who would have suspected Davenport ordered a hit on your brother? It would be a reach at best. Then that takes us back to the original question. What's Davenport's motive for wanting Kane dead?"

"Too many questions for three in the morning," she replied simply.

"Then allow me to speculate what I believe happened," Rayner announced. "Davenport knows he wasn't behind Kane's murder. He wants to make sure he's cleared beyond all doubt, so he hires several private detectives to poke around the murder and prove he wasn't involved. Davenport *didn't* order the hit on Kane."

She pulled back and eyed him with surprise. "Do you think it was Rico?" Scorpio practically gasped and became interested. "Do you think Rico was the mastermind and Davenport was his scapegoat?"

"I don't think Davenport is completely innocent either," Rayner informed her, "but I think it's possible Davenport didn't have anyone killed. Rico may have been working an angle, and it backfired."

"So why did Davenport run?" she asked. "If he were innocent, wouldn't he have--?"

They exchanged stares. Rayner raised his brows as if silently answering her question.

She read the look in his eyes and was surprised by what she saw. "You think Davenport's dead, don't you?" she gasped.

"It's possible Rico wanted to take over his entire operation, which he has successfully done," Rayner announced. "As his second in command, he would control the business in Davenport's absence whether that be on the run from the law or in prison for murder."

"Because if he's dead--"

"Everything goes to his wife."

"Have you seen Celine?" Scorpio announced boldly. "She's young and gorgeous. Rico could even have had a thing going with her. Together they could have the assets and the business."

"I'm not so sure I'd go that far as to pair up those two," Rayner remarked. "Remember Rico went to great lengths to get Amber back. If he had something going on with Davenport's wife, he would have welcomed being rid of Amber."

She stared at him a moment and considered everything he'd said. "You make my head hurt," Scorpio announced while touching her temple. "I think I'd rather take a bath and not think about it." She kissed him quickly on the lips and then smiled slyly. "You're welcome to join me."

Rayner seemed slightly surprised then hid his smile. "That sounds *romantic*."

Scorpio straightened and groaned while rolling her eyes. "You went and ruined it," she remarked while climbing out of bed.

He didn't bother looking up from his laptop. "Nope," Rayner casually replied. "You can't have a romantic bath for two without the romance. Either we're playing by your rules or we're not."

"Seriously?"

He finally looked up. "Yes, seriously."

She folded her arms across her chest and wasn't entirely sure how to respond to his comment. "You aren't going to back off until we're officially in a relationship, are you?" she practically demanded.

"We *are* in a relationship," he corrected. "You just refuse to acknowledge it. I realize I can't compete with your feelings for Cal, and I've accepted that. I don't expect you to love me the way I love you, but I can't keep suppressing my feelings for you. I can't limit my emotions to behind closed doors. It's soul-crushing."

She stared at him a moment as his words sank in. "Did you just say you loved me?"

"Are we going to fight about crossing that line too?" he practically demanded then groaned and cast his laptop aside. "I didn't know how emotionally draining our non-existent relationship was going to be. I guess I thought the sex would be enough, and I could easily hide my feelings. Well, it's not so easy."

Scorpio groaned and ran her fingers through her hair. "Rayner," she announced while fidgeting and avoided looking at him. "I--"

His laptop lowly wailed a radiation leak alarm. Rayner immediately turned over on the bed and pressed a button on the keyboard.

"What is that?" she asked with surprise and approached him and the bed.

He stared at the laptop with concern. "Someone has remotely disabled the downstairs security alarm," he informed her and pressed a few buttons on the keypad. "After that last fluke, I reprogrammed the system to alert me if anyone tampered with it, which also included any attempts to deactivate it remotely."

She stopped near the bed and stared at him. "You mean someone--?"

He pressed another button and pulled up the security cameras. Scorpio stared at the screen and witnessed several heavily armed men entering through the kitchen door. Rayner switched cameras to bring up the second breach. More men came through the front door. He eyed Scorpio, and they exchanged horrified looks.

"A dozen armed men just stormed the hotel," he informed her while springing up from the bed. "You phone the police; I'll wake the guys."

Scorpio bolted for the bedside phone and picked it up. She suddenly looked at Rayner as the color drained from her face in a déjà vu moment.

"The phone lines are dead," she gasped.

"Wake the guys," he ordered and returned to his laptop. "I can notify the police from my computer."

She nodded and hurried from the room, making certain she locked the door behind her. She knew she only had minutes before the men came up both sets of stairs. As she ran along the second floor hallway in her bare feet, she could hear men attempting to run silently up the grand staircase. She bolted into Maverick's mostly dark room and locked the door behind her. A startled Maverick leaped up in bed and stared at her with surprise.

"What's going--?"

"We have company," she informed him. "The worst kind."

Scorpio ran through the connecting bathroom and entered Stone's bedroom. As she crossed Stone's bedroom to lock his door, Stone was already jumping from the bed and pulling on a pair of pants. Her presence was enough to send him into action.

"What is it?" he asked while rushing to dress in his discarded clothes from the floor.

"A dozen armed men," she announced while barely glancing at him. "They're coming from the front and up our ass from behind."

Maverick ran into the room with a massive, frightening looking shotgun in his hand and a shoulder holster containing his semiautomatic.

"Remember our midnight intruder contingency plan?" Stone announced while eying Scorpio as he pushed open a hidden compartment in the headboard revealing his intimidating shotgun.

As he pumped the shotgun, she jumped at the sound then nodded in response. "Yes, I'm aware of the contingency plan, but there are a dozen men out there," she blurted out her concerns. "There are only two of you. I can't just sit by. I have to do something."

Stone removed his shoulder holster from the bedside table and slipped into it. "The plan is you hide in your secret passageway," Stone reminded her. "That's why you had them installed, remember?"

She frowned and nodded while rubbing her chilled, bare arms. "I remember," Scorpio muttered. "I referred to Kane as being paranoid, yet I'm the one who had two secret passageways installed in my hotel." Horror then crossed her face. "Rayner. I left him in the bedroom across from my bathroom. What if they find him?"

"He knows where the secret passageway is in your room, right?" Maverick asked.

"We never actually discussed it," she remarked and immediately felt concerned that she hadn't shared that information with him.

They could hear the men in the hallway.

"We need to do this now," Stone announced and hurried to the nearby wall.

He moved a book from the bookcase, and the secret doorway popped open. All three hurried inside. They no sooner shut the door behind them when there was a thump against the bedroom door. On the second strike, the doorframe cracked, and the door flew open. One of the armed men entered the room with his gun aimed. He hurried for the bathroom and was nearly startled by another man coming from Maverick's bedroom.

"There's no one here," the first man announced, seeming slightly surprised.

"They have to be here," the second man gruffly responded. "The bedroom doors were locked. Check the closets and under the beds."

The first man returned to Maverick's room while the second searched Stone's room for the missing occupants. A small peek hole within the bookcase vanished.

Chapter 53

Just down the hall, another armed man kicked in the bedroom door and entered the room where Scorpio had left Rayner. He immediately aimed his weapon at the rumpled bed, but it was empty. The intruder noted the condition of the bed, indicating someone had been there and then hurried for the bathroom, which took him into Scorpio's room. He looked around with his weapon aimed, but the connecting room was empty as well. Another man entered Scorpio's room through her unlocked door. They aimed their weapons at each other then relaxed and simultaneously lowered them. The second man removed his mask to reveal Rico.

"They were here," Rico snarled. "The beds were slept in. How did they know we were coming?"

"They must have heard us coming up the stairs," the first man replied.

"Allowing them to escape unnoticed with a two second warning?" he demanded then shook his head. "No, they somehow knew we were coming."

"Do you think we've been double-crossed?" his partner remarked while looking around with concern.

"I don't know," Rico muttered while sinking into thought. The possibility must have occurred to him as well. He then glared at his partner. "Stay alert just in case."

§

The library bookcase moved away from the wall revealing the secret passageway. Stone stepped out with his shotgun aimed and ready for action, but fortunately, there was no one there. He motioned to Maverick, who stepped out of the passageway to join him. Scorpio remained in the entranceway as concern swept through her.

"The secret passageway in the game room leads to my bedroom," she informed them. "If we can get to the game room--"

"You're not going anywhere," Maverick firmly insisted. "You stay hidden as we discussed. Stone and I will clean house."

"You don't understand," she attempted to explain while twitching with alarm.

"I understand there are a dozen heavily armed men running around this hotel, and we're not letting you get caught in the crossfire," Maverick bluntly informed her while glaring demandingly. "We need to provide backup for Deputy Gaines and whatever men he brings to this little party. He'll be here soon, and this will all be over. There's no reason for you to get yourself killed."

"I've lost everyone, Maverick," she announced then drew a deep breath. "I can't lose the two of you and Rayner. I can't lose any more people I love. I'm the next domino to fall. That's the way it's supposed to be."

"And talk like that is why you aren't coming with us," Stone informed her and pointed a demanding finger. "You, girl, have a death wish."

"I don't," she insisted.

"Well, you'll need to prove that and stay hidden," Stone replied.

Maverick smiled warmly and kissed Scorpio on the forehead. "Stone and I will be fine," he insisted, obviously pleased with her concern for their welfare. "You just wait inside the passageway until everything is clear. We'll find Rayner; I promise. We won't let him die." He then grinned playfully. "He's too much fun to torment."

She reluctantly nodded knowing every minute she spent arguing with them was another minute the armed men could find them. Scorpio returned to the secret passageway and shut the bookcase behind her. She leaned against the slightly dusty wall in the dark, hidden passageway, which was lined with glow-in-the-dark stripping. She finally opened the peek hole, which was located in the library on the shelf just above some books. She peered into the library and watched Maverick and Stone leave the room. Scorpio returned the cover over the peek hole and looked at the glow-in-the-dark stripping on the wall near her, which outlined a small opening within the wall. She felt inside the cubbyhole and removed one of two flashlights within the opening.

When she had the construction men install the secret passageways, she also had them put in a few safeguards. One of those safeguards was a holder for two small, three-inch flashlights to help navigate the dark passageway. Scorpio turned on the flashlight and shined it across the passageway to reveal a cupboard of sorts. Since it wasn't marked, someone within the passageway had to know it was there in order to find it in the dark. The built-in cupboard was her second safeguard. She opened the small cupboard to reveal two semiautomatics, two additional magazines, and two extra boxes of bullets. Scorpio was 'scary prepared' for this day, and her friends weren't going to sideline her. She removed the handgun that was already loaded and contained one in the chamber.

Her only regret was not having pockets or wearing something that she could easily carry an extra magazine. She'd need to be content for now with the few bullets she had. With use of her flashlight, she followed the passageway a short distance to the vertical ladder they had come down from Stone's room. She climbed the ladder in her bare feet while carrying the small flashlight in her mouth. The gun proved more of a burden, clinking against each rail along the way, but she managed to reach the second floor without dropping it. Arranged somewhat like a submarine, the vertical shaft and ladder continued up to the third floor, which would come out in Kane's room.

When she had the passageways installed, she assumed Kane was still coming back. Given his paranoia, he would have gotten a kick out of the secret passageway in his room. He would have been so proud of her. She was sad he never got to see them. Each passageway entrance contained the same emergency equipment. Two small flashlights, two handguns, and extra ammunition. Had she considered she'd have co-conspirators, she would have stocked walkie-talkies as well. Had she considered she'd be creeping around in her sleep attire, she would have bought shoulder holsters for each weapon as well. Scorpio hurried along the second floor passageway and paused near the exit within Stone's room. She opened the peek hole and scanned the empty room.

When nothing moved, she drew a deep breath and quietly opened the passageway entrance, knowing the intruders had to be around somewhere. She stepped into Stone's bedroom and silently shut the bookcase behind her as an added security measure. The intruders couldn't be allowed to discover the passageways. Scorpio hurried across Stone's room to the bedroom door and stood alongside it, listening for any sounds. She could hear the ceiling creak above her, indicating someone was in the third floor hallway. From her position in Stone's bedroom, she could see across the hall to the room where she had left Rayner.

Although it was only a short, twenty-foot sprint down the hallway, she felt the wiser option would be to go through Maverick's room, via the connecting bathroom, since it would put the bedroom she sought directly across the hall. She'd only be exposed in the open hallway a few feet at most. She slipped through the connecting bathroom and into Maverick's bedroom then paused alongside his doorway and peered out. An armed man dressed in black appeared in the second floor hallway, having come from the main stairs. She had been fortunate. Had she entered the hallway from Stone's room, she would have run into him and gunfire would have been exchanged, which would have alerted his many friends.

With a dozen armed men running around the hotel, any gunfire would immediately bring more men with weapons. Considering she was such a bad shot, exchanging gunfire wasn't in her best interest. She remained hidden alongside the door and listened to the man walk along the hallway. Although he attempted to make little sound, she heard every footfall. She swore she could hear the leather of his boots with each step. The sound of his leather shoulder holster creaking as he pivoted was almost deafening to her. She shut her eyes while clutching her gun close to her chest and concentrated on the tiniest sounds he made, which told her his position in the hallway. He was getting closer.

When she heard the familiar creak of his leather shoulder holster, she knew he had pivoted left directly before her doorway. She didn't have to look; she knew he was there. She opened her eyes and looked at the floor. She could see the appearance of his shadow blocking the light from the hallway into Maverick's nearly dark bedroom. By the length of his shadow on the floor, she knew his exact position. He was just inches from the doorframe. Her pounding heart told her she needed to remain perfectly still and silent in hopes he'd continue onward, avoiding a confrontation. Her body twitched as her instincts disagreed with her pounding heart and shouted for her to attack. Attack now!

Although she couldn't see the man, she saw him in her mind. She knew where he stood, how he stood, and exactly where he held the weapon. Her senses frightened her. She used to get the same feeling when she and Kane played war games as kids in the hotel when it was abandoned. He always hunted her down, and she always knew when to attack. That was just play; this was real. Kane won fifty percent of the time, and their fights often came with an excessive amount of noise. She wrestled with her instincts. She couldn't afford to make any noise this time. Based on her play fighting with Kane, she only had a fifty percent chance of beating this man.

Why were her instincts fighting her on this? She heard him pivot away from the room. Her instincts cried out for her to *attack now*! Her head told her he was walking away, and she was safe. Attacking would be foolish. Scorpio was almost stunned when she realized she had stepped out of safety and into the doorway. The man immediately turned, catching a glimpse of her from the corner of his eye. She caught his right wrist in her left hand and twisted his arm with force, preventing him from shooting her. She then spun into a high, roundhouse kick, striking him in the face and dropping him to the floor. She caught his gun before it hit the floor, although his body striking the floor to her sounded like a boulder crashing. In reality, it wasn't that loud.

Scorpio bolted across the hall for the open bedroom door and slipped inside just before two more men ran down the hallway to see their fallen man. Scorpio was already running through the empty, dark bedroom, through the connecting bathroom, and into her bedroom. She slipped into the secret passageway, shutting it behind her only seconds before an armed man ran into the room, attempting to find whoever had attacked his man. Scorpio remained silent within the passageway with both guns in her hand. She listened to the man run across the room. She could hear him frantically searching the closet for whoever attacked his man.

The distinctive sound of leather creaking from his boots, shoulder holster, and his leather belt told her he was now looking under her bed. She controlled her breathing, so she could concentrate on the sounds within her bedroom since she didn't dare open the peek hole at that moment. She had to preserve the sanctity of the secret passageway. Once the man left her room, she opened the peek hole and looked into the bedroom. She saw the man hurry out the door and listened to the mild commotion in the hall as the fallen man told them what had happened to him.

"It was the girl," the man insisted. "I swear it was the girl."

Scorpio eyed the two guns she now held. The intruder's gun contained a silencer, which would better serve her. She felt the passageway wall for the cupboard and placed her own gun inside the cabinet with the others. Her journey through both bedrooms had been brief, but she was able to remember every detail of the rooms. There wasn't any blood, and she didn't see any sign of Rayner, so he was still alive. She wasn't sure how he escaped. If he had figured out there was a secret passageway then she should find him on one of the floors. Remembering the creaking floorboards from the third floor, her instincts told her to go upstairs. She hurried along the short passageway, leaped onto the vertical ladder, and made her climb to the third floor, which would bring her out in Kane's room.

Once she reached the passageway opening to Kane's room, she looked through the peek hole, saw everything was clear, and quietly opened the passageway door. As she stepped into the room, she sensed something and immediately spun with her gun aimed. Rayner held a baseball bat, prepared to swing, and then realized it was her. He sighed with relief and lowered the wooden bat.

"You scared the shit out of me," he gasped and pulled her into his arms.

She returned the warm embrace only for a second then pulled away and met his gaze. "Did you get the emergency call to the police?"

"Yeah, they should be here soon," he replied in a hushed voice. "I said to bring plenty of backup and mentioned how many armed men there were. I'm adding an additional ten minutes to their response time in order to find reinforcements. Where are Stone and Maverick?"

She groaned softly and rolled her eyes at the question. "Defending the fort," Scorpio muttered. "I hope they don't do anything stupid and they're as crafty as they seem to think they are. They want to make sure Deputy Gaines is properly backed. He's going to need all the backup he can get." She then eyed him suspiciously. "How did you know about the secret passageway in my bedroom?"

Rayner grinned almost slyly. "When you mentioned you called my guy, I had to figure out what you'd done," he announced. "I found the passageway in the game room in under ten minutes. Naturally, I had to see where it went. The one in the library took a lot longer. Too many bookcases to explore. We should probably wait in the passageway entrance in the game room. That'll enable us to hear when the police arrive."

"I agree," she replied. "I just want to stop in my room and grab a few things."

"I left my laptop in the passageway entrance to your room," he informed her. "I'd like to grab that as well. We can use the security cameras to our advantage and find their locations throughout the hotel, even if I can only view one camera at a time."

"That's a great idea," she announced then took a moment to grab a leather jacket from her brother's closet.

Rayner watched with a bewildered look as she slipped into her brother's jacket. "What do you need that for?"

She indicated the semiautomatic and placed it in the inner pocket. "It's not easy climbing up and down that ladder with a gun in my hand."

"That's why I had to leave my laptop behind too," he replied. "My briefcase is in your bedroom near the nightstand. If I can grab that, it'll help."

"We need to move," she insisted.

They hurried into the secret passageway, safely hiding before anyone would stumble upon them.

Chapter 54

Stone and Maverick approached the grand staircase while listening to the sounds of creaking floorboards above them. If any of the men were on the first floor, they were somewhere near the back half of the hotel. Stone checked out the front lounge and took a stakeout position just beyond the doorway, while Maverick ventured into the downstairs powder room with a view of the grand staircase. Stone had eyes on the stairs up to the second floor landing, while Maverick could keep an eye on the grand hallway and the elevator. Both had full view of the foyer and front door.

There was a knock on the front door. Maverick and Stone exchanged bewildered looks from across the hall. It couldn't be the police. They certainly wouldn't knock after receiving a dire call for help involving multiple gunmen. An intruder appeared on the stairs, hurried partway down them, and paused with his gun aimed at the door. He was waiting to ambush the person on the other side of the door. When there was no response, the front door finally opened, and Deputy Gaines poked his head inside. Despite the gun in his hand, he looked frightened as he scanned the immediate area.

"Hello, Scorpio?"

The man on the stairs was about to take his shot. Stone stepped into the lounge doorway and fired the shotgun into the grand stairs without aiming. The man took the full brunt of the buckshot to his abdomen, practically tearing him apart, and tumbled down the broad stairs. Deputy Gaines saw the carnage, cried out, and darted back outside, slamming the door behind him. Deputy Gaines ran down the porch steps screaming like a maniac with his gun in the air. Two other deputies with weapons drawn remained by their cruisers.

"We need the staties," Deputy Gaines cried out while clinging to his hat and gun as he ran toward them. "We need the staties!"

Back inside, Maverick and Stone remained in their respective hiding places and waited for the war that was about to come to them now that the entire hotel heard the shotgun blast. Two men ran down the grand hallway toward the foyer to investigate. They ran to their fallen man at the bottom of the stairs. Stone and Maverick had them in a kill hole and took their shots. Shotgun blasts echoed throughout the first floor, dropping the two men on top of the first dead man. The sound of footfalls running along the upper floors was loud and urgent as everyone was now alerted to the firefight. Maverick and Stone patiently and quietly waited, but no more men appeared either in the hallway or on the stairs.

§

Rayner remained crouched against the wall within the second floor secret passageway and worked on his laptop while Scorpio changed into a pair of jeans near the passageway entrance to her bedroom. She slipped into a pair of soft soled, black boots that would produce the least amount of noise for sneaking about. She put on her brother's leather jacket, which still contained the gun in the pocket, and grabbed both extra clips from the built-in cupboard in the passageway wall. She handed Rayner one of the guns from the cupboard. He stared at it a moment then accepted it, placing it down the back of his pants. The faint sounds of shotgun blasts from downstairs alerted them to the war that was about to unfold.

"That's our guys," she informed Rayner, recognizing the sounds as shotguns, and then eyed his laptop. "I definitely heard shotgun blasts coming from the first floor. Are they okay?"

Rayner switched video feed on his laptop. "Looks like they took out some bad guys at the bottom of the stairs," he informed her while watching the security monitor. "If I'm correct, they took lookout positions in the lounge doorway and the hall bathroom."

He pressed several buttons and changed cameras multiple times. "We have bad guys on second. There are two at the top of the stairs. Judging by their reactions, they can see their fallen men, but they're not taking the bait. They must realize it's a trap." He watched a moment in silence. "They're turning around, probably heading for the back stairs."

Both remained quiet and listened. They could hear the men running in the hallway outside Scorpio's room. Once they were gone, Rayner pressed several more buttons.

"I have more guys at the back stairs heading down them as well," he announced then switched cameras. Rayner suddenly groaned. "Two are heading out the kitchen door. If enough of them come at them from both the back hallway and the front door, they'll be outnumbered and cornered. If the curtains are open in the lounge, someone sneaking around outside may see Stone through the window and take a shot at him."

"We need to warn them," she announced.

"We don't have any way to contact them," he informed her. "What we need is a diversion."

"Where are the police?"

Rayner pressed a few more buttons then groaned discovering more bad news. "Deputy Dumbass is out front with two men," he muttered.

She suddenly glared at him. "That's all?"

"Hopefully, they're waiting for additional backup," Rayner remarked. "I specifically said to bring reinforcements. What was that idiot thinking?"

"We need to divide and conquer," she informed him without hesitation.

"What?" he asked with surprise while looking at her then vigorously shook his head. "No, Scorpio. You're not going out there."

"You see who you can contact online," she insisted. "I'll alert the guys and give them a chance to make it to the game room or the library. Once we're safely hidden in the secret passageways, we can wait it out."

"There are already two men in the kitchen heading for the hallway," he informed her. "They'll be near the game room by the time you reach the secret passageway entrance. They'll be in the perfect position to ambush you."

"I didn't intend to use the secret passageway," she announced.

Rayner suddenly eyed her. "Whatever it is, Scorpio, no," he insisted with horror in his eyes. "You can't go out there. There are too many of them."

"Are there any men in the second floor hallway?" she demanded while ignoring his protests.

He pressed several buttons. "I don't see any, but that doesn't mean--"

Scorpio opened the passageway to her bedroom. She was about to bolt out the opening when she suddenly hesitated, turned back to Rayner, and kissed him quickly but passionately on the lips. She pulled back, affectionately touched his face, and closed the passageway behind her before he could protest. She hurried for her bedroom door, peered into the hallway, and then silently scurried several doors down to the elevator. She pushed the button. The elevator creaked and groaned before loudly making its way to the second floor from the first.

§

Deputy Gaines sat half inside the cruiser and radioed for backup while frantically yelling into the receiver. The two remaining deputies took cover behind the open doors of the same cruiser with their weapons aimed at the hotel. A familiar car pulled up the driveway and stopped several yards behind the police vehicles blocking the driveway. Scorpio's grandfather got out of his car and stared at the armed deputies.

"What's happening?" he demanded, clearly concerned for his granddaughter.

The first deputy motioned for him to come closer and get down. Newman hurried to join them while keeping low. The look of horror was evident on his face.

"Something's happened. I tried calling from the hospital but couldn't get through," Newman gasped with alarm. "Is my granddaughter in trouble? Is she okay? Damn it. What's happening?"

"We received a distress call about multiple intruders," the first deputy informed him without taking his eyes off the hotel. "There's gunfire coming from inside, and someone was killed on the stairs. We're calling for backup."

"You're waiting for backup while my granddaughter could be in there dying?" Newman suddenly demanded. "We have to go in there and help her."

"I see someone," the second deputy from the opposite side of the cruiser announced. "There's someone coming around the side of the house."

"Wait until we see who it is before firing," the first deputy responded and again aimed his weapon for the house.

"It could be Scorpio," Newman practically cried out. "Anyone shoots my granddaughter--"

The first deputy motioned behind him for Newman to keep his voice down. He frowned and remained silent while watching the house.

Chapter 55

The two men within the kitchen bolted down the hallway and stopped not far from the noisy elevator as it descended. Both men aimed their weapons at the elevator and waited. Maverick peered out the bathroom doorway and saw the men by the elevator, but he didn't have a clear shot. As the elevator made its way to the first floor, Maverick exchanged looks with Stone across the hallway. They heard gunfire from outside, stopping either from stepping out of the safety of their rooms. It sounded as if the two men who had gone around the hotel ran into the deputies out front. Despite the gunfire outside, neither intruder moved from their position in front of the now stopped elevator, waiting to shoot the first person who stepped out of it.

Maverick and Stone saw movement on the stairs, despite not hearing anything. Scorpio paused halfway down the steps and crouched on them so she could see Maverick in the bathroom. She indicated the hallway and the foyer entrance. He raised his brows and nodded, indicating he already knew they were out front. Scorpio then heard the gunfire out front as well. She nervously ran her fingers through her hair. There was little chance the deputies were winning the firefight. Scorpio knew she had to get off the stairs before someone came up behind her. She hurried down the steps while clinging to her gun and joined Stone inside the lounge.

"We need to move before we're surrounded," she informed them.

The front door was thrown open with surprising force, causing Scorpio and Stone to jump.

"Too late," Stone remarked and aimed his shotgun at the front door. He waited, but no one rushed inside.

Scorpio crouched down on the opposite side of the door from Stone and aimed her gun at the stairs to keep them safe from a surprise attack.

"Son-of-a-bitch," Stone suddenly groaned.

Scorpio looked toward the front door to see what had Stone concerned. Her grandfather took a step into the foyer with his hands raised in the air and a deeply concerned look on his face. A masked intruder stood behind him with a gun aimed at Newman's head and looked toward the lounge doorway, where he could see Stone, who had been mostly hidden.

"Come on out and drop the weapon or gramps gets his head blown off," the man announced to Stone.

"Don't do it, Scorpio," Newman called out. "He'll kill us all!"

Somehow, they saw Scorpio as well, but they didn't seem to know about Maverick. The two men in the hallway near the empty elevator realized they'd been played and approached the foyer. They passed the bathroom without seeing Maverick, who remained hidden just inside the doorway. Stone cursed under his breath and lowered his shotgun. Scorpio stared at him with surprise from her crouched position.

"You can't go out there," she gasped just loud enough for him to hear. "They'll kill you."

"They're going to kill your grandfather," Stone whispered back.

"And after they kill you, they'll kill him anyway," she insisted.

"Go out the window, Scorpio," he announced softly. "Just run for the woods and don't stop."

She stared in horror as Stone stepped into the hallway near the dead men piled at the bottom of the stairs. He kept the shotgun in his hand but no longer had it aimed. There was a creak from the stairs. Stone didn't bother turning. It didn't matter who was on the stairs since he was already in enough trouble. One more intruder with a gun didn't matter at this point.

The man with the gun aimed at Newman's head looked at the stairs and immediately tensed. "Drop the gun," he shouted with conviction.

Scorpio and Stone both looked toward the stairs at the command, realizing his words could only mean one thing. Scorpio stared in horror at Rayner standing on the stairs with the gun she'd given him aimed at the doorway. As the men in the hallway turned toward the stairs, Stone bolted back into the lounge, again aiming the shotgun at the men. Maverick pumped his shotgun behind the two men in the hallway, causing them to freeze. Newman appeared horrified at the situation that was about to unfold.

"Everyone drop their weapons, or the old man gets it," the man behind him now screamed.

To everyone's surprise and horror, Rayner fired his weapon at the doorway. As the bullet struck her grandfather in the shoulder, Scorpio cried out with alarm. The man in the doorway was left exposed without his human shield. He aimed his gun at Rayner. Rayner fired again, hitting the gunman in the doorway between the eyes. His head snapped back from the shot, and he fell backward onto the porch. The two remaining men in the hallway attempted to take out Stone and Maverick, but both fired their shotguns and took them down with a spray of buckshot, spraying the entire area with blood. When the last of the men in the hallway fell, Scorpio bolted from the safety of the lounge and ran for her grandfather. Newman was huddled in a small ball in the foyer entrance clutching his bleeding shoulder. A bullet struck the floor just before Scorpio's feet causing her to stop in her tracks. She spun around and looked back at the stairs where Rayner kept his gun aimed.

"Leave him," Rayner cried out, surprising everyone.

Stone immediately spun and aimed his shotgun at Rayner. Maverick did the same.

"Drop the gun, Rayner," Stone shouted, "or so help me; I'll cut you in half."

"Her grandfather shot the deputies out front," Rayner announced without taking his gun off Newman. "I saw him on the security camera. He's behind everything!"

Scorpio stared at Rayner with horror then looked at her injured grandfather. He now held a gun in his hand and fired a shot at Rayner before darting out the open door. Rayner fired two shots at him, but he was already running across the porch. Stone ran for the door and saw Newman dart around the side of the house. Stone shut and locked the door then looked at the others.

"There are still at least six more men inside this house," Stone informed them. "They can still ambush us. We can't afford to go after Newman."

Scorpio stared at the closed foyer door with horror. "My grandfather?" she gasped and shook her head in disbelief. "No, it's not possible."

Rayner hurried to her side and gently touched her arm. "I'm sorry, Scorpio," he announced. "I saw him shoot the deputies in the back from the security cameras. He ambushed them, and they never saw it coming."

She couldn't look up. A thousand thoughts and images flashed through her mind. What had her grandfather done? How far had he gone? Did her grandfather actually send someone to kill her grandmother? Was he responsible for Cal's murder? Did he order the hit on her brother; his own grandson? She felt every muscle in her body suddenly twitch. Rayner was talking to her, but she didn't hear a word he said. She wasn't even aware that all three men were staring at her while practically shouting out orders.

"Scorpio, we need to get out of this hallway," Maverick announced. "The remaining men will be coming any minute. We have to go."

"Scorpio?" Stone announced attempting to get her attention but was unsuccessful. He looked at his friends. "I think she's in shock."

Rayner attempted to lead her to a safe place while Stone collected the discarded weapons. Scorpio suddenly pulled away from Rayner, startling him. She met his gaze for the first time. Her look was wild and unpredictable. Without a word, Scorpio turned and approached the front sitting room door.

"That's locked," Maverick reminded her while looking around with concern. "We have to go, Scorpio."

Scorpio violently kicked the door. The doorframe cracked with a loud snap, and the door flew inward, slamming against the inside wall with tremendous force. She entered the room with determination and purpose. All three men hurried to the sitting room, a room they had never been inside. Stone kept an eye on the hallway from the sitting room doorway. Maverick and Rayner watched in bewilderment as Scorpio crossed the dusty room to the wall beyond the grandfather clock. She paused before the samurai swords where they hung and stared at them only a moment before removing them from the wall. She twirled both swords in her hands and turned to face the men now staring at her.

"I know you're upset," Maverick gently announced while attempting to calm her, "but this isn't the time to seek revenge. This is a kill or be killed moment."

"Which is exactly what I'm going to do," she scoffed while glaring at him with what could only be described as the devil in her eyes. "Now get out of my way."

Maverick was about to protest when Rayner gently pulled him from her path.

"She knows what she's doing," Rayner announced timidly. "Let her go."

Maverick stared at Rayner with surprise by the comment. "I'd think you of all people--"

Scorpio walked past Maverick and Rayner and headed toward Stone in the doorway.

"She's capable of defending herself," Rayner insisted while watching her. "*Immensely* capable."

Stone stood aside and allowed her to leave the sitting room. He then looked back at Maverick and Rayner. "It wasn't just sheer luck the night Cal died, was it?" Stone asked with surprise. "She knew exactly what she was doing when she went after those men."

"By her own admission. She's in predator mode," Rayner informed them. "We can offer her backup, but it's best if we just stayed out of her way."

All three men hurried after Scorpio. When they entered the hallway strewn with blood, Scorpio was gone. An armed intruder appeared in the hallway and aimed his weapon at the three men. Before any of them could react, Scorpio lunged out of the carefully hidden closet beneath the steps and kicked the gun from the man's hands. He spun to face her with surprise. She slashed him across the throat then spun into a roundhouse kick and struck him in the face, sending him to the floor. All three men stared at the dead man on the floor and watched the blood collect into a pool around his slit throat. Scorpio turned without comment and headed down the hallway for the kitchen. Maverick, Stone, and Rayner exchanged concerned looks then hurried after her.

Chapter 56

Scorpio walked across the kitchen with her bloodstained swords then suddenly paused alarming the three men following her. Maverick was about to speak when Rayner silenced him by holding his hand up as he watched Scorpio. She turned her attention to the open basement door, which was always closed. She headed through the basement door and silently crept down the stairs. The three men hurried after her, attempting to make as little sound as the woman they followed. Each time they made even the slightest sound, she glared at them. They reached the bottom of the steps without running into anyone, but they could hear voices echoing from the main room just down the hall. She paused by the entranceway and listened a moment before peeking into the room.

Muddy and Blain had Davenport bound and gagged while on his knees not far from the body drop pit. Schmidt paced the room with earbuds attached to his walkie-talkie, which hung from his belt.

"Can we off this bastard yet," Schmidt announced then listened to the response. "Copy that."

He turned to the other men then looked at Davenport, who looked up at them with concern.

"The boss says to hold off killing him just yet," Schmidt announced. "It has to look like one of *them* killed him in self-defense."

"So what's the holdup?" Blain demanded with some irritation.

"No takers yet," Schmidt responded.

"You mean all that gunfire going on upstairs, and we haven't taken down any of them yet?" Muddy practically demanded.

"How many men have we lost?" Blain suddenly asked with concern.

"He didn't offer, and I didn't ask," Schmidt replied. "If you want to survive in this game, you need to keep your eyes open and your mouth shut."

Blain was about to respond when he looked across the room. Scorpio was already standing in front of him. He gasped with surprise and attempted to aim his weapon. Scorpio swung her right sword, easily slashing his throat. Schmidt and Muddy saw their accomplice go down and noticed Scorpio too late. She kicked the gun from Schmidt's hand and slashed Muddy across the arm with her left sword the moment she regained her footing. Schmidt attempted to lunge for her. She slashed crisscross with her swords, slashing his abdomen and throat at the same time.

As he fell to the floor, she lunged forward, impaled Muddy through the gut, and spun, slashing him across the throat with the other sword. She pulled her sword free as Muddy spit up blood before sinking to the floor. She turned to face Davenport still kneeling on the floor. He stared at her with horror in his eyes and attempted to beg for mercy through his gag. Scorpio removed his gag.

"Please, I didn't kill anyone," Davenport insisted. "Rico turned on me. Him and Celine."

Scorpio was surprised to hear the last part of his confession and immediately looked back at Rayner while raising a cocky brow.

Rayner shrugged. "Okay, so I was wrong about Celine and Rico," he announced.

Scorpio stepped behind Davenport and used her blood-covered sword to cut the rope binding his wrists. He was a little slow moving to his feet then indicated one of the discarded guns.

"May I?"

Scorpio nodded. Davenport grabbed one of the dead men's guns and checked the clip before slamming it back into place and cocking the weapon.

"Rico's here somewhere," Davenport informed her while looking around.

"He's here with at least two more men," she informed him then sneered, "and my grandfather."

Davenport stared at her with shock and surprise. "Newman," he gasped. "He's behind all of this?" He shook his head in anger. "I should have known he was too squeaky-clean. Always paying someone else to do his dirty work." Davenport's expression suddenly dropped. "Kane. He couldn't possibly have--" Davenport eyed the three dead men then Scorpio as she walked across the room to join her men. "No wonder you're pissed." He hurried after her. "Your mother's death finally makes sense."

Scorpio suddenly stopped and spun to face Davenport with a horrified look in her eyes. "What do you mean?" she demanded.

"Didn't you put it together yet?" Davenport asked. "Your uncle was starting to renovate this place. He must have gotten too close to your grandfather's death pit. When he contracted the hit on your uncle, he probably hadn't contemplated his unexpected trip to Boston. Your uncle just happened to be with your mother when his hired guns carried out the hit." He shook his head. "That's far more believable than someone from your father's past coming back to kill your mother for no apparent reason."

Scorpio let the comment sink in and it suddenly made sense to her. Davenport was right. Her uncle was the target, not her mother! Her anger consumed her. She glared at Maverick as she approached him.

"*Now* we can clean house," she scoffed.

Scorpio twirled the swords aggressively in her hands and walked past him. Davenport hurried after them with his own weapon in hand. Stone brought up the rear behind Davenport, showing less trust than Scorpio. They'd been betrayed one too many times already, and he wasn't about to make that mistake again.

§

Once they entered the kitchen, Stone took a lookout position at the bottom of the back stairs while Maverick took one at the main kitchen door. Scorpio eyed Rayner and realized he was without his laptop.

"Can we make it to the office and see their location on the security monitor?" Scorpio asked Rayner.

"No, I'm afraid I was forced to disable the main monitors remotely from my laptop," he informed her. "I didn't want Rico's men to steal my idea and post a lookout on the main monitor in order to find us."

"Where are they?" she asked with surprise. "Why aren't they down here looking for us?"

"I may have that answer," Davenport boldly announced. "I overheard some of their conversations while they held me hostage at Muddy's house. I heard them say before Kane left town, he stopped at your grandparent's house. Apparently, he mentioned something called Midnight Requisition. I don't know what that is, but it's possible your grandfather thinks it had something to do with the hit he took out on your uncle all those years ago. If he thought Kane was acting stranger than usual, it's possible he's been killing himself trying to find where Kane hid Midnight Requisition."

"So he's looking for Midnight Requisition?" Scorpio practically demanded. "Well, he's not going to find it here. We looked. Even with Rayner's superior brain, we couldn't find it."

"I'm guessing it's a file of some sort. The guys seemed convinced it was on Kane's laptop," Davenport informed her. "All evidence of it must have burned in his laptop along with the car."

"No, his laptop wasn't with him in the car. I assumed they stole it before setting the car on fire," she informed him. "Is that why he had his men try to kill my grandmother? He feared she'd remember something when your private detective stopped by the house."

Davenport stared at her with surprise. "He sent men to kill Patricia?" he gasped then appeared concerned. "Is she okay?"

"She's fine," Scorpio announced and then became concerned while considering the comment. "At least I hope she is. We left her at the hospital with him." She looked at Rayner for reassurances.

"There was a guard outside her door," Rayner reminded her, hoping to comfort her. "I'm sure he wouldn't attempt anything at the hospital."

"So Kane said something that day, and he feared his wife would remember their conversation if it came up again," Davenport announced then shook his head. "I suspected Celine was screwing around with Rico, and I never once thought about killing either of them. It takes a cold man to order a hit on his own son, grandson, and his wife."

"Are you sure Celine was having an affair with Rico?" Rayner asked not seeming convinced.

Davenport frowned in response. "She was having an affair with someone," he replied. "Knowing Rico, I assumed it was him. I thought she'd put an end to it months ago, but when Scorpio told me Celine was talking to her cousin at the diner, I knew she was still seeing him. She'd borrow the keys to her cousin's houseboat for her rendezvous. It was the only time she talked to her cousin."

"I really can't picture Celine with someone like Rico," Rayner remarked.

Scorpio suddenly frowned then glared at Rayner. "How about someone like my grandfather?"

After hearing the comment, all eyes were suddenly on Scorpio. It was a surprising revelation that seemed to strike a chord with everyone.

Davenport sneered and shook his head. "Yeah, that makes sense."

"She probably overheard my conversation with Daniel at the diner and alerted Newman," Rayner remarked.

"Celine's affair with Newman is the least of our concerns right now," Stone announced. "If she's involved in this, the authorities can deal with her later. We have more pressing concerns at the moment."

"If they're looking for Midnight Requisition, they'll be in Kane's room or searching for my laptop," Rayner announced. "They must think I found something of importance."

"They'll be watching the stairs for us," Maverick announced from the doorway then raised a sly brow. "I'm thinking we take the back way."

"They'll be watching the back stairs too," Davenport corrected.

"Not that back way," Maverick announced while grinning. "The other back way."

Scorpio nodded. "And I have just the plan," she announced.

§

The old, creaking elevator was heard moving up the shaft for the upper floor. An armed man positioned at the back stairs on the third floor looked down the hall toward the loudly moving elevator. He radioed the man positioned by the grand stairs since they couldn't see each other due to the long hallway with multiple smaller corridors.

"You copy?"

"Yeah, what is it?" the male voice asked from over the radio.

"The elevator's moving. I think it's coming to this floor," the man by the back stairs announced with concern. "Should I check it out?"

"Negative," the man by the grand stairs announced through the hand radio. "They're creating another diversion. They'll be coming up one or both of the stairs while they think they have us waiting by the elevator."

"Copy that."

"Stay alert," the man responded. "I'm sure it's another trap."

Once the elevator stopped on the third floor, the man by the stairs kept an eye on it as well as the back stairs. When the gate didn't open, he focused his attention on the stairs and kept his gun aimed down them. The familiar sound of the gate opening was then heard. He spun around with his gun aimed, but Maverick was already in the hallway outside the elevator with a borrowed semiautomatic containing a silencer. Maverick fired two nearly silent shots into the man with one of their own weapons. No one was alerted to the unheard shots or their falling man.

Stone and Davenport appeared from one of the bedrooms on the right side of the hallway, where the second passageway came out, and headed for the main stairs. The man by the grand stairs saw them and turned with his gun aimed. Stone fired two muffled shots into the man and watched him tumble down the stairs. Stone grimaced at the loud thumping the man's body made while falling down the steps. Davenport frowned at Stone and shook his head.

Chapter 57

Rico routed around within the closet in Kane's bedroom and carelessly tossed objects across the floor. Scorpio's grandfather attempted to pull out each dresser drawer while only using his good right hand. Blood had soaked through the shirt on his left shoulder, but a crude patch job seemed to have stopped the bleeding. The contents of the desk were already scattered on the floor. Newman gave up and raised his hand radio to his mouth.

"What's the status on the hotel residents?" he asked. "Are they out of the way?" There was no response. "Anyone copy?"

He waited, but there was still no response.

Rico appeared from the closet with the locked box. "Found this in a hidden compartment inside the closet," he announced and set it on the bed.

Newman saw the box and immediately became excited. He hurried for the bed to join Rico. Rico examined the box and shook his head.

"There's no quick way of getting into this thing without the code," Rico informed him.

"I'll try his birthday," Newman announced. "Scorpio uses her birthday for everything. That's how I remotely accessed her security system from my cell phone. Being they're twins--"

He pressed the number into the code panel. It turned red, signaling it wasn't correct.

"We don't have time to mess around here," Rico informed him and appeared irritated. "Why aren't the other men responding?"

"I don't know," Newman remarked, "but we have to get out of here in case Deputy Gaines got that backup call through before I shot him."

"My men can handle any backup from this town," Rico informed him.

Newman spun to face Rico with fire in his eyes. "Your men couldn't even handle the computer geek," he announced while indicating his bleeding shoulder. He attempted to use the hand radio again with rising anger and frustration. "Anyone copy? We need to terminate Davenport and purge the hotel ASAP."

There was still no response.

Newman glared at Rico. "We need to completely sanitize this hotel," he announced revealing his anger and frustration. "We'll disconnect the gas line, let her fill up with gas, and blow this godforsaken building off its foundation. This bitch of a hotel has cost me my entire family."

"We should have done that in the first place," Rico remarked.

"I never should have sold this place to my son. I can't believe he found that pit. Son-of-a-bitch. I looked for it for weeks and couldn't find where my security team stashed the bodies. I thought I was safe," Newman informed him.

"You'd think after ordering a hit on your own son, you'd destroy the evidence once and for all," Rico muttered.

"Hey, I honestly thought the hotel would convert back to me once he was dead," Newman lashed out. "I didn't know he'd willed it to Scorpio and Kane. Christ; they were only babies."

"You should have burned it to the ground then and there," Rico scoffed.

"Too many questions," Newman replied. "It'd come back to me. Besides, now that I know where the bodies were hidden, it's a good thing I hadn't burned the place down. Would have led the police right to the bodies once the structure was gone. The police I can handle; it was answering to some very angry mafia families that would have been hazardous to my health. Since Horton removed the evidence, I can finally get rid of anything else hidden in these walls."

"You should have let the men take care of that the night you sent them to kill Cal," Rico informed him. "Would have saved yourself a lot of headache. This entire Midnight Requisition thing has been one tough bastard to find."

"I thought I could save my granddaughter," Newman announced then frowned. "She actually meant something to me. Just like her mother. It wasn't supposed to be this way. None of this was supposed to end this way. I don't know why Kane had to keep poking around. If he'd just spent his money and lived a playboy's life like any normal twenty-something with a million dollar trust fund, none of this would have happened. He wouldn't have found this Midnight Requisition bullshit."

Just beyond the secret passageway entrance, Scorpio listened to the conversation being held within Kane's bedroom. Rayner watched her with anticipation of her next move. She was surprisingly in control despite the way she gripped her swords. Rayner once again looked out the peek hole and watched the two men within the bedroom. He silently closed the peek hole and turned to face her.

"They're leaving the room," he whispered. "They intend to destroy the hotel. We need a plan."

Scorpio finally straightened and turned to face Rayner in the mostly dark passageway. "We have a plan," she informed him. "You get down to the game room entrance and get out of the hotel the first chance you get. I need to a have a little *talk* with Grandpa."

"I'm not leaving you," he insisted.

She impatiently glared at him. "We don't have time to argue about this," Scorpio informed him.

"You're right; we don't," he replied. "So stop arguing with me."

"You don't understand. I can't lose another man I love," she launched then realized what she'd just said.

Rayner stared at her a moment with surprise. She immediately fidgeted, uncomfortable with her confession. He kissed her quickly on the lips then met her gaze with a serious look.

"You need me," he boldly announced and raised his brows. "I'm a better shot than you are."

Scorpio managed a tense smile at the comment. He knew she didn't have time to argue with him. Rico and her grandfather had to be stopped before they reached the back stairs, which would offer cover until they made it to the kitchen. At that point, they'd already have access to the gas stoves. Scorpio decided against arguing with Rayner. She opened the passageway entrance and hurried across Kane's ransacked bedroom for the open door. Stone and Maverick approached them within the hallway and indicated the back stairs.

"Rico and your grandfather just went down the back stairs," Stone informed her.

She cursed under her breath then looked around. "Where's Davenport?"

"We sent him to the police cruiser to call for backup," Maverick informed her.

Scorpio indicated the grand stairs across the building. "The three of you take the front stairs," she announced. "I'll take the elevator. Meet me in the kitchen."

Maverick and Stone hurried down the hall for the main staircase that was just out of sight. As Scorpio headed for the elevator, Rayner joined her. She cast a glare at him then groaned, knowing she didn't have time to argue. She needed to use the elevator while her grandfather and Rico were on the back stairs and still couldn't hear the rickety monstrosity moving.

§

Rico and Newman entered the kitchen from the back stairs. Newman set the locked box on the island counter and hurried for the two large stoves while Rico kept watch with his gun securely in hand. As Newman approached the gas stoves, the interior kitchen door was heard. Both turned toward the door with their guns aimed. The swinging door swayed slightly, but there wasn't anyone there.

"Check it out," Newman ordered.

Rico nodded, hurried across the kitchen, and cautiously entered the hallway through the swinging door.

Newman set his gun down on the counter and again turned toward the stoves, crouching before it to turn out the pilot light. He heard something alongside him. He was about to speak when he looked to his left and saw the tip of a samurai sword only an inch from his eyes. Scorpio held her sword in both hands above her shoulder directly in her grandfather's face. Newman slowly straightened and watched as the sword followed. Scorpio's look was cold and without emotion as she stared back at him.

§

Rico crept along the grand hallway with his gun in his hand and looked around. He glanced into each of the nearby rooms but didn't find anyone. Further down the hall and closer to the grand staircase, two of his men lay in bloody heaps. He didn't even give them a second glance. He paused before the closed elevator and looked through the gate. The old elevator was one level down, placing it in the basement. Rico turned away from the elevator and nearly collided with Stone, who stood directly behind him. Stone twisted his wrist, forcing him to drop his gun, and then punched him in the face, sending him back against the rickety elevator gate. The old gate rattled in response. Rico touched his bleeding lip and straightened while glaring at Stone. Stone didn't appear to be armed. Rico suddenly grinned and read the cold expression on his adversary's face.

"This is about Amber, isn't it?" Rico suddenly chuckled. "You have feelings for the little slut, huh?"

"Actually, I saved Amber from you the moment I planted that diamond necklace in her apartment," Stone boldly announced. "Kicking your ass is purely for my amusement."

Rico sneered in anger, realizing what Stone had done. "She wasn't yours to save!"

He lunged for Stone and tackled the big man into the opposing wall with enough force to knock several framed photos to the floor. Rico punched Stone twice in the side while he had him pinned to the wall then stepped back to punch him in the face. Stone immediately straightened and swung first, punching Rico in the mouth. Rico stumbled backward. Stone swung hard and fast with his right then lift fist, repeatedly striking Rico in the face. Rico fell to the floor. He panted a moment while on his hands and knees then snatched the discarded gun near him. He sprang to his feet with the gun in his hand, although swaying slightly from the hard hits.

"You should have killed me when you had the chance," Rico snarled then grinned with bloodied teeth.

Stone jumped back a step as Rico's finger tightened on the trigger. The second dead man on the floor suddenly sat up with a gun in his hand. Maverick, who had been posing as the second dead body, fired his weapon. Rico took the bullet to his shoulder, forcing him to drop the gun. He clutched his bleeding shoulder and looked from Maverick just down the hall to Stone standing before him.

Rico sneered with anger. "Two on one is hardly a fair fight," he growled.

Stone shrugged, took a step forward, and pulled open the elevator gate. "Yeah, but I don't play by those rules," he announced.

He kicked Rico in the abdomen, projecting him backward and into the open elevator shaft. Rico cried out as he fell down the shaft and landed with a thump.

Maverick rolled his eyes and shook his head while standing. "You're sadistic."

"No, I have anger issues," Stone corrected while glaring at his friend. "And I'm working on that."

§

Newman stared at the bloodstained sword Scorpio aimed at his face. Her anger and hate was directed at him, and there was no telling what she intended to do. Newman remained calm while staring at her, talking to her as he did when she was a child.

"I know you're confused and upset, honey," Newman announced.

"You don't get to call me honey anymore," she snarled without so much as twitching.

"You've got this all wrong," he attempted to explain. "Rico and I were trying to save you by pretending to conspire with those men. We were trying to flush Davenport out."

"By attempting to blow up the hotel?" she launched back. "Sorry, *Grandpa*. Rayner's in the basement shutting off the gas as we speak."

He hesitated a moment while staring at her. "Is that what you think I was doing? You know I'd never do anything to hurt you," he insisted sympathetically. "You know I didn't kill anyone. Do you actually think I killed your brother? My own grandson?"

"Is that the best you've got?" Scorpio scoffed while glaring at him. "I heard you in Kane's bedroom. You told Rico you had Kane killed. And Cal? You hired those men to kill him too, didn't you?" Her eyes suddenly narrowed with hate. "You ordered a hit on your own son and daughter! You killed my mother!"

"It wasn't like that, Scorpio," he announced. "I swear."

She sneered at him. "Midnight Requisition had nothing to do with you."

The expression drained from Newman's face as a horrifying realization swept over him.

A twisted, hateful smile crossed Scorpio's face. "That's right," she snarled. "You killed your entire family, everyone you loved, over something that wasn't even about you."

Newman immediately reclaimed his calm demeanor then shook his head with confidence. "You won't kill me," he announced boldly. "I'm unarmed, and I'm your grandfather. I raised you, remember?"

"You killed everyone I've ever loved," she snarled. "What makes you think I care about any of that?"

Newman drew a deep breath and stood proudly. "Because if you kill me, you'll never know the truth," he informed her. "You want to know things only I can answer."

Scorpio stared at him over her sword blade. She took several deep breaths then lowered the sword. Her grandfather relaxed as well. He suddenly lunged for the gun on the counter.

"The head of the beast," she snarled and swung the sword.

Newman aimed the gun at her with a strange smirk on his face, as it would seem she had swung and missed. He stood motionless a moment, the smile never leaving his face as blood trickled down his neck, revealing the slice. His head slid from his neck, and his body collapsed to the floor just seconds after it. Scorpio stared at her dead grandfather without any emotion.

"I already know the truth," she scoffed.

Rayner bolted through the basement doorway with a semiautomatic in his hand. He suddenly stopped and stared at the decapitated man not far from Scorpio's feet.

Rayner held his breath a moment then met Scorpio's gaze. "Are you okay?"

She opened her hand, releasing the bloodied sword, and allowed it to drop to the floor into the quickly collecting pool of blood. As her emotions returned, Rayner hurried for her and gathered her in his arms, allowing her to sob on his shoulder.

Chapter 58

Scorpio, Maverick, Stone, and Rayner sat on the porch and watched as the paramedics loaded the stretcher with Deputy Gaines into the back of the ambulance. Not far from the ambulance, Davenport gave his statement of accounts to the state police while in handcuffs. He could have fled the scene and been well on his way to some remote country, but he chose to assist the severely wounded deputy instead. Not innocent by any means, Davenport wasn't quite as bad as he had been portrayed, which was mostly brought about by Scorpio's grandfather. A state trooper approached the porch. All four moved to their feet.

"Your grandmother is perfectly safe in her hospital bed," the trooper informed Scorpio. "I suppose she wasn't the bigger threat to your grandfather at the moment, so he didn't waste time finishing her off."

"Thank God," Scorpio remarked with a sigh of relief. She then cringed at the question she had to ask. "Does she know about my grandfather?"

The state trooper nodded. "We couldn't get around not telling her that he was behind the murders and tried to kill you and your friends."

"Was she okay?"

"A little on the angry side," the trooper replied. "The doctor had to give her a sedative."

Scorpio frowned somehow feeling guilty about the pain she may have caused her grandmother. "Does she know *how* he died?"

He gave a sympathetic nod.

"She's going to resent me," Scorpio whispered.

"I doubt that. Her exact words were, 'now Kane can rest in peace'," the trooper informed her. "She can't wait to see you."

"All of this," Scorpio announced and looked around with disgust. "All the killings were so he could protect his interests from the horrors he'd committed decades ago. Starting with my uncle and mother just because my uncle stumbled upon his secret in the basement."

"But why did he kill your brother?" the trooper asked while putting away his notebook.

"A misunderstanding," Scorpio replied while studying the trooper. "My brother was discussing what he'd found about my father's death with my grandmother, and my grandfather overheard something about a file Kane had found. He mistakenly thought it was something that would implicate him in my mother's murder. I guess he had one of his hitmen follow Kane to Virginia. I suppose we'll never know since his laptop is gone."

The trooper nodded, gave his condolences, and headed past them into the hotel. Rayner, Stone, and Maverick stared at Scorpio. She met their strange looks with an emotionless expression.

"You could have told him what you suspect happened at your grandparent's house the day Kane left," Rayner informed her.

She shook her head. "No, if he left something there, I want to find it myself and see what it is," Scorpio replied. "Then I'll contact the police and let them know what I'd found."

"Well," Stone announced with a sigh. "The hotel is officially a crime scene. We could invade your grandmother's house and clean ourselves up there before heading to the hospital to see her."

"No, the police have her house sealed off as well," Scorpio reminded them. "Now with new evidence against my grandfather, I'm certain they'll be poking around there half the night as well."

"You realize Stone and I could be in her house, find what your brother left behind, and be out before the police ever realized we were there," Maverick informed her while offering a devious grin.

"No," Scorpio remarked. "There's no reason to risk getting caught there tonight. We'll have plenty of time to search Kane's room at my grandmother's house once the police have finished their investigation."

"We can't stay here tonight," Stone reminded her. "We need to find someplace to stay."

"We'll go to my house," Rayner suggested.

Both men eyed him, appeared curious, and then chuckled in response.

"That's right," Maverick announced. "You do have your own place. I almost forgot, since you practically lived here the last couple of weeks."

"Rayner's house it is," Scorpio announced with a sigh then eyed Rayner and raised a curious brow. "Do you have *everything* we need?"

Rayner collected his bag containing his laptop and unzipped it while offering a sly grin. Scorpio saw the locked box tucked inside the bag.

"Right here," he announced then zipped the bag. "Ready when you are."

Scorpio looked back at the open front door as the blue and red police lights flashed across the front of the hotel. She frowned and shook her head.

"I'm having doubts about this place," she muttered almost to herself.

"We're going to fix her up," Maverick insisted while gently rubbing her shoulders.

"Yeah, you've already sold us on the dream," Stone informed her. "I finally have a family, and I'm not giving that up."

"Me either," Maverick announced proudly while smiling at Scorpio.

Scorpio then looked at Rayner as if silently asking him the same question.

"I'm not going anywhere," Rayner insisted without hesitation. "I'm whipped, remember?"

Scorpio smiled, kissed him warmly on the lips, and then pulled away while extending her hand. Rayner eyed her hand, understanding the significance, and then placed his hand in hers. They walked from the porch together. Maverick playfully extended his hand to Stone and smiled while batting his eyelashes. Stone chuckled, slapped his hand, and walked off the porch.

Chapter 59

The following day, Stone and Maverick helped Scorpio's moderately bruised grandmother limp into her living room. The two men made her comfortable on the antique sofa and propped her sprained ankle onto a pillow on the coffee table. Scorpio and Rayner stood in the foyer doorway and watched without comment. She gave him a slight nod to the stairs. Rayner hurried up the stairs while Scorpio entered the living room and watched the two men attend to the injured woman. Scorpio couldn't help but smile as the moderately tough men fawned over her grandmother.

"I'll make you some tea," Maverick announced and hurried from the room.

"Do you want the television on?" Stone asked while grabbing the remote control.

"No, but I would like my cordless phone, please," Patricia replied.

Stone left the remote control on the arm of the chair then went for her cordless phone. Scorpio approached her grandmother and sat on the sofa facing her.

"Are you sure you wouldn't rather come to the hotel and stay with us?" Scorpio asked in a sympathetic tone. "The crime scene clean-up crew did an excellent job sprucing up the place. I'm thinking about putting them on retainer."

"As tempting as that sounds, I'd rather be here," she insisted.

"I could stay here with you," Scorpio informed her while placing a hand on hers.

"I'll be fine," Patricia replied and smiled sweetly. "The hospital is sending a nurse to stay with me for a week or two. I already met with him. He likes those television judges. We'll have a good time."

Scorpio's brows suddenly rose. "He?" she asked with surprise. "Your visiting nurse is a guy?"

Patricia suddenly grinned. "Yeah, a real handsome one too."

Scorpio laughed and shook her head. "No wonder you're so adamant about this visiting nurse."

Her grandmother's eyes lit up as she leaned closer and whispered, "The girls at the hospital say he dances like Elvis. You know; hips swinging." She then shrugged. "It's possible he's gay too, but it doesn't matter, I can still enjoy his swinging hips."

"Yeah, you go ahead and enjoy that," she announced while grinning. "You've earned it." Her look then turned serious. "Are you going to be okay, Grandma?"

"I'm feeling much better already," she replied. "But don't be surprised if I have a sudden relapse. I may be able to get another week out of the visiting nurse."

"That's not what I meant," Scorpio scoffed. "I meant about--"

"I know what you meant," Patricia replied then drew a deep breath. "Your grandfather had us all fooled. Deep down, I knew there was something going on with him. I just never suspected he was capable of putting out a hit on his own son." She then hesitated. "And your brother." She rolled her eyes and shook her head. "It's too horrible to imagine he could do something like that."

Scorpio shifted uncomfortably and stared at her grandmother. "Is there anything else you can think of that I should know? No matter how trivial it may seem."

"Not off the top of my head, dear," she replied.

Rayner sheepishly entered the living room while holding the shoebox with a picture of women's shoes on front. "I, uh, found it in the closet."

Scorpio stood and hurried toward him. He handed her the box.

"I'll be with the guys in the kitchen," he announced then left the room.

Patricia eyed the shoebox as Scorpio returned to the sofa. "What is that?" she asked. "I remember seeing it in Kane's closet."

"I'm guessing this is the last piece of the puzzle," Scorpio informed her grandmother. "Kane must have left this here the day he stopped by and asked to borrow your travel bag. It could be what Grandpa hoped his hired men would find at the hotel."

"But it was here the whole time," Patricia replied. "Right under his lying nose." She appeared interested and leaned forward. "Well, what are you waiting for? Let's have a look inside."

Scorpio opened the lid and removed several recent photos on top. She looked through them. One was of their mother's cemetery headstone taken when they were teenagers. Kane was sitting on the ground before their mother's headstone. Scorpio remembered it well since she was the one who took the photo. The second photo was the same as the one Rayner found in Kane's bedroom behind the framed photo of his car. That photo had the date written on it. It was weeks before he left. Scorpio was slightly puzzled by the significance of the photos. She compared the two pictures side-by-side.

The photo taken years ago didn't have the heart carved into the stone. The recent one did. At some point during the last five to ten years, someone carved a heart into their mother's headstone. In the recent picture, Kane was pointing to the carved heart with his brows raised almost demandingly. It was almost as if he was attempting to tell her something. Was he anticipating Scorpio would find the box? Was he sending a message to her? She set the pictures aside and removed a brochure for Colorado.

Scorpio remained confused as she paged through the brochure. What did it mean? What did Colorado have to do with anything? She paused on a page with Colorado Springs circled. The same heart was drawn alongside it. Scorpio twitched. Her brother had been sending her a message. Did he want her to go to Colorado Springs? Did *he* go to Colorado Springs? Her mind was suddenly swimming with so much information; she could barely process it. The dead detective may have held the key to Kane's death. What had the detective learned that he was never able to tell them? She stared at the heart symbol a moment longer.

Kane believed their father carved the heart symbol into their mother's headstone. If he believed that, the photos indicated it happened within the last ten years. If Kane had Colorado on the brain, why was he killed in Virginia? What was in Virginia? There was nothing to indicate he had intended to go to Virginia. So why the last minute change in travel plans? She finally looked at her grandmother, who stared at the two photos with complete bewilderment.

"How did my father die?" Scorpio asked.

"I told you before," her grandmother replied and appeared uncomfortable. "He was murdered. Someone from his past killed him."

"Yes, you told me that many times," Scorpio remarked. "But *how* did he die? What happened?"

"Your mother never talked about it," she replied. "It upset her too much. We didn't press the issue."

"It had to be in the papers," Scorpio insisted. "You must have heard something. You had to be curious. We're not that far from Boston."

"I don't want to talk about your father," her grandmother announced with a fearful look in her eyes that immediately turned stern. "It was your brother's obsession with that fantasy that probably got him killed."

"Probably? If there's a chance my brother is still alive, I have to find him," Scorpio remarked while staring at her grandmother. "Why would he believe our father is still alive? Why would he risk his life chasing ghosts?"

"Kane refused to believe your father was dead," her grandmother reluctantly informed her. "He never listened to anyone. Who knows what went through his head the day he picked up and left."

Scorpio continued her search of the old shoebox. She removed a black and white photo, studied it a moment, and then looked at her grandmother with surprise.

"What's this photo?"

The older woman eyed the picture of several men in uniform. The alarmed expression on her face was enough to answer the question.

"That's nothing," she nervously replied. "Just an old photo your mother kept."

"According to the date on this photo, it was taken a few years after I was born," Scorpio insisted. "My mother died *before* this was taken. This wasn't hers. Where did this come from?"

"Who knows? I'm sure it's nothing," she replied while waving her off. "Must be something your brother found."

Scorpio glared demandingly at her grandmother. "It says Whiskey Tango Foxtrot. What does that mean? Who are these men?"

Her grandmother immediately fumbled on her words. "I'm not sure. I think they were some men your father knew."

"No, Grandma," she announced and indicated the picture. "My father is in this picture, isn't he? That's why my brother left. He went to find our father because he found proof he was still alive."

"Don't dig up the past, Scorpio," her grandmother begged. "Losing Kane was enough. I don't want to lose you too."

Scorpio shook her head. "I don't think Kane's dead, Grandma," she announced.

"We found evidence that your grandfather ordered the hit on him," Patricia announced timidly while trembling. "Your grandfather identified what was left of the burned car. Everything indicated it was Kane's car. According to the police, the car's VIN and plates matched. They found Kane's wallet with his identification partially intact. It had to be Kane in the car."

Scorpio frowned knowing there was no reasoning with her grandmother. She didn't want to believe Kane was still alive, because it would get her hopes up. Scorpio believed something different. She believed Kane wasn't in the car. She suddenly doubted he even went to Virginia. She was almost positive her brother went to Colorado, but she had to find something to substantiate her theory. She rummaged through the box and removed an old newspaper article, although it was printed more recently. Scorpio stared at the article from the Boston paper about the death of her father. Her grandmother became silent as she watched Scorpio reading the paper in her hand. She seemed almost troubled by it.

Chapter 60

Twenty-three years ago. Maggie Wayland entered her Boston apartment and set her bag down on the nearby chair. She looked around the unusually quiet apartment.

"I'm home," she called out, but there was no response. "Are you taking a nap?"

Maggie entered the bedroom and looked around. The bed was made, and the room was empty. She was about to leave the bedroom when she saw a red greeting card envelope on the pillow. Maggie smiled and hurried to the bed. She picked up the envelope and removed the card. A note fell onto the floor. She glanced at the card then picked up the note and read it. Her expression dropped. She tossed the note aside and ran from the room.

§

Maggie jumped out of her car near the dock and ran toward the boats past several fishermen, who gave her bewildered looks. The familiar boat, Dame Margaret, was still docked in her slip. Maggie sighed with relief and ran along the dock. She was about to board the boat when she heard a familiar voice yelling in the distance. She spun around and searched the dock. She caught a glimpse of her boyfriend running while another much larger man chased after him. Maggie gasped with alarm and ran after them, although they were too far away.

Several fishermen stopped to watch the excitement and nearly got in Maggie's way as she attempted to keep the running men in sight. She saw them run up the path leading to the cliffs. She was still too far away to catch up to them. Her boyfriend, who was being chased, was almost to the woods, running past several whale watchers standing on the cliffs with their binoculars. Her boyfriend was by no means a large or impressive looking man. He was shorter than average and not built very muscular, but his outward appearance was deceiving. He was strong and fast. His additional ten years on the man pursuing him made little difference since he was the faster man. Maggie's heart was pounding. He was going to make it. He would get away!

A gunshot rang out. Maggie suddenly stopped in her tracks and watched her boyfriend fall to the ground. He immediately sprang back up while clutching his bleeding leg. He attempted to limp for the woods then stopped and gasped for breath, no longer able to run. He turned to face the man pursuing him. Maggie ran for them and stopped when she saw the man, who couldn't be more than twenty years old, raise the gun.

"No," Maggie screamed.

Her boyfriend stood before the cliff and stared at her with surprise as his expression shattered. Three gunshots were heard. Maggie watched in horror as the bullets struck her boyfriend in the chest. He fell backward over the cliff as the onlookers watched.

"Zack!" she screamed and ran for the cliff.

One of the men who had been standing nearby watching whales caught her and kept her from running too close to the edge. The young man with the gun took off, disappearing into the woods. Maggie attempted to reach the cliff while sobbing as the large, bald headed man held her back.

"No," she wailed and attempted to pull free from the strong man's hold but ended up sinking to the ground.

The powerhouse of a man assisted her to the ground and attempted to comfort her while cradling her in his arms as she sobbed.

"He's gone," the man announced softly into her ear as he held her head to his chest, comforting her like an old friend. "I'm sorry."

§

Present day. Scorpio stared at her brother's handwriting at the bottom of the copied newspaper article. It simply read Midnight Requisition with a question mark behind it. Scorpio stared at her brother's handwriting a long moment then finally eyed her grandmother.

"I need you to be honest with me, Grandma," she announced firmly. "What do you know about Midnight Requisition?"

She was about to speak and seemed to change her mind. Patricia hesitated then groaned and appeared defeated. "After your father was murdered, your mother came here to have you and your brother," she announced. "She always believed her life was in danger from the people who killed your father, that's why she didn't want you anywhere near her. She felt you were safer here with us. She stayed only a couple of weeks before heading back to Boston. The day she left, something had her upset. At the time, I thought it was just because she was leaving her children behind. Turns out, she'd left something else behind that day." She drew a deep breath and reluctantly nodded toward the bookcase. "Last book in the corner on the top shelf."

Scorpio stood and hurried to the bookcase. She climbed the small, wooden steps built into the case and removed the last book. It was a book on combat strategies. She flipped through the book to an envelope hidden between the pages. She returned to her grandmother on the sofa while staring at the discolored envelope.

"Did you read this?" Scorpio asked.

Patricia frowned and nodded. "I never told your grandfather about it. I suspected he would have destroyed it," she announced then shook her head. "It probably should have been destroyed."

"If you felt that way, why didn't you tell Grandpa and let him destroy it?" Scorpio asked.

Her grandmother drew a deep breath. "Because," she replied softly. "He did it out of love."

Scorpio eyed her suspiciously then opened the envelope. She removed the official-looking documents and read through them. It was the missing papers from the Midnight Requisition folder.

§

Twenty-three years ago. Zack trudged through the surf onto shore not far from the cliff while shedding his jacket. The young man who had shot him a few minutes earlier walked across the beach toward him. Zack saw the man and immediately sneered as his shooter approached him without his weapon in hand.

"We have to hurry," the man announced while pausing before Zack on the beach. "If anyone sees you, this entire operation will have been for nothing."

Zack looked up, met his gaze, and suddenly punched the man in the mouth, stunning him. The young man held his mouth and stared at Zack with surprise. Zack tore off the special vest he wore containing bullet holes with fake blood and tossed it onto the beach. He straightened then pointed a warning finger at the stunned man, who gingerly rubbed his bleeding mouth.

"She wasn't supposed to be there, Abbott," Zack cried out in anger. "She wasn't supposed to see that. I didn't want her to see me die!"

Abbott wiped the blood from his mouth and glared back at Zack. "It wasn't my fault. It was planned perfectly," he announced. "That new guy, Gil, was supposed to be at her apartment building and make sure she didn't leave after she got home."

"And I told you not to use the new guy on this mission. He has the attention span of a puppy," Zack snarled. "He's a pilot for Christ's sake." His anger continued to rise. "The plan was perfect. Your execution was sloppy."

Abbott shook his head defensively and with some anger. "We did everything according to the book. Either way, the mission was a success. You're officially dead, and your girlfriend is free from your past," Abbott informed him although harboring some resentment from the accusation. "Jackson should be on his way to the marina where Ross is waiting for us. We should go before someone comes this way and sees us here."

Zack pulled his pants leg up and removed the wrap containing the fake blood from his perceived leg wound. "That's the last time I count on you, Abbott," he growled. "You never should have taken the shot with her there. I won't forgive you for that." He snatched the special vest and walked along the beach with both wraps containing fake blood.

"I'll add it to the list, Zack," Abbott muttered then followed him.

§

Present day. Scorpio's eyes widened as she read the classified information on the papers in her hands. She finally looked at her grandmother with shock on her face.

"This is the mission file for Midnight Requisition. According to this, Midnight Requisition was a government-sanctioned mission for my father to fake his own death," she gasped with astonishment. "He did it to protect my mother from people who wanted him dead. This means my father could still be alive."

"Perhaps he did it to protect your mother," Patricia replied then raised her brows. "Of course, maybe he did it because he found out she was pregnant and needed an escape."

Holly Copella

"Grandma, this was government sanctioned," she informed her with some irritation. "The government isn't in the habit of going to such great lengths to help a man get out of a relationship." Scorpio sank into thought then considered the entire situation further. "The empty folder was in Kane's bedroom at the hotel. Where would he have found the folder?" Her thoughts suddenly reeled. "How did my mother get ahold of classified files?"

"Perhaps from the lawyer who stopped by the house shortly before she died," Patricia announced then shook her head. "I really don't know. After she met with your father's lawyer, everything went south."

"So my not really dead father had a lawyer who suddenly showed up at your door?" Scorpio asked. "Was he really a lawyer?"

"I suppose so," Patricia remarked. "She said she met with him a few weeks after your father died. He gave her a large check from your father's estate. Apparently, he named her as his beneficiary. We set it aside for college for you and your brother. That's why it was strange that he showed up again all those months later."

"What did this guy look like?" Scorpio asked. "Did you see him?"

"Oh, yes," she replied. "He was a strong, strapping young man in his early thirties. Very handsome. Had a head like Mr. Clean. Shaved bald."

"Do you remember his name?"

"Jack something or another," she replied. "It was too long ago."

"So what did this Jack something or another say he wanted all those months after my father's death?" Scorpio then questioned.

"That's just it," Patricia announced. "Maggie didn't say what he wanted. Two days later, I saw her putting that book on the top shelf of the bookcase, and then she headed back to Boston."

"Then after she died you read those papers in that book." Scorpio thought about everything her grandmother had just admitted then shook her head with disappointment. "So you

366

knew the whole time? You knew my father was still alive. Why didn't you tell us?"

"Because I didn't want Kane running off trying to find him. I feared both of you suffering the same fate as your mother. I didn't know who that guy was and if he was responsible for getting her killed," she insisted with noted anger. "For whatever reason, your father faked his death. If he wanted everyone to believe he was dead, there was a very good reason for it, and I didn't want Kane getting killed because of whatever it was your father feared."

Scorpio attempted to remain calm about the whole incident, since she understood her grandmother was only doing it to protect them, especially Kane.

"You always told us our mother was getting her Boston affairs in order before she moved back home to be with us," Scorpio announced while staring at her grandmother. "Yet you just admitted she really left us here to keep us safe. She wasn't coming back to stay with us, was she? When she died in that car with my uncle, where was she really going?"

Patricia drew a deep breath and tensed. "After I'd found those papers, I suspect she intended to search for your father," she replied delicately then shook her head. "All these years, I believed she died because she wanted to learn the truth about your father. It was never about him, was it? Your mother died because your grandfather didn't want his son putting things together and exposing his dirty secret. I'm sure he never meant for your mother to die with him. He couldn't have known they'd be together when the hit was carried out." She drifted out a moment as all emotion drained from her face. "When I wept at our children's funeral and he held me, I wonder if he ever felt any guilt about what he'd done?"

"Maybe briefly," Scorpio replied then studied the lost look on her grandmother's face and took her hand, snapping her out of her trance. Scorpio stared into her eyes. "I believe Kane is alive."

Patricia squeezed her hand while offering a sympathetic look. "You're setting yourself up for disappointment," she gently announced. "Everything points to him dying in his car. The evidence is all there. What makes you think it wasn't him? Why do you think he's still alive?"

Scorpio offered a timid smile. "Because I can still feel him," she replied with conviction. "I keep having dreams that he's alive."

"If Kane were alive, don't you think he'd have contacted us by now?" her grandmother practically demanded. "It's been over nine months since he left. We haven't heard anything from him."

"If he discovered someone was trying to kill him, he may have decided to stay away for our safety," Scorpio informed her then drew a deep breath. "Rayner found several fake IDs and passports with different names in a locked box in his room. He knew our father was alive and being hunted by bad men. Kane was paranoid just enough to have been prepared for something like this. If there's a chance he's alive, you know I have to find him."

Her grandmother stared at her with tears in her eyes. "Yes, you may be right, there's a chance he's still alive," she whispered and squeezed Scorpio's hand. "Bring my grandson home to me. You both come home to me, you understand?"

Scorpio nodded. "I promise."

Chapter 61

Eight months earlier. Kane left the trucker diner and headed across the remote parking lot where his black 1967 Chevy Camaro muscle car was parked almost hidden among the massive eighteen-wheeler trucks. He removed his keys from his pocket and manually unlocked the driver's side door. He was about to toss his backpack inside when he heard someone approach. Kane instinctively turned to see two men standing before him.

"Nice car," the unfamiliar man in his early twenties announced while grinning. "How about letting us take her for a ride?"

Kane lowered his backpack from his shoulder and dropped it the rest of the way to the pavement then casually folded his arms across his chest. He indicated the open car door and gave a slight nod while grinning.

"Sure, be my guest," he announced almost playfully as his smile mocked the men.

The two young men exchanged bewildered looks then focused their attention back on Kane. The taller of the two men pulled a switchblade knife and held it up.

"I don't know what game you're playing," the man announced, "but you won't win."

"I assure you," Kane announced with confidence as he grinned. "I've won every game I've ever played." He then reconsidered his own comment and thought reflectively. "Except against my sister. That girl's got a bit of the devil in her."

The two men again exchanged baffled looks, uncertain what to make of their victim.

"I think we should kill him on principle alone," the first man announced while shifting looks from Kane to his friend with the knife. "Wouldn't you say?"

"Yeah, let's kill him," the friend agreed and lunged for Kane with his switchblade knife.

Kane darted to the left, allowing the man to fall partially into the car. Kane grabbed the door and slammed it on the man's legs that were sticking out. He howled in pain as his friend leaped to his aid and threw his fist at Kane's face. Kane ducked the punch, spun into a roundhouse kick while crouched low, and nailed him in the side, sending him flying into the hood of the car. The metal groaned from the hard hit creating a massive dent. Kane straightened and frowned at the large dent on the hood of his precious car.

"Not my car--"

The second man scrambled out of the car with the switchblade still in his hand and again slashed at Kane. Kane snap kicked his hand, sending the knife into a pinwheel through the air. He punched the man in the face then caught the knife on the way down, flipped it in his hand, catching the tip, and then threw it down. The knife embedded itself through the man's boot and into his foot. He screamed and cursed while attempting to grab his foot. Kane kicked him in the face and sent him backward onto his ass. The man across the hood lunged for Kane while he was preoccupied with his friend. Kane saw him out of the corner of his eye, darted left, and allowed him to strike the open car door face first.

Kane made a face as the man clutched his bleeding nose. "Ouch, that's gonna leave a mark," he muttered.

The man on the ground screamed while pulling the knife from his foot. Despite the blood, he scrambled to his feet, cried out, and lunged for Kane with the knife high above his head prepared to strike. Kane threw himself to the pavement, grabbed his discarded backpack, and rolled across the parking lot, allowing the man with the knife to stab his friend in the shoulder. His friend cried out and clutched his bleeding shoulder.

"I'm sorry," the man with the knife cried out. "He moved and--"

"Jerk each other off later," Kane snapped from behind them.

The man clutching his bleeding shoulder looked behind his friend and suddenly gasped. "Look out," he cried out as he ducked.

The man with the knife turned just in time to see a set of three shuriken throwing blades flying at him. The throwing stars connected with his face, throat, and chest simultaneously. Kane took a step forward revealing a pair of nunchucks in his right hand.

"Now, about that ride," Kane announced while casually twirling the free nunchucks as he approached.

The man with the bleeding shoulder cried out and jumped into the car. He slammed the door and locked it. Kane hesitated and felt his pockets for his keys. He immediately frowned and looked around.

"Damned keys," he muttered.

The man in the car felt beneath his buttocks and removed the lost keys. He managed a weak laugh and started the car. Kane groaned with disgust.

"Great," he scoffed and twirled the nunchucks in his hand then struck the driver's side window.

The man behind the wheel screamed as the window cracked but didn't shatter. He put the car in gear and burned out. Kane watched with annoyance as his cherished car flew from the parking lot. He eyed the dying man by his feet and indicated his car.

"Your friend is a real prick," Kane informed him. "Stole my car and left you to die."

The man gasped his last breath. Kane suddenly felt his pockets and groaned.

"Son-of-a-bitch," he scoffed. "My wallet was in the glove box." Kane sighed while shaking his head. "It's a good thing I have a few more identities left to my name." He crouched alongside the dead man and pulled the throwing stars from his body. "Mondays suck."

As Kane pulled the last throwing star from the young man's chest, he saw a piece of paper sticking out of his inner jacket pocket. He removed the slightly bloodied paper and unfolded it. The paper contained a description of his car, the license plate number, and Kane's name.

"Kill Kane Wayland; recover laptop," Kane read the scribbled words on the bloodstained paper. "Fifty thousand dollars."

Kane kneeled motionless alongside the young man a moment. He heard voices coming from the diner, which was out of view. Kane placed the paper in his pocket, collected his backpack, and hurried past the trucks.

"I'm sorry, Scorpio," he muttered aloud to himself while running his fingers nervously through his hair. "You're better off on your own until I figure out who wants me dead and why."

§

Present day. Three days had passed since Scorpio's grandmother had been released from the hospital. After everything that had happened, the older woman was able to pick up the pieces and erase Newman from her life. Scorpio and her friends had spent the entire three days restoring the hotel to its pre-war ravaged state. After many hours, Scorpio had finally finished tidying up Kane's bedroom on the third floor. It took some time to get the room back to its original condition, but it was almost the same way he had left it. She heard a commotion in the third floor hallway and was about to investigate when Rayner hurried into the room with Stone and Maverick on his heels.

"Damn it," Stone lashed out in frustration. "Tell us what you found."

Rayner carelessly sat on the neatly made bed and set his laptop down as all three eagerly gathered around him to have a look at what he'd found.

"I've been cross-referencing Kane's fake IDs over the last couple of days," Rayner informed them. "Each of them turned out to be dead-ends. It's as if he wanted each of his alternate personas to have their own life so anyone poking around would never find anything."

"Yeah, we knew this yesterday," Maverick muttered while folding his arms across his chest. "You better have something worthwhile this time."

"Oh, I hit the mother lode," Rayner announced while grinning. "While I was busy chasing ghosts of your brother's alter egos, I was more consumed with what I saw rather than what I didn't see."

"I'm going to hit him," Maverick muttered then glared at Scorpio. "Tell me I can hit him."

"Okay, Rayner," Scorpio groaned while feeling her anxiety rise as well. "Get on with it."

Rayner smiled proudly. "There were five IDs and passports, but there were eight credit card statements," he informed her. "Three IDs and passports are missing from the box. I pulled up the credit card statements for all three cards and discovered one has been used excessively in the last eight months."

Scorpio leaned forward while staring at him practically ready to jump out of her skin. "And?"

"Kane Templeton checked out of a motel two days ago in Colorado Springs," Rayner announced while grinning.

"It's him," Scorpio gasped.

"I'm almost positive it was your brother," Rayner informed her. "According to Kane Templeton's old credit card statements, he caught a flight from Boston to Denver eight months ago."

"I knew he was alive, that son-of-a-bitch," she announced excitedly and hugged Rayner across from her. She then pulled away while maintaining her smile. "If you gentlemen will excuse me; I'm going to Colorado Springs and find my brother." Her smile immediately faded. "And then I'm going to kill him."

"I guess we should start packing," Maverick announced with a sigh.

Scorpio looked at Maverick with surprise. "You don't need to go with me."

"Actually, we do," Stone informed her. "He's been on the run for eight months. There's no telling what sort of trouble he's gotten into. You're going to need our help to track him down."

"*All* our help," Rayner insisted.

She eyed her three friends and smiled in appreciation. "Thank you."

The End

Coming Soon!

"Midnight Requisition 2"
Amateur Night

§

"Witness Protection 7"
Bravo Foxtrot

§

"Witness Protection 8"
Midnight Requisition

Other books by Holly Copella!
Reviews left on Amazon are appreciated!

"The Battle for Andrea Maria"

A cruise ship attack turns six survivors into overnight celebrities after they take credit for the heroic act of a stowaway who died saving them.

The cruise is just what Jess needed--a bit of harmless fun far from her daily grind. But what begins as a relaxing vacation turns into a desperate fight for her life when terrorists take over the ship and start piling up bodies. Teaming up with a mysterious stowaway, Jess attempts to send out a distress call but knows they cannot wait for help to come. If she or the few remaining passengers have any hope for survival, Jess must act now. The papers dub it "The Battle for *Andrea Maria*," but to Jess it is the moment she fought side-by-side with her enigmatic Romeo, saving the ship--and losing him. She thinks the story ends there, but really, the nightmare is just beginning...

"Insanely Deadly"

When the dead return to life, it's up to an admiral's daughter and a mildly insane, former war hero to save their small town.

Jetta Cross, a Navy Admiral's daughter, is tasked with keeping her father's comrade, a former war hero turned town crazy, grounded in the real world. Capt. John Hunter is still fighting the war in his head, where imaginary dead people are part of his world. When a viral outbreak brings about a zombie uprising, Hunter is left to his own devices. He must resume his role as a one-man commando unit in order to destroy the ravenous undead. With Hunter still fighting his own inner demons as well as the undead, the townspeople fear their zombie neighbors may not be the only threat. Stranded at the island's luxurious resort with a handful of workers, Jetta is forced to live up to her father's reputation and take charge of the deteriorating situation at the hotel. She must wage her own war against the infected before the government declares her hometown a total loss.

"Deadly Institution"

A town recluse suspected of killing his wife teams up with a young woman in order to stop a killer.

After being accused of murdering his wife, Konrad Asher turns his back on the town that once adored him. Ten years later, he still holds his grudge and the title of the most feared man in town. With the reopening of the burned mental institution, where his wife had died, former employees are now murdered one-by-one, throwing suspicion back on Asher. A young local reporter, Jacey, is forced to reveal her long-time friendship with the infamous recluse in order to clear his name not only in the recent murders but to exonerate him in the death of his wife as well. Will Jacey's relationship with Asher invite the killer closer to her? Or is the killer already in her life?

"Death Displacement"

A grief-stricken man travels back in time to seek revenge on the woman who murdered his girlfriend but inadvertently falls in love with her.

Kane is about to marry the woman he loves. His life is perfect. A few weeks before the wedding, a vindictive woman from his girlfriend's past mysteriously arrives and kills her. He learns of a traumatic accident that happened five years earlier, which triggers Riley's hatred for his girlfriend. Distraught over his girlfriend's death, Kane uses an antique time machine to travel into the past in order to find and destroy the woman responsible. When he runs into Riley's younger self, he realizes she's not the monster she later becomes, and he can't bring himself to destroy her. With a little help from his oddball friend from the past, they formulate a plan to prevent the accident that sends Riley down her destructive path. Kane's plan backfires when he falls for the younger Riley. His new tortured existence is further complicated when future Riley, his girlfriend's killer, shows up with her own devious agenda that doesn't include him. Will he be able to stop the time ripple, which ultimately ends with his girlfriend's death? Or will future Riley take him out of the timeline forever--

"Dead Village"

After strange happenings isolate a small resort town from the rest of the world, nearly one hundred residents seek refuge at the closed hotel. Only eight survive the night. And that's just the beginning...

One day after the entire population of Fox Ridge Village disappears, a car wreck forces several unsuspecting crash victims to seek help at the closed summer hotel. Within the hotel, they discover the grisly aftermath of a brutal slaughter. Crash victims Vander and Devon, a reluctant clairvoyant, team up to solve the riddle of the "haunted hotel" and the mass hysteria plaguing the remaining survivors. By the time they discover the hotel's secret, they're already drawn into the hysteria. As the body count continues to climb, it's a race to isolate the source and bring everyone back to reality before they kill one another. Will Devon be able to communicate with the traumatized spirits before their fate becomes her own?

"Town Darling"

After surviving a brutal attack that claims the lives of those she loves, a young woman seeks revenge on a corrupt town.

Going back home is never easy, but for Casey, it means returning to her corrupt hometown where she barely survived a brutal attack. Accompanied by two family friends, she seeks justice for the night that destroyed her life. Her physical scars are nothing compared to her emotional ones, forcing the local sheriff to believe that the town darling is back for revenge. As the conspiracy for her revenge appears to be leading up to the coveted town fair, the sheriff is determined to stop her from fulfilling her vengeful scheme...but guilt over his role on that fateful night continues to haunt him. Will his desperate need for Casey's forgiveness be his undoing? Or will Casey's desire for revenge destroy them both?

"Basement Dwellers"

A viral outbreak at a hospital leaves a mortician, sheriff, and coroner fighting for their lives against a horde of undead and the CDC.

After a massive car wreck leaves several survivors in critical condition at the local hospital, a surgeon uses experimental drugs on his critical patients and accidentally causes a zombie outbreak. When local mortician, Lexx, receives an infected corpse as her client, she becomes stranded in the hospital basement during CDC quarantine along with the local sheriff and the coroner. The infamous surgeon struggles to find a cure for his infectious blunder by using the other survivors as test subjects. Meanwhile, Lexx and the sheriff attempt to locate his missing sister, who's stranded somewhere in the battle zone that once was the emergency room. It's a race against time and the ravenous undead. Can they survive the undead before CDC sanitizes the hospital of all infection?

"Misfits, Inc."

A seemingly ordinary, young woman meets four misfits who claim she has given them supernatural powers.

While on a business trip to a remote island paradise, a bored secretary, Hailey, has her world turned upside down when her path collides with a psychic freak, Skyler. He attempts to convince her that they had met in his dreams, and she had chosen him as one of her four mystic warriors. After Skyler foresees a woman's death, they discover an unidentified creature has killed one of the guests. They are joined by a lounge pianist and a rich playboy, who also claim they had met her in their dreams. If Skyler's prophecies are genuine, the evil entity controlling the ravenous creatures needs to destroy Hailey to ensure its survival. Reluctantly accepting her fate, Hailey has to locate the last and most powerful of her chosen warriors, The Guardian. Their fate is in doubt when The Guardian turns out to be a self-absorbed, former cat burglar with a bad attitude. Can Hailey turn her company of misfits into an elite team of mystic warriors? Or will The Guardian's secret agenda destroy them all?

"Deadly Institution 2"

When blackmail turns into murder, a young woman finds herself caught in the killer's crosshairs.

The small town of Stony Ridge is no stranger to scandal and persecution of the innocent. When a brutal killing shakes the town's prestigious country club, Jacey McMurray seeks help from a self-proclaimed vigilante, Konrad Asher. As her professional and personal worlds collide, Jacey fears the stress of the country club killings have finally taken their toll on Asher. Can a stressed out vigilante stop the killer before he strikes again?

"Witness Protection"
Also available in audiobook!

After witnessing an execution, a resourceful young woman attempts to disappear while being pursued by a hitman and a handsome federal agent.

A helicopter pilot, Jackie Remus, reluctantly agrees to go on a date with one of her clients, but her date is unexpectedly cut short when she witnesses a man being murdered. After narrowly escaping with her life, she is placed into protective custody. When the safe house is breached, Jackie makes a daring escape from both the hired killers and the handsome FBI agent, who wants to return her to protective custody. With a little help from her sly and crafty friend, Monroe, Jackie is convinced she can disappear until the trial. While on her journey to meet with her friend, she solicits help from a few shady but lovable characters along the way. Although she manages to stay one-step ahead of the hired killers, the federal agent remains in hot pursuit. Will Jackie reach Monroe before she's captured by the FBI and returned to protective custody? Or will the hired killers silence her first?

"Unconditional"

A young woman puts her life on hold to care for an unstable, highly skilled combat soldier, who believes someone is trying to kill him.

A botched military coup leaves a team of elite fighters injured with one clinging to life in a coma. When Harlan wakes from his coma, he's left with no memory of his past life. His commander's daughter, Indy, takes it upon herself to care for the fallen war hero. She's challenged with more than just his physical care as she combats with not only his memory loss but also his newly found desire for her. His infatuation with her becomes the least of her worries when he sinks back into his role of a combat soldier. Believing his life is in danger, his fighting skills surface, turning him into an unpredictable and dangerous man. Will his memory return to him before Indy is forced to commit him? Or will he finally find his nemesis, "the coyote", and possibly claim the life of an innocent person?

"The Pen Pal"

In order to save her friend, she must enter the mind of a serial killer.

When her best friend is abducted, no one believes Jolynn saw it in a psychic vision. With nowhere to turn, Jolynn reluctantly joins Agent Harris Slade and his team on their hunt for a sadistic serial killer known only as "The Pen Pal". Finally confronted with the killer, Jolynn realizes she must enter the mind of the psychopath in order to stop the brutal killings. But when her vision reveals a particularly disturbing death, can Jolynn sacrifice her lover for her friend?

"Witness Protection 2"
The Return of Whiskey Tango Foxtrot

Believing she holds the clue to millions in missing laundered money, a young woman is placed into the protective care of a former Navy SEAL team.

Feeling sorry for her recently separated co-worker, Leeann invites Wiley to join her and her friends on their night out. Little does she know that finding her co-worker murdered is just the beginning of her nightmare. Leeann unknowingly holds the key to fifty million dollars in potentially laundered mob money. With hired killers pursuing her, the FBI places her into a different kind of protective custody. Former Navy SEAL team Whiskey Tango Foxtrot reunites to keep Leeann alive at their secret hideaway. What should be an easy assignment takes an unscheduled turn when secrets, lies, and betrayal threaten to derail their mission. Is the team prepared for a war on their own doorstep? Will Leeann's misguided trust endanger the lives of those sent to protect her?

"Witness Protection 3"
Alpha Mike Foxtrot

A helicopter pilot risks her life to help a team of retired Navy SEALs rescue two girls from a killer.

When former Navy SEAL team Whiskey Tango Foxtrot asks for a simple favor, Jackie reluctantly offers her air-taxi services. What could go wrong? What begins as a search and rescue for two girls turns into a fight for survival against a heavily armed drug cartel. Wanted by the law with the cartel in hot pursuit and their home base breached, the team is forced to call in a favor from a questionable ally. Unfortunately, their new safe house isn't what it seems. Without knowing who the real enemy is, can Jackie and the team save their young witnesses from the hands of a killer?

"Already Dead"
Supernatural Collection

From the already dead to the undead. Three supernatural tales of "things that go bump in the night".

"Bloodletting" - A vampire themed resort allows guests to *participate* in their Bloodletting Ritual to celebrate the island's legendary vampires.

"Reaper of Souls" - A young woman must outwit an evil sorcerer in order to save her brother or become one of his minions forever.

"Already Dead" - When Flight 220 crashes, ten passengers make it to an isolated island, but only one man lives to tell the lie.

"Witness Protection 4"
O-Dark-Hundred

A simple assignment turns deadly when a retired Navy SEAL team uncovers a plot to kill a notorious mob boss.

When Whiskey Tango Foxtrot embarks on a simple stalking case, they're not prepared for a trip to a private island paradise owned by an infamous mobster. With one of their own suffering from traumatic head injuries, the team is left scrambling to decide what is real or imagined. The situation escalates even further when they uncover an assassination plot where everyone is a suspect. Now targets themselves, can the team survive their trip to paradise?

"Witness Protection 5"
Outside the Wire

After suffering several casualties on their last assignment, a retired Navy SEAL team discovers their misery is just beginning.

When Whiskey Tango Foxtrot returns home after suffering a devastating loss, they're hit with even more bad news regarding the rest of their team. Their grief is cut short when they discover their names are all on the same hit list. Hunted by relentless assassins, the scattered team must decide whether to remain safely hidden or find the man who put the price on their heads. Against the wishes of her teammates, Jackie strikes out on her own in order to save a friend who wants her dead. In a kill or be killed situation, will Jackie's emotions finally betray her?

"The Murder of Emily Fisher"

After finding their favorite teacher murdered, the lives of two teenage girls are forever changed.

Everyone loved Emily Fisher. While walking home one afternoon, two teenage girls, Sidney and Trisha, stumble upon a gruesome murder scene. The brutal murder of Emily Fisher, a young, attractive schoolteacher, shocks the small town of **Marilina**. After graduation, Sidney moves far away from the memories of the small town while Trisha retreats deeper into denial. Eight years after the murder, Sidney receives a desperate call from her childhood friend, forcing her to return home. Trisha believes Emily's killer was falsely accused and she manages to turn the entire town against her while attempting to prove it. When Trisha receives a death threat, Sidney realizes there may be some credibility to her friend's wild accusations. Is Trisha's mental breakdown a result of childhood trauma? Or is the real killer actually attempting to silence her? In order to save her friend, Sidney must answer the eight-year-old question. Who murdered Emily Fisher?

"Once Upon a Disaster"

A young homicide detective finds herself at the mercy of a hitman in the aftermath of an earthquake

While investigating the murder of a hitman, Detective Jade Wesson pursues a lead connecting the dead man to a break-in at a computer programming company. She's drawn into the world of nightclub owner and front man for the mob, Cody Riley. Her investigation keeps pointing to Cody's right-hand man and possible hitman, Vahn Lott. Despite her efforts to keep her investigation on track, Vahn has plans of his own for the attractive detective. When an unprecedented earthquake rocks their east coast town, Jade must put her life in Vahn's hands if she wants to survive. Can she trust a man who might be the killer she's hunting?

"Awaken the Dead"

A grieving innkeeper struggles to keep her haunted hotel out of foreclosure.

After losing her parents in a suspicious boating accident, Harley Brandon is determined to keep the family hotel out of foreclosure. Unfortunately, the hotel ghosts have other plans. Built with tainted money, the century old Horizon Hotel thrives on a tradition of murder, scandal, and suicide. As the paranormal activity increases to alarming levels, Harley discovers the truth about the hotel and its residents. Can Harley save her friends from the hotel's frightening hidden secrets?

"Castle Bloodshed"
Murder Collection

From a deadly island paradise to haunted castles. Three novella length tales of murder, mystery, and malicious intent.

"Castle Bloodshed" – A tour of Wesley Castle turns into a fight for survival as six stranded tourists discover the haunting secrets within the castle walls. A mystery writer teams up with an uptight butler in order stop a killer who may already be dead. Novella length paranormal murder mystery.

"Fleshies" – Is Uncle Rutger crazy? Five years ago, four business partners died within their newly purchased, fixer-upper castle. Their bodies were never found. The surviving partner, Rutger, claims a demon keeps him as its slave. Rutger's nephew schemes to save his uncle by sacrificing the lives of a group of stranded motorists and a high-profile novelist. Novella length supernatural murder mystery.

"Demon Island" – A group of strangers are invited to a remote island for the reading of a will. The guests soon discover they were brought to the island to be executed one-by-one. It's up to a private detective and a tenacious young woman to solve the murders and find a way to escape paradise. Novella length murder mystery.

"Brighton Island"

When a psychic visits a haunted island mansion, he inadvertently awakens the ghosts' tortured souls.

Something's not right with Simon. When Jacklyn brings her eccentric friend to her uncle's island mansion, she didn't expect him to slip into psychic overload. As Simon attempts to solve a decade-old, double homicide, Jacklyn is confronted with the possibility that she could be next to join the mansion ghosts. When they find themselves stranded on the secluded island, her Uncle Hyland wages his own war to save them from a flesh and blood killer. Will her uncle's "shock and awe" military tactics save them or get them killed? Can Simon bring peace to the tortured souls or unexpectedly join them?

"A.L.F. Resort"

A fantasy vacation turns into a nightmare when the resort's artificial life forms are compromised.

Welcome to A.L.F. Resort where you can live out your fantasies with safe, state-of-the-art artificial life form robots! When a young journalist and a photographer are sent to A.L.F. Resort to do a story for their magazine, Shay and Becka believe they've hit the jackpot of all work-cations. The engineers pull out all the stops to make their fantasies memorable. Unfortunately, the newly designed A.L.F., the Gen X, is smarter than his programming and creates havoc within Shay's fantasy. A computer malfunction removes their safety inhibitors and the A.L.F.s play out their own hostile fantasies. Zombies, bikers, and mobsters run amuck, turning fantasies into nightmares. Shay gets more of a story than she anticipates, but will she survive long enough to write it?

"Jungle Princess"

While stranded on a prison island, a young woman discovers a creature of "unknown" origin.

After their cruise ship sinks, Alex and two of her shipmates are stranded on a deserted, tropical island. Unfortunately, the castaways soon realize they're not alone. They discover an abandoned prison with over two dozen inmates living on the island's south side. While avoiding the prison on the far side of the island, Alex discovers a strange but loveable creature of unknown origin. When one of her fellow castaways is in trouble, Alex reluctantly seeks help from the prisoners. After the brutal murder of several inmates, their questions surrounding the abandoned prison are about to be answered. What really killed over one hundred prisoners? And is it still out there?

"Murder in Wax"

A series of brutal murders plague a quiet farming community when beautiful women audition for the same acting job.

While all the young women in town are fighting over a once-in-a-lifetime acting opportunity, Devon Vincent is excited about her new job at the local wax museum. Although supportive of her friend's acting aspirations, Devon has a hard time understanding the rivalry among the women in town. When the aspiring actresses are brutally murdered one-by-one, Devon fears her friend may be the next victim. Devon finds herself in the middle of a murderous revenge plot that leads back to the wax museum's doorstep and possibly implicates her boss as the killer. Will Devon's newly found feelings for her boss bring a killer closer to her? Or is the killer already in her circle?

"Witness Protection 6"

Alpha Dogs

An easy rescue turns into a wild ride for retired Navy SEAL team Whiskey Tango Foxtrot when everyone wants to kill their client.

It was a simple task. Rescue a young woman from her mob boss father-in-law. Little did Jackie and company realize that rescuing the young woman was the easy part. Keeping her alive would be a massive undertaking, especially when everyone wants a piece of the mafia heiress. The team fights for survival against their toughest adversaries yet. How many innocent people must die in order to save one woman? Can the team survive the ultimate battle between mercenaries and assassins?

ABOUT THE AUTHOR

Holly Copella has been writing since the age of twelve when her frustration at a book's poor plot drove her to author her own story. Over the last decade, she's written a number of screenplays, some of which she's now adapting into novels. Her fascination with zombies and other darker material lends an edge to her writing, which tends to lean toward horror. As a fan of Agatha Christie, she appreciates the craft of a good plot and the importance of creating significant characters.

Hailing from Pennsylvania, Copella lives in the Endless Mountains on a farm with her rescue horses and other animals. In addition to writing and reading fiction, she enjoys riding horses and traveling to Las Vegas and Disney World.

www.ingramcontent.com/pod-product-compliance
Lightning Source LLC
Chambersburg PA
CBHW071424260626
47162CB00014B/215